Are We Nearly There Yet?

Also by Sheila Hayman

Small Talk

SHEILA HAYMAN

Are We Nearly There Yet?

Hodder & Stoughton

Copyright © 2003 by Sheila Hayman

First published in Great Britain in 2003 by Hodder and Stoughton
A division of Hodder Headline

The right of Sheila Hayman to be identified as the Author of the
Work has been asserted by her in accordance with the Copyright,
Designs and Patents Act 1988.

2 4 6 8 10 9 7 5 3 1

All rights reserved. No part of this publication may be reproduced,
stored in a retrieval system, or transmitted, in any form or by any
means without the prior written permission of the publisher, nor be
otherwise circulated in any form of binding or cover other than that
in which it is published and without a similar condition being
imposed on the subsequent purchaser.

All characters in this publication are fictitious and any resemblance
to real persons, living or dead, is purely coincidental.

A CIP catalogue record for this title is available
from the British Library

ISBN 0 340 81889 1

Typeset by Palimpsest Book Production Limited,
Polmont, Stirlingshire
Printed and bound in Great Britain by
Clays Ltd, St Ives plc

Hodder and Stoughton
A division of Hodder Headline
338 Euston Road
London NW1 3BH

To my father and mother, who taught me the importance of taking my own bread, butter and Spam to France.

Are We Nearly There Yet?

1 December – McCallum family Christmas lists

Helen

Leonidas – plain and milk only, no white chocolate, definitely no marzipan, and absolutely NO creams please.

. . . or maybe Neuhaus, except you only find them in obscure places, so you can't be sure they're fresh. And there's nothing more tragic than chocolate past its prime.

. . . which is a point in favour of something a bit more heavily marketed e.g. Godiva, especially if you can find the one with the crossed tennis rackets on it, or the other fat disc-shaped one with the double shell and the soft caramel centre and the blob on top.

. . . but then what about Charbonnel et Walker? Nobody else makes hard chocolate caramels any more, and they're worth the trek at Christmas, because they have samples.

. . . if any of that is too much effort, I actually do like Quality Street, naff it may be but you do get a huge tin for not very much money, and people kind of expect it, don't they, when they drop round?

. . . even Jack and Tamsin could afford a KitKat.

(Oh dear. I'd forgotten that a Christmas list is a merciless mirror, magnifying and reflecting back every tiny personal flaw. Let's try a spot of camouflage)

Helen (revised)

Classical CDs: Brahms, Beethoven, Berlioz, Bruckner. All the nintheenth-century masterworks you catch sampled on Classic FM and think how novel it would be to hear the whole thing, even if it does drag in places.

Leonidas – plain or milk only, and absolutely NO creams please.

Important Books: *War and Peace*, *A Tale of Two Cities*, *Remembrance of Things Past*. I must stop reading rubbish, sadly no excuse now Des is four and sleeping properly, at last. And my new career as librarian would probably be assisted by at least a passing familiarity with the standard texts of world literature.

. . . or how about Neuhaus? So long as they're fresh . . .

Health Club Subscription (again). Just passing the changing room mirror in Georgie's old candy-striped bikini should fuel at least eighty laps.

. . . and possibly Godiva, as before . . .

Deliriously fragrant bath potions. This is the year I restore myself to the sleek, desirable womanhood I binned with the first dirty nappy. But no cheap rubbish and ABSOLUTELY no vanilla – I am not going to bed sleek, desirable and smelling of custard.

. . . not forgetting Charbonnel et Walker hard chocolate caramels . . .

Sensual, luxurious robe for intimate evenings a deux: Remember, before there was Des, there was Colum and I. But better make it machine washable, given that there is now, indisputably, Des. In fact, why not get it from M&S, because if it doesn't fit or something, I can always swap it for underpants, I don't know how they get through so many. (Nor do I want to know).

. . . Quality Street, or KitKat – even Jack and Tamsin can afford that.

(There, that'll do. Frankly, anything I haven't bought and wrapped for myself would be lovely. I bet nobody bothers giving presents to poor old Santa, either. I wonder what he'd have on his list?)

Special Agent 'Santa Claus'

Late-model V8 turbo sleigh with night vision, all-weather tyres, anti-lock brakes, cruise control, autopilot, radar, GPS, fax, phone, 18-CD changer, and instrument landing gear.

Army spec, polar-fleece-backed, bright red (IMPORTANT!) Gore-Tex all-in-one, size XXX large.

Matching hat, with earflaps, Wap aerial and built-in hands-free mobile headset.

Knee-high, warm-lined, waterproof boots with ankle supports, multigrip cushion soles and quick-release Velcro fastenings.

Several spare pairs lightweight Thinsulate socks (NOT reindeer patterned, please).

Black, double-zipped, inside-pocket money belt, packed with assorted platinum credit cards, in case of sleighjacking in hostile territory.

A new Thermos, a big reindeer-proof bag of Trail Mix, and a couple of those US military long-life sandwiches, in case of forced stopovers due to bad weather. A person can get very, very tired of mince pies and sherry . . .

Anything by Dick Francis or Stephen King, in case of air traffic snarl-ups or stubbornly wakeful children.

New Year's in the Maldives.

Colum (Helen's husband)

No, to be honest, I'd rather not. Well, if you insist, I suppose you can't go far wrong with a good single malt.

Oh, and while you're out, I noticed we're short of Jif, the yellow one for bathrooms, not the cream but the clear liquid, the cream's bloody useless, and the trigger pack not the bottle. And could you mebbe pick up some Scotchbrite scouring pads? Please don't try to economise by getting the own-brand ones, it's me who ends up using them every night, after all. Ta, then, and if I think of anything else I'll call you on the mobile.

Des (Helen and Colum's son)

Pirate ship, a real one with real guns and blood and knives.
A whale for playing Moby Dick only it has to fit into the bath.
Some more elephants, African ones with big tusks and ears and stamping their feet.
A cowboy outfit with real guns and a horse to ride and real guns.
Ice cream every day, it has to be Magnum, I don't like those Sainsbury's choc ices like last time, and hamburgers and meat and sausages and more butter on my toast.
Not have a nap.
Some books about guns and weapons and fighting and blood.
DVDs about guns and fighting and battles and about dinosaurs and about Godzilla and about elephants.
A DVD player EVERYBODY else at nursery school has a DVD player and I need to play all those DVDs.
Stay up until very late after supper every day and have hot chocolate every night at bedtime and go to bed when I want to.

Bertie (the cat)

Roast turkey with plenty of skin, dragged across the floor with puddles of gravy and carpet fluff.
Fresh newspaper to sit on with muddy paws before anybody else gets to it.
Stupider birds in the garden, or at least slower, heavier ones with more meat on them, after all that bother.
A mouse colony, preferably in the kitchen where they're easier to sneak up on.
A collar WITHOUT a bell on it, my life is hard enough as it is without being the laughing stock of the entire street. I might as well do my hunting with outriders and sirens.

Alison (Helen's mother)

Really, you don't need to bother, I'm not going to be around for long and it'll all have to be thrown away then anyway.

And you know what I'd REALLY like is to see my grandson a little more often, after all you're not so far away, I'm virtually the only grandparent he has and I'd hate him to realise too late what he missed out on and blame you like you blamed me, yes, you did, you know, I . . . sorry, where were we?

. . . Well, if it's just to be a token present then don't go to any trouble just pop down to Boots and get me some Shalimar, I do hate cheap scent but if you feel it's too much the bath soap wasn't dear last time, I had to buy it myself so I know.

Georgie (Helen's older sister)

Goodness is it that time of year already I haven't even begun to think about it to be honest but let's see, well I always need tights. Just loads of black and navy and dark brown tights, and I get through tons of hand cream at the clinic so any old hand cream you can find, and now Tamsin's at secondary she's always bloody swiping my lipstick so more lipstick, I don't do well with purply colours they make me look green but coral provided it's not pearlised, I can't stand shimmer it's so tacky isn't it? And you might as well get lipstick for her too, might give me a chance of keeping mine longer, and you know Jack he'll just want a game cartridge as usual but don't bother with Brian, he certainly won't be bothering with you lot, and I've told him last year was definitely the last time I'm being Santa for him and saving him from public exposure for the tight-fisted selfish layabout he is, buying and wrapping my own present is one thing but putting it on my own Switch card is one thing too far, Christ is that the time, is that enough sweetie?

George (Colum's father)

Well, ye ken, there's everything here now since young Gus McCluskey took to the drink and got himself bought out by Tesco's. He'd the devil's luck always, they had to pay a fortune wi' him being the only shop here and squaring it wi' the elders and the parish council an' all. Yer mother and I tried that Fruit and Fibre wi' freeze-dried raspberries last week, can ye credit raspberries in November, I'd a job stopping her from scoffing the lot.

Fiona (Colum's mother)

Don't heed to a word yer father says, we'd be glad of anything at all from London in this god-forsaken corner of the wurld. They're all the time for promising us a bright new dawn of Internet shopping, but what's the good of putting down yer name a week ahead to get online at the post office, I'd like to know, when the delivery vans stop at Stornoway? The day one of yon bright sparks in Silicon Glen figures out a way to send a new winter-weight mattress cover along his modem, I'll sign up for their digital revolution, but in the meanwhile I thank the Lord God for ma catalogues and Consignia or whatever damn name they've given it today.

10 December – Helen

Unexplained seasonal lull in enquiries at the Reference Desk today gave me a chance to plan the Siege of Stalingrad, aka Christmas shopping trip. After an hour spent decoding the veiled threats, passive-aggressive hints and unhelpful ellipses of the various lists, I spent the next hour on a time-and-motion calculation of which shops in which streets in which areas of the capital and beyond I'd have to visit to get everything, only to conclude, just before chucking-out time, that I might as well take the keys to our house straight down to the Nationwide and tell them to do the bloody shopping for me. That's what forward planning gets you – an early warning of a four-figure overdraft. So much for the season of good cheer.

At least if I was spending it on myself, I'd come out of it with something I wanted. Maybe I'll just call everybody, suggest we all do our own shopping and circulate the bills instead of Christmas cards. Never did see the point of Christmas cards – if I haven't spoken to somebody for a year, it's highly unlikely that I'll want to again, and if I see them all the time anyway, what's special about Christmas?

So, thinking about it all as I battled home on the Northern Line, it seemed the only kind thing to do was put a £10 spending limit on everybody's presents, including my own (Tolstoy! Who was I kidding anyway?) to give us all at least an odds-on chance of a New Year unbesmirched by the merry carolling of the creditors. I feel safer buying my own chocolate, anyhow.

12–14 December – E-mail exchange: Colum and Billy (old friend and father of four)

From: ColumMcCallum [colum@laverda.demon.co.uk]
Sent: 12 December
To: Billy Giddens [billy@goat.freeserve.co.uk]

```
Hi Bill
I've been wondering what to get the bike for
Christmas - quite fancy one of those carbon
fibre fairings but not sure if the ones Steve
imported are quite up to Monza spec, and it's
not a question I can exactly ask him without
offence. Otherwise I suppose there's always the
usual total service and hand-wax but that seems
a bit boring - what are you doing for yours?
```

On which subj, clouds have been massing of late with the thought that Her Indoors will be expecting some lavish gift-wrapped object, and as usual I have to psychically channel the one thing that she has failed to think of for herself, despite daydreaming about nothing else for the last year. Frilly undies are clearly a minefield, as they will not only give offence if either too large or too small, but will also lead to accusations of only being interested in one thing. Nightgear sensible or otherwise ditto. Food is an obvious no-go area, booze is coals to Newcastle, nostalgia CDs might work if I could remember what she liked listening to ten years ago. This year we have the added complication that she's decided to spring a New Puritan £10 spending limit on the entire family. I suspect this of being some kind of trap, designed to lure me into revealing the natural meanness she insists on associating with my origins, though I have reminded her more than once that this kind of racist slur is now legitimate grounds for a quick call to the European Court of Human Rights.

What do you advise?

Col

From: Billy Giddens [billy@goat.freeserve.co.uk]
To: ColumMcCallum [colum@laverda.demon.co.uk]

col old miucker
intrestign qustio re teh fiairing = - I could call Steve pretending not to know he has tehm

in and ask te qeuisiton re identical p[aint etc., no reason for him to know you wre behind it. otherwsie it loks like you and i mihgt be obliged to take naother jaunt to Italy soem tiem – early Spring is always god tooling weather down there.

   as for theotehr thing – do not waste another second worrying about iut, whatever you buy she will wabnt to change anyway so teh logical thing is to dig out one of her many cerdit card bills, find out hwre she shops most often and buy her someting from there. The onloy thing you have to worry about is the size of the pacjkage, make sure its big enough to mpress her under the tree, but what's inside is immaterial as she will take it stright back anyway and change it for something totqly different but witouht telling you so when you complimetn her on it she wil have an ecsue to berate you for failng to remember oyu gave it to her in the first place.

   we are as usual off in a few days to a p[art of teh world where they thrpow you inside for 99 years if oyu even mention Chrsitams. Expensvie but wothr ever penny belive me.

   see you on our return
   cheers
   bill

----

16 December – Urgent message: Des McCallum to Santa Claus

Hello Santa Claus I know you are very busy now and I hope you did get my list, I made Mum send it properly with a stamp and everything because only little babies believe that it gets there by itself up the chimney, and I am not a baby, I am nearly four and a half now. Plus we do not have a chimney, I have to talk to you about that too.

Only I was a bit worried because I heared her on the phone to Auntie Georgie and to Grandma saying nobody was to spend more than ten pounds on anybody's present or on mine which is not very much money even though it is a lot more than I have in my elephant bank, because I found out that the cowboy outfit will be more than that and I think maybe a DVD player is as well, so please I'm sure you can spend as much as you like, and I know you are very generous and kind, and I have told Mum that you like brandy not sherry and it has to be chocolate cake not a horrid mince pie and remember the carrots for Rudolph and she promised

Oh I forgot to have a pee before bedtime, night night.

17 December – Helen and best friend Ernie, on the phone

E: So how're the festive preparations going?
H: Hang on. (Des, four and a half is quite old enough to poo on your own. I'll be there to check your bum in a minute.) Oh, you know, emptying the bank account and tripping over drunks in Santa hats, but Des is so excited it's almost worth it. I'd never bother with it all except for him.
E: Mmm – hang on, just getting on to the massage table. (Neck and shoulders, please, darling, and lots of that lovely ginger oil like last time.) God, yes, nothing I loathe more than a family Christmas – bankrupting myself on presents nobody wants, disgusting turkey dinner, dreary afternoon in front of the telly with people I'd send off under the next Eurostar if they weren't related to me . . . (Up a bit, sweetie – yummm, perfect.)
H: Oh.

(*Pause*)

H: Well, I was going to ask if you wanted to come, as Des is your godson and everything, and I'd hate to think of you all alone. (NO, I'm BUSY, Des, and there are NO SPIDERS in the bathroom!)

E: Christ, I've no intention of being alone, no offence or anything, and of course I'd love to see my yummy darling fairy godson the minute I'm back . . .

H: Back?

E: Yup, in FACT I was going to tell you . . .

H: Will it keep till later, sweetie, because I'm just rushing off to Pricecheck for more tinsel? (Des, you DO NOT have to flush it twenty times, how often do I have to . . .)

E: Pricecheck? Helen, darling, if you're that short of cash, let me . . .

H: Pricecheck is an emporium of delights culled from the premier sweatshops of the globe, and all designed to self-destruct within two weeks, which is just perfect for this time of year.

E: I'll have to trust you on that one.

H: (Des, if you don't have your wellies on in two minutes I'm leaving you behind with a HUGE pile of ironing – no, it's okay, sweetie, Mum's only joking – yes, really . . .) Look, I've gotta go but I'll see you tonight.

E: Tonight? Oh Christ, it's Marla's party, isn't it. (Mmm, perfect, you're a star.) I have to say, it turns into a bit of a chore, doesn't it, at this time of year?

H: God, yes, I'm so exhausted by the time I get home from work and with Des still waking up at six . . . In fact I wasn't going to go either but I thought you . . .

E: I mean the first few are okay, but when it's two or three a night, every night, you almost long to be back at A.A., don't you?

H: Well, um, actually I haven't been to so many this year,

since I left the Archive, you know. (*hastily*) Not that I'm sorry to see the back of that bunch of old lushes or anything, and the hours at the library work much better with Des's school . . .

E: Jeez, if I'd known you could have gone to half of mine! But honestly, darling, you're not missing anything, especially as you're not exactly trawling any longer, are you? . . . I mean, in your situation, what's the point of parties?

H: (What's that, Des? Are we going where? Oh – of course we are, right now. Silly Mum was miles away.) Well, we'll be at Marla's anyway. You may find it hard to believe but I have a sister who's even sadder than I am, so sad in fact that she's free to look after Des. So . . .

E: Hey, doll, I never said you were . . .

H: . . . I'll see you tonight. If you can drag yourself there. *(Sound of phone being slammed down, very hard.)*

17 December – Marla's party

The party venue is a large family house in a part of London that's always up and coming but somehow never arrives. The street is totally parked up with estate cars and people-movers, so all the party guests have to tramp miles in the sleet in their skimpy clothes and stupid shoes, which does not deliver them in the best of spirits.

The dining table has been covered with an old sheet and a mixture of M&S canapés, chopped-up raw vegetables and limp baguettes. The remaining furniture has been cleared to make room for the expected heaving crowd, so the first dozen guests feel like ants on a football pitch. And needless to say, in order to optimise on the baby-sitter, the first two are . . .

8 p.m.   Helen and Colum. No one else is there. Colum immediately pours himself a large Scotch and

turns on the telly to catch the end of *Driven*. He remains here with a bunch of like-minded married males for the remainder of the evening. Helen disappears to the loo to check that she hasn't overdone her make-up, and stays there as long as she dares, hoping somebody else will arrive meanwhile.

8.30 p.m.   Ernie arrives. Helen and Ernie have a huge reconciliation, during which Helen discovers that Ernie has booked herself on the ultimate Caribbean winter break *à deux*, hence her unavailability for Boxing Day leftovers.

8.45 p.m.   Helen decides she needs to phone Georgie, just to check everything's okay. Hangs up and immediately phones back again, having remembered the stew she left in the oven, so she won't have to cook after late opening at the library tomorrow night.

Ernie goes to find another drink, and has an enjoyable tussle over the corkscrew with Marla's husband Tom.

9 p.m.   Helen remembers she needs to write her 'to do' list for tomorrow before she gets too drunk to remember what to put on it.

Ernie exchanges business cards with the CEO of an indie record label, who needs consultancy advice on optimising his digital property.

9.15 p.m.   Helen is deep in a fascinating conversation with a part-time teacher about how to get pre-schoolers to think number work is fun.

Ernie and Mr Music look out some cool grooves for dancing.

9.30 p.m.   Helen finds herself still trapped in what has gradually become an interminable exchange about arithmetic with the world's most boring woman.

	Ernie comes up to her in the nick of time and drags her off to dance.
9.45 p.m.	Helen falls off her heels, which she hasn't worn since last year, and goes looking for a corner quiet enough to call Georgie and make sure Des really is in bed and asleep.

Ernie decides she needs to keep a professional distance from Mr Music, and drags Helen up to the bedroom, where all the cute boys and girls are huddling round the SciFi Channel. Helen takes one look and flees in terror.

10 p.m. Helen, her feet killing her, and almost unable to keep her eyes open, decides not to join the subcommittee solving the child-vaccination dilemma round the last few carrot sticks, and goes to find Colum. Who is exactly where she left him, only a lot cheerier, either because of the Scotch or the telly or both.

Ernie decides she's chill enough, and luckily meets the male au pair under the mistletoe on the way back down.

10.15 p.m. Helen and Colum decide they may as well nod off in front of their own TV, and leave.

Ernie decides the party may not be a total waste of time after all.

18–19 December – E-mail exchange: Colum and Billy Giddens

From: ColumMcCallum [colum@laverda.demon.co.uk]
Sent: 18 December
To: Billy Giddens[billy@goat.freeserve.co.uk]

```
Hi Bill
Things at the office slowing down most
```

satisfactorily, never felt more in agreement with whoever said that most of the probs of the world are caused by people working. Think it may have been Keynes? Might even manage to get down to see Steve and pick up those bits I need to rebuild the Aero Caproni over the hols.

Meanwhile Madam, having nagged me for two weeks to rush back to base yesterday in time to be frogmarched off to some old girls' reunion in Muswell Hill, spends the entire evening remotely monitoring the progress of Des's bedtime routine, suddenly decides to leave just when it's warming up, and then spends the journey home berating me because she's going to feel terrible tomorrow morning. This being a somewhat unseasonable period for the delivery of divorce papers, do you have any other suggestions?

Col

From: Billy Giddens[billy@goat.freeserve.co.uk]
To: ColumMcCallum [colum@laverda.demon.co.uk]

col old miucker
if your gnoig to see Steve you might pick up that goretex cover he's got in for me, fnially decided hairyness odf Hyde Park corner february skidfest to much for an old codger. in fact i have even been pndering one of those Beamer scooters with the little roof, the Dog already treats me like a wheelchair case so mighs as well live up to it. but better not tell Steve, need to hang on to

remainig shreds of credibility in that quarter.

   as for yoursa, sounds to me liek she needs a few weeks in kennels somewhre with eighteeen hours of sunshien and no nagging opportunites. while your saving up, try givibng her a luagh, sending the odd funy postard etc, thy like to think we're thinking about them even when they're not there so lnog as what we're thinkng doesnt' involver sex in any shape or form, no danger with mine i have to say

   yrs bill

---

19 December – Joke postcard, 'A Busy Day at the Office', sent by Colum to Helen:

(Note: 'office' has been crossed out and the word 'library' substituted. This document has been reconstructed with some difficulty from many small fragments.)

10.00	arrive, catch up
10.15–10.45	coffee break
10.45–11.00	lavatory break
11.00–11.30	phone calls
11.30–12.00	plan lunch
12.00–13.00	lunch
13.00–13.30	walk round block to work off lunch
13.30–14.00	return phone calls
14.00–14.30	return e-mails
14.30–14.45	lavatory break
14.45–15.00	cigarette break
15.00–15.30	make to-do list
15.30–16.00	tea break . . .

(The remainder has been defaced and/or lost)

20 December – Helen

Stimulated by highly amusing 'joke' postcard from certain persons whose socks I intend never to wash again, to realise that what I would really, really like for Christmas is to swap lives with Des.

7.00   Woken by big hug from Mum, lie around in bed kicking stuffed animals on to floor and picking nose while she tidies up and removes my dirty clothes, water glass and other detritus.

7.20   Dressed by Mum, more hugs as tell her all about various and colourful dreams. As usual, she thinks they are the most fascinating and exciting thing she's ever heard. Bask in her admiration for a few extra minutes. After all, I'm not going to get blamed if we're late again.

7.30   Fed breakfast by Mum, made exactly the way I like it. Absolutely refuse to eat last two spoonfuls until she pretends they're express trains going into a tunnel, and reward her and Dad with my famous imitation of an elephant blowing muesli out of his trunk. They pretend to be shocked but I know better, and anyhow they're the ones mopping up.

7.50   While Dad does the washing-up, sit on Mum's knee while she reads me a story. Finish picking my nose while she's not looking.

8.00   Mum gives me my packed lunch, all ready, and buttons me into my snuggly coat, brand new because I conveniently outgrew last year's before it had time to get worn or boring. Kiss Dad goodbye and leave for nursery. Huge breakfast has given me surge of energy, which I use up running in circles round Mum, kicking old leaves, and playing chasing games with best friend Archie who lives on the way. Archie and I talk about what we're getting for Christmas. We don't have to get anybody anything as we have no money and Mum will do the cards for us, in the end.

8.30   Arrive at Paint Pots. Mum and teacher Patti help me off with my coat and boots and on with my Paint Pots overall. Now comes the stressful part of the day – pouring water, fitting shapes together, painting, and even sticking my tongue out while copying letters. Very glad when it's time for . . .

11.00   Hot chocolate and biscuits for break. I can have as much as I like because I am growing and always hungry and however many biscuits I eat I never get fat. Then more hard work until . . .

12.30   Lunch-time – delicious packed lunch with extra cereal bar. Mum keeps pretending they're bad for me but she keeps giving them to me anyway, and Archie is weird and he doesn't like food so I eat most of his lunch too, and then dump my bread crusts and carrot sticks in his lunch box – nobody will know.

13.00   Patti bundles us into our coats and we go to the playground to run off our giant lunch.

13.30   Nap time. Aaaah . . . sleep like a baby – no worries to stop me.

14.30   Wake refreshed and bounding with energy. More hard work – music or dancing, followed by story-time and another run around.

17.00   Mum collects me from Paint Pots. Archie comes home to tea. Archie and I build giant train track all over my bedroom while Mum makes favourite pasta and cheese and courgettes.

18.30   Archie goes home. Mum tries to get me to clear away train track but I keep finding new bits to add on instead, so in the end she does it herself, which I knew she would. Then Mum gives me lovely hot bath with bubbles and we play Baby Whale while she dries me on the big soft towel.

19.00 Dad comes home. Watch half an hour of my favourite video sitting on his knee and rubbing his prickly chin with my hair while Mum washes up tea and gets their supper.

19.30 Toothypegs-time and lots of hugs and bed, with personalised bedtime calypso improvised by Mum on the spot. Tell all my toys what I did today. Sleep deeply for eleven hours.

19 December – Excerpt from phone call: Ernie to Helen

H: Where are you?
E: *(sound of Capital Radio playing at full volume in background)* At home. I'll just turn it down, hang on. *(Capital diminishes slightly)*
H: What? What's wrong?
E: What d'you mean, what's wrong?
H: Well, you're never at home. In fact, thinking about it, I realise I don't even imagine you having a home.
E: Where do you think I sleep?
H: Don't ask me to answer that! (Second floor, between sanitary engineering and mortality rates. No problem.)
E: You know I have a home, you helped me decorate it.
H: So I did. (This is my lunch hour, if you don't mind. No, that was yesterday's that I missed and saved up. Do you mind?) Rude bastard. Is it still that colour?
E: It is. And it's still fab.
H: If you say so. Anyhow, to repeat, what's wrong?
E: Nothing. No, in fact it's brilliant, I had this brilliant idea.
H: Oh yes?

E: You know that superfit boy I told you about at the party?
H: The one you're going on hols with? (No, Chick Lit's upstairs, it's basically the whole of General Fiction . . .)
E: Yeah, exactly, well, that's it. It turns out he's not actually very . . . well, to be honest he's a total tosser and . . .
H: I knew there was something. D'you need a mop-up?
E: God, no, I'm thrilled about it, only it means, you see, I have this . . .
H: (Sorry, I thought you said Chick Lit. Lit Crit is in the basement with Semiotics and all that rubbish. Okey-dokey.)
E: HELEN! I'm trying to offer you the holiday of a lifetime!
H: You are? How come?
E: Well, I bought the extra ticket and the hotel reservation and everything and I'm certainly not going on my own, so I thought . . .
H: ERNIE! (Sorry, did I startle you, Mr Pargiter? Yes, it is that time of year, isn't it.) You're amazing! Where is it again?
E: Barbados. Two weeks, the first in this fabulous . . . Here, let me read it to you.

'Breezy, hilltop plantation house brimming with eighteenth-century atmosphere, with canopied beds, open verandas and three-hundred-and-sixty-degree views. Your second week will take you to the beachside bungalow of your dreams, where you'll sleep amidst bougainvillaeas and hibiscus, lapped by the gentle waves of the coral lagoon . . .'

Pretty fine, or what? Rum punch, steel bands, boogying in the New Year on the beach . . .
H: It sounds to die for.
E: So get packing, girl.
H: God, you've no idea but . . . two weeks, that's an awfully long time.
E: Not half bloody long enough, if you ask me.

H: Yes, but I'd be away for Christmas, and for New Year . . .
E: That's the whole idea.
H: But I mean, leaving Des over Christmas, when I've promised him Santa Claus and the zoo and . . .
E: Colum can do all that, you're always saying he's the perfect father. Let him prove it.
H: I just don't know . . .
E: Look, I do know one thing, and that's that Des will love you a lot more if you're happy and sun kissed and rested and cheerful than if you're a miserable ratbag stewing around full of resentment that you didn't go.
H: Well, when you put it like that . . . (Actually, I've only had forty-five minutes, and no, I won't be leaving early again, since you ask, not that it's any of your business.)
E: There, it's done, then. We don't leave till the twenty-third, so you've got lots of time to pack.
H: I'll have to talk to Colum about it. I've no idea what I'll say to poor little Des.
E: Poor little Des! You're not sending him into slavery, you're giving him two weeks to bond with his dad and discover just how much he owes you. Promise me you'll come?
H: I'll talk to Colum, okay?

19 December, late – Helen and Colum: in the kitchen

An almost empty bottle of wine and two glasses sit on the table between them. Helen is sticking white cotton-wool balls on to an ancient pillowcase. Most of the glue is ending up on her fingers. Colum has spread three sheets of kitchen roll on his side of the table. On these he has arranged a large collection of tiny, jewel-like metal and rubber bike parts, which he is meticulously coating with calliper grease from a toothpick.

Helen sighs dramatically, and puts down the pillowcase. Colum looks up.

C: I said I was sorry. It was supposed to cheer you up.
H: I bet Billy put you up to it.
C: He . . .
H: Anyhow, it's not that. It's . . .

She pauses, and tries to look mysteriously tragic. Unfortunately Colum has gone back to his advance-and-return controls, and misses it. Helen tries again.

H: It's . . .
C: You're having second thoughts about that ten-pound limit, aren't you? Don't worry, I never thought ye meant it.
H: Oh, it's hopeless.

Colum looks up again, racks his brains, and assumes she must be talking about the pillowcase.

C: Well, but it's not done yet, is it? What's it supposed to be?
H: It's a sheep. For the nativity play. I copied it from *Teletubbies*. Only I've run out of white cotton balls, and it still looks a bit . . .
C: Mangy?
H: Thanks. D'you think he'd mind if I mixed in a few coloured ones? I mean, you do see sheep with coloured splodges on them, don't you?
C: Sugar pink splodges?
H: Maybe not in the Outer Hebrides, but I bet those Home Counties sheep, in Sussex and Kent . . .

Colum's look is not encouraging. She sighs, again.

H: Well, I'm not going out in this weather to find more white ones. He'll just have to be mangy. After all, a sheep's life in ancient Palestine'd probably make modern Sussex look like . . . *(meaningfully)* like a holiday in Barbados.

She bites her lip on this and stares at Colum, who's reloading his toothpick and misses it again.

C: D'ye think the peer group'll buy that line?
H: It's the peer group's parents I'm scared of. No I'm not.

She puts down the bag of balls, and sniffs.

H: Honestly, look at me, I'm so pathetic. D'you think Madonna spends her evenings worrying about sheep costumes? Or Cherie Blair? No wonder I've never made anything of my life. I'm a ludicrous failure, and I'm about to turn my son into a social outcast, too.

Colum finally realises that something is seriously up. He replaces all the parts in their right places, wipes off the toothpick, wipes his hands, and only then comes over and sits her on his knee.

C: I'd not want either of them in bed wi' me. And I bet their kids don't love them half as much as young Des loves you.

He tries to kiss her. She turns away, trying very hard to muster an affecting tear or two, and sighs, again.

H: That's just it! That's why I can't! I just can't!
C: Can't what?

He notices that he's left the cap off the grease, and leans over to replace it, which makes her cross.

H: Oh, you don't care, anyway. You're perfectly happy to stew in boring NW5 every day and every night, letting the world pass you by.
C: Leaving aside the matter of the world in my head, which is far from boring, at least to me, what is this all about?

H: It's . . . Ernie.
C: Ah. Ernie envy. The woman with no family, no husband, no son, and no obvious idea of how she's going to spend her days once her chin's finally been ratcheted up to her hairline.
H: God, you're mean. Anyhow, it's not, and she's not. If you must know, she's . . . she's offered me something absolutely wonderful, and I can't . . . (*almost a real sob*) can't have it!
C: What's his name?

Helen tries to hurl down the pillowcase, which she's been clutching all this time, and leaps off his knee. The pillowcase sticks to her hand. She tears it off, furiously, and stalks across the room.

C: Hey . . .
H: I'm boiling a kettle.

She does so, covering the handle liberally with glue.

H: DAMN. It's not a he, it's a holiday. It's two weeks, in a luxury Caribbean paradise, with plantation houses and rum punch and rainforests and steel bands and pineapple massages and fans and canopied beds and it's absolutely free and . . .
C: Sounds great. Off ye go.
H: What? No, you don't understand, it's over Christmas! And New Year! She's leaving in four days, and I wouldn't be back until . . .
C: So?
H: So . . . so, I'd be abandoning you and Des and . . . I've booked us in to see Santa, and what about his stocking, and . . .
C: I can take him to see Santa. And I should think a respectable degree from Scotland's premier university is probably just about enough training to get a stocking filled.
H: But . . .

She stands there, a teabag stuck to her finger, the wind entirely out of her sails.

H: But . . . but wouldn't you miss me? And what about Des, he'll hate me, he'll never want to speak to me again!
C: Of course I'll miss ye, and so will young Des, but I'll make sure he has a great time, and you can bring him back some wildly exotic Caribbean present . . .
H: He wouldn't . . .
C: Or failing that, something pricey from the airport shopping mall, and he'll be more thrilled than if you'd stayed. Trust me.

He comes over and kisses her. His shirt now has glue on it, too, but he puts up with it.

H: Really?
C: Really.
H: *(Big, happy sigh)* Wow!

She hugs him back, pulls the teabag off her finger, scattering tea dust everywhere, and dashes for the door, grabbing her coat on the way.

C: I thought you said you'd four days?
H: I have to get to Pricecheck before it closes. I just remembered they sell cotton-wool balls.

20 December – Paint Pots nursery school nativity play

Twenty adoring parents try to look comfortable on a semicircle of children's chairs in the Paint Pots classroom. The protagonists, in various home-sewn and papier-mâché disguises, huddle to one side, giggling. Patti, the teacher, is mustering them.

Barney, a beefy boy in a red cloak and a cowboy hat, suddenly shouts:

B: Patti can I start Patti is it ready yet?

Without waiting for a reply he charges into the middle of the semicircle and bellows:

B: THIS IS THE STORY OF THE BABY JESUS WE ARE TELLING IT TODAY BECAUSE IT IS NEAR CHRISTMAS THERE ARE LOTS OF STORIES AND LOTS OF RELIGIONS IN THE WORLD THIS IS ONE WE HOPE, WE HOPE . . . YOU LIKE IT!! Was that good, Mummy?

He suddenly looks very embarrassed and rushes to the other end of the room. His mother looks in her bag for a tissue.

Patti whispers into the ear of a very small girl, Sukie, dressed as a star, who staggers out in front of the others, blushes, and says in a rush:

S: I am the magic thtar thent by God to guide Mary and Jotheph to where they can ummm can . . .
P: (*whispers*) . . . can have their baby Jesus safely.
S: Can have their thafely Jethuth! Bye-bye! Follow me!

She twirls around in triumph and goes back to the cluster. Now her mother suddenly has a cold, too. The tissues are passed down the row.

Patti whispers to a girl wearing a blue towelling dressing gown and a nun's veil – Mary – and a boy in a brown dressing gown and a long cardboard beard – Joseph. They walk into the middle, holding hands, but unfortunately facing away from the audience.

M: Good morning, Joseph! Today I'm going to have my baby Jesus!!

Mary's mother doesn't even pretend she's not in tears.

J: Oh good Mary let's go to Be . . . Bel . . . Bellyham.

Joseph's mother and father burst into tears. By now almost every adult in the room is trying to suppress sobs, and Patti is visibly near the edge, too.

Joseph tears off his beard which is obviously very scratchy, and Mary and Joseph, still clutching hands, run off. Mary trips on her dressing-gown cord, falls flat and howls loudly. Her mother immediately sobers up and calls out, 'You're fine, Serena, no need to fuss!' Serena instantly swallows her sobs.

Two more children in dressing gowns and carrying large walking sticks – the shepherds – now come on, followed by three sheep. Evidently all the mothers get their creative vision from *Teletubbies*.

Helen sits up and gets out her camera. Sukie the Star pirouettes back into the circle and twirls around among them, hogging the limelight.

S: That'th a funny thtar, isn't it, sheep?
SH1: Baaaa!
SH2: Baaa!
SH3: ROOARRR!

One of the sheep doesn't seem to want to baaa. Helen looks worried and lowers the camera.

S: I think that thtar ith for baby Jethuth what do you think sheep?
SH1: Baaaa!
SH2: Baaa!
SH3: ROOOWWWRRR!! RUFFF!!

The third sheep has suddenly begun attacking the others, which fight back enthusiastically. Helen looks more worried, then starts to laugh.

SH: POW!!   RRROOOAARR!!   BANG   BANG!!! CHAAAARGE!!!

The shepherds shriek delightedly and join in the fray. Patti tries to restore order as Mary and Joseph tear off their annoying costumes and join in. Sukie, realising that her moment in the spotlight has been snatched from her, stamps her foot and shouts:

S: Thtop it! Thtop it! I'm the Thtar of Birmingham!! It'th not fair! Patti make them thtop it'th not fair!

Sukie's mother, furious, rounds on Helen, who stops laughing, but then unaccountably bursts into passionate howls instead, and rushes from the room. Patti finally succeeds in breaking up the scrum.

P: (*brightly*) Well done, children, come and take a bow! Let's all have some juice and flapjacks, shall we?

20 December – Voicemail message left on Ernie's mobile

H: I can't, I just can't! He looked so sweet in his sheep costume and he's so wonderful and he's going to grow up so fast and if I miss a Christmas I'll never forgive myself and how would I look him in the eye and tell him and I'm so so sorry to mess you around and I KNOW you're going to have an amazing time and I'll be thinking about it night and day . . .
(*At this point Helen's voice disintegrates into sobs again, with the result that the remainder of the message was not recorded.*)

20 December – Helen, Colum and Des having supper

Helen and Colum are eating pasta and drinking wine, in quantity. Helen still looks somewhat red around the eyes, but is gazing at Des as though he is himself the baby Jesus.

Des has somehow managed to eat all his grated cheese, pasta and bacon, while leaving the tomatoes and mushrooms.

C: So after Mary and Joseph got ambushed by the robbers, what happened then?
H: *(sniff)* Eat your lovely vegetables, Des darling.
D: So THEN the robbers said, 'We're going to EAT your baby all up, and then we're going to kill it!'
C: So this is after the baby's been born, then, is it? Mebbe on the way home?
H: Would you like some more cheese on them, darling?
D: *(absently)* Yes.
H: *(autopilot)* Yes please.
D: *(on autopilot back)* Yes please.

Helen grates some more cheese over the tomatoes and mushrooms. Des forks in the cheese in one mouthful, still talking. The tomatoes and mushrooms remain intact.

D: No no no they weren't going HOME they were going to the TOYSHOP with the baby Jesus.
C: Aha, stocking up with the basics, I suppose.
D: No no no it was Christmas they were buying his Christmas presents! And do you know what he got?
H: Eat at least some of them, sweet.
C: D'ye know, I've always wondered what was on baby Jesus' Christmas list but it just doesn't say anywhere in the Bible. I've looked . . .
D: He got chocolate and some guns and some soldiers and a pirate outfit and . . .
H: Baby Jesus always ate ALL his vegetables, Des sweetie. Look . . . *(reaching over with her fork)* Look, I'll have some *(eats a forkful)* and now YOU have some.
D: *(ignoring her)* . . . and a fort and an ambylance with some blood and . . .
C: All that? I hope they'd a spare donkey or two to get it all home.

H: IF YOU DON'T EAT YOUR VEGETABLES, DES, YOU'LL GO STRAIGHT TO BED NOW WITH NO PUDDING!!

Des and Colum both look at her, astonished, and stop talking.

C: (*to Des*) D'ye know, elephants really, really like mushrooms. They grow in the jungle all over the place, it's that hot and swampy and damp.
D: Do they like tomatoes too?
C: I happen to know that tomatoes are absolutely an elephant's favourite food.

Des immediately picks up his fork and clears his plate. Helen leaves the table, bangs into the kitchen, and starts doing the dishes, very loudly.

(Some time later)

Helen has decided to make herself really miserable by getting out all the filthy old baking tins and scouring every single one of them. She's up to her elbows in greasy black dishwater when Colum comes in behind her.

C: What are you . . .
H: AAAAAARGH!!

She jumps about three feet in the air.

C: . . . up to, petal?
H: Don't do that to me!
C: Come into the kitchen without an exchange of diplomatic letters in advance?
H: Creep up on me like that! Can't you see I'm busy?
C: Looks like fun. I won't disturb ye, then.

He turns away.

C: Come on, Des, we'll just have to force ourselves to eat it.

Des appears round the door, looking more than usually adorable, fresh from the bath.

D: No! It's for Mum you said it was you said! And you don't like it anyway!

He runs up to Helen, holding out a large cardboard object, and buries himself, and it, in her skirt. Helen turns round, and leans down to investigate.

H: Oh! Oh, Colum! Oh, Des!

The object is a Godiva chocolate advent calendar, somewhat battered but heavy with promise. Des jumps up and down, tugging at her.

D: Look and look Mum look what I did too!

He opens one of the cardboard doors and pokes out the chocolate, which promptly falls into the dirty water. Helen retrieves it, wipes it on her sleeve, and eats it, challenging Colum with a look. Behind the chocolate is a little scrap of tightly folded paper, which Des hands her, eyes bright with anticipation. Helen unfolds it and reads:

H: 'I love my Mum because she's cuddly and wears tight skirts.'
D: D'you like it Mum d'you like it? I did it all with Dad, there's one for every day that's why . . .
C: That's why ye're only getting it now, it took bloody ages, but better late than never, eh?

Helen shrieks and holds out her arms, and everybody has a big soggy hug.

C: Happy Christmas, ye mad bat.

Editor's Letter, *Traditional Living* Magazine – December issue

Written in August five years ago when she first got the job, and recycled with minor variations every August since, in time for the December issue.

> A very warm seasonal welcome to all our readers, new and old. This is the time of year we at the magazine most look forward to, as the fashion department spills over with sparkly and shimmery creations to set our pulses racing, the art department comes in with seasonal baubles and decorations, and the Home and Hearth department fills the office with irresistible sweet and savoury aromas.
>
> But even the most diehard party-goer must pause occasionally to wonder whether, in this giddy merry-go-round of shopping, eating, drinking and present-giving, the real meaning of Christmas is in danger of being forgotten.
>
> With this in mind, we've decided to devote this year's Christmas issue to the traditional Christmas rituals and activities that families used to enjoy together, when they made their own entertainment on those long, snowy winter nights. We've decorated our tree with papier-mâché candle-holders, clove-studded clementines and silver- and gold-painted nuts (p. 124). Our Christmas tea table features a home-made gingerbread house from the easy-to-follow instructions on p. 145. Children will love sticking the chocolate buttons on the front door! And we have Christmas present suggestions galore to make yourself, from this season's trend-setting embroidered silk ties, to cosy ethnic slipper-socks and jewellery baskets woven from ribbons and lace. There's something for everybody here, and the best news is that this year the preparation will be as much fun as the day itself!
>
> So get stuck in – I know I can't wait!

The new second paragraph of this letter, with its implication that consumerism is in some way a bad thing, had the immediate effect of halving the advertising revenue of the following issue of the magazine.

For this error of judgment the editor lost her enormously lucrative job with immediate effect, and discovered a whole new side to the season of goodwill, in the ranks of the unemployed.

21 December – Helen, back from the supermarket

The phone is ringing as Helen staggers in through the door and up the stairs, laden with plastic bags and wrapping paper. Eight bags hit the floor, followed by a yowl and skittering of claws as Bertie emerges from beneath them, and makes for the door.

Helen gets to the phone, just too late.

H: Sorry, Bertie.

She picks up the phone and retrieves a message from Ernie.

E: (Dollface! Here I am at the airport just wanting to say I'll miss you and I'll have double everything for you and bring back loads of pineapples and big Rastafarians to massage away all those winter blues. Oh God, there's my final call now. Byee!!!)

Helen puts down the phone, stares at it dolefully for a minute, then pulls herself together, heaves off her damp, heavy coat, hangs it up and looks at her bedraggled self in the hall mirror.
H: No you don't. Bad, bad girl. Think about somebody else. Aha!

She goes to the phone again and dials a number. Her mother.

H: Mum?
A: Helen, dear! How unlike you to remember . . .
H: God, it's like the siege of Grozny out there today. Sometimes I envy you the rural calm of Aldershot. Almost. But I think I've got everything, more or less, now. How are you?
A: I'd be better if I didn't spend the best part of every morning opening the post.

H: How lovely that you've got so many people who remember you at Christmas! I suppose that's one positive thing about being old, isn't it, that you've had all those years to accumulate friends.

A: Funnily enough, I never feel old except when I'm talking to you. But of course, you're not the only one. Half of the pile is charity Christmas cards from third cousins who clearly regard me as a seasonal duty alongside the Salvation Army collection bucket, and the rest are thoughtful reminders from various government agencies that this is the time of year I'm most likely to freeze to death, break my hips on black ice, contract killer flu, or lie undiscovered after a household accident for a week or more, while the rest of the world celebrates heedlessly without me. Not the most uplifting start to the day, as I'm sure even you can imagine.

Yowling and scuffling outside the door. Helen walks over, phone in hand, and opens it.

H: (In or out, Bertie, for goodness' sake, I'm not the doorman here.) What you need, Mum, is a megadose of Traditional Christmas. I've tracked down the perfect present for you, and Des and I are stuck into all the fabulous craft activities and little rituals that Christmas ought to be about, but so rarely is! We've made the puddings and the cake, and most of the potato-print Christmas cards, and next we're going to do the pomander balls and the gold and silver walnuts for the tree.

A: And Des has been helping you with all of that?

H: Oh yes, he weighed the raisins and currants and ate the ones that fell on the floor – at least, he shared them with Bertie – and then he scraped out the mixing bowl, and he did three and a half cards all on his own – well, almost.

A: How many did you need?

H: Umm – well, he's only little and Christmas cards are such a waste of time, aren't they, but he's really looking forward to painting the nuts and making the gingerbread house.

A: Well, I sincerely hope you all have a lovely time, if that's really what you want. I have to say it all seems a bit artificial to me, this harking back to happy times that never were.

H: Mum! It'll be lovely, and especially with you there and Georgie and her lot, all together like a proper family. Of course, it'll be a bit crowded but I did think it was our turn, and Colum's getting the tree this afternoon . . .

A: Me? You're not expecting me there, surely, dear? Even you can't have forgotten already . . .

H: Forgotten what?

A: The cruise that dear Brian found for me, bird-watching in the Norwegian fjords. He came across it when he was booking their skiing holiday. In fact, I believe we're all going to meet up on New Year's Eve.

H: Georgie and Brian are going skiing?

A: Of course, dear. You know they're always trying to improve young Jack's co-ordination, and this year apparently your sister's reflexology work's been picking up – one born every minute, it would seem – so anyhow, they . . .

H: When?

A: When what, dear?

H: When are you going?

A: I'm off tomorrow. In fact I had thought, foolishly, that you were calling to wish me bon voyage.

Helen sits, heavily.

A: I think the others are leaving on Monday. Is something wrong, dear? You sound a little strange.

22 December – Helen

Bird-watching! She hates birds! In fact the only reason she

doesn't have a cat is that she hates cats even more than birds. (Nothing to do with Colum's impulse purchase of Bertie a couple of years ago, of course.) And absolutely bloody typical of her to spend half an hour telling me off for calling her old and then spring her Christmas cruise on me, when everybody knows a cruise ship is just a giant floating wheelchair for people who can't go anywhere unaided any more.

As for Georgie taking her brood skiing – all I can say is I hope everybody else at whatever resort they've booked into has been warned to take out triple accident insurance, because if ever I saw a multiple pile-up on a double black diamond waiting to happen, it's Jack being encouraged to improve his co-ordination.

Well, at least I can dump the painted walnuts and the gingerbread house now. I'll give Des the Smarties in his stocking, that'll make him happy. I wonder if it's too late to head off Column with the tree?

Better go and see how Des is getting on with his ambush plan for Santa Claus. I'm sure I'd never heard of hostage-taking at his age.

23 December – The Santa Claus kidnap and ransom demand calypso

> There was once a scary man, in a red coat and a beard
> Who wanted to be liked, but was more often feared.
> He used to get small children to sit on his knee
> By bribing them with presents that he said were free.
>
> *(Yes, I know you didn't want a pull-the-string Wibbly Pig. If he'd been the real Santa he'd have given you a Kalashnikov at the very least, wouldn't he? . . . No, probably too late to add that to the list now, but there's always next year. Now lie down and close your eyes.)*

But Mum knew better, 'cause she'd had to pay
To take Des through a queue that seemed to last all day.
When Santa made Des hug him just to get a prize
Mum said, 'I know a way to see through his disguise.'

There's only one real Santa, and he's not human
He knows a thousand ways to get into a room, an
D'out again without making a sound or a mark
And he never bumps or clatters, even in pitch dark.

So Des has made an ambush that will trap a fake
And he's lying here, determined to stay awake.
But I bet the real Santa will come instead.
And he'll leave a big fat stocking right here on the bed!

(Night-night, pudding . . . Yes, you know it's a funny thing, that milk tonight made me very sleepy too . . . No, no horrid man with a fake beard can get through the double glazing, I promise.)

Traditional Living Magazine: 'Countdown to Christmas' – December issue

So you've done the bulk of the shopping, bought and wrapped your presents, invited friends and family, got the tree home and chosen the decorations. It's time to kick back, cosy up in your softest Christmas housecoat and spend an enjoyable two days finishing those last-minute jobs that will ensure The Day goes smoothly and happily from stockings to port.

23 December

Morning	Last-minute shopping for perishables: milk, salad, tangerines, cream or custard, and of course fresh flowers – a fragrant midwinter luxury.
Afternoon	Stuff goose with chestnuts, fennel and figs mixed with a few brown breadcrumbs and a drop or two of Calvados.

	Make Potato Purée Savoyard, pipe into whorls and freeze. Finish silver gilt walnuts and pomander balls for tree.
Evening	Why not do something totally un-Christmassy tonight? You've done enough cooking – order in a curry (an empire tradition!), find a photo album, and get out all those summer holiday snaps jumbled in a drawer (we know they're there!). You'll enjoy reliving memories of fun in the sun as carollers come and go and Christmas music plays in the background.

24 December

Morning	Make apple sauce and mince pies. Make orange jelly boats – lighter alternative to Christmas pudding. Stuff prunes with walnuts and cream cheese for an original appetiser.
Afternoon	Decorate tree. Time to go through your address book for somebody who may be feeling lonely and left out this Christmas. Why not pay them a surprise visit or cheer them with a goodwill phone call?
Evening	Wrap presents. Fill stockings (after the little ones are safely tucked in bed, of course!). Put champagne on ice. Slice smoked salmon and interleave for ease of serving. Pour yourself a drink and relax – the hard work's over!

25 December – The Day

8 a.m.	Put crumpets and muffins on to toast. Light oven, remove potato whorls from freezer.
8.30	Serve light breakfast of crumpets and muffins with home-made preserves and compote of winter fruits.
9.00	Goose into oven. Slice red cabbage with onion, peel apples and slice, derind bacon

10.00	Boil water for pudding, wrap pudding with clean, dry cloth and tie tightly with string. Lower into water and keep simmering. DO NOT boil dry and DO NOT allow to go off simmer.
10.15–12.30	Open presents, play games and make those special Christmas phone calls to loved ones. Meanwhile every twenty minutes check pudding doesn't boil dry or go off simmer, and baste goose.
12.30	Remove stuffed prunes from fridge. Put red cabbage and other vegetables on to simmer. Glaze potato whorls with butter and Parmesan, pop into oven above goose. Put sugar lumps, bitters and brandy into champagne cocktail glasses.
13.00	Remove goose and allow to sit for half an hour while you serve stuffed prunes, smoked salmon and caviar blinis and champagne cocktails to your guests.
13.30	Remove potato whorls from oven. Grill bacon and chop finely. Remove pudding from pan but leave tightly wrapped. Carve goose, finish red cabbage with star anis and crispy bacon.
14.00	Luncheon is served!!!

27 December – Helen

Never. Never again. I seem to remember having said this before, but this time I REALLY mean it. This is what I get for chancing on *Traditional Living*. It's not often you find a current magazine in a doctor's waiting room. I thought it was a sign. How was I supposed to know it was a sign to leave the country?

As I'd spent the 23rd 'clearing my desk' into the recycling bin in Periodicals, the 23rd's recommended schedule had to be fitted in on the 24th. The morning began harmlessly enough with Colum breezing off to work to 'tidy up' and Des and me setting off to Sainsbury's for 'last-minute bits and pieces', which would have been less of a problem had the shelves not resembled those of a Dresden corner store immediately after the firebombing. Suffice it to say that 400,000 other readers of *Traditional Living* had swept it of everything but forlorn little heaps of spaghetti hoops, pork chops and frozen sweetcorn niblets. The traditional goose had already got the elbow after Colum expressed an uncharacteristically craven reluctance to eat anything larger than his own child, and I managed by some fluke to remember to buy a guinea fowl instead, possibly because I fell off my bicycle right outside the butcher's shop after the office Christmas lunch on Monday.

However, such was the heaving throng of locals fighting over the last packet of crumpets that assembling our modest haul took nearly an hour, though actually we needn't have bothered, because while we had to leave it in the trolley inside the negative-gravity area to walk half a mile to where we had parked the car (rather farther away than home, but in the other direction), Santa and his Elves decided there were needier persons than us and whisked the lot off to the great soup kitchen in the sky. (At least, I assume it was he. None of the several thousand putative eyewitnesses admitted to having seen anything.)

At this point I decided to scale back a little on the grand plan, especially in view of recent revelations that not since the early days of the Great Plague had so many people left London so suddenly and for so long. So we popped into Tesco Express at the petrol station for the basics – bacon, extra-thick custard and two cans of squirty cream.

And as the silver nuts and the pomander balls had already been given the heave-ho, and Colum hates potato purée, the afternoon was enjoyably free for experimenting with the optimum concentration of Calvados in the fig-and-fennel stuffing. What with all the scaling back and changes of plan, the entire recommended schedule for Christmas Eve was binned too, which left the evening free for *Traditional Living*'s one good idea, which we got past Des by persuading him that he'd never get to see elephants en masse in India until he could eat curry.

After that it looked like the only hard part was going to be keeping Santa awake longer than Des, but for once our firstborn, agog with his kidnap plan, could hardly wait to join the four elephants, stuffed iguana, pair of Colum's old boxer shorts and sticker book from the last Disney magazine which are his bed mates of choice, and as I'd taken the precaution of spiking his bedtime milk with the Christmas pudding brandy, it was only minutes before Santa and Rudolph, or Renata as she prefers to be known these days, were able to dump the satisfyingly lumpy and heavy stocking on his bed and tiptoe off up the chimney, in squiffy anticipation of the joys of the morrow.

We didn't have long to wait. At 1.33 a.m. by the clock radio a banshee wail echoed through the house and we found Des puce, terrified and shaking with the trademark 106° temperature which he saves for special occasions such as this.

So it was rather a good thing, all in all, that we had no winter fruit compote, potato whorls, roast goose, stuffed prunes or salmon and caviar blinis to get ready, as between changing the sheets and digging stubborn bits of curry out from the sisal matting, Colum discovered that the queasy feeling he'd been attributing to bad choices at the cocktail bar was, in fact, the selfsame flu, a seasonal tradition that somehow even *Traditional Living* forgot.

So this is how 25 December – The Day – actually went.

6 a.m.	First in line outside emergency pharmacy at local hospital, only about twenty minutes down the motorway at this time on Christmas morning. Obtain industrial quantities of Calpol. Spend return journey reflecting gloomily that it's come to something when you don't know a single

	neighbour you can borrow a non-prescription drug from.
8.30	Fancy a light breakfast of crumpets and muffins with home-made preserves and compote of winter fruits – but make do with old hot-cross bun M.I.A. in the freezer since last April.
9.00	Colum has first nosebleed for thirty years over wedding-present linen sheets. Change them around his groaning body, and put worst blood-soaked bits (sheets) to soak in giant pan.
10.00	Remember giant pan needed for Christmas pudding. Re-evaluate chances of eating Christmas pudding this, or any, Christmas. Consider alternative uses for pudding, e.g. weight-training.
10.15–12.30	Des decides repeatedly that he's well enough to open a present and, in manner of small household god, stamps his foot and demands that little plates of goodies be put in front of him, which, sadly, he is unable to make disappear. Chocolate he can eat, though not, alas, keep down.

Meanwhile loved ones are making those special Christmas phone calls to let us know what a fab time they are having in Bergen, Bolzano and Barbados.

| 12.30 | Remove guinea fowl from fridge, realise too hungry to wait until it cooks, replace in fridge, stick bacon under grill and stuffing in microwave. |

Put sugar lumps, bitters and brandy into champagne cocktail glass. Fill up with remaining Calvados. Nursing goes much more smoothly when you're canned. Ask any NHS ward sister.

Take sheet out of pan and stuff into washing machine, along with two sets of Des's sheets, two pairs of his pyjamas, one lucky iguana and one pair

	of Colum's boxer shorts, possibly unsalvageable.
13.00	Remove Des from bed after persistent promises that he's better, and allow to sit for half an hour in front of *Charlie and the Chocolate Factory* while serving champagne cocktails to self. Realise, too late, that *Charlie and the Chocolate Factory* may not have been wise choice. Put Des back to bed, and attack new abstract pattern on living-room carpet.
	Realise have been subliminally aware for some time of pathetic bleeping and increasingly acrid smell from kitchen. Look up to see smoke wisping around kitchen door. Remember bacon and stuffing. Cooking, unlike nursing, not recommended on empty stomach and half a bottle of Calvados.
13.30	Remove stuffing from microwave. Attempt to remove bacon from grill pan. Lightly toss entire thing into bin, and eat Tesco ready-made custard from pot instead. Bertie arrives back from carol singing, makes beeline for bin, and gives self third-degree burns all over front paws and nose. Discover brandy butter much more soothing to burns than regular variety.
13.45	Mysterious clanking noise heard from direction of washing machine, reminiscent of Santa's sleigh disintegrating. Water pours out over kitchen floor. Washing machine shudders to terminal halt.
14.00	. . . and it's still only lunch-time . . .

So I now know
a) Where to go for Calpol on public holidays.
b) Which local launderettes are open on Boxing Day.
c) Not to believe a four-year-old when he says he's better.
d) (REALLY) Never again.

Boxing Day – Ernie, on the beach in Barbados

Ernie is lying on a palm-fringed beach of blinding white sand, which borders an azure ocean, lapping a soft breeze on to the sunbathers. Outside the lagoon, kite-surfers weave round little fishing boats, and pelicans dive for scraps.

The beach is scattered with expensively bronzed tourists in minuscule body ornaments, big shades and miles of gold chain.

Ernie's perfect, jewel-studded body and tiny minikini blend right in. But something's wrong. There's no perfect male body lying beside her. She sighs, and, making the best of it, carefully applies sunscreen to her inner thighs, then lies down with her legs bent, her nose in her towel and her bottom in the air.

A voice behind her says:

A: That is so gross!

The voice, with a whiny mid-Atlantic tone, belongs to a girl of about twelve, chalk-white all over, in a black floppy T-shirt, black Greek sandals and a huge black sunhat. This is Angel. She's wandering along the beach, and she's bored.

Ernie turns her head to peer over her shoulder.

E: Excuse me, have we met?
A: You want to be careful. Some guy's going to come right up and give it you doggy style.
E: I think I can take care of myself, thank you very much.
A: But, like, what is this?
E: Not that it's any of your business, but it's yoga for sides and cracks. A little invention of my own. You'd be amazed how many people spend a fortnight bronzing and entirely forget about their sides and cracks.

Angel flops down on the sand under a palm umbrella.

A: You sound like my mom. That tanning boloney, it's so, like – over.

E: My darling, some of us can do Goth, and some of us prefer not to try. Where is your mum anyway, and how come she let you out of your cage?

Angel doesn't answer. She's spotted Ernie's mobile, which is gold, to match her thong, and propped beside her in a dinky little gold solar-powered charger. Angel reaches over to pick it up.

A: You've got mail. Shall I . . .

Ernie snatches it from her . . .

E: Absolutely not. Bloody cheek.

. . . and replaces it on its stand.

A: Cool phone.
E: Yeah, it is nice, isn't it? Windproof, sandproof and solar powered.
A: So you can, like, surf and – like, surf at the same time?
E: It's the wave of the future.
A: Hah.

Ernie squints at her watch and changes her position so she's propped on her shoulders with both legs splayed in the air.

A: I guess I better go find Mom.

She reaches out a hand with nails the colour of dried blood, and tickles Ernie's belly.

E: Hey!

Ernie collapses in a heap beside her.

E: You, my darling, are what we used to call a juvenile delinquent. Come on, I want to find out what demon gave you birth.
A: She'll love that.

They trail languidly up the beach, between couples whispering, kneading and eating each other. Ernie looks more and more glum. Then she looks up and sees a blur of incongruous activity, figures scurrying towards and away from the biggest palm umbrella, carrying towels, suncream, drinks, fruit plates, phones and pieces of paper. As they approach, Ernie sees that the figures are all young boys and men. More, that they are all stunningly good looking. And positively fighting for the attention of whoever's under the shade.

A: There she is.
E: In there?
A: Yup.
E: Christ, they're like ants on a mango.
A: That mango is my mom. Wanna meet her? Hey, Mom! This is . . .

The young men flutter and part, and Ernie finds herself face to leather face with a woman in huge black shades and a black baseball cap, with a black hands-free mobile clipped to her black bikini, into which she is speed-talking in a weird accent somewhere between Birmingham and *Baywatch*. This is Madge. She flaps her hand at Angel, indicating she's far too busy to meet anybody.

But the thing that's got Ernie's attention is that this human honey pot is a good fifteen years older than herself, and not nearly so good looking.

M: Yeah, and for the pet store clerk I've gotten Val Kilmer, he'll do anything since that Dr Moreau bloodbath, believe me . . . Yeah, wants to eat a couple goldfish on-screen, so I said . . . I know it's been done but . . . Okay, terrapins, what the heck . . .

Angel, realising she's still not visible, wanders off again. Ernie, intrigued, intercepts a Greek god bringing a smoothie, takes it from him with a hundred-carat smile, and sinks on to the sand next to Madge, listening and watching very attentively.

New Year's Eve – Helen, Colum and Des at supper

The three of them are sitting around the kitchen table. A bowl of (unpainted) walnuts is in the middle, with three plates of fish pie around it. Helen and Colum are eating. Des's plate is untouched. He is playing with a toy elephant, apparently one of the spoils of Christmas.

H: *(putting down her fork with a happy sigh)* Isn't it lovely that Christmas is over and nobody's ill and it won't be Christmas for another whole year!
C: We could always ignore it from now on.
D: . . . and the hunters SEED the cowboy and the elephant went . . .
H: *(to Des)* Saw the cowboy, darling. Eat up. *(to Colum)* Only by renting a nuclear bunker. Or leaving the planet. I always wanted to be an astronaut.
C: Ye'd never stick it out.
H: And why not?
C: No cake. Crumbs and zero gravity not mutually compatible.
D: When will it be my birthday?
H: Not for a long time yet. Goodness me, you can't be thinking about presents again already!
D: Why not?
H: Eat your supper, darling. And put the elephant away, no toys at the table now, Christmas is over.

Colum puts the elephant to one side, carefully positioned so it can still see what's going on. Des stops eating completely and looks miserable.

C: And ye're okay with it being New Year's Eve and all, and us being in?

Helen leans across the table to kiss him.

H: Of course. I'm just very, very happy the washing machine is mended and you managed to heave that Christmas pudding into the skip.

Des is sitting looking glumly at his food.

H: Come on, Des, you love fish pie, you know you do. And I made it all creamy just specially, do you want me to help you eat it?
D: I don't like it.
C: *(mouth full)* He'll eat it, just leave him. Will I fetch myself some more?
D: It's got bits in it.

Colum goes to the cooker to help himself.

H: *(to Des)* What do you mean, bits? It's just the same as I always make it.

Des gingerly sticks his fork in and removes one of about ten thousand tiny flecks of red, which he then picks off with his fingers and carefully deposits on the rim of the plate.

D: Those bits.
H: That's sun-dried tomato, Des, that's what makes it taste lovely! You love tomatoes!
D: Not these tomatoes, they're horrid.

Colum returns with another heaped plateful.

C: He's got a point. They're a mite salty if ye're not used to 'em.
H: *(muttering)* Whose side are you on?
C: I just said . . .
H: It's all very well for you, when it's your turn to cook you just do sausages or cheese on toast, if it was down to you he'd be one of those children who . . .

Colum ignores her, lifts a forkful of Des's pie and whooshes it around in front of him.

C: (*to Des*) Here ye go, son, here's the harpoon coming at Moby-Dick . . .

Des giggles delightedly as the fork approaches his mouth, then at the last minute ducks his head sideways. The food slops off the fork and all over the table. Helen shoots back her chair and jumps up to fetch a cloth.

H: Oh, for God's sake, now look what you've done! *(to Des)* You're not going to bed till you've eaten it.
D: I'm fed up! I'm just not having it! YOU're not going to bed till YOU've eaten it!

Colum, having finished his meal and most of Des's, tries not to laugh out loud. Helen whirls on him.

H: I work all day at the library, and half the time even then when I should be thinking about work I'm figuring out things I can make that will be nutritious and balanced and good for him and that will give him all the vitamins and minerals he needs and not be monotonous and that you'll eat too and that don't cost an arm and a leg and that I can make in the bare half-hour I get between scrambling out of my coat and hearing your Neanderthal footsteps approaching the serving hatch . . .
C: What serving hatch?
D: What's a serving hatch?
H: . . . I don't ask you to cook every night, or even every other night, all I ask is that I get a BIT of support in my attempt not to have our only child grow up an immune-suppressed, cholesterol-sodden ball of lard, and . . .

Des is looking with detached curiosity from Helen to Colum. The more worked up she gets, the more impassively Colum carries on eating. Des takes the opportunity to sneak a foil-wrapped chocolate novelty from under the pile of walnuts. Bertie, who's been sitting under the table throughout, pads off outside.

Helen shoves her own half-eaten plate across the table and jumps up.

H: ... and I'm just BLOODY FED UP with it, that's all!

... and rushes out of the room.

New Year's Day – Bertie's inventory of his past week's diet

Mon: 1 dish Felix Liver Delight, biscuits on side
1 bowl water
1 puddle
Tues: 1 dish Felix Liver Delight, biscuits on side
1 bowl water
half HobNob (dropped on carpet when she realised her watch had stopped)
Wed: 1 dish Felix Liver Delight, biscuits on side
1 bowl water
1 beetle
Thurs: 1 dish Felix Tuna Delight, biscuits on side
1 bowl water
1 leaf (mistaken for mouse in half-light)
1 puddle (stale)
Fri: 1 dish Felix Tuna Delight, biscuits on side
1 bowl water
1 saucer of tea, 1 custard cream (from Irish neighbour; have to lap and run to avoid unpleasant stroking – hardly worth it)
Sat: 1 dish Felix Lamb Delight, biscuits on side
1 bowl water

Sun: crusts of cheese on toast (left in sink while they mated on sofa in other room)
beer and carpet fluff (licked up in haste before they realised that noise was the bottle going over)
1 bowl water (Felix apparently forgotten – maybe after-effects of mating, who knows?)
1 sparrow (I had to eat something)

Not exactly what you'd call a varied diet, and if it was left to her it would be a good deal worse. All that trouble she lavishes on her own young, and it doesn't even appreciate it. It should try eating what she gives me! I don't know what sort of animal a Felix is, but clearly it's bred to expect the worst.

However, until now this has only appeared to be a problem of monotony and occasionally erratic supply. Now it appears from their conversation that this limited diet is jeopardising my entire health and well-being. If I notice any worrying symptoms I may be reduced to going hunting again, which would entail leaving the house, something I haven't done since . . . well, since it started raining, a long, long, long time ago.

5 January – Ernie and Helen, on phone

H: . . . so I stomped round to Georgie's to view her photo archive of classic Alpine bone-crunchers, and then he called and said he was sorry, I went home for a cuddle and we were all asleep by ten. Totally standard New Year's.

E: Oh dear.

H: No, it was fine, really. Call me a dreary pragmatist, but when I know baby Tarzan will be pogoing on my chest at 6 a.m., that third martini begins to look less like a treat and more like a divorce waiting to happen.

E: How is my darling fairy godchild?

H: Learning to start his buttons from the bottom up, and trying to grow a beard. Colum's latest ruse to get Des to wash more is telling him it'll only grow if he waters it.

E: *(sighs)* I adore him! Oops, hang on, just paying this nice car valet. (Here you are, and here's another twenty. Make sure it stays out front for me, would you, sweet – thanks!) So where was I?

H: Eavesdropping on a paradise beach.

E: Yes, well, it turns out she's from England originally, but now she's one of the top casting agents in Hollywood, and a total poppet, but worked off her ass, and of course she's constantly jetting back and forth so she needed somebody to help her out over here . . .

(Sound of a male voice asking a question at Helen's end.)

H: Hang on. (Yes, Mr Pargiter, lovely, thank you, and I've saved all the classified sections for you, they're by your favourite chair.) Go on.

E: . . . So, in a word, the job consists of prowling the streets of London looking for gorgeous boys, picking them up and promising to make them rich and famous.

H: So what's new?

E: I get paid, and there's even a smidgeon of truth in it. It fills in the gaps between consulting jobs and pays my Jo Malone bills. All in all, *très* satisfactory.

H: So how come all these movies are entirely populated by men under thirty? Don't you have to cast the drooling hags and balding middle managers too?

E: I think it's something to do with the target demographic – and I do have a special gift, you know. On which subject I think – yup, code green north-north west, gotta go, love you, byee!

H: *(a trace wistfully)* Bye. *(Hangs up)* Jo Malone bills indeed! What's wrong with E45?

20–23 January – E-mail exchange between Colum and Billy

From: ColumMcCallum [colum@laverda.demon.co.uk]
Sent: 20 January
To: Billy Giddens [billy@goat.freeserve.co.uk]

Hi Bill
Christmas thankfully over and done with – in the end I opted for the Peruvian deerskin tummy pad, polypropylene racing bungs and a new pair of carbon fibre exhausts, which seemed to hit the spot. Steve is threatening me with a test ride on the new Bluell – told him I hate Harleys but he insists. Would be a lot more fun pacing you on your blade – fancy a run this weekend?

Her Galactic Huffiness went into a major skid the other week over the ingredients of a fish pie. Up until then she's been relatively rational of late, though turning down a free fortnight in Barbados in favour of forty-eight hours of mopping vomit and wringing sheets would not be everybody's idea of sound judgment.

What do you advise?
Col

From: Billy Giddens [billy@goat.freeserve.co.uk]
To: ColumMcCallum [colum@laverda.demon.co.uk]

col old miucker
this wekend is out as at least two of our four ar shoving to go karting and the Dog sesm to requrie my repsecne at the supermarekt and/or the toolcupbraod from dawn till dusk on sunday,

but how about folowngi weekend, they ar all off with her verminosu cousnsi in cornwall for the duration, we ocudl make a run of it.

Your Dog is defnitely overdue for a walkies in the sun etc. looksl ike she wants you to cough up for it so i woudl wtstart saving now, if not for a holss you will need it for the divroce ha ha. meanwhile avoid all refence to her size, wiehgt etc as they alwayus think they'er fat after chrsitmas wahever the evidnece eithe way.

speaking of hquich I noticed some major ammuniation against the browmn rice lobby in your second favaroute periodical this month. check it out . . .

give us a tinkel next week okay?
Bill

Excerpt From *Scientific American* – February issue

. . . on, or immediately after, the third week of the experiment, it was discovered that the guinea-pigs who had been given free run of the two food sources (i.e. both the nutritious and the nutritionally invalid) spontaneously gravitated towards the former, even when the latter was more frequently refreshed and enhanced with extra aromatics and other appetisants. . . . although wary of drawing literal parallels, we feel safe in inferring from this that it is at least within the realm of the possible that children given a wide choice of foods, including the so-called 'junk foods', will in the course of time diminish their consumption of the latter. We might even go farther and speculate that the process could be accelerated by actually encouraging the consumption of junk food in quantity . . .

24 February – Text message: Angel to Ernie

> HI ERN. GLD JB GONG WLL. WLD RTHR WRK 4 JCK TH RPPR THN MOM MYSLF. CMNG 2 TWN SAT 4 ALLNGHTR @ BRXTN, PLS TLL MOM IM @ YRS OK. U OWE ME RMBMR? X A

3–6 March – E-mail exchange between Madge and Ernie

> **From:** Madge Handelman [madge@handy.com]
> **To:** Ernestine Short [ernie@ernie.com]
>
> Sweets
> Just a quickie re 'Bending Time' (btw now called 'Channelling Christine') – enclosed revised cast list, you will see we still need those supermarket backgrouders, and now also a gross old man with a big nose, the new dirextor seems very hot on this. Particulary mentioned those English teeth – you know yellow and uneven and a few gaps. Well done with rteh club scene types, you certaibly have a gift just like you said. Let me know and don't forget to invoice your expenses, you can pad 'em a bit on this one they have agood deal with the Studio.
>   weather here glorious as usual.
>   big kiss M
>
> ---------------------------------

Revised cast list for 'Channelling Christine' – 3/15

PRINCIPALS
CHRISTINE – female lead, sweet bookish type – Uma

	Thurman? Winona – is she up to the accent?
HARVEY –	male lead, English gent type – Hugh Grant? Richard E. Grant? Any other Grants out there?
ADRIAN –	antagonist, needs some menace, maybe Continental? Antonio Banderas? Vinnie Jones?
SUZANNE –	Christine's mom, Adrian's lover. Dignified but sexy. Helen Mirren?

CHARACTER PLAYERS

OLD MAN/GRANDFATHER – male, big nose, falling apart (?drink/etc.) – Alan Bates/Richard Harris equiv.
STALKER – insane/delusional – Gary Oldman?
WAITRESS – funny/sad – Dawn French? No US profile. Tracy Ullman?

WALK-ONS/DAY PLAYERS
Club scene types – English but clean
Wait staff, smart restaurant
Supermarket customers, bus passengers etc.

From: Ernestine Short [ernie@ernie.com]
To: Madge Handelman [madge@handy.com]

Hiya
Will get working on the supermarket and the disgusting old man. Not my major areas of expertise I'm afraid, but I have a friend in Kentish Town who should be able to help. Party boys absolutely no problem. We have them in all shapes, sizes and colours and they normally clean up pretty well.

    Weather here absolutely vile. I was
wondering - do expenses cover protective
gear/shoe leather? Only I've had to do quite
a lot of walking in the wet the last few
days, not something my wardrobe is actually
kitted out for, as you can imagine, and
there's a silver PVC mac at Versace, plus
some rather sweet little fur-lined boots in
the Manolo sale (BTW, want me to look out for
anything for you?)
    Angel came to stay on Saturday. What a
great kid she is, you must be very proud.
    Thanks again - LOVing it!
    big kiss E

----

21 March – Helen

Honestly, first Ernie comes on the phone all sweet to me and says she'll take me out to dinner at Odette's if I scour Kentish Town for a dirty old man with a big nose, and then Colum tries to persuade me that the best way to improve Des's diet is to force-feed him junk food. Sometimes I feel I'm the only sane person left around here. Colum went on to back up this obviously ludicrous theory by producing an article in *Scientific American*, which claimed that if we let Des choose he would eventually opt for the healthy food all by himself. I said that if Des was going to get there in the end anyway, it would be a lot more efficient to cut out the junk-food stage and go straight to the eight-grain muesli and sheep's yogurt, to which Colum replied that now he knew why I had never been promoted to a managerial position. What does he mean by that? Nobody at the library has ever called me a food nazi. All

I know is that total responsibility for the developing brain platelets of our two-legged retirement insurance is a heavy burden to bear. If Des doesn't eat properly now, he'll never get a decent job or earn any money, and assuming those crooks at Marchant Godspeed are on course to squander Colum's pension fund, we'll both be living out of shopping bags in forty years' time. There's no way the Holborn and St Pancras Public Library Service'll finance a retirement home in Malaga.

Speaking of sunny places, or lack of them, today is what we used to refer to as the first day of spring. What it looks like is the fortieth day of Noah's carpentry project. Raining and cold, again, and the sky that flat greyish white, as though somebody forgot to colour it in. Can't even cheer myself up by shopping (even if I had any money), as all retail outlets, demonstrating an admirable intransigence in the face of the obvious collapse of climate as we knew it, are suddenly full of skimpy garments in eye-hurting shades of pink. A person could get pneumonia just window-shopping. At some point, presumably, the penny will drop and the British fashion industry will undergo a total re-evaluation of the idea of seasons, now that we are reduced to one (wet).

24 March – Helen, Colum and Des at breakfast

Colum and Des are chomping their way through large bowls of muesli, while Helen bustles about making tea. In the background, John Humphrys is talking on the radio.

> (*'Seriously, Minister, do you expect to come on this programme with a load of old bollocks like that and shove it down the throats of our millions of . . . Minister? . . . Are you there? . . . Sorry, we seem to be having problems with the radio car . . .'*)

H: You're having problems with your temper as usual, you old fart.

D: What, Mum?
C: Your ma's talking to the radio again. Take no notice.
D: What video did we watch last night?
C: *A Bug's Life*, wasn't it? Just for a change . . .
H: Eat your breakfast, Des, I put lots of banana in it for you.
D: *(mouth full – sounding surprised)* It's yummy! Can we have this every day?

Helen, smirking, brings the tea and embarks on her own cereal. Colum takes a large spoonful, then another.

C: I gather extra-thick double cream doesn't count as junk food, then.
H: Junk food? Those fatty acids are the guarantors of our old age. Anyhow, it was on special offer.
C: That'll be all your save-the-planet friends going over to soy. Sainsbury's must have a mountain of cream to get shot of.
D: Can we go there? Do cowboys have swords?
C: Finish your mouthful before you talk. From my memory, only the rare Japanese samurai cowboys have swords. The others have guns. And knives, of course. And lassos, and probably the odd catapult.
H: Cowboys are really farmers, you know. They only use their guns when they have to.
D: No they're not! They fight! FIGHT, FIGHT, FIGHT!!!
H: Shhhh!!

John Humphrys is talking about global warming. Helen jumps up to turn the volume up.

> 'What started out as a peaceful protest at the abandonment of the accord on climate change has turned into a major confrontation, as anti-American elements charged the barriers at . . .'

D: FIGHT, FIGHT, FIGHT!!
H: Shhh, darling, I'm trying to listen!!

Colum finishes his breakfast, looks at his watch and gets up, carrying his bowl to the sink and giving Helen a friendly squeeze en route.

C: If you're going to recycle those papers and mags, could you mebbe make it some time before paper is entirely superseded by digital storage?

H: Oh God, yes, I meant to do it yesterday, only it was so wet they'd have been papier-mâché before I got near the bins. I'll do it tonight, I promise.

Excerpt from *Scientific American* – March issue

> . . . 2,000 of the world's leading climatologists at their conference in Calgary last month revealed an unprecedented consensus in their updated evaluation of data relating to greenhouse gas emissions and global climate change . . .

25 March, 12.15 a.m. – Helen

Oh God. Oh no.

One minute I'm sorting out old copies of *Bike* and *Disney Time*, and the next life has changed for ever. How can humanity continue to turn out such selfish, greedy, short-sighted fools! A beautiful, lush planet, the confluence of a set of evolutionary circumstances unique among billions of galaxies, and we have to ruin it! And most of the Third World doesn't even drive yet, what's it going to be like when all the Africans and Chinese are tooling around belching out hydrocarbons? . . . How can everybody else be so blind, so nonchalant, about this? How can they go on havering between sandwich options at M&S, or evaluating the effect of Pilates on their bums? Talk about deckchairs on the *Titanic*, fiddling in Rome, etc.

I have to talk to Colum about it. Right now.

25 March, 12.30 a.m. – Helen and Colum, in the bedroom

Helen, fully dressed, comes rushing in and wildly pummels the snoring lump in the bed.

H: Wake up, wake up, I have to talk to you!
C: (*muffled groan*) Now?

She turns on the bedside light, blinding him.

C: Ouch!

He buries his face in the pillow to shield his eyes.

H: Don't try to hide from it. None of us can, any longer! This is the only thing that matters! We must DO something! We must stop everything and devote all our energies to this and give all our money to environmental charities!!!!!!

Colum rubs his eyes and takes in her state.

C: Oh no. That copy of *Scientific American*.
H: So? You left it out for me to recycle. In fact, you left it open at that page, don't tell me you didn't mean to.
C: That's likely, isn't it? The reason I normally only bring home carefully selected excerpts is to spare you stuff like that. Takes an iron nerve to read a whole issue of *Scientific American*.

Lies down again and closes his eyes.

C: Can I go to sleep now, please? Des'll be awake in, in . . .

. . . struggles to get a squint at his watch – groans again.

C: . . . five and a half hours.
H: You haven't been listening to a word I've said! We're in the grip of a major disaster, and it's about to be too late! We have to give all our money away!
C: So far as I'm aware you have no money, and I've been wearing the same three shirts to work since the first nappy bill.

H: Shirts! How can you talk about shirts! You won't need shirts soon, you'll be wearing bearskins and down jackets in the office. If there is an office come to that, yours won't last long right by the river I'm telling you. How can you go on finessing contracts and arguing about copyright on cookery books when human selfishness and greed are dooming our child to life on a blighted, frozen wasteland?
C: Believe me, there'll be copyright on survival manuals too. Come here.

He lies down again and switches off the light, pulling Helen to him as he does so.

C: If we have to sort out the world we can at least do it in comfort.
H: But if we don't act now . . .
C: Might as well make the most of our last hours . . .

He kisses her. She reluctantly, and then more enthusiastically, kisses him back.

C: I've been thinking . . .
H: Mmmm?
C: You've been having a tough time of it, with running the household and doing your job, and growing Des's brain, and saving the world, and all . . .
H: Finally you notice.
C: . . . and I wondered if you'd like a holiday, after you missed out at Christmas?

Helen shuffles away from him, ready to get in a huff.

H: Did I complain about that? Did I, once?
C: I'm not . . .
H: Even when I was hand-washing that iguana in disinfectant at 2 a.m.?

Colum reaches out and grabs her back.

C: You were a saint. Which is why you deserve a treat. I've saved a bit since I don't get to the bike shows.
H: A holiday? Really? Now?
C: Well, mebbe not at one in the morning, but you could start thinking about it . . .
H: A holiday! How wonderful! But what about the fossil fuels? We'll have to . . .

He shuts her up with another kiss.

C: . . . tomorrow. Night-night.

Helen's Holiday Wish List

Essential:
- not a resort complex – too many other Poundstretchers
- local open-air restaurants for romantic dinners with simple fresh fish and salads
- reliably sunny
- accessible without flying – one long-haul flight dumps as much poison as a family car does in its whole lifetime. Not much point jumping in a plane to escape a disaster that cheap flights are only making worse
- not too expensive
- safe swimming with no huge breakers, undertows or rip tides

Desirable:
- greenery
- quaint local towns for wandering in during midday hours when too hot to loll about in sun, preferably laced with shady little shopping streets where the ancient peasantry peddle their traditional crafts in the form of sandals, bags etc. that other people back in England will covet and NEVER BE ABLE TO GET!!!

Colum's Holiday Wish List

Essential:
- decent sanitation
- not too hot
- cheap local wine of quality, not something apparently left open since a first communion in 1923
- opportunities to observe local bikes and their owners
- does not require inoculation six weeks in advance against every plague ever recorded on the planet

Desirable:
- no television in hotel or surrounding area
- local dealer in rare and ancient bikes with generous test-drive policy
- local restaurant serving aforementioned decent wine within rolling-home distance of hotel (and open to supplying retail at generous discount)
- bedroom walls more than 3mm thick

Des's Holiday Wish List

Essential:
- lots of other children my age especially boys no babies not too many girls unless they have guns and dinosaurs and squirt guns and good sand toys and they must share
- I can eat the food and as much as I like and pudding every lunch and every night time
- and ice cream in between – IMPORTANT – MAGNUM!!
- and not funny food
- sunny
- no bugs
- childrens swimming pool with warm water and not too deep and steps all round like that one I saw on TV

- all the children stay up as long as they like except the naughty ones
- *Bob the Builder* on TV in the room and *Tweenies* and *Pocket Dragons* but not *Teletubbies* I'm too grown up for that.

Desirable:
- can we go to Disneyland?

20 April – Helen

Compilation of the selection criteria for our first-ever family holiday reveals almost total incompatibility between Colum's choice (expensive hotel in central Bologna), mine (undiscovered Mediterranean fishing village) and Des's (Disneyland). What used, in my days as maths whiz of Year 11, to be known as the Empty Set. Still, having made the decision and seeded the fantasy, and with the rain still bucketing down day and night, I decided the best hope of finding a compromise was on an island in Greece – for a start, there are about a million of them. There must be one that combines quality vineyards, bikers and simple local cuisine in peaceful fishing villages, which happen to have one charming, well-plumbed small hotel with a sea view and just the right number of well-behaved other children gambolling around the tepid, crystal-clear pool sharing their inflatable dinosaurs.

The matter of *Bob the Builder* on twenty-four-hour tap in the thick-walled, simple, affordable yet surprisingly comfortable bedroom I will have to leave to fate. After all, one has to be a bit flexible, starting out.

So I've ordered all the brochures and bought the *Rough Guide to the Greek Islands*, and I shall cross-check them until I come up with the goods. Plenty of time between now and July.

Lemnos – the Brochure	Lemnos – the *Rough Guide*
With just enough foreign visitors to give the island a holiday atmosphere . . .	Lemnos is not a popular destination, nor likely to become one . . .
. . . Lemnos offers a truly different experience to the discerning traveller.	. . . with its unique combination of impassable mountains in the west, and mosquito-plagued swamp in the east.
The main town is so self-contained and with so much to do that you may feel no need to stray farther . . .	Outside the main town itself there's little for even the most diehard explorer . . .
If you do decide to go farther afield . . .	. . . unless you have access to your own boat . . .
. . . you will discover deserted, pristine beaches . . .	. . . to get to the otherwise inaccessible beaches . . .
. . . and rugged, breathtaking coves.	. . . and rocky coves hiding treacherous rip tides and constantly overflown by jets from the island's resident air force base.
The hotel we have selected, the . . . Aeghia Nikia . . .	Of the many indifferent hotels in the main town . . .
. . . where we have built up a close relationship over the years . . .	. . . most of which are the products of downmarket package tourism . . .
. . . will offer you the warm welcome and comforts of home.	. . . at all costs avoid the Aeghia Nikia, which serves English beer and chips to a constant stream of locals and bewildered British pensioners.

(One down and 224 to go . . .)

29 April – Helen

This may be a little trickier than I had realised. Comparison of the brochures with the invaluable, but dispiriting, *Rough Guide* reveals that there is, in fact, no Greek island not fatally let down by rip tides, killer jellyfish, swarming mosquitoes, malarial swamps, filthy beaches or parched desert landscape, or free of hordes of yachtspeople, religious nutcases, Australian backpackers, downmarket package tourists and hostile, monoglot peasantry.

Wish I knew somebody else with small children and approximately similar world view who might have done it before. All the other Paint Pots parents are well outside our price bracket, judging by the late-model eight-cylinder tinted-glass megajeeps which disgorge their little darlings every morning. Library colleagues, where they've spawned at all, are polarised between total capitulation to CenterParcs and reading tours of Slovenia. No point consulting Georgie, who just spends three weeks in Cornwall every year, along with most of the population of London.

But at least if we fail, we shan't be burning fossil fuels or tramping over the few as yet untarnished acres of the earth's surface.

Maybe Colum, Des and I should just take it in turns to have our dream holiday – if one of us went each year, we'd have three times as much to spend. I wonder how much Ernie paid for her Christmas in Barbados?

5–7 May – E-mail exchange: Madge and Ernie

    From: Madge Handelman [madge@handy.com]
    To: Ernestine Short [ernie@ernie.com]

Sweets

Don't sweat it over supermarkets — stuido has product placement issues so that whole scenario is histr=y. New director (yes another one) ADORED the boys though — papered his thailer with the headshots. Need I say mor . . .

   meanwhile I've a minor snafu on the personal front, ion fact it's Angel, I need to get here to Tuscany for our vacation en famill in July and entre nous tere's a humungous alan Parker job coming up from Dreamworks that I just canNOT aford to pass up on, and as you and she have palled up so brilliantyl, I wonderd if you might liek to drive her down, take in a bit of La Cultur Fransaise en rout, practice her languages, and then naturalmente you'd have a free vacation with us at the end, can't remember but I think at last eight bedrooms and a pool and maid of course . . .

   weather here glorious as usual.
   big kiss M

From: Ernestine Short [ernie@ernie.com]
To: Madge Handelman [madge@handy.com]

Hiya

Great relief to be off the hook with grocery emporium. As for the boys, it's not the heads he needs shots of, if you get me . . .

   I may have a problem getting away myself with Angel, but I do have another idea — I'll get back to you on it.

```
    Weather here still stinks. Blahniks major
consolation - thanks!
    love ya E
```
----

12 May – Angel and Ernie: shopping

They're inside Urban Decay, a very, very noisy Goth hang, deep in the sordid heart of Camden Market. The only lighting is ultraviolet and low. Blank-faced youths hunch around racks of fetish gear, waving to the beats like seaweed. This is not Ernie's preferred browsing location. She's trying to make the best of it, in designer jeans and a black lace stretch top, which is way closer to Goth than she'd ever normally allow herself, and a big pair of Persols, just in case, God forbid, somebody she knows is here.

Angel is right at home, hair all over her face, shoulders hunched in a ripped top, skinny fishnet legs teetering on eight-inch soles which carry the thumping bass right to her brain. She's spent the last twenty minutes riffling through a rack of coats, finally brings out something and holds it up for Ernie to appraise.

A: *(shouting over the music)* Whaddya think?

There are no words for what Ernie thinks. She smiles gamely and removes her shades.

E: It looks like the doormat from a Glasgow pub.

Angel hasn't heard a word. She smiles in triumph and dumps the coat on Ernie.

A: Okay, you can get it for me.
E: I beg your pardon?
A: *(shouting again)* Look . . .

She gives up and drags Ernie and the coat to the checkout, where, before she knows it, Ernie's platinum Amex has been given a good thrashing, and the coat is in the bag. Then Angel marches a stunned Ernie outside, where the noise is marginally less, but the sun has finally come out. Angel hunches, frowning, and mutters quickly:

A: Look, I know why you're being so, like, palsy with me suddenly.
E: You do?
A: You want to dump me on some rancid troglodyte mates of yours, so you won't have to drive to Italy. They're cleaned out, but they're gagging for 'Continental glamour', and you want in with my mom. Right?
E: I'd watch who I was calling a troglodyte, if I were you. But, broadly speaking, you've got it.
A: So basically it's, like, a done deal, right? I'll go along with it, but in exchange . . .
E: Yeeees?
A: . . . you buy me stuff and cover for me on weekends, okay?

Ernie, speechless, gazes over Angel's head, and suddenly sees something wildly exciting retreating behind her. She grabs Angel and hurries away from the shop.

A: Okay?
E: One simple condition.
A: Yeah? What?
E: You go up to that disgusting old man with a hook nose over there, and tell him I'm going to make him a movie star.

20 May – Helen

Wondrous life-saving Ernie has once again salvaged things at the eleven-and-halfth hour in the shape of her friend Madge, or rather Madge's daughter Angel. (Poor girl, with a name like that you have to like her right away, don't you?)

Anyhow, it turns out that helping Ernie stalk old men in Sainsbury's paid off, because she found the perfect one just up the road by the recycling bins, and Madge is so grateful she wants us to share her luxury villa in Tuscany for two weeks. Great food, wine and major motorbike culture for Colum, a private pool for Des, dappled sunshine and beautiful fifteenth-century architecture for me to wander about in when the lifestyle alone palls (ha!) and a positive cornucopia of cultural artefacts (and shops) at a safe distance, just in case. Why I didn't think of Tuscany before escapes me, though Colum pointed out it could be to do with the forest of noughts on the rental prices. Well, that's not our worry now, in fact Madge seems positively eager to subsidise the journey down as well. We can potter through France in our own car, not filling the upper atmosphere with toxic waste, take in château country and amazing Gothic cathedrals, shop for lunch in quaint covered markets, and eat delicious regional home cooking at night in those auberges dotted all around the French countryside.

Typical Colum had to play it all suspicious at first – why would she want to shift her only child on to a bunch of total strangers for a week and then invite us on holiday too? – but I said look at all those parents who happily consign their pre-pubertal daughters to French exchanges every year, where they're lucky if it's the father of the family who makes the trip memorable. And obviously, when we've driven her all that way, Madge isn't just going to drag her out of the car and wave us off. If the villa's anything like Ernie claims, we can probably spend a week there without meeting up once. Anyway, Ernie, Madge and I are having lunch next week, so we can all check each other out.

And the best thing of all is that Des gets to have some company in the back seat. Ernie says Angel is very quiet and not at all like most twelve-year-olds – she's probably lonely too, all by herself at boarding school, poor thing. I told him about it at bedtime and he immediately wanted a Tuscan Holiday with Inflatable Dinosaur in the Pool Bedtime Calypso.

I kind of dodged the specifics on the inflatable dino, but I'm sure between now and July I can find one somewhere.

20 May – The holiday in Tuscany with inflatable dinos by the pool calypso

> Holidays in Tuscany
> Are pretty good fun as you will see!
> After the rigours of a year at nursery
> It's time for a drink or two *(and of course an ice cream and
>   probably some crisps)* under a tree.
>
> *(in fact I seem to remember that in France they have a wicked bright green thing that you're only allowed to drink if you're under six, that tastes of peppermint and is very, VERY sweet . . .*
>   *. . . oh, France? Well, that's on the way . . .)*
>
> We'll drive down in our motor car
> And every day we won't go too far.
> That way we can see the countryside
> With the castles where the knights of old used to polish
>   their armour and write poems and have jousting
>   matches and, er, hide. *(And fight. Of course.)*
>
> *(Yes, I should think there'll certainly be some knights there still, or at least some suits of armour – will they kill you? Goodness, no, there won't really be any knights – yes, silly old Mum was only joking. Now go to sleep, precious.)*

Then when the mountains are far behind
The road to our villa will be clearly signed *(it's been a long day, okay?)*
And when we get to the swimming pool
We'll have a big splashy soak to get ourselves lovely and cool.

(Night-night, sweetheart . . . oh yes, the dinosaur . . .)

And by the pool, well, what have we here?
A squashy blow-up dinosaur is lying very near!
He's waiting for Des to take him into the water
And after that perhaps he'll have a swim with Madge's daughter.

(Whew! Do I get a laureate for that? No? Then I guess it'll have to be the Shiraz again.)

10 June – Madge, Helen and Ernie at lunch

They are sitting at a low table in the Oriental Fusion food bar of a very fancy London hotel.

Madge is talking into her chest – actually, her phone – and taking notes in a black organiser. She's wearing black baggy pants, a black polo shirt, late-model black Pumas, and her signature black backward-facing cap. The tan has evolved from cherry to mahogany.

Ernie, in a black leather suit with discreet Goth influence in the lace tights, is touching up her face.

Helen, in whatever fell out of the washing machine that morning, is reading the menu, avidly.

M: *(still in the weird accent)* (No, no, like I told ya before, Tommy, ya can't text me on this phone . . . No, the mail on the Palm's bugging out . . . Haveta send it to my car . . .

Whaddya mean? . . . Yeah, it's parked right across the street, the valet dude can bring it in.)

Helen makes an attempt to establish eye contact with a waiter, who immediately glides to the farthest end of the room. She tries Ernie instead.

H: God, I'm starving. Do you think autumn rolls are like spring rolls?
E: (*through her lipstick*) More bracing.

Madge finally finishes her call, puts down her pad, pushes up her eye shade and gives Helen 2.45 seconds of lower-face-only smile.

H: This is lovely!
M: Hopeya don't mind coming here, only I haveta get the asshole director to commit to who I've found so I can get going on the next job.
H: Is everybody having two courses?
M: Sure, whatever ya want, be my guest.

Her phone rings again.

M: (Hi, André!!! Amigo!)

She ducks down and begins scribbling again. The waiter coughs discreetly, right by Helen's ear. She jumps.

H: Oh! Shall I go first, then? So – the crispy pigskin and wood-ear wilted salad to start, and then the autumn rolls, please. And the ginger and mandarin juice, that sounds fab. And could I have some bread and butter, please?

The waiter whispers in her ear.

H: Oh yes, of course, steamed Chinese buns and extra virgin olive oil will be great. (*to Ernie*) Get us in the mood for Tuscany! Are you sure you can't come, even for a bit?

As Angel's such a pal of yours?
E: I'll see what I can do. (*to waiter*) Just a San Pellegrino sparkling, please.
M: (Yeah, the team's standing by . . . Right here, yeah.) (*to waiter*) Double hazelnut espresso. That's it.

Too late, Helen realises that once again she'll be scarfing a large meal on her own. The waiter glides off.

M: (Gotta go. Busy busy. Loveya!)

She looks up – 2.57 seconds of smile this time. Helen smiles bravely back.

H: So this is so nice of you! I'm so sorry not to be meeting Angel . . .
M: Yeah, she was bummed too, but she's real excited and she knows if you're Ernie's pals you're cool, right, Ern?
H: (*to Ernie*) So you've spoken to her about it already?

Ern seems to have something in her eye. Madge has gone back to inputting.

H: (*to Madge*) Do you speak every day? You must miss each other terribly!
M: (*distracted*) Yeah. Or every few days anyhow. Whenever. She texts me. She's cool, she understands.

The waiter brings a forest of bitter leaves, a basket of buns, a flask of soy-garlic-chilli olive oil and a plate of mini-sashimi, and clusters them around Helen. It's just as well nobody else is eating, because the table is now full. Madge's phone rings again.

M: (Hi? Where?) (*to Ernie*) Where the heck is Shropshire? I've been gone so long . . .
E: Three hours. M5.
M: (*into phone, looking at watch.*) (Five thirty? He's ONLY there

until five thirty? And he won't travel? How much do we want this guy? . . . I get it. A lot. Okey-dokey, I'm there.)

She hangs up her phone, gathers her things and drains her coffee.

M: That's it then, right? Just send me the bills, spend whatever ya need to – Angel doesn't do too great with like, economy – and I'll catch y'all there! (*to Ernie*) I'll get ya the script and a breakdown later, hon.

And she's gone, still talking to the air. Ernie steals a piece of Helen's bread.

E: There you go! Sorted!

12 June – Story synopsis and cast breakdown of major studio picture *Thief of Life*

STORY
Joe Mitchum is a regular guy, sweating it out as a car mechanic to keep his wife Kelly and his adored only daughter, Fawn. The only thing that marks Joe out is his amazing good looks, and from working on cars he's developed a physique that makes women swoon. But Joe has eyes for nobody but Kelly. He's a one-woman, straight-up kind of guy. Then tragedy strikes, as Fawn develops a life-threatening illness, and Kelly is forced to reveal the secret she's kept from Joe since they met – she is carrying an incurable disease which killed her brother and two aunts. Joe spends every penny he has scouring the world for a solution, but to no avail, as Fawn gets weaker by the day. Finally, Joe hears of a doctor in Switzerland who may have the answer.

Joe sells his beloved vintage Mustang to pay the air fare for himself and Fawn. Fawn barely makes it, but when they meet the doctor, Dr Ingrid Goldpfinger, she immediately produces a drug made from a secret formula known only to herself which relieves Fawn's symptoms. Dr Ingrid, who has an aloof beauty to match her world-class skills, agrees to treat Fawn, and Joe, unknown to Kelly, remortgages his house to pay the bill. Back home, Fawn progresses by leaps and bounds. Her parents and her beloved collie Laddy are delighted to see her back to her old self. But all too soon the drugs are about to run out and Joe goes back to Dr Ingrid, this time alone. Dr Ingrid knows he has no more money. But unknown to Joe, she too has a secret: she can never have children, and she is violently jealous of any woman who does. She tells him she'll treat Fawn anyhow. He's overjoyed – how can he thank her? Then she tells him her price. For every month's supply of drugs, a night of passion with him . . .

(NOTE FROM MADGE – that's it so far, they're finessing it at the studio, but we have our principals nailed so you and I can get going.)

PRINCIPAL CAST:

Joe   -   WM/Caucasian, mid-30s, regular guy type
          (George Clooney? Pierce Brosnan?)
Kelly -   WF/Caucasian, early/mid-30s, homebody
          (Julia Roberts? René Russo – too old?
          check w' agent)

Dr   — WF/Caucasian, late 20s/early 30s, aloof, intellectual beauty (Catherine Zeta-Jones? Julianne Moore?)

Fawn — WF kid, adorable but fragile, big eyes, etc., some wiggle room on age — say 5 up to 10 (Haley Joel Osment got a sister? Any girl Culkins coming down the pike?)

15 June – Madge and Angel: on phone

A: Mom, I'm not going, like, on vacation with a bunch of strangers, okay? If Ernie comes along then maybe, but I am not . . .

M: And the boy!!! Wow, wadda hunk!

A: *(mumbling, suspicious)* What boy?

M: *(sound of hand slapping forehead in disbelief)* I canNOT BELIEVE I didn't mention him until now? He is . . . I'm telling you, their son . . . Who's that guy you girls all go crazy for, Ricky someone . . .

A: *(even lower mumble)* Ricky Martin? He's, like, old!

M: Yeah, but take him back ten years, and their mothers couldn't tell 'em apart!

A: *(pause, then reluctantly)* So how old is he?

M: *(vaguely)* Well, let's see, Heath Ledger is eighteen now and Ryan Philippe's . . . I'd take a shot at sixteen? But hey, ya wanna spend the summer studying instead, so . . .

A: It's only for, like, a week, right? It only takes a week to get to Italy?

M: I'd say four days, tops. In that Maserati of theirs.

A: They have a Maserati?

M: Could've been an Aston Martin — took off like a rocket, hard to tell.
    (Pause. Madge seizes her advantage.)

M: So that's a grand I owe ya for colour therapy, two grand for the art history trip at Easter, five hundred for clothes for this vacation — now ya see why ya never see me, I'm working day and night to pay the bills here . . . I'll bank five grand in your account today and I'll . . . There goes the other line — I'll tell the McCulkins to expect ya on July tenth. Loveya, hon!!

16 June – Text from Angel to her best friend Leila

SMR PLANZ FINLZD, TRNG URP W MJR HNK(18) !!!

16 June – Text from Leila to her friend Rowan

NGL SEZ SHS SPNDNG HOLS W 18 YRLD MLE. 8 YR LD MR LKE I BT. IS SH SAD R WHT?

16 June – Text from Rowan to her friend Mandy

ANGEL SPNDNG HLS ON BLND DTE W MOVIE * !!! IDNTTY SCRT, FMLY FRND. DNT MNTION 2 LEILA!

16 June – Text from Mandy to her friend Trina

LEILA SPTTNG NLS, ANGEL GNG TRVLLNG W MVIE * THS SMR, WLL TRY T FND OUT MR.

17 June – Text from Mandy to Trina

NT SRE BT THNK MY B RYN PHLPP R HTH LDGR.

17 June – Text from Trina to Angel

RYN PHLPP? HTH LDGR? PLS CNFRM R DNY ASAP . . .

17 June – Text from Angel to Trina

    SWRN 2 SCRCY – SRRY!

30 June – Letter from Colum's parents

Mull of Spottie,
Beinn Na Foaghla
Outer Hebrides

Twenty-first of June

Dear Son,

It will probably surprise you to hear from your father and myself, as you know well we do not put pen to paper very often.

    Things here go on much as usual. The post van blew into the church vestry last Sunday during service, but as luck would have it the postman was taking his dram with the vicar's wife the while and Mrs McMurdo had been waiting that long for the replacement china being sent to her from Fraser's in Edinburgh that she had bought something else already, not such a nice pattern but quite good enough for the cattleman's tea, so it was not a big matter when it arrived broken. Your Auntie Megan's Hereford had triplets again. That will be the fourth time. Your Uncle James says he is minded to write to the paper about it in case it is a record, but it is my belief he is too lazy to get round to it this side of Christmas.

    Now before I go rambling on any longer, I will get to the point and say that your father has taken it into his head that he wants to see The King and I one more time before he dies, and we looked in the Sunday paper for the notices and it says that the run will end at the end of July.

    So he has been at me to write to you about coming to London to see it and also to see you and our grandson and of course dear Helen, in case we are snowed in once again at Christmas time which we are beginning to expect as normal owing to this Global Warming you will have heard of no doubt.

We have booked our tickets on the ferry and the train and we will be arriving into King's Cross on the Ninth of July at six thirty in the morning, all being well.

I hope this is convenient for you son and I will be bringing your new pullover along, I hope the colours are to your taste this time, also the Old Spice aftershave as I know it can be hard to find in London.

We will take it that no news is good news unless we hear from you in the next week.

With best wishes to you all,

Your Loving
Mother

1 July – Colum's list of jobs to do before leaving house to parents

- rerun wires of all electrical appliances, so nothing trails across floor. Unplug VHS player and answering machine, and hide remotes and instruction manuals, just in case. Hide electrical heaters and hairdryer, in case they're tempted to use them in bathroom.
- hide all books, mags, and videos with any reference to sex, also Des's *Bob the Builder* annual, and my valuable collection of vintage bike magazines.
- sort out all medicines, wines and spirits, and store well out of reach. Relabel all cleaning materials in big letters, and store in prominent place.
- buy, and label clearly, three weeks' worth of cat food. Buy new, idiot-proof, safe can-opener. Make sure dry food is opened and scoop clearly visible next to it.
- make list of regular deliveries, e.g. milk, newspaper, post. MAKE CLEAR absolutely NO other deliveries to be accepted.

- read all meters, and send readings in so no danger of people arriving to 'read meters' during absence.
- list phone numbers and names of known neighbours and trusted friends. MAKE CLEAR NOBODY ELSE to be allowed in house. WARN ALL ON LIST.
- BUY: porridge oats, honey, Marmite, Ovaltine, Horlicks, oatcakes, mince, butter, onions, carrots, Table Cream, jelly cubes, custard powder, Dream Topping, ginger wine, Nice biscuits, Milk of Magnesia.
- DEFLEA CAT.

4 July – Message left by Ernie on personal voicemail of Pierce Brosnan

E: Hi, Pierce. Ernestine Short here. Hope you'll forgive me – mmm – *ambushing* you at home, but the lovely Cary at ICM gave me the number and said you'd be fine with it. Well! I'll get straight to it. I'm working with Madge Handelsman in Hollywood on this major show for Dreamworks, we'll be shooting probably mid to late September with I think Ridley or perhaps Tony, it's a rather fascinating take on a medical/psychological thriller, and it has this just to *die* for megajuicy male lead – you know the kind of thing, tough but caring, sexy but sensitive, brilliant but down to earth. Well, of course, we all IMMEDIATELY thought of you. I mean, who else is there? And as you're in town and I happen also to be in town just now, it seemed like a brilliant chance to – mmm – hunker down over a script and a cup of coffee – or whatever you'd prefer, of *course*. I'll leave you my mobile number, call me on it absolutely any time, I know how crazed you must be. And do please feel free to throw any questions you have at me – mmm – any questions *at all*, okay?

Thanks a bunch, Pierce – hope I can call you that? –

and I hope to hear back from you – *real* soon.
(This message, in an unrecognisably husky, smoochy tone, was also left, with appropriate minor variations, on the personal phones of Jude Law, Rufus Sewell, Jonathan Rhys Myers, Daniel Day-Lewis and Ewan McGregor, just in case . . .)

7 July – Helen

Well, I have to say I'm amazed at the enthusiasm of this little girl – I suppose I have to start calling her Angel – for coming on holiday with a bunch of dreary suburbanites like us. Here she is, flitting between Los Angeles, London and her upmarket boarding school in Sussex, with side trips to visit her diplomat father in Nigeria or Argentina or wherever he happens to be, and Ernie says she's counting the days before we set off. Rather sweet, really – all goes to show that however sophisticated they look and act these days, they're still just little girls underneath. When I think back to when I was twelve I was . . . well, now I remember, I was drinking Bacardi and blackcurrant and having very detailed erotic dreams about Simon Le Bon. But then I wasn't closeted at a Sussex boarding school.

I must say I didn't take to her mother, and where she got that accent from I wouldn't like to say, but I'd have thought there were people in Hollywood who could have sorted it out for her. Which reminds me, the one thing I haven't sorted out is Angel's passport. Must call Madge to get hold of it, unless Angel looks after it herself.

But apart from the delightful prospect of leaving Colum's parents in residence for two weeks, and persuading Bertie to give them a second chance, all the knotty stuff seems dealt with. It is extraordinary, sometimes I could swear that cat understands a lot more than he lets on. Ever since we got the letter, he's been running away on a daily basis, and only the extraordinary repulsiveness of one of our neighbours, and the hostility of the other, brings him back even at mealtimes. Surely he must have forgotten the cocoa incident by now?

Still, I remember when Des was a baby, thinking he understood every word, too. Maybe Bertie's planning a little holiday of his own. Anyhow, having taken two extra days off work to 'prepare', I had to fill the time somehow, so I researched the current literature for tips and did a spot of last-minute shopping.

I always think bright colours work better than neutrals in the sun, especially as everybody's already looking at you through dark glasses, but the palazzo pants are plenty covered up enough for the odd cathedral or, indeed, palazzo.

Excerpt from *Marie-Claire* – July issue

> . . . There's an art to packing for that perfect, romantic summer break, and the key words to remember are 'versatile' and 'easy-care'. After all, there's nothing *less* romantic than waiting at the carousel for a huge pile of bags, and then spending all your holiday money on dry cleaning! The great news about this summer's holiday classics is that they've been updated in great new synthetic blends which literally shake off creases and dry in minutes. Make sure to respect local customs by including something loose and covered up, and if you stick to a few neutral colours for the mix'n'match basics, you can let yourself live a little when it comes to T-shirts and accessories . . .

6 July – Bills from Helen's holiday shopping

```
Welcome to Top Shop
06/07/02

1 x hot pants (12), aqua            £13.99
1 x bra top (34c) matelot stripe    £10.99
1 x wetlook stud belt, wht (M)       £8.99
SUBTOTAL                            £33.97
```

```
PAID VISA                    £33.97
CHANGE                       £00.00
```

Thank you for shopping at Top Shop
(for refund and credit terms see over)

H&M
ESSENTIAL FASHION AT ESSENTIAL PRICES
06/07/02

14.22

1 x palazzo pants,
Sizzling Tangerine (12)   £24.99
1 x crop top,
Bubble Gum (12—14)   £19.99
SUBTOTAL   **£44.98**
PAID VISA WITH THANKS   £44.98

Come back soon!

Shelly's Shoes
'The World Walks Our Way'
Oxford Circus Branch   06 07 02   15.44

1 x cork platform
'Rock Chick'   (pink/38)   £34.95
1 x sparkle slide
ShaNaNa   (silver/38) £24.95
1 x spike sandal
'Basic Instinct'   (navy/38)   £44.95
1 x wedge sandal
'Laguna Blu'   (purple/38) £36.99

SUBTOTAL   £141.84
PAID TOTAL MASTERCARD   £141.84

Thanks - Walk the Walk

```
Agent Provocateur Broadwick Street W1
06/07/02
16.16

Bra, 'Voulez-Vous?' purple-orange (34c)      £45
Tango, 'Pourquoi Pas?' purple (med)          £25
Baby-doll set 'Lolita' purple/black (med)   £105

SUBTOTAL                                    £175

Paid VISA                                   £175
Credit or exchange only – sorry!
```

Of course, Colum took one look at that lot and had to ask whether we were still going on the same holiday, or was I in fact going on a make-your-dreams-come-true singles package, while everybody else melted in the antique family saloon in solid motorway traffic for four days?

Luckily this at least deflected the conversation from the bill, but when I tried to tell him it wasn't going to be like that, owing to my detailed and expert route planning, and that most people just stick to the motorways because they're like lemmings who can't think for themselves and don't speak any languages, he just wandered off muttering about lemmings having more sense than they're given credit for, and by the way, if I'm so smart, what's the French for 'lemming'? Honestly, where's his romantic spirit?

I mean, take a look at *his* packing list . . .

7 July – Colum's packing list

    2 pairs trousers, one lightweight, one heavy
    2 pairs shorts
    5 T-shirts
    1 jumper

1 pair swimming trunks
4 pairs underpants
1 pair sunglasses
1 pair sandals
1 book.

Never mind, all the more luggage space for me – I can't imagine a twelve-year-old girl will bring a lot with her, and Des is young enough to be told, thank God.

7 July – Des's packing list

- All my dinosaurs – the large carnotaur and two small carnotaurs and the big soft tyrannosaurus from the museum that time and the baby one from the zoo, and the triceratops Grandma gave me and the spinosaurus that you always say is a stegasaurus because you're so HOPELESS Mum and it's not and why can't I have a pteranodon yet it's ages till my birthday please can I have a pteranodon if I'm good on holiday do they have dinosaurs in France?
- My new swimming trunks and my armbands with the frogs on because I can nearly take my toes off the bottom already, you know, now that I am an Adult.
- Where are my goggles Mum you promised to buy me some goggles and some jellies where are my jellies Mum are they blue I only want blue? If you didn't find any jellies I'll have to wear my wellingtons in the pool otherwise I'll get wet won't I?
- Regrettably, I need to take some nice white bread and cheese sandwiches in case I don't like the food. Dad says they eat funny things and they are frogs.
- All my story tapes for the car in case I get bored will I get bored Mum?
- Teddy wants to come so he can broaden his mind too and

he wants the elephants to come as well because they'll be lonely without me and because they'll be scared of Grandma and Grandpa because they make funny noises in the night when they're sleeping, shall I show you how, they go WHHHEEEEEEE!!! UNK UNK UNK WHEEEEEE!!!

— Look Mum! I've packed all my suitcase myself already am I a good boy NO DON'T NO DON'T I NEED ALL OF THAT YES I DO I DO I DO I'M NOT GOING UNLESS I CAN TAKE THEM ALL NO I WON'T I WON'T I WON'T I'M NOT HAVING THIS I'M TIRED AND CROSS AND I'M FED UP AND I'M JUST WAHHHHHHH!!!

7 July – Bertie's packing list

    21 tins Felix

(no way am I catching my own food, this is meant to be a holiday)

    4 packs biscuits

(though if I find anything better en route I shall dump them without regret. The ones they've been forcing me to eat lately are, to be frank, well nigh unpalatable)

    blanket

(of course, I was hoping for a new one for Christmas – I've long since given up expecting them to remember my birthday – but in vain, as usual. Who is always passed over when Santa comes to call? You've guessed it, poor flea-bitten old Bertie. Those motorbikes get more consideration than I do, and have you ever tried cuddling up to a motorbike on a chilly winter night? If only they bothered to think of me as a sentient being instead of a hot water bottle on legs . . .)

But look here! Maybe I'm misjudging them. She seems to have done the packing for me, or at least it's all piled up ready, with a new bowl, no less. Funny that she would have piled it in the kitchen, though, and on a piece of paper like that. And what's that tucked in with the biscuits? It's a note of some sort (of course I can read, there's precious little else to do all day long in this house – why else do you think cats make straight for the newspaper the minute it's opened? You'll be telling me you didn't know I could play the piano next). Here goes . . .

'*Dear Mother and Father, here is . . .*'

No.
I don't believe it. It's true, then. They're leaving me. And with those maniacs. That cocoa, at that temperature, was a lethal weapon in highly practised hands. Accident my scrotum!

Ah well, no time to lose. I thought they were bluffing, which is why I came back – that and the difficulty of digesting sparrow after years of Felix – but now it seems they have indeed abandoned all scruples in pursuit of their own selfish needs. I almost regret leaving them like this, after so many years of loyal attention and companionship, but now that their apparent hospitality stands revealed as the hollow sham it undoubtedly always was, dignity if nothing else constrains me to flee with nary a backward glance, before the boiling cocoa maniacs can get me in their sights.

Ah, but the times we've had in happier days! Some would call me a sentimental old fool for . . . Hey! Put me down! I'm LEAVING, I tell you, I'M . . .

9 July – www.countdowntosunshine.com

> COUNTDOWN TO SUNSHINE! Your site for holiday planning that does the hard work for you and leaves nothing to chance!
>
> Six Things to Do a Week Before You Leave
> 1 Check driving licenses and passports for

>validity. Check all necessary visas etc. Make two photocopies of each document and keep them separately, one at home and one in a safe place in your luggage or locked moneybelt.

(Okay, that's at least six things already . . .)

>2 Order spare glasses or prescription sunglasses from optician, spare contact lenses and fluid.
>(Remember! Many countries now ban certain prescription sunglasses and certain coloured or photoreactive lenses on ANY sunglasses for drivers.)

(They're bluffing. Where would the French be without their turquoise Reactolites?)

>3 Check contraceptive pills and other prescription drugs you may need on your holiday to make sure you have an adequate supply. Check what other medicines, e.g. children's fever suspension, you may need to take with you, ALWAYS REMEMBERING that they may be legal here but NOT in the country you are travelling to, and that you may find yourselves in serious trouble with local officials if you don't check in advance — at the very least, your holiday could be curtailed or badly delayed.

(Or you could sell them and make the cost of your holiday back. I wonder what the Marseilles street value of a bottle of Calpol is?)

>(Refer to 'DRUG AND MEDICINE GUIDE FOR PRINCIPAL WORLDWIDE DESTINATIONS' for details of

> banned drugs and their local equivalents, where they exist.)

(Aha! The street-corner dealer's handy online route planner. I'll come back to that.)

> 4 Buy your maps, guidebooks, town guides and phrase books. Briefly discuss your proposed route in general and the detailed plan for Day 1. Write down the roads you will be travelling on this day, in the order you will reach them, and also the names of the principal towns, especially the last one before a road or route change.

(Not much point in that if they're building roads at the rate they were last time. Just take a compass and hope they join up in the end.)

> (See DETAILED ROUTE PLANNING under THINGS TO DO THREE DAYS BEFORE YOU LEAVE for more specific guidance on this.)
> NEVER travel with outdated maps – you may find yourself suffering serious delays. Remember that roadbuilding attracts major EU subsidies and is therefore constant and rapid. Consequently, you should always allow for possible delays due to construction and roadworks.
> (See LAST MINUTE CONSTRUCTION UPDATES under our ONLINE ATLAS OF EUROPE for up-to-date details on this.)

(What did I tell you? I'll book somewhere for Day 1 and we'll just have to wing it after that.)

> 5 Set aside a 'Car Bag' that can go as hand

luggage on the ferry and be carried inside the car while driving. Some items you may want to include:
- change of clothes for all family members in case of accidents en route, thicker and thinner clothes in case of sudden changes of weather (particularly common in southern Europe in early and late summer), spare nappies and knickers, sunhats, preferably with folding neck flaps to protect children, flipflops or other lightweight sandals for quick trips to the bathroom over hot ground. Lightweight night clothes for all, for night ferry crossings or emergencies.
- sunblock, both kids' and adults', aspirin and paracetamol (but see previous notes on banned drugs), Evian or other refreshing aerosol, sticking plasters and gauze pads, sting reducer, hand cream, hand wipes or refresher towels.
- toothpaste (adults' and kids'), toothbrushes, dental floss, soap and handwashing detergent, in tubes if possible, shampoo and conditioner (a good idea to transfer these into small containers before you set out to make space).
- fruit, dried fruit or Trail Mix, savoury crackers in case of delays or traffic jams. Boiled sweets and plain sweet biscuits, e.g. Marie, in case of car sickness. Water bottle (NOTE: do not be tempted to refill plastic water bottles, especially if children have been drinking from them directly - they very quickly become breeding grounds for bacteria).
- torch and spare batteries.

> – one book or toy per child and adult, preferably ones that can be shared and passed around, and one game that the whole family can join in . . .

(What game would that be, then? Pass the Buck?)

> . . . Pencils and spiralbound pad for all those other games – Hangman, I Spy, Consequences, etc. – in case of unexpected delays.

(There isn't room in a sixteen-wheel truck for that lot. Surely the major bonus of ferries, and indeed holidays in general, is that kids can be entertained for hours on the quest for items that you secretly know all along will be impossible to find, and don't in fact need.)

> 6   Eating en route. Pack another hamper or cool box with the following items, then add food, drinks and perishables at the last minute on the day you leave: cups with lids and straws, plastic or Microban plates and bowls, plastic boxes or other containers for your favourite tea or other nonperishables, salt and pepper dispensers, bottle opener/corkscrew (though of course no drinking by driver), icepacks to store in hotel fridge overnight, clingfilm for wrapping leftovers, wipes, paper towels and toothpicks (wood, not plastic, is safer with small people around).

(Or buy delicious, cheap, ready-made sandwiches at any local patisserie.)

> For further ideas on in-car entertainment and . . .

(Seven days? The moon landing could have been planned in less time than this lot. Let's see what else we have here . . .)

```
'Seven Things to Ask Yourself Before You Put
the Key in the Ignition'
```

(Apart from 'Where the hell is the car key, I had it a moment ago?' I'll print this off and save it, I'll never remember from now till then.

Anyhow, it may well be Colum asking himself the gnarly questions. We haven't really discussed in detail the allocation of roles on this particular top-level mission, except we all know he'll be the one navigating by the Waitrose Ten Superb French Reds list.)

```
1   Which side is the petrol cap on?
```

(I'd have thought it was easier to ask the passengers in the back. All they have to do is look out of the windows.)

```
2   Is the petrol leaded or unleaded, and do I
    know the words for them?
```

(There's no way I'm letting a French petrol station attendant near my filler cap. I'll just make for the green nozzle.)

```
3   Where or when will be my first stop?
```

(Why on earth should the driver ask that when there's a perfectly good navigator taking up valuable snack space right there in the front seat?)

```
4   Have I checked the weather conditions ahead?
```

(Short of snow on mountain passes, what difference does it make? It's not like we're going to say, 'Oh dear, showers forecast for later, let's all go home again.')

```
5   Has the car hire office got any sugges-
tions en route?
```

(Car hire office? What demographic do they think we're from?)

```
6   Are the water bottles filled, and has
everybody been to the restroom?
```

(A minute ago they were telling us not to refill water bottles. Honestly, who writes this rubbish?)

```
7   Have I bought a local phone card or
tokens? Do I need local currency for tolls?
```

Local currency? When was this thing last updated? I guess in that case I can discount the rest, too. Who'd have guessed driving through France had overtaken circumnavigating the poles via the summit of K2 as the Worst Journey in the World?

There's always the alternative of popping down to Sainsbury's for Valrhona, Beurre d'Isigny, Petit Pont L'Eveque, Bonne Maman, a couple of baguettes and the VHS of *Chocolat*, and holing up for a fortnight. I almost miss the old days when croissants and Camembert were rare foreign treats. How we pitied the French their tasteless unsalted butter! And how we laughed at them for having to buy drinking water in bottles, and put up with gas in it!

MUST remember to ask about Angel's passport, MUST . . .

9 July – E-mail exchange: Colum and Billy

```
From:   ColumMcCallum [colum@laverda.demon.co.uk]
Sent:   9 July
To:     Billy Giddens[billy@goat.freeserve.co.uk]

Hi Bill
Well, we're finally off tomorrow - don't much
fancy the prospect of eight days of nothing
```

to look at but overweight Frenchmen on Harleys, but at least there should be a few choice MMs and MotoRumis in between. And from memory the French motorway stops sell half-decent plonk which should deaden the pain somewhat. Madam is locked in an elaborate fantasy dating from her early childhood that we'll be bypassing the above in favour of charming vine-covered auberges serving *cuisine bourgeoise* – no point bursting her bubble when two days will do it for me.

She's also been behaving like a starving squirrel in search of its last nut for the past week, but the good outcome of this packing frenzy is that she's had only limited time to nag me about my choice of swimwear. She also seems to think that travelling with children is an Open University course in itself. You've had four – any tips?

Col

From: Billy Giddens [billy@goat.freeserve.co.uk]
To: ColumMcCallum [colum@laverda.demon.co.uk]

col old miucker
those frog harleys are indeed a pain but luckily they are such pispoor mecanics they're usually in teh shop. you will notice they spend a lot more time standnig around them at gas statinos than acutally riding teh buggers.
   as for kids in cars – it's more or les hell any way you cut it, no point in going to

```
any trouble but rmember no milkshakes until
the day's travel is well past.
    yrs bill
```
---

10 July – Helen, Colum and Des, with George and Fiona

George and Fiona are standing in the front hallway with their two small plastic holdalls. The way is barred by Colum, busy fixing an elaborate wire gate across the passage a couple of feet in front of the door. Beyond, the living room is piled with bags and suitcases, while Des, wearing only swimming trunks and a pair of frog-shaped sunglasses, jumps up and down on his own bag.

Meanwhile Helen, holding Bertie by his fat neck to stop him escaping, rushes through before he can spot the visitors. It's clear they've arrived before the household is entirely ready for them.

D: Grandma and Granddad are here! Mum! Dad! We're going to Franceanitaly! I can count to nearly eleven! Shall I tell you what time it is on your watch?

H: *(from behind the door)* George! Fiona! How lovely, do come in! Can you move that OUT OF THE WAY, Colum, your parents are here?

Colum looks up, and speaks through a mouthful of nails.

C: Hi. Just thought I'd run something up to keep the cat in when you open the door.

H: *(still out of sight)* Not that we think he doesn't want to stay with you or anything, of course. Here, Bertie, let's . . .

She peers out and sees them, still standing there.

H: COLUM! Can you get the bags and let your parents IN the house, do you think?

C: Half a mo . . .

Helen, holding Bertie away from George and Fiona, rushes through to the kitchen.

H: I'll just make us all a lovely cup of coffee, or would you prefer tea? Did you have a good journey?
G: *(around the unlit pipe in his mouth)* Tea'd be just fine.
F: I'm sure we don't have to stay if we're in the way, Helen, dear. Though the next ferry back isn't until tomorrow night, and . . .

Colum finishes, stands up, opens the wire gate and grabs the two bags.

C: Don't be daft, Mum.

Gives her a big kiss and his father a manly handshake.

C: You don't want to be running around after a lost cat every five minutes, now, do ye?

The two grandparents allow themselves to be ushered beyond the cat trap, where Des immediately rushes up to them and covers them with kisses.

D: Did you know mummy elephants hit their baby elephants with their trunks when they're naughty? Did you bring me a present? Can I have it now?
H: *(from kitchen)* Des!
F: *(indulgent grandmotherly chuckle)* Och, don't nag the boy, Helen, dear, it's only high spirits.

A sudden sound of cupboards being opened and doors rattled very loudly.

F: *(rummaging in her bag)* Now, let's see – what have we here?

George meanwhile takes the opportunity of handing Colum a plastic carrier bag.

G: Ye'r ma was sure ye'd not have any o' this by ye.

Colum peers into it.

C: Porridge oats, honey, Marmite, Ovaltine, Horlicks, oatcakes, mince, butter, onions, carrots, Table Cream, jelly cubes, custard powder, Dream Topping, ginger wine, Nice biscuits, Milk of Magnesia. How thoughtful. And all things we use all the time. Come and sit, Dad.

F: Aha!

Grandma has found what she's looking for – a plastic sword and shield that manage to look simultaneously lethal and shoddy.

F: Here y'are, Grandson – off ye go now and kill us a few Germans.

Colum looks anxiously towards the kitchen, where Helen is managing to spend a very long time making the tea.
   This is because she is, in fact, chopping fillet steak and calves' liver into Bertie's bowl, while holding him clenched between her legs.

H: There you go, Bertie. Early dinner.

Bertie, looking as surprised as a twenty-pound furball can, dives in.

D: Wah!!!! KILL KILL KILL! MUM!! Look MUM!!!

Des rushes through the kitchen door, straight into Helen's armful of cups, saucers and teaspoons, which crash to the floor.

F: (*conversationally, from the next room*) Were ye no' expecting us, Helen, dear? Only I thought I'd made a special point of letting ye know the time we . . .

Luckily at this moment the phone rings.

H: Sorry! Could be an emergency!

Helen stops sweeping up broken china and grabs the phone, as Des continues to careen round Bertie.

H: (Hi, can I call you ba . . . Ernie? What's up? . . .)

She covers the mouthpiece and stage-whispers to Colum.

H: Ernie – crisis – won't be long.

Colum comes into the kitchen and takes over making the tea. George produces a folded newspaper from his bag and unfolds it very slowly. Des rushes back in to Grandma.

H: (. . . so Pierce didn't – yeah, but he's a creep, look at that last thing he did, what was it . . . Oh, but Ewan did, well, that's good, isn't it? . . . Breakfast? What, this morning? . . . And he didn't . . . Oh, he *did*? Well, then, what's the . . .)
D: KILL KILL here you are Grandma lots and lots of Germans all chopped up and all covered in bleeding and wounds!!
F: How nice, Lewis, dear, at least somebody is willing to keep us company after our long trip. *(to George)* He's a real wee man now, is he not, and the spit of his father too. *(raised voice, to Colum in the kitchen)* Don't trouble yerself wi' the tea if it's too much bother, son, surely there'll be a café round these parts if ye'd just point us the right way . . .

In the kitchen, Colum piles more cups and saucers on to the tea tray and opens a packet of HobNobs. Back in the living room, George is looking for something. He methodically tries every pocket with no luck.

H: (He turned up and then spent the whole time chatting up the waitress? . . . Not even the waitress . . . I don't believe it! Hang on, darling . . .)

Noticing Bertie's finished and is making for the doorway, she grabs the HobNobs from Colum and empties them into his plate. A moment's incredulity, and he dives in again.

G: *(to Fiona)* Have ye seen ma reading glasses?
F: Well, ye had them for sure in the taxi – you've no' left them behind again?

Bertie, having finished the HobNobs, begins to pay attention and realises where he's heard that voice before. He raises his head, looks into the living room, and his hair prickles. Colum peers out through the kitchen window as Bertie backs towards it, hissing.

C: The cab's just up the road. I think I can catch him . . .

Helen, still stuck to the phone, is gesturing frantically, but he doesn't notice. Before she can grab Bertie, Colum opens the window to call out to the taxi. The cat, with amazing agility, leaps straight through the open window.

H: Bertie! DON'T!

A frozen moment after he disappears while they all wait for a crash, or a plop or squish, which thankfully doesn't come.

H: (Ernie, darling, I have to go, I'm so sorry, MAJOR emergency, I'll call you later, okay? Love you too . . .)

10 July, bedtime – The St George and the Dragon and the Puking Cat Calypso

> There once was a brave knight, he was called St George
> He used to help the poor and sick and other unfort-
> Unates, and one day he heard about a princess who
> Had a dragon that she needed to send to the Zoo.
>
> Now other knights had come but they'd all made the
>   mistake

Of trying to kill the dragon, which made her heart break
But St George loved animals and hated to kill
Making friends with fur and feathers was his greatest
   skill.

(What bit? The sword and shield and killing bit? Well, you know, not all knights — okay, here goes.)

As I said, the other knights all shed a lot of blood.
But brave St George knew that was no good.
He had a sword and shield but just for self-defence, and
   every
Time he met a beast they ended up best friends.

(You're perfectly welcome to kill as many as you like, Des, I'm just telling you about St George, the well-known pacifist and animal lover.)

So St George took the dragon safely to Princess Doreen
(yes, that was her name, really — well, maybe they only just
   found that out)
And though they were both shy, she became his queen.
They married right away and had a lovely feast, to
   which
They asked every dragon, lizard, bird and beast!

(Wasn't that the story you heard last time? Well, that's definitely the authentic version. No, he definitely didn't kill the dragon, I'd have remembered. Yes, I know it was supposed to be about your sword and shield, but that was only part of the story. Which zoo? Umm — that is one detail I have to admit I don't remember. Your poor mum has a head like a sieve sometimes, doesn't she? I do NOT have a head like a banana! But it was quite a long time ago, so I'm afraid it is possible, whichever zoo he was in, that the dragon has died of old age by now. Like the dinosaurs, yes.
   Oh, the cat bit. Hmm. Let's see.)

Well, Bertie the cat had a big feast too
And without him really noticing his tummy grew
Until he couldn't fit where he had gone before, and he
Got stuck when he tried to come in through the door.

He wriggled and he wiggled so he would unstick
But sadly in so doing made himself quite sick
When Grandma went to help she was right in the way
And that was the end of her lovely day!

(Yes, poor Grandma, we did feel sorry for her, didn't we? Almost. Night-night, sweetie – go to sleep now, big day tomorrow, you're meeting your lovely new friend Angel. Love you too, big hug.)

11 July – E-mail exchange: Ernie and Madge

From: Ernestine Short [ernie@ernie.com]
To: Madge Handelman [madge@handy.com]

```
yo sista
Just a quickie to say not sure Ewan McGregor
really has the range and depth for the part,
and Pierce Brosnan is so three years ago, but
how about Jude Law or Ben Chaplin? Both defi-
nitely have the physique for Joe's line of
work and Jude L especially would be an
exciting, cast-against-type kind of idea for a
motor mechanic, don't you think?
   Still working on the other parts. Couldn't
quite make out from the story outline where
it's set - might help if I knew what sort of
accents I'm aiming at, we have most of 'em
here in London, as you know.
   Isn't today the day they leave? Bet you
can't wait to see her again!
```

```
    Weather still vile. Incredible, but at least
I'm getting more mileage than I expected from
the Versace raincoat.
   love ya E
```

From: Madge Handelman [madge@handy.com]
To: Ernestine Short [ernie@ernie.com]

```
sweets
don't sweat it over the accents - like some-
body said, if the audience notice the
dialogue, there's something wrong with the
sixpacks. Studio accounts department still
determining actuarially optimal setting for
movie - current thoughts seem to be Turkestan
or southern Austria, but could rewrite for
anywhere they have motor mechanics, and will
also depend on where director and talent
willing to work. So plan on Malibu.
   who's leaving today? Didn't get it, sorry,
brain fried.
   weather here glorious as usual.
   big kiss M
```

----

11 July – Helen, Colum and Des, in car en route to pick up Angel

It's raining. The car is piled high with bags and suitcases. Colum is sitting in the passenger seat, in jeans and a T-shirt, with a brand-new atlas of Britain (unopened) and a copy of *Autosport* (which he's reading). Helen is in the driver's seat, in her new palazzo pants and stripey top, looking cold. Des is in the back, in his shorts, T-shirt and a pair of fish-shaped swimming goggles, playing an elaborate game with a toy gorilla and a cowboy on a horse.

The car isn't moving. Helen takes a deep breath, holds it, and closes her eyes.

C: So — are we off, then?

No reply.

C: Only, my understanding was that packing and loading the car was the preparation stage of this holiday, and the actual event involved travelling to another place. Or several.

Helen, lungs bursting, turns to glare at him.

C: Have it your own way.

He returns to his magazine.

D: Mum! Mum! Can we stop for lunch soon?
C: We haven't actually started yet. Your mother's having second thoughts.

A rush of air explodes from a puce-faced Helen.

H: If you must know, I'm just taking the recommended five minutes of calm and peace before starting on what is undoubtedly going to be a very stressful experience.
C: So you are having second thoughts. Should I unpack the car?
D: Mum! I'm hungry!

She wheels on him.

H: Remember those four sausages and that big baked potato and those carrot sticks and the two biscuits and that apple you had half an hour ago? That was lunch.
C: So much for the calm and peace. Will they help us get to West Sussex in *(looking at his watch)* an hour, do you suppose?

Helen starts the car. Des is thrown violently back in his seat.

C: He's not strapped in.

Helen stops the car again and Colum clambers out and opens Des's door.

H: If I'd had five minutes of calm the first time, we wouldn't be so late already.
C: How do you make that out, then?
H: Well, I'd have had a chance to notice we didn't have any petrol before I set out to drive once around the block to make sure we hadn't forgotten anything.
C: If you'd driven the other way around the block, we'd have got to the petrol station before it ran out.
H: Exactly!

Colum looks baffled, fastens Des's belt buckle and clambers back in. Helen starts the car again.

H: Wave bye-bye to Grandma and Grandpa, Des!
C: (*back in his magazine*) They went to the shops about forty minutes back.
H: But the house was full of food! What about all that stuff they brought?
C: I have the impression they were trying to dump it on us.
H: Cheek!
D: Hello, Bertie! You're not strapped in.
H: (*whispering, to Colum*) So sweet the way he makes things up!
C: Look in your rear-view mirror.

As she does so, an unmistakable big fat furry head appears between the two front seats. The car screeches to a halt.

H: Bertie! You CAN'T COME!!!
C: You'll break his heart.

Helen wheels the car around violently, narrowly missing a cyclist, and heads back the way she came.

H: I'll break his legs. How d'you fancy three weeks in traction at the vet's, Bertie?

Bertie miaows piteously and tries to hide behind the back seat.

C: He understands every word you say, you know!
H: Don't be ridiculous!

(Two hours later – at Angel's school)

The car pulls in at the gates of a big country house. As they drive towards it, they see a huge pile of luggage, and a group of what appear to be under-age Calvin Klein models in minutely differentiated versions of wispy T-shirt and sprayed-on jeans, watching out for the car and ragging each other.

Suddenly Colum looks like a child who's found a fiver in the road.

C: Which one is she? Not that it matters . . .
H: How would I know? *(nervously)* D'you think those are all her bags?
C: The bags would seem to imply she's in there somewhere. Hey, this holiday could turn out all right after all.

Helen gives him a withering look. The car pulls to a stop. The girls stop their giggling and preening, and stare. Among them are Leila, Trina and Ramona.

L: Here you are, Angel! Here's the Maserati!
T: You are SO, like, mean, Leil!

It's definitely not a Maserati. Helen, brave smile on her face, clambers out. Angel, in the middle of the group, backs away and hides behind the rest. They're shrieking with laughter. She's not.

Leila, an Egyptian princess with a tart's purple lipstick, saunters towards Helen.

L: Hi! We've heard *all* about you. Come on, Angel, your date's here.

The other girls push a protesting Angel forward. She's dumped the Goth thing and redone herself as an Anglo Destiny's Child. Pure twelve-year-old jailbait.

C: (*to Des*) Watch and learn, son. Your education begins here.

There's a knock on the car window. Trina — who could be Claudia Schiffer's baby sister — smiles in at Colum. He smiles back and opens the door.

T: Hi!

But the smile is evidently for somebody else's benefit. She licks her lips, sticks what there is of her chest forward, and peers into the back of the car.

T: And you must be . . .

Des, who has been chasing the cowboy after the gorilla on the seat back, turns around and smiles adorably.

T: . . . Desi? Omigod! Oh, this is, like, hilarious!

Angel allows herself to be pushed in front, pretending shyness. Des squishes his face, still in swimming goggles, against his window. Angel screams, then tries to recover her cool.

A: (*Home Counties posh, like all the others*) That's not him. Desi's eighteen.

Helen is busy trying to wrestle at least some of Angel's bags into the car boot.

H: (*from behind the car*) Open the door and say hello nicely, Des.

T: He's about three! Des is three, everybody.
D: I am not! I'm four and more than a half!
A: *(small, icy voice)* That is NOT Desi. My mum told me . . .

Colum suddenly realises what's happening.

C: You're absolutely right . . . Angel, is it? I'm Colum. Des is meeting us at the . . . later. This is . . . *(whispering at Des)* Pretend time, okay? *(to Angel)* . . . Sam, our youngest.

The girls are still screaming and giggling, clearly not convinced. Helen comes round to introduce herself and catches the end of this.

H: What's the problem? *(to Angel)* Hi, I'm Helen.

Angel doesn't move or shake hands. Helen shrugs.

H: Come on, Des, stop making faces and be . . .
C: *(whispering urgently to her)* Sam!
H: Who's that?
C: This is Sam, isn't it. Say hi, Sam!
D: Hello, I'm . . .
C: . . . and this is my wife, Helen. Come on, we'd better be off, we've a ferry . . . um, a Concorde to catch.

Helen looks totally baffled, but picks up the last two bags. Angel is frantically dialling a number on her mobile.

A: Mum? Mum! . . .

She listens to what is obviously a recorded message.

A: Mum, you have to call me back, okay? This is urgent, there's a BIG problem.
H: *(to Angel)* There! I shan't be able to see, and you won't be able to put on any weight, but who wants to eat funny foreign food, ha ha?

She holds the door open for Angel, still smiling gamely.

A: I'm not moving until I've spoken to my mum.

The other girls begin to drift away, giggling.

L: Have a lovely time!
R: Send us a postcard!

Des wriggles across the seat to make room and smiles up at Angel, who looks about to burst into tears.

D: Don't be sad! Are you missing your teddy? Would you like to play with my gorilla?
A: My mum said . . . she SWORE to me . . .

Helen climbs into her seat and slams the door, rather harder than necessary. Angel is still standing there.

H: I don't know what she said to you, but she told us you were really looking forward to it, and one thing none of us is going to enjoy is sitting on the dock all night waiting for the next ferry.

Colum gets out and tries to put a friendly arm around Angel. She shrugs him off. The girls have vanished, and there's nobody else around.

C: Come on. I'm sure she'll call you back as soon as she's off the phone, and we can sort something out.

Angel, realising she has no option, very reluctantly squeezes in beside Des, who holds out his gorilla to her. She ignores him, fumbles in her bag and brings out an MP3 player and a set of headphones.

C: So who's for pizza in Portsmouth?
D: Me! I am! Can I have doughballs AND garlic bread????

11 July, evening – Mobile phone calls from car in Portsmouth

COLUM TO DIRECTORY ENQUIRIES
　Hello? Directory? ... Portsmouth, please. Pizza Express ...

ANGEL TO MADGE
　(*back to mall rat accent*) ... Mom? Mom, I'm being kidnapped by these like total drongy strangers in this totally heinous beat-up old car, and they're taking me, I don't even know where, and you have to ...

COLUM TO DIRECTORY ENQUIRIES
　... No? Nothing? Well, where's the nearest one? ... Chichester? ... No, that is rather far ...

ANGEL TO MADGE
　... I've been, like, calling and calling and leaving messages and there's this psycho kid in with me ...

COLUM TO DIRECTORY ENQUIRIES
　Directory? Can you give me Pizza Hut for Portsmouth, please? ... Nothing? You're quite certain about that?

ANGEL TO MADGE
　... You CAN'T DO THIS TO ME, MOM!! I'm telling you, once they get me out of the country even Dad won't be able to get me back ...

COLUM TO DIRECTORY ENQUIRIES
　Hello? Hello, Directory? ... Portsmouth ... Well, I don't have an exact name, but anything with 'pizza' in it ... Ah! Where's that, then? ... It's takeout only? ... Better not, I think, but thanks anyway.

ANGEL TO MADGE
　I HATE YOU, MOM!!!!

11 July – Bill from Charlie Chimichanga's Mexican Grill and Tandoori

Ola Amigos! El Party Comienza Aqui
TABLE: 12
No. in party: 4
YOUR SERVER IS: Ryan

1 × Pepitos guacamole/chips	£2.45
extra chips	£1.50
1 × Tony's Special Spicy nachos/chips (hold chilli)	£4.50
extra chips	£1.50
1 × Charlie's Special Mega burrito	£6.99
extra cheese	£1.00
extra sour cream	£1.00
1 × tortilla salad (hold sour cream, hold cheese, hold guacamole)	£7.50
1 × pina colada cheesecake	£3.99
side ice cream	£1.50
1 × Diet Coke	£1.99
1 × orange juice	£1.50
2 × Dos Equis @ 3.50	£7.00
1 × Cuervo Gold shot	£4.00
2 × black coffee @ £1.99	£3.98
1 × Cuervo Gold shot	£4.00
1 × Diet Coke to go	£1.99
SUBTOTAL:	£56.39
OPTIONAL SERVICE @ 12.5%	£7.05
TOTAL:	£63.44

PAID VISA WITH MUCHAS GRACIAS!
Hasta La Vista! and Come Back Soon!

11 July, late – Bertie 'Escape from Colditz' McCallum: battle strategy

List of options:

1 Escape
Well-nigh impossible, and even if I did, what then? Two weeks on that ledge above the bus stop seems, quite frankly, an even less attractive prospect than two weeks with the cocoa assassins. The alpha male had enough of a struggle getting me down, so this lot would probably not even attempt it, if they bothered to come looking, which is not at all guaranteed. I am NOT risking the humiliation of rescue by the Fire Brigade at my time of life. I've avoided it until now, and I intend to keep this record unblemished.

2 Attack
Now, here's a more attractive concept. After all, there's plenty of fight in me yet! Instead of bemoaning their feebleness, senility and general decrepitude, turn it to my advantage in one deadly attack.

All it would take is to wait until they fall asleep – any minute now, by the look of them – then leap on their faces and claw out their eyes, leaving them helpless to resist while I tear their flesh in ribbons from their wizened bones . . .

I don't think I can continue with this, it's making me quite queasy. I am definitely not the warrior I was. Even the sight of my own vomit has lost its former appeal. The prospect of two weeks in here with a pair of decomposing corpses makes the ledge above the bus stop look like Marbella (whatever that is).

Which leaves . . .

3 Capitulation
Has it really come to this? Is Bertie, the proud scion of a noble litter, to be reduced to a craven collaborator, abandoning loyalty,

dignity and principle for a measly tin of Felix? How could I even eat it without gagging in shame?

But wait!

There is another option!

4 Passive Resistance

Not that I've ever tried a hunger strike, but it has to be admitted that I have lost much, if not all, of my former sleekness, and with it that agility which defines a cat as opposed to, for instance, a cushion. And by merely refusing the Felix I would not only lose weight but attack the enemy where they are most vulnerable – their psyches. I'll drive them mad with worry, crazed with guilt, until they will do anything – anything at all – to see me eat again.

Then I shall have them in my power. And who knows what they may offer me as temptation? That steak today certainly hit the spot.

Pity they're not around to witness the chilly superiority with which I am even now eschewing the food bowl. Might as well have a nap until there's an audience . . .

11 July, late – Helen

Well, I have to say those travel websites are a total waste of space. I spent hours packing that bloody bag with pyjamas, toothpaste, nourishing snacks, emergency knickers, a bouquetière of foreign mini-dictionaries and secret documents on which the addresses of British consulates in every capital of the world were inscribed in invisible ink, but where on any website does it say 'Whatever you do, don't forget to pack a spare toy animal in case the one he was playing with gets inadvertently left in the car on the locked car deck for the duration of the voyage'?

Des is a sweet and reasonable child, but four hours of Angel's company had reduced his reserves of cheer to a dangerous low, and apparently only the gorilla was maintaining his will to live. Colum bravely volunteered to investigate the consumer paradise known as Deck 7 Gift Shop, which was quite useful as Angel flatly refused to undress in front of anybody else, and with Colum out of the way I was able legitimately to retire with Des to the cabin's cunningly miniaturised bathroom, while she decided which of her various designer T-shirts she was going to designate as night-time cruisewear.

But eventually we had to come out, partly because Colum had returned, *sans* any kind of gorilla but proudly waving a POdge, the P&O Sailor Teddy, on the basis that this was at least an animal. Only a parent could make such a crashing error of judgment. A teddy, Des patiently informed us, is not an Animal, but a Toy.

Anyhow, thank God they're all asleep now, or at least they're not demanding anything and the lights are out, so I for one intend to get some shut-eye while I can.

Timetable of P&O Night Ferry, Portsmouth/Le Havre

20.45	All cars and passengers to report to ferry port.
20.46	Industrial action by French dock workers announced.
21.15	Scheduled departure time.
21.45	Industrial action cancelled (management caves in, as usual).
22.30	Actual departure time.
22.40	Find cabin. Spend fifteen minutes getting excited about dinky bathroom and ladder to top bunks. Begin to undress and prepare for bed.
22.50	Cabin steward bursts in with baby's cot, intended for family two cabins down. Get half dressed before realise it's all a mistake.

23.00	Undress all over again, clean teeth, get into bed and lights out.
23.05	Tannoy reminds everybody to put their watches forward one hour.
23.15	Tannoy reminds everybody that arrival time in Le Havre is now only six hours and twenty minutes away.
23.25	Tannoy informs all passengers of emergency procedures in case of evacuation and warns of impending fire alarm test.
23.45	Fire alarm goes off, apparently inside cabin. Forty-five babies on Deck 10 burst into simultaneous wails of pure terror.
00.15	Tannoy thanks everybody for their cooperation with fire alarm test.
00.35	Tannoy announces Calvados promotion, proudly sponsored by Normandy Tourist Board, to commence on Deck 8 in half an hour.
01.00	Reminder of Calvados tasting.
01.30–02.00	Revellers return from Calvados tasting.
02.00–04.40	Ship's foghorn sounds every five minutes.
05.00	Tannoy announces that Continental breakfast, coffee, tea, hot beverages and other light snacks are now available in the Boulevard Café on Deck 7.
05.45	Every light in every cabin on the ship goes on at once. Forty babies start to scream again.
06.15	All passengers required to go immediately to rejoin their cars for disembarkation. Tannoy thanks everybody for travelling P&O and hopes they've slept well, enjoyed their crossing and will repeat the experience in the near future.

11–12 July – 'The Abduction' (Angel's Dream): Episode 1

From the first moment the Empress came to her with the plan, Princess Xandar knew that something was not right. All her instincts were to resist, to stay where, though suffering cruelly, at least she knew her gaolers. But the Empress was so persuasive, so reasonable, so, like, apparently sweet and kind. There seemed nothing to object to in the plan – at least, the way she told it. And – here's the bit that sucks – the Empress knew that Princess Xandar knew that, for a few more endless years, she had the power to decide the Princess's fate.

Oh, the tragic foolishness of the nobly born! The Princess, who would never have dreamed of, like, lying or deceiving anyone herself, was utterly unprepared for the villainy, the cruelty and shittiness, of those who now surrounded her. The rich, gorgeous and ultra-cool companions she had been promised for her arduous journey were but yet another sick joke. Too late, Princess Xandar realised she had been tricked. But what could she do? Her compadres, her so-called friends, had vanished like – like, smoke. The Empress was far away, working the phones in a distant galaxy. Once again, as so often in her young life, the Princess found herself utterly alone.

Alone, but not defeated. No way. 'They may have enslaved my body,' she told herself, 'I may be forced to travel in the company of rancid low lifes and dwarfish mutants to who knows what totally gross and dangerous destination. But they cannot break my noble spirit. Sooner or later, the Powerful One will recognise me and bring me to his court to be among my own kind. Until then, I must have faith, and wait.'

With these thoughts in her heart, she allowed herself to be forced into the ratty old StratoCar for the journey to the Galactic Cruiser. The transfer was swift and ruthlessly efficient – no chance of escape or a last farewell. Until at last, strapped into her pod with those cool little earplugs, the Princess could do her complexion exercises and try, as best her agonised nerves would allow, to rest.

12 July – Colum, Helen, Des and Angel

They're sitting in the car, still inside the hold of the ferry. Nobody has slept. Angel's retreated into MP3 land again. Colum is in the driver's seat. Helen is still trying to be brave and positive.

H: Well, here we are. Almost in France! Well done for finding the car, Des. That would have been funny, if all these people had been stuck behind us, and we'd still been on the other deck looking for it.
C: Funny?
D: It wasn't me found the car it was Teddy POdge.
H: But Teddy POdge had never seen it before, darling.
D: Yes he had!! He had!!
H: Okay, of course he had.
D: Teddy POdge is hungry.

The lights on the cars in front flick on.

C: Here we go.

He starts the engine. Helen leans over to Des and holds out her empty hand.

H: Here's a yummy honey-and-banana sandwich for Teddy!

Des gives her a withering look.

D: Not PRETEND hungry, REAL hungry.
H: Well, we're just driving off the ferry now and in ten minutes we'll be in France, where they have delicious croissants and hot chocolate on every corner.
C: We've got to get through customs first. Can you chuck me the passports?

Helen's face loses what colour it previously had. She makes a weird choking sound.

C: Excuse me?

He starts the car and drives off the ship. Helen hands over three passports.

H: Here they are.

She nerves herself, turns around and touches Angel's arm to get her attention. Angel jumps, shrieks, and reluctantly removes her headphones.

H: Angel, sweetheart, do you have your passport handy?

Angel squirms around, rummages in several of her bags in turn, and produces a passport. Helen's face clears.

H: Great! Terrific! Look, Colum, Angel's passport! Look, Des! Isn't that wonderful! Clever you, Angel!

She hands it to Colum. The others look at her as though she's mad.

The car pulls up to the customs shed. Colum hands the four passports to the immaculate officer. Helen smiles winningly at him. He flicks through the first three passports, and then looks at Angel's. Doesn't like what he sees.

H: Is there a problem? We're taking her to her mother . . .
CO: *(caricature French accent, almost unintelligible)* Zees passpor' ees freum Patageunia!!
H: From where? It's not!
A: Sure it is. So what?
H: It is?
D: What's Pata . . . Patagum? Why is that man talking like that?
A: I have dual nationality. My dad's a diplomat, okay? I was born in Patagonia, okay? So? Mum said to bring my passport, she didn't say WHICH passport, okay?

Helen is speechless. Colum clears his throat and prepares to speak Man to Man.

C: I'm extremely sorry we're causing you difficulties, Officer. What do you need us to do now?
CO: Feerst, yeu meuve out euv ze way euv ze ozzair carrz. Ai weel ceum teu yeu whain Ai 'ave taim.

Colum drives on to the deserted customs dock. Rain drizzles over them. They wait. Angel, unperturbed, reaches into a huge pink crocodile-skin vanity case and starts doing her make-up.

D: Teddy POdge is REALLY hungry now. Can we go and have croissants? Can I have a chocolate croissant and one for Teddy POdge?

Helen, a Queen's Guide to her fingertips, unzips the overnight bag and produces three cereal bars and a water bottle.

H: Here we are! Good thing I packed some nourishing snacks for emergencies!
C: Shouldn't we wait till we know how long they'll be holding us in the illegal aliens' detention centre?

Helen, mouth full, turns and fixes the oblivious Angel with a baleful stare.

H: What d'you mean, 'us'? Eat up, Des, it's lovely.
D: You said . . .

The customs official strolls elegantly past the car and into the shed. Ten minutes later, he emerges, wearing an Yves Saint Laurent raincape over his uniform. This time he comes up to them. Angel finishes her face, kisses her reflection, gets out her mobile and dials a number.

CO: Monsieur. Ai 'ave ascertained zat citizens euv Patageunia are requaired teu 'ave a visa teu enter France . . .
H: A visa? How long will that . . .
CO: . . . Ze leetle gairl meust return teu England and apply freum zaire.

H: (*brightening up*) Go back to England? Just her?

Angel stops dialling.

A: All right!!
C: No, it's not all right. Look, we can sort this out. D'ye have a number for the British consul, by any chance?

Angel starts dialling again. The customs official leans into the car and takes a look at Angel, who in addition to her mascara, blusher and shimmer lip gloss is wearing a low-cut mini-T-shirt trimmed with sequins spelling 'DevilChick'.

CO: I seenk maybe I 'ave a talk weez zee gairl een mai bureau 'ere and we can wairk out some agreement, heh?
H: No!
C: No!

Angel waves her hands at them to be quiet. She's still on the phone.

A: (Okay, Dad, hold it there! Hold it! I'm passing you over now!)

With a small smug smile she hands her phone to Colum.

A: My dad. He's in Nigeria. He's the US ambassador. He wants to talk to him.

Colum passes the phone to the customs officer, who looks suspicious, but puts it to his ear.

CO: ('Allo?)

A stream of expressions races over his face – puzzlement, shock, discomfort, pure terror. The others wait. Angel nonchalantly goes back to her music.

D: Mum, Teddy POdge has got a tummy ache from that food.
H: Shh!

CO: (Vair' well . . . M'sieu, you do not undairstand . . . No, no, m'sieu, *pas du tout, mais* . . . *Très bien* . . . *D'accord* . . . *Très bien. Merci mille fois, M'sieur l'Ambassadeur.*)

He hands the phone back to Colum, who hands it back to Angel, who puts it away, looking even more smug. He clears his throat.

CO: Ai am pleased teu be abel teu inform yeu, messieursdames, zat exceptionally we can allow yeu and yeur friend . . .
H: Good, that's settled, can we go now, please?

He holds up his hand and pulls a little booklet out of his immaculate pocket.

CO: . . . but zair eez a penalty payment euv . . . four 'undred fifty euro payable, and . . .
H: Four hundred and fifty? That's – that's a fortune! He's asking for a bribe, Colum! We don't have . . .
C: *(loudly)* Certainly, Officer – cash or traveller's cheques?

A shrug of supreme indifference. Colum glares at Helen, who meekly produces some cash.

CO: . . . and zee young lady meust 'ave 'air Americain passpor' sent teu a French address wizin sree days so it can be presented teu ze Gendarmerie for stamping. Where do yeu wish teu deu zis?

Colum looks at Helen, who's still in shock over the money.

C: You're the one with the village-by-village itinerary all planned out. Where are we going to be in three days?
H: Three – that's . . . Where are we now? Tuesday. Er, Lyons!
C: Lyons?
CO: Lyon! *Très bien!*

He writes something on a printed form, signs it, tears it off, takes the money, and hands the form and the passports to Colum.

CO: Ai 'ave teu warn yeu, eef yeu deu nut show zees passpor' in Lyon by Fraiday, zee yeung lady weel be deported and yeu weel be in serious treuble. *Bonjour, messieursdames, et bienvenus en France!*

12 July – Travelling through France

The view through Des's window
Here, Teddy POdge, look out of the window, look – let him look, Gorilla, he's your friend, be nice to him, you have to share now. Look the cows are a different colour. Look they look like toffee. Maybe their milk tastes like toffee too. Watch out for the French cowboys, they are very fierce. Are you hungry too? I'm very hungry too.

The view through Colum's window
I see France doesn't get any less boring. Or empty. I'd be thankful for a Peugeot to look at. Or even a Simca. Well, maybe not. How am I supposed to keep awake for the next four days?

The view through Helen's window
Thank God for that. Is Lyons anywhere near where we're supposed to be on Friday? I think it's about the right direction, anyhow. Better make sure she gets on the phone to organise somebody to send her passport out pronto. Safest to send it poste restante, I guess. Does poste restante still exist?

I ought to speak to her about it now, really. Or – maybe I'll wait until the shock has worn off. Poor thing, she must be feeling very forlorn and abandoned. I just wish she had a more appealing way of showing it.

Come on, Helen, here we are in France, make the most of it. It's very tidy, isn't it? Not a scrap of litter anywhere. Makes a change from Kentish Town. Goodness, this road is brand new. Amazing how they can just get permission to drive a road through the countryside here. You'd never get away with that in England. Thank goodness. We really are a lot more civilised, even if the croissants are better here. God, I could murder a croissant.

That's the thing about the French, though, isn't it? They're obsessed with their bourgeois material comforts. That's why there aren't any vegetarians. They'd rather have *faux filet* or *blanquette de veau* than principles.

Stop thinking about food.

So I suppose if there aren't any vegetarians there aren't any tree-huggers, either. Stands to reason, nobody flies the flag for the poor plants. So there's nobody to stop them building these bloody great boring superhighways.

Christ, I bet Angel is a vegetarian. Well, she'll just have to eat a lot of omelettes. I wouldn't mind an omelette right now. There's got to be a village or something soon.

I am NOT making our first stop at a motorway service station . . .

The view through Angel's window
. . . dhu dhu duh DUH DUH – duh duh duh DUH DUH – AAAARGHHH!!! GETITOUT GET IT OOOUT!!

H: Jesus, what's going on?
D: AAARH!!! MUM!! IT'S A BEE IT'S A BEE NO NO NO!!!
A: AAAAARGHHH!!!

Angel and Des are clinging to each other, screaming. Colum pulls the car over into the slow lane. Helen turns around. No bee is visible. The children continue to scream.

H: BE QUIET!!!

Helen spots a very small fly clambering around on the back window.

H: It's a FLY, okay? Des, Angel, it's a FLY. Des, you're supposed to love animals, it can't possibly hurt you.
D: It's not a fly it's a bee it's a BEE SEND IT AWAY MUM!!!!

All three of them are now shouting. Colum spots a sign and zooms off down a slip road.

12 July – Bill for breakfast: Le Sandwich Village

```
Bienvenus au Sandwich Village de l'Aire de
Grottin Nord!
le 12/07          09.45

2 x croissants beurre        @ €3.50     €7.00
2 x pains au chocolat        @ €4.00     €8.00
1 x chocolate chaud Nestlé               €6.00
2 x grand crème Kenco        @ €5.50    €11.00
1 x Diet Coke                            €5.50

MONTANT                                 €43.50
SERVICE @ 12.5%                          €5.44

TOTALE                                  €48.94

au revoir à très bientôt!
```

12 July – Captain Des 'Blackbeard' McCallum, in service station playground, surrounded by enemy pirate fleet

Yo ho ho ho, ho ho, me hearties! And a bottle! First thing very important is to take note of all key enemy positions and equipments in sight. 1 pirate ship (climbing frame) 1 x walk-theplank (slide) 1 rigging (net). Enemy outnumber Captain

Des's ferocious pirates quite a lot but we are more cunning than them! So this is what we do we pretend to be climbing the rigging up up up now they are all coming down off the ship to climb the rigging too they think they will capture me this way so I JUMP!!! down and now I have the walkthe-plank all to myself up I go, youch! what is this? Enemy pirates have treach . . . treach . . . they have naughtily maked it hot, slide is too boiling hot to go on with my shorts, so Captain Des makes a retreat to the pirate ship instead. Excuse me! Please may I come up? EXCUSE ME I said PLEASE you have to let me up I said PLEASE! These pirates are very hostile and rude now he is saying something I don't understand WHAT???? Now they are all saying it, why are they talking in code, NO I will not get off why should I get off I am Fierce Captain Des Blackbeard and I FIGHT to the DEATH FIGHT FIGHT FIGHT Ha ha ha, I'm the king of the castle and you're the dirty rascal! Now it's your turn, you come up and you say it! What's your name? Go on, YOU CAN COME UP why are you running away? Why are you crying that's no fun I didn't hurt you! Mum? Mum what . . . MUM PUT ME DOWN it's not fair I didn't do anything, I said Please I did, I did say please I did!!!!!!

12 July – Angel's text messages from car parked outside Le Sandwich Village

```
TO LEILA:
SRRY 2 DSAPPNT U BT STTNG HRE N PVMNT CAFE N
CHC FRNCH TWN DRNKNG KR RYLE W XXXX DES. HE JND
S IN PARIS WHR CR RPLCD BY GGNTC LIMO. HP U R
HVNG FN N SSSX HA HA.

TO MANDY:
TP SCRT DNT TLL ANYBDY!!! BT I HVE BN BDCTED BY
```

```
AGNTS WRKNG 4 MY DAD I M CGHT N TUG F LUV BTWN
DAD N MUM BTH WNT ME WTH THEM PRESSUR V HRD ND
NT SURE I WLL BE BCK AT LL F U HV NT HRD FRM
ME N A MNTH PLS CLL INTERPOL.
```

12 July – Colum, in car park outside Le Sandwich Village

While Angel finishes off her Diet Coke and sends text messages, Colum is meticulously cleaning every last scrap of fly and bug off the windscreen of the car. This is, of course, a cunning ploy to spy on a group of fifty-something French bikers standing around in skin-popping black fringed leathers, all labelled (in studs) 'Le Club Harley de Las Vegas', comparing bikes. Their licence plates are French, but they also carry Stars 'n' Stripes-patterned USA vanity plates, and various other Hell's Angels slogans and stickers.

Eventually, one of them spots Colum looking at them and, drawing himself up to his full five feet, plants a big boot nonchalantly on the starter pedal and tears open a Gitanes pack with his teeth, flipping a lit match on to it with perfect timing. Colum sniggers.

C: Bonjour.
    (Hiya)

The Frenchmen stare.

C: Je vois que vous avez des plaques françaises?
    (I see you've got French plates on those hogs)
F1: Oooai???
    (So?)
F2: Quoi?
    (What's he on about?)
C: Mais vous avez aussi cette petite etiquette qui dit 'USA', non?

(But – ahem – you've also got that dumb 'USA' tag)

F1: Et alors?
(What's it to you?)

C: Alors, vous êtes français ou americains? Je me trouve un peu confus.
(Nothing, nothing at all. Just a bit confused whether you're actually French or Americans – or something else. That's all.)

The Frenchman begins to see a trap opening up.

F1: Je suis français moi? Vive la France! Et qu'est-ce que ça à faire avec vous?
(I'm French, right! Vive la France! French, get it? And what the fuck business is it of yours, anyway?)

C: Mais non, rien du tout, c'est parfait. Et ça vient d'où, Le Club Harley de Las Vegas? De Las Vegas aux Etats Unis, alors?
(Fine. Great. And so, this Harley Club of Las Vegas, that'll be based in the States, right?)

F1: Mais non. Je viens de vous expliquer . . .
(No, clothhead, I just told you that we're French)

C: Alors, il y a peut-être un Las Vegas ici en France même?
(Oh, I get it, so there's a Las Vegas in France somewhere? Funny, I've never heard of it.)

F1: (unintelligible mutter)

C: Mais vous êtes au moins allés à Vegas, je suppose? Peut-être que vous avez achetés là vos motos?
(No? Then you've at least been to Vegas on holiday? 'Course, there aren't any decent bikes in France, so I guess you must have bought these there.)

The Frenchmen both look very cross by now.

C: Non? Excusez-moi! Je m'interesse aux motos, vous savez. C'est tout! Merci pour l'information!
(Or did I get it wrong? Sorry to butt in, just taking a friendly interest. Thanks a lot!)

F1: Salaud d'un Anglais! Je suis français, moi, vous savez? FRANÇAIS!!!! Vive la France!!
(Fucking English wanker! I'm French, get it? French!)
F2: Vive la Belle France!
(Vive la France!)
C: Exactement, c'est ça. Parfait! Excusez-moi, messieurs!
(Right, got it. Well, I'll be off, then.)
F2: Crétin!
(Fuckhead!)
C: Bonne journée!
(Nice meeting you!)

He ducks back into the car.

C: Beautiful one, McCallum!

The Frenchmen look after him, shaking their fists. They're not going to let a sorry Brit in a family saloon get the better of them . . .

12 July – Colum, Helen, Des and Angel: en route again

Everybody apart from Angel looks a bit happier after the pit stop. Des is dozing and Angel, in desperation, is playing with the animated frog on her mobile screen.

H: . . . but if there was one thing you could rely on them for, it was a decent croissant. Otherwise what on earth is the point of all the snobby crap the rest of the world has to put up with from them? Wherein lies French cultural superiority, if not in croissants and coffee?
C: What cultural superiority?
H: Well, that's just it. Apart from public transport. And cinema. And bras, of course. And sunscreen, which reminds me – damn, I could have bought it back there. Will you remember next time, not that we're going to one of those

shitty motorway places again, but when we hit a town?
C: Remind you of what?
H: Sunscreen, of course.

She settles back into random musing-out-loud mode. Colum is watching a movie in his head of himself riding through Vegas on the latest racing MotoGuzzi.

H: But we're better at gardening, pop music and advertising. And crumpets. I've never even seen a crumpet in France.
C: You've not been looking in the right places.
H: And language, look at the languages! You can't compare them. On the one hand you have English, with its richness and variety of inconsistencies, irregularities and mediaeval obscenities, and on the other . . .
C: On the other, you have the language that gave us Jacques Brel and Edith Piaf.
H: And Johnny Halliday. Vroom vroom. Why were those bikers looking so cross, by the way?
C: I have no idea.

Angel, who has for some time been staring out of the back window, turns to speak.

A: They're following us.
H: Nonsense.
A: Have it your way.

She goes back to her mobile and begins texting.

H: Which reminds me, I thought of something.
C: Should I call the cops?
H: Ha ha.

Nerving herself, she turns round.

H: Angel? Angel, about your passport . . .
A: That's what I'm doing now, aren't I?

H: Are you?
A: Poste restante Lyon in two days, right?
H: Er, right. Good. Thanks. You okay?

No reply. Helen turns back to Colum.

H: No, what I was thinking was, you know the French make this huge deal about their national spelling competition every year?
C: Not sure I . . .
H: . . . and there was that big scandal a few years back when it was won by a Japanese. Anyhow, it's administered by the Ministry of Culture and it's a very big deal indeed.
C: So?
H: So, what is the point of a spelling bee in a language that's totally phonetic? I mean, how hard can it be?
C: I have no answer to that.
H: (*happily*) They're all bonkers.

In the back, Des yawns and stretches.

D: Mum, Gorilla is very bored, can he go home now?
C: No problem. Rwanda, is it? There's bound to be a cross-country route. (*to Helen*) You and Angel can hitch to Tuscany from here, right?
H: How about a story tape, Des?

She fumbles in the glove compartment.

H: Here we go – *Robinson Crusoe*, *The House at Pooh Corner*, and – er – that's it! Which do you want?
D: Can I . . .
H: *Robinson Crusoe*'s all about a shipwreck on a desert island.
D: Does it have pirates?
H: Loads of pirates. You'll love it.
D: (*to Angel, excitedly*) We're going to have a story tape, Angel! Do you want to listen?

Angel is rocking back and forth in her seat like a trauma victim to the thumping beat from her headphones. Des grabs her arm and shakes it.

D: Angel! Story tape time!

She glowers and shakes him off. Des looks as though he might cry.

H: Don't worry, she probably prefers her music – you can tell her all about it afterwards.

She switches it on, and after a few crackles a sonorous male voice begins:

(RADA-trained famous thesp)
    'My story begins in the Year of our Blessed Lord . . .'

D: I don't like it.
H: Oh, come on, pud, it's lovely, we can maybe skip the introduction . . .

. . . scrabbling for the fast-forward button . . .

H: . . . here, now we'll be well into the story.

(Famous thesp)
    '. . . and lo, as I pondered the abominable concatenation of circumstances that led me hither, I marvelled at the . . .'

D: I still don't like it, and it's giving Gorilla a headache in his elbow. Can we have another one?
H: It's just written in old English, love, because the man who wrote it died a long time ago.
D: Can dead people talk on tapes? Is that a dead person? I know about dead people they're ghosties, I don't want to listen to a ghostie. *(voice rising in panic)* I'm scared!
H: Okay, maybe it is a bit grown-up for you, we'll keep it for when you're older, all right?

Leans forward, removes the tape and looks in the glove compartment again.

H: Oh look, here's Pooh, shall we listen to Pooh?
D: YEEEEAH!! Hooray! Angel, we're . . .
H: Leave her be, sweetheart . . .
C: (*mutters*) . . . or Hallowe'en won't just be Hallowe'en any more . . .

Helen puts in the next tape. After a few more scratches, Alan Bennett's woolly-tea-cosy tones fill the car.

(Alan Bennett does Winnie the Pooh)
 '*It was a blustery, windy day at Pooh Corner, and . . .*'

Helen gives a little sigh of pure nostalgia and settles happily to listen. Colum grips the steering wheel a little harder. Des shuffles about.

(AB)
 '*. . . just the time of day for a Little Something. And at that exact moment, who should come knocking on his door marked "Ring f no nsr is requird", but . . .*'

D: He doesn't sound like Pooh. I saw Pooh on that video, he sounds like . . .
H: Shhh, darling. This is the real Pooh. That was some awful Disney travesty, this is much, much nicer, believe me.

She leans forward and turns it up.

(AB in squeaky falsetto)
 '*. . . oooh Pooh, you are brave and clever! Shall we go and tell Rabbit now? . . .*'

D: I DON'T LIKE IT MUM!
C: He doesn't like it.

Helen leans forward and hits the 'off' button.

H: Well, that's that, Des. There aren't any other tapes.
D: That's not fair! Why aren't there? I'm . . .

Colum leans over and opens the glove compartment.

C: I'm sure I saw . . . let me just . . . Ouch! Woman, what are you doing?

Helen is glaring at him, jamming it closed over his hand.

H: *(stage whisper)* There are No More Tapes!

Colum extracts his squished hand, with another tape in it.

C: Here we go, *Jack Jiggley's Jangley Jingles.* Your sister brought it by – said it never fails.
H: To do what?
D: Hooray!! Jingley Jangles! Are they like nursery rhymes? Gorilla likes nursery rhymes.

Helen very reluctantly extracts *Winnie the Pooh* and inserts *Jack Jiggley.*
    The car fills with the sound of an electronic keyboard at high volume, playing a couple of bars of 'Here We Go Loobie Loo' with kazoo and party-popper effects, followed by an eager male Rolf Harris soundalike.

(Eager male voice)
    'Hello, children!'
(Children's chorus)
    'Hello, Jack Jiggley! Hooray!!!'

D: *(enthusiastically)* Hooray!!!

Helen leans forward to switch it off.

H: Well, we certainly don't want THIS, do we?
D: I do I DO I like it!!!!
C: *(to Helen)* It's this or I-Spy for six and a half hours . . .

Helen slumps back, defeated.

(Eager male voice)
    'So, children, shall we start with an old favourite?'
(Children)
    'Yesss!!'
(EMV)
    'Are you all ready to shake yourselves about?'
(Children)
    'YEEES!!'

D: Yes!!! Angel, are you . . .

Angel's glare could clot blood. Outside the car, the French countryside speeds by, featureless and unappreciated, and not a monument in sight.

(EMV and children)
    'Here we go Loobie Loo! Here we go . . .
    '. . . You don't wanna knaaaaow!!!! You don't wanna hearmee!!!! . . .
    '. . . All on a Saturday . . .
    '. . . I'm going craaaazeeee . . .!!!
    '. . . left foot IN! Put your left foot . . .'

Something very odd is happening to the tape. The Jingley Jangleys keep breaking into heavy guitar beats and anguished teen wailing. Des looks puzzled and stops putting his left foot IN to the back of Helen's seat.

H: Horrid cheap tape, there's a fault on it . . .

She's got her hand over the button.

C: No there isn't, it's Angel's MP3 file breaking in. I could go for it myself – Mixmaster Jiggley's Hip-Hop Jingles . . .

Helen rips the tape from the player.

H: Sorry, Des – tape's broken, but we're nearly at the lovely town where we're going to have lunch, shall I read to you about it?

Tourism Guide to the City of Rouen, 2002 edition

> Nestled in a winding valley of the lovely river Seine, Rouen, its ancient streets and town centre immaculately rebuilt after World War II, remains a jewel in the crown of Normandy. With its ancient churches and massive Horloge or Great Clock as it is known . . .

(Helen notices she's losing her audience and speeds up a bit)

H: 'famous as the site of the trial and execution of Joan of Arc, the Maid of Orleans in 1431' . . . da da da . . .

(audience still not totally won over)

H: . . . Here Joan of Arc was tried and burned and killed horribly at the stake with a lot of screaming and blood. There's a big big cross at the place it happened and a waxworks museum of it and . . . a place selling giant waffles stuffed with cream and jam and . . . patisseries and . . . duck, their speciality is duck how delicious and you can have it for lunch too AND there's a restaurant called Jumbo! Des, there's a restaurant named after an elephant, would you like to have lunch there? . . . Hey, Colum, did you know Flaubert's father was chief surgeon, and there was a cholera epidemic when he was only eleven and he used to scramble around in the morgue and the autopsy room? . . . And they have one of his parrots, stuffed. He really did have parrots!

Colum has spotted the sign for Rouen and moves across to take the exit.

C: Remarkable.

H: Hey! Look, here's the exit, sorry for the short notice but, Colum, can you . . . Oh, well done, you spotted it clever you. Okay, come on, what does it say, Toutes Directions . . . keep going, Toutes Directions again . . . Well that sign still says Toutes Directions but it seems to be going out of town that can't be right, what does the other one say, Autres Directions let's try that . . . Didn't we come this way before? But . . . oh, we were going in the other direction . . .

C: Left or right?

H: . . . Hang on a mo, I'm trying, but it's very difficult when . . . So if that was this way and this is that way, if you just take the next left . . .

C: I can't.

H: . . . Oh, you can't turn left here, damn, well maybe the next left . . . No, that seems to be the way back to the motorway, what does this . . . Toutes Directions and Autres Directions again! For God's sake, don't these people WANT any tourists to visit their pathetic towns?

C: Calm down, you're not helping yourself . . .

H: I'm perfectly calm, let's just turn round and start again . . .

C: It's a one-way street.

H: Of course I know it's a one-way street, I was just . . . It can't go on being a one-way street for ever, can it?

C: No?

H: Oh, I see, it can, it's a dual carriageway . . .

Colum takes control, and swings the car back on to the autoroute slip road.

C: Lunch-time, everybody!

D: Hooray!!!

H: What are you doing, this is the way back to . . . I am NOT having ANOTHER meal in a motorway service station!

The Parents' Handy Pocket English–French Phrase Book – 2003 edition

Chapter 1: In the Motorway Service Station Restaurant

At the Entrance ('L'Entrée')

Excuse me, monsieur/madame, where is the 'no smoking' section? The 'no smoking' section?? Excuse me, is there a 'no smoking' section at all? Yes, that was indeed my question. Yes, I am unfortunately a person from a foreign land.

Please, monsieur/madame, could you make way for my child to look at the food? He is not French and it is not familiar to him. No, my child was not brought up in a sewer. I believe he was frightened by your dog. In England we do not allow dogs in restaurants. No, nor do we serve them in restaurants. Ha ha. Yes, it is indeed a blessing to have a sense of humour.

In the Queue ('La Queue')

Excuse me, monsieur/madame, where are the trays? Oh, I see, right in front of me. No, I was not trying to reach for yours, any tray will do. Yes, I have plenty of time, please push right past me. Here is your tray, my little cabbage. What would you like to eat? No, the nice gentleman does not understand, you must point to what you want. No, he is not the Hunchback of Notre Dame, that is just an apron he is wearing.

At the Servery ('La Serveraie')

What are those? Those are French beans like you have at home. Yes, we are now in France, where the French beans come from. No, we cannot go to Switzerland and eat Swiss roll instead, nor to Denmark to eat Danish pastries. That slimy stuff on them is dressing. It is very nice, see! All the French people are eating it.

No, those carrots have not been eaten already, they are just very finely grated so they are easier to chew. Yes, French people have teeth just like yours. Do not stare at the lady's teeth, she probably smokes many French cigarettes each day, and drinks several litres of strong French wine, also.

Does that cheese smell like a doggie's bottom? Perhaps this cheese will be nicer.

Look, here are the bread rolls. Excuse me, how many bread rolls come with the meal? Ah, the bread rolls are extra. Where is the butter, please? Yes, butter for the bread. Yes, for the bread. No, do not worry, we too are used to eating our bread without butter. Yes, it is indeed exceptionally fine bread, quite possibly, as you say, a thousand times better than our factory-made abomination of an English loaf of bread, and to spread it thickly with flavourless unsalted French butter would undoubtedly ruin it. That is too much bread, my little cauliflower, please put it back. Excuse me, monsieur/madame, my child is too small to reach the tongs. No, we English do not commonly have many fatal communicable diseases. Nor do we feed our chickens on raw sewage sludge. No, I said nothing. Yes, I am sure.

At the Till ('La Caisse')

Pardon me, monsieur/madame, by all means go ahead of me, I am merely trying to carry three trays, pay my bill and look after my only child at the same time.

Pardon me, monsieur/madame, but could you possibly reach me a Diet Coke/two Diet Cokes/three Diet Cokes from the chiller over there? No, I am sorry, I have only just been asked to get them. Yes, I would rather not have to go back to the beginning of the queue. Yes, indeed we British do understand what it is that is a queue. Thank you a thousand times, monsieur/madame.

How much do I owe you, monsieur/madame? That is more money than I earn in a week. Oh, excuse me, my mistake, that is in fact very cheap, please keep the change. No, I am not insulting you, monsieur/madame, I am just very tired and hungry.

Thank you, monsieur/madame, I will certainly attempt to enjoy my meal.

12 July – Bill for lunch at 'Le Carillon de Rouen' motorway service station

```
Bienvenus au Carillon de Rouen!

12/7/02              13.43

1 x assiette Héros, jambon cru       €10.50
2 x frites @ €5.00                   €10.00
1 x plateau de fromages               €7.50
2 x petit pain @ €1.00                €2.00
1 x grande assiette de crudités      €12.00
3 x mousse au chocolat @ €4.50       €13.50
1 x petit assortiment de fromages     €5.00
1 x pichot de rouge                   €6.50
1 x Orangina                          €4.00
1 x eau gazeuse                       €3.00
2 x Diet Coke @ €4.00                 €8.00
2 x café @ €2.50                      €5.00

MONTANT                              €87.00
SERVICE 15%                          €13.05

TOTALE                              €100.05

Merci et au revoir!
N'oubliez pas nos specialités gstronomiques
de la région à emporter du magasin!
```

12 July, after lunch – The view from Helen's window

Why is it that you see your children totally differently when there are other adults present? Is it that a person is literally blind to the truth until she sees it through another's objective eyes, or do they in fact behave worse on these occasions, and if so, why?

Somehow Des's antics wouldn't have bothered me a bit if those English people hadn't been at the next table with their two perfect children, delicately forking up the *carottes râpées* and *salade de betteraves aux deux moutardes* like natives, while conversing sedately in perfect French. '*Zut, Perdita, ces carottes sont vraiment croquantes!*' '*Mais oui, Edgar, et j'adore cette arome de persille dans les betteraves!*' Edgar and Perdita! I ask you!

Meanwhile Des is getting the Babybel IN and OUT of its little red wax coat for the twenty-fifth time, and claiming that the cowboy can only save the gorilla from the killer poodle by fording the chocolate mousse on a raft of vanilla wafer. Still, you have to marvel at his imagination. I bet those other children have zero imagination, they obviously spend far too much time doing private-school homework and far too little daydreaming.

I wonder how worried I should be about Angel? So far she has taken no nourishment except Diet Coke since we picked her up. At least Des eats his props after the game.

The view from Des's window
I liked that chocolate stuff, but it was a bit deep for you wasn't it, Ride'em? Well done you got through it before the alligators found you. Did you see they sell Magnums in France too and you can just reach right in and pull them out! I nearly did it before Mum came back, I'm sure I can next time, you can be lookout.

What is a holiday? Do you know Teddy POdge? Did you talk to those other bears in the shop? Fascinatingly, they were speaking in that funny code too. And they had clothes on just like those hedgehogs did. I don't have any hedgehogs, d'you think Mum will buy them for me? Why do all the toys in France wear clothes?

I think a holiday must just be when you stay in the car all day. We must be nearly home by now. I do miss Bertie. I hope he's guarding my toys.

12 July – Back in England: Bertie's journal

Passive resistance is indeed a noble path, but nobility, now I remember, was never cheaply bought. It appears that neither of the senile old humans has even noticed my stoical and heart-breaking refusal to let a morsel cross my lips. Either that, or their eyesight is even worse than I feared, and any moment could be my last. I've been sitting here for a day and a night, with a look that would melt a heart of Caledonian granite, but you'd think from their behaviour that they fancied them-selves entirely unobserved.

Meanwhile, the fortifications remain in place and I'm not even allowed out to perform my, ahem, ablutions. Modesty forbids me to explain the alternative arrangements, but if you, dear reader, had to do it in public, next to your dinner, in full view of hostile humans and on a pile of damp sawdust, you'd probably have difficulties, too.

Meanwhile, duty calls. Those toys, alas, cannot be trusted alone for a minute. How many times already have I had to return lost jigsaw pieces to their mothers? I just hope that maudlin old monkey on the window sill doesn't start on again about his childhood in the jungle. If he's from the jungle, I'm the King of Siam.

12 July – George and Fiona: with the cable guy

George is at the living-room table, surrounded by the dirty dishes from the last twenty-four hours, finding out whether

CocoBanana ChocFlakes really are even better than Freeze-Dried Berry Buds. Bertie is sitting in the kitchen doorway, balefully watching every spoonful into his mouth.

Meanwhile Fiona, who's been rifling Helen's leftover wardrobe in celebration of the tropical southern weather, squats in eager conversation with a cable guy, who is just refining the tuning on a new TV and VCR that take up most of the room.

CG: There you go, you've got your adult movies here on twenty-nine and thirty, your sport from thirty-five to thirty-nine, and your cartoons on eight to twelve. Anything else?
F: Aye, where would I find ma home shopping?
CG: Aha! Glad you asked me that, it's right here on fifteen to eighteen, and we've got an amazing special on that at the moment. Anything you buy within a month of signing up we give you absolutely free delivery!

George stops eating. He's finally spotted Bertie.

G: Woman, can ye no get rid of yon cat?

Fiona is deep in conversation.

F: That's verra interesting! And there'll be no limit on that at all?
CG: Nah, any size, any weight, the bigger it is the more money you save.

Fiona snatches the remote from him and changes channel. The cable guy produces his worksheet and a pen. George turns his chair away from Bertie, who immediately moves round into sight again. George eats another couple of spoonfuls and gives up.

CG: Right, then, I'm off. Just sign here for us, would you?

Fiona reluctantly tears herself away and signs.

CG: (*reading*) 'Helen McCallum.'

He suddenly looks embarrassed. Fiona has turned back to the TV. He coughs, quietly and then a little louder. George turns his head.

G: Will ye have a spot of whisky to wet yer whistle afore ye go?
CG: Oh, er, no thanks. Um, I hate to ask you this, I always think it's a bit of a liberty with pensioners, but . . .

George reflexively covers all his pockets.

G: I've not a penny on me since . . .
CG: (*blushing deeply*) God, no, it's just . . . Your wife wouldn't happen to have anything by her that would – er – prove who she is?

Fiona turns round, the sweetest little old lady ever to wear a miniskirt.

F: Why, that'd be no trouble at all, laddie. I'd hate to be getting you into trouble wi' yer bosses after all yer hard work today. Just give me a minute, will ye?

She skips into the kitchen, where various unpaid bills are stuck on the notice-board, and brings one back.

F: Here ye go, laddie – Helen McCallum, forty-four Fabian Crescent. Will that do ye? No, I can see ye're still worried. Dinna fret . . .

She moves to her handbag and rummages in the bottom.

F: Here – the card I bought it on, how'll that do ye?

The John Lewis account card does indeed say Helen McCallum. The cable guy hastily writes down the number, gathers up his things and sprints for the door. Fiona is eager to get shopping. Bertie's stare is beginning to rattle George.

G: Can ye no put him out fer a wee while?
F: Can ye no see I'm busy? What's wrong wi' teh puir wee pusscat?
G: He's giving me the wullies.
F: Well, stop looking at him like that!
G: And he's no' eaten any of his food.

Fiona sighs deeply, finding the male sex helpless once again in the face of a simple problem. She goes into the kitchen, followed by Bertie, doing his utmost to look thin. She peers at the biscuits and the Felix, which has developed an unappetising dark brown crust.

F: The puir creature'll never eat that muck.

She moves to the freezer, opens it up and begins rifling it.

F: Yon Helen's a cruel streak in her, I've said it many a time.

She pulls out a couple of packages and scrutinises them. Bertie quivers with anticipation, unable to believe his luck.

F: He's shaking wi' hunger, puir beastie. Guid thing one of us is paying him heed. *(reading a label)* Steak – that'll do fine, and here's smoked salmon, export rubbish, of course, but it'll do for a cat. *(to Bertie)* There's plenty more, laddie, when ye've that down ye. *(to George)* Come away, George, will ye, and gi' us a hand figuring out yon microwave.

12 July, after lunch – Back in France:

The view from Colum's window
Amazing how the French have sorted out their act on the plumbing front. Finally it's safe to piss and breathe at the same time. That red wasn't bad either.

Thank Christ Helen gave up on her plan to drag us into

some claggy tourist trap for microwaved duck. I wonder how long Lolita can sustain life on Diet Coke? You can't help but feel for the poor kid, it's pretty clear her folks don't give a monkey's about her.

The view from Angel's window
How come all the French girls have longer hair and longer legs than me and how do they get to be so thin eating all that bread? I WILL NOT eat I WILL NOT eat, I WILL be thinner than anybody else at the villa. Omigod, I could NOT BELIEVE the amount the dwarfish alien abducters ate back there, no wonder she's so gross and fat. Even if I ever get to be as old as her I'm not EVER going to let myself go like that.

The view from Helen's window
Oooh, look, *le soleil brille enfin*, now I can finally remove this hideous big woolly jumper of Colum's that he smugly insisted on packing against my carefully researched advice. I'm really quite pleased with this matelot/palazzo look, it's ridiculous how dowdy and middle aged I've let myself get these last few years since Des arrived. Somehow in my head I'm still hauling around all those extra pounds, whereas the fact is, as radiantly evident in the mirror at Top Shop, that it's possible to be a mother and a glamorous woman, too. A young, glamorous woman, indeed. I noticed I got quite a few looks in that place we stopped for lunch. There was one guy I could definitely have possibly gone for, if he'd gargled for about a week first.

Perhaps I should ask Angel what she likes to eat. Something to talk about, anyhow. But I read somewhere that people with borderline eating disorders can be tipped over the edge if you draw attention to them. She's bound to eat tonight, isn't she?

How can I be so terrified of somebody less than half my age?

The view from Angel's window
Omigod she's taking that jersey off, what DOES she have on underneath? Yeech! It's like she doesn't even watch makeover shows on TV or anything, didn't anybody tell her that old people are supposed to dress classic, with high necks and long sleeves? It's almost like she thinks she's, like, still young or something? I mean, it would be almost tragic if it wasn't so embarrassing, and the way people were looking at her in the café, I honestly nearly did feel sorry for her.

I mean, why would you want to look sexy at her age anyway, it's not like she's going to actually HAVE sex. Oh yuck, what a totally gross and disgusting thought, I wish I hadn't thought of that. Think of something else quick, where's that copy of *heat*?

The view from Helen's window
Where are we? No way of telling, landscape totally featureless. Oh, here we go, *prochaines sorties* Le Bille, Bouffecoeur – Chartres!

Guidebook to the City of Chartres, 2003 edition

> Of all the jewels in the precious crown of France, the diamond must certainly be the breathtaking city of Chartres, with its quaint alleys, overhanging eaves, peaceful atmospheric squares, and above all the . . .

C: I have a horrible suspicion you're not just reading aloud to keep yourself company.
H: '. . . above all the incomparable beauty of its cathedral, miraculously spared in two world wars and many centuries of previous conflict, to delight both the casual tourist and the dedicated student of architecture today'.

She closes the book and looks at Colum in triumph.

H: It's one of the wonders of the world, and we're going right by it.
C: We've been right by Wembley Stadium about four thousand times without going in and it's never bothered you.
H: But we promised Angel . . .

Colum looks in the rear-view mirror. Angel is asleep.

C: We'll be way past it before she wakes up. She'll never know.
H: . . . and we promised Madge . . .
C: Madge doesn't know she's not locked in the cells in Le Havre. Nor care, apparently. She's not going to bar the door to the villa over a cathedral here or there.
H: Well, I want to see it. I mean, it's one of the glories of the medieval world – an incredible product of a forgotten culture . . .
C: Did you not get enough of those at lunch-time?
H: . . . it'll uplift our spirits and take our minds off the petty problems of our daily lives.

Colum sees she really means it.

C: How about the petty problem of finding a parking space in the middle of a mediaeval jewel in high summer? What does the book have to say about that?

Helen opens the book again and searches through the pages.

H: 'opening hours . . . changing money . . . first aid . . . youth hostels . . .'
There doesn't seem to be anything here about parking.

She closes the book disgustedly.

H: Honestly, they're such rubbish these guidebooks, they lure you in with their purple prose which quite frankly anybody could write, and then they don't give you the most basic factual information. But anyhow, it'll be fine, it's not Camden, they're all Southern and *très décontractés*. Just park at a funny angle and block the pavement, and they'll think we're local and ignore us.

The car approaches the turn-off to Chartres.

H: And it's not raining!

Colum puts on his indicator and moves across.

C: One thing.
H: What's that?

Colum hands her the woolly jumper she just removed.

C: You're not exactly dressed for a cathedral.

12 July – Helen: inside Chartres Cathedral

This is truly beautiful. At last, the reason we spent two weeks packing and entrusted our lovely house to those two ungrateful derelicts from . . .

Come on, Helen, don't think about that, they're very nice and I'm sure the house is fine.

Ooh look, that must be the famous rose window. Pity about the rain, I'm sure it would be even more magnificent if there were actually some light coming through it. Still, at least I'm not boiling in this heavy jumper. Where's Des? Oh. Well, there's plenty of space here, I'm sure nobody will mind the odd baby elephant marching through the jungle. He's a bit young to take in the whole meaning of it, but the general atmosphere and the beauty and stuff are bound to seep in somehow.

Don't worry about him, he's fine. Concentrate on the cathedral now we've finally got here.

These choir stalls are lovely, aren't they, you can see all sorts of detail about how they lived in those days that you wouldn't get just reading a book. Oh look, that one's mending a cart, he looks a bit like Colum's mechanic friend Steve in fact, same stunted posture and scrunched-up face. I wish Colum were here to see it.

Very convenient for him that the only place to park was in a loading bay, so he just had to stay with the car. I don't see why he couldn't have left Angel in there on her own, but he said it wouldn't have been fair in case she got towed or something. My guess is that anybody who towed Angel would bring her back pretty quickly.

Don't be mean, Helen, you're supposed to be being a surrogate mother to her. If only she weren't quite so snotty about everything. Can I have been so snotty at her age?

FOR GOD'S SAKE HELEN CONCENTRATE! You said you'd be back in half an hour and it's . . . Can't see my watch. Goodness, it really has got dark.

Let's just take a quick look at that huge painting. Ooh, that's interesting, baby Jesus in a nappy, I don't think I've ever seen that before. It must have been a nightmare boiling nappies in those days, no wonder they usually didn't bother.

CHRIST (sorry, baby Jesus)!!! You can't even look at a painting for FIVE MINUTES without making it into something about babies!!

My brain really has rotted into a pulp, I used to be able to sit and look at paintings for hours before Des. And now I don't even have the excuse of sleep deprivation. Nobody told me the loss of function was permanent . . .

But I wouldn't swap lovely Des for a brain. Of course I wouldn't. Not for good, anyhow. The odd day or two might be nice. Where has he got to? He's being very quiet . . .

12 July – Des: in Chartres Cathedral

The giant's castle was huge and guarded by lots of men with

walkie-talkies and evil yellow toothypegs. But the brave St Des wasn't afraided, he knew that if he defeated the evil giant and tooked the giant's Treasure home, he would be king and live for ever and watch lots of TV and never have to go to bed or eat baked beans, ever again ever.

Far far in the distance he could spy the Treasure gleaming over there. A big gold cross and some gold bowls and some huge gigantic candle thingies, all piled up on a big table with a white cloth. The brave knight creeped and creeped, up to the tall high mountain. But there was a rope round the mountain, with spikes and very difficult to get past. Brave Sir Knight Des wished he had his real sword not his pretend sword with him, but maybe if he wriggled down very low he could get under the fence to the steps of the mountain . . .

Just then he saw the giant!! Huge scary giant with a long beard and holding a big heavy rope of stones, and disguised in a white dress with lace on it like a lady! And coming right towards the brave knight, looking very ferocious, but he was nearly at the Treasure, if he just ran and ran he might just . . .

HELP OW OW NO PUT ME DOWN I DON'T LIKE YOU PUT ME DOWN WHERE'S MUM I WANT MY MUM WAHHHHHHHHHH!!!

12 July – Colum reading *Bike* while listening to Angel on her mobile, outside the Cathedral

> You have to feel sorry for the G25/2000. There it was, happily banging fairings and spec sheets in the 650 class, next thing it knows the 650 class has turned into the 850 class and it's all Firestorm this and R2 that, and the poor old 750 . . .

A: No no, you should never use Mondaine it's too harsh it's like a kitchen cleaner or something honestly . . . No no l'Oréal's the best all the hairdressers use it I swear to

God, my hairdresser I went to, you know in Bond Street said . . .

With all those revs and all that noise, it's easy to get sucked into riding like a nobber – that's why GSX riders have got a rep as single-brain-celled rather than single-minded . . .

A: . . . so what d'you think, has Julia Roberts had plastic surgery? . . . She has she has, omigod those lips, they've got huge . . . only no listen, I saw a photo from ages ago and she had really big lips then, but she's had more, honestly I swear to God . . . Omigod yes . . . absolutely like, the worst lip job ever was Liam Gallagher's ex-wife what is she – Patsy Kensit that's it . . .

. . . but we TD900 riders can afford to slow down, pose a bit, pull a few wheelies then go nuts as and when . . .

A: . . . my hol? . . . Ooooh it's absolutely brilliant, we're in St Tropez right now . . . yeah, baking hot and right by the ocean . . . yeah (*giggles*) you could say he's here . . . in fact . . .

She looks over to make sure Colum isn't listening, then whispers:

A: . . . he's taking me out on his bike this evening to this like, truly romantic restaurant where, like, you have to be a movie star or a gazillionaire even to get a reservation . . . yeah, just us two . . .

. . . the only bike that comes near it in terms of no-compromise, head-down, mindless boogie is the 925 . . .

A: . . . what? . . . She said WHAT? . . . That is just SO not true, it's total lies omigod she's always been so jealous of me and . . . He is not, he's eighteen and he's had two Oscar nominations already and . . . No I can't, he's having a massage but I . . . You're a stupid cow too . . . You're worse and your legs are fat and . . . No I don't, who'd want you for a friend anyhow . . . Bitch! You rotten horrible bitch!!!!'

Angel slams down her phone and is about to burst into tears when she remembers Colum, who seems still to be engrossed in his mag. She sniffs, tosses her head, puts away her phone, pulls it out again. Dials a number. Nobody there. Puts it away again.

Colum goes on apparently reading for a couple of minutes, then looks out of the window, puts down the magazine and turns round.

C: Rain's stopped.

No answer.

C: There's a café on the corner, d'you fancy a Diet Coke or anything?
A: No thanks.
C: I get a terrible head stuck in a car all day long, don't you?
A: I'm fine.

Colum opens his door.

C: Well, I think I'll get a bit of air while I can. You're welcome to stay.
A: Thanks.
C: If they come to tow the car, just scream loudly and burst into tears, okay?
A: Is that supposed to be a joke?

She finds a copy of *OK* and buries her nose in it.

C: Fine, well, back in five, then.

He leaves. Angel gets out her phone again, tries the number again. Still on voicemail.

12 July – E-mail exchange: Madge and Ernie

From: Madge Handelman [madge@handy.com]
To: Ernestine Short [ernie@ernie.com]

```
Sweets
Here's updated scrit outline - much more
dramatic, as you'll see from italics - AND we
now have a favulous kid. She's black, which
may involve some more minor futzing depend-
nigvon who we cast as the mom, but will keep
you oosted.
   Also re the 'mechanic to the stars' thing -
might be good to scare up a few more humks
for walk-on mechani potential. I know I can
rely on you for this.
   weather here glorious as usual.
   big kiss M
```

----

12 July – Story Synopsis of Major Studio Picture *The Price of Love*

```
STORY
Joe Mitchum is a guy everybody envies - chief car
mechanic to one of the biggest stars in
Hollywood, with a stunning wife, Kelly, who is a
person of colour, and an adored only daughter,
Fawn, he spends his days polishing Ferrari engine
blocks and his nights singing his baby girl to
sleep and making passionate love to Kelly. The
only other thing that marks Joe out is his
amazing good looks, and from working on cars he's
developed a physique that makes women swoon. But
```

Joe is a one-woman, straight-up kind of a guy. Then tragedy strikes, as Fawn, *who has inherited her mother's coloration*, develops a life-threatening illness, and Kelly is forced to reveal the secret she's kept from Joe since they met – she is the carrier of an incurable disease *which tragically only attacks people of colour, and* which killed her brother and two aunts. Joe forgives her and spends every penny he has scouring the world for a solution, but to no avail, and time is running out as Fawn gets weaker by the day. Finally, Joe hears of a doctor in Switzerland who may have the answer. Joe sells his beloved vintage Mustang to pay the air fare for himself and Fawn. Fawn barely makes it, but when they meet the doctor, Dr Ingrid Goldpfinger, she immediately produces a drug made from a secret formula known only to herself that relieves Fawn's symptoms. Dr Ingrid, who has a stunning beauty to match her world-class skills, agrees to treat Fawn, and Joe, unknown to Kelly, remortgages his house to pay the bill. Back home, Fawn progresses by leaps and bounds. Her parents and her beloved collie Laddy are delighted to see her back to her old self. But all too soon the drugs are about to run out and Joe goes back to Dr Ingrid, this time alone. Dr Ingrid knows he has no more money. But unknown to Joe, she too has a secret: she can never have children, and she is violently jealous of any woman who does. She tells him she'll treat Fawn anyhow. He's overjoyed – how can he thank her? Then she tells him her price. For every month's supply of drugs, a night of passion with him . . .

But Joe's boss, megastar Silvano Stallion, has always secretly lusted after Kelly. And one day Joe, overcome by the agony of his dilemma, reveals to Silvano that without truckloads of cash their beloved Fawn will die. The next time Silvano gets Kelly alone, he offers to pay for Fawn's treatment, if she becomes his mistress.

So now both of them, unknown to each other, are racked by the same terrible agonizing dilemma. But neither dares confess . . .

* CASTING NOTE: CONSIDER BRUCE SPRINGSTEEN FOR LEAD ROLE? COULD WORK, E.G. 'BORN IN THE USA' INTO A GARAGE SCENE, SOME NEW JERSEY BACKSTORY, ETC.

NOTE: MEMO MARKETING RE DEMOGRAPHICS OF SPRINGSTEEN AUDIENCE

From: Ernestine Short [ernie@ernie.com]
To: Madge Handelman [madge@handy.com]

'Ssup Madge babes
Glad the junior element is working out – had midnight inspiration for new source of hunks in background, and have obtained details of all A-list personal trainers in town for one-on-one casting interviews.

God, I hate this job, but somebody has to do it.

If Springsteen doesn't happen, how about Robbie Williams, or I hear David Beckham is quite keen to get into acting – you can fix the voice thing, right?

Sun finally came out for two seconds. Pavements of London now choked with stomach-churning pasty males in ripped singlets

```
    drinking iced Guinness. Not sure I didn't
    prefer the rain.
       love ya E
```
----

12 July – Helen: in car after Cathedral

Well, I got Des into a monument – pity about the forced departure, but I did sort of see the sacristan's point about the treasures having survived on the altar for eight hundred years without any looting and pillaging from three-foot-tall foreign invaders.

Colum seemed to be making a bit of progress softening Angel up, until he insisted on telling his Harley Davidson joke, which even I didn't find funny – I mean, I may not be the world's expert on men, as Ernie endlessly reminds me, but even I know that your average engineering student, faced with a half-naked girl on a brand-new Harley, would take the bike and leave the girl. What's so hilarious about that? Anyhow I suppose we might have guessed that her father has five Harleys, one of them an export-only model he had crated and shipped out to Lagos. So that didn't exactly fly like Concorde.

Maybe she'll relax with a night's sleep – I'm sure I will. This hotel in Orléans sounds lovely, I must say – v pleased with self for getting two doubles, even after it had been in that Sunday supplement.

Guidebook Entry for Hôtel de l'Horloge, Orléans

> Located in a most atmospheric and desirable location right by the historic town clock in the central market square ... Seventeen rooms each distinguished by its own character ... Cosy en suite bathrooms or convenient facilities close by ... Unspoiled by

the modern intrusions that ruin the character of so many hotels today . . .

It sounds great. Surely even Angel will succumb to the romance of that little lot. Better make sure Colum finds it this time . . .

The Parents' Handy French–English Phrase Book – 2003 edition

Chapter 3 – At the hotel

Arrival ('l'Arrivée')
Good evening, m'sieur. We are the family X you have been waiting for. We telephoned two weeks ago. Yes, you most certainly have a reservation for us. No, our name is not Dubois. No, the reservation was not for tomorrow/next week/next year. Please may my little boy use the lavatory? He has been travelling all day. Yes, I know there are public lavatories three streets away, but he is very young. Your carpet looks very beautiful, m'sieur, I would hate it to be ruined by an accident. Thank you so much, we shall be right back.

At the Check-in ('Le Check-in')
Ah, you do indeed have our reservation? No, that is not how we spell it, but it is of no matter. Yes indeed, you are welcome to our passports/our driving licence/our credit cards/the keys to our car/our house.

Is there perhaps somebody who could help us with our luggage? No, we are not disabled or crippled. Yes, I understand that the hotel is not equipped to deal with disabled or crippled people. Yes, we would still like the rooms. Please. Yes, the hotel is indeed ancient and beautiful. Naturally it would be ruined by an elevator or a staircase wide enough for a normal modern human.

Finding the Room ('*l'Accès à la Chambre*')

Come this way, children. No, I do not smell cheesy feet/old cabbage/stinky cigarette smoke/cat's pee. The hotel is ancient and full of atmosphere. No, that is not our room. That is an expensive and luxurious suite currently occupied by another family. Ah, look, here are our rooms. How convenient, they are right next door to each other! We shall be able to converse with each other without even opening the door! Yes, that was a joke. No, perhaps that was not a joke.

In the Room ('*Dans la Chambre*')

Ah, how charming. Yes, it is indeed cosy. Look, you can reach the wardrobe/clean your teeth/lean out of the window/open the door without leaving the bed! No, that is not a swimming pool for pet turtles, that is a bidet. What is a bidet? Ask Papa. Ah, did Papa tell you? French people do not have dirty bottoms. It is possible indeed that French people think that we have dirty bottoms, ha ha!

No, children, there is no television in the room. If there were television in the room, it would be in French. I do not know if the Teletubbies can speak French. Perhaps they have cousins here in France, who knows? No, there is no minibar in the room. This is a traditional hotel. Yes, the plumbing is indeed traditional also.

My goodness! How loud is that clock! Ah, it is the famous horloge of the town, famously right beside the hotel. How lucky we are, our rooms are just below the famous clock. Now we shall not need to look at our watches all night. How lucky we are to have found the last two rooms in the hotel!

In the Bar ('*Dans le Bar*')

Excuse me! *Pardon*, m'sieur, but is there any chance that you, or one of your esteemed colleagues, might be free to serve us a drink? What is that? Ah, you do not serve children in the bar. Is there perhaps somewhere else where we could have a drink with our children? No, I quite understand, the hotel is small and traditional. Yes indeed, it would probably be more convenient for us to progress directly to dinner. You are probably right that many people who dine later would prefer not to have their dinner in the company of our so charming children. Thank you for your advice, we will indeed change our clothes before entering the dining room. Yes, I see the sign right here. Yes, my command of French is indeed adequate to understand it.

12 July – Colum, Helen, Des and Angel, at dinner in the hotel

The hotel dining room is elaborately papered and upholstered in floral chintz, with a heavy patina of tannin and nicotine. Although they are the only people there, they have been squashed on to a table in a dark corner, crowded with fragile, expensive glass and china. Des is still in his turtle goggles, but he's swapped the swimming trunks for shorts and a reasonably clean T-shirt, and Angel is texting determinedly into her phone, in Lurexed denim cut-offs, a Hello Kitty halter-neck T-shirt, Cleopatra braids and a glitter make-up job worthy of the Vegas Strip.

Des has built an elaborate landscape out of napkins and cutlery through which the cowboy is stalking the toy alligator, while Colum and Helen read through ten pages of broadsheet-size menu.

H: Isn't this nice? Such a good idea to eat early, we'll get much faster service.

She looks around the deserted dining room.

H: I wonder where that waiter went? I'd love some bread to keep me going.
C: They'll be waiting to see whether we order enough to justify it.

Helen looks alarmed and consults the menu again.

H: Wow, forty euros for a green salad, that's . . .
C: . . . quite a lot of bread, anywhere else.

Angel tires of texting and looks up from under her Cleopatra fringe.

A: Can I go now? It smells like, weird in here.
H: You really must eat something, Angel, you're probably ill from starvation.
A: (*sigh*) I'm fine.

The waiter reappears and stands in the far corner of the dining room, staring loftily out over their heads. Helen vainly attempts to catch his eye, first by waving, then with a demure, strangled cough. Seeing her about to resort to tinging her wineglass with her fork, Colum calls out loudly.

C: Monsieur!

The waiter reluctantly glides towards them.

H: Err, *pouvez-nous*, no, that's not right — er, *commander des* drinks — *des boissons, s'il vous plaît!*
W: *Oui, madame, je vous apporte la carte des vins.*

He's about to disappear again. Helen clutches at his sleeve.

H: No, no!

He freezes. She removes her hand and hides it under the table.

H: *Non, pardon, je voulais*, er, *des boissons très simples. (to Des)* Des, d'you want apple juice or that nice fizzy orange stuff?

D: Can I have the fizzy orange stuff only without the bubbles?
H: *(automatically)* . . . without the bubbles PLEASE.
W: *Je regrette, madame, mais nous n'avons pas de jus de fruits ici. Nous sommes un restaurant, vous savez.*
H: Ah. *Très bien.* Des, it's water, I'm afraid, but we'll buy some orange juice tomorrow, okay? Now, Angel?
A: *(heavy sigh at this fresh torture)* Diet Coke, I guess.

The waiter is staring meaningfully at Des, who has happily returned to his game and is leading the cowboy down the table leg to safety.

W: *Non, madame, je dois vous expliquer que ceci n'est pas un café, mais un restaurant gastronomique de très bon genre. Peut-être que vous seriez plus confortables . . .*

. . . meaningfully indicating the doorway . . .

W: *. . . ailleurs?*

He makes to whisk the menus away from them. Helen grips hers tight.

H: *Non, non, pardon, je comprends, excusez-nous,* it's fine, sorry. Des, put those away now.
A: It's cool, I'm feeling, like, nauseous anyhow.

She gets up to leave.

H: But Angel, sweetheart . . .

The waiter is about to depart again. Colum takes charge.

C: *(to waiter)* So, an iced Chambéry, a Kir, not too strong, a bottle of mineral water with gas, and the wine list, please.

Helen looks mortified. The waiter allows a condescending smirk to creep over his face.

W: *Très bien, monsieur. J'arrive.*

And disappears.

H: You let him think we're ignorant tourists!
C: Nonsense, I welcomed him into the global confraternity that is McDonaldspeak.

Angel has also disappeared. Helen looks worried.

H: Perhaps I should go and make sure she's okay?
C: She'll eat when she's hungry. I'll go up later.
H: I'm hungry now. What d'you fancy, Des darling? Lovely . . .

She's still trying to figure out the prices.

H: . . . soup? Ummmm – I expect we could stretch to the onion tart, it's only an hors d'oeuvre, or . . .
C: I thought Madge was picking up the tab for this.
H: Oh God, so she is, I'd totally forgotten – but I mean, if Angel isn't eating?
C: That's hardly our fault.
H: (*off the hook*) Well then Des, what's it to be? Haunch of venison? Fillet steak?

Des looks at her with patient contempt.

D: Mum! You silly bumface forgot I'm a vegetarian!!!
H: You are? Since when?
D: Angel's a vegetarian. What is a vegetarian? I want to be one!
H: No you don't darling, you love meat. Yummy chops and bacon and sausages . . .
D: (*excited shriek*) Sausages! Can I have sausages? Can I have ice cream?? Can I have a Magnum?

The waiter reappears with the drinks, dumps them on the table, hands Colum the wine list with a microscopic bow, and prepares to vapourise again. At this moment, another family arrives in the dining room, an English couple with two children, a boy of fourteen and a girl of ten. All four are perfectly turned out in expensive English classic style. Instantly, the waiter hurries over to them, wreathed in smiles . . .

W: *Ah! Messieurs Loxley! Vous avez passé une bonne journée, alors?*

. . . seats them at a large table with a view over the square, and within twenty seconds reappears with water, wine, bread and menus. They begin conversing in low voices, in perfect French.

H: (*loudly*) My God!
C: (*buried in the wine list*) He's right next door in the cathedral, remember? He can hear you fine.
H: No, but . . . aren't those the English people who were next to us at lunch-time? What an amazing coincidence!
C: (*still browsing the Grands Crus*) Amazing. Unless of course there are more than two people who read the *Independent on Sunday*.

The waiter is about to disappear again. Helen nudges Colum urgently.

C: *Monsieur! S'il vous plaît?*

The waiter reluctantly leaves the other family and approaches them, staying at a safe distance.

H: Er – *nous – prêts – commander, oui?*

He stands there, notepad in hand.

H: Oh, look, this looks nice, Des. (*to waiter*) *Qu'est-ce que c'est que 'torchon de brunailles'?*
W: *Saucisses* . . .
C: Perfect. Sorted.
W: . . . *de poumons.* (*to Colum, in perfect English*) Sausages of lungs, sir.
D: Sausages! I'll have that, Mum!

H: Perhaps not, sweetheart. Um . . . *(frantically turning the pages)* Wild boar, blood pudding, partridge, kidneys, *cervelles*, oh no, that's brains isn't it, don't worry Des we'll find you something . . . Ah! Here we are, it's veal but needs must. *(to waiter)* Okay, here, '*le miniminou de veau avec sa sauce*', twice, er, *deux fois, s'il vous plaît*.

The waiter leans over a fraction and mutters to Colum.

C: Miniminou appears to be local dialect for . . .

His voice is drowned by Des jumping up and down and shouting . . .

D: Please sausages! And ice cream do they have Magnum??

The English family are now all staring at them . . .

H: Dialect for what? I can't hear you! Stop muttering!
C: *(loudly)* Balls!

12 July, after dinner – Helen and Des, in Des and Angel's bedroom

Des is sitting up in bed in his T-shirt, looking adorable. Helen is sitting on the end of the bed, looking tired. Angel is nowhere to be seen.

H: She went to the bathroom?
D: Yes she did can we have our song now please Mum?
H: She's been there ages. Still, it took long enough to get that lot on, her face, no reason it should be any quicker to get it off. What was it again you wanted for your calypso?
D: Willy sausages and cowboys killing nasty men in white dresses.

From outside, a loud burst of raucous male laughter, accompanied by the revving of several motorbikes.

H: Ah. Okay. Do my best. Jesus, for a quiet hotel in a sleepy old town this rivals the Bog and Badger on a Saturday at closing time.

12 July – The Willy Sausages/Cowboy and Angry Priest Calypso

> A cowboy once went for a holiday
> And through a French cathedral he happened to stray
> And while he was there, without even a falter
> He decided on a daring plan to rob the altar.
>
> There were candlesticks and dishes of the purest gold
> A jewelled cross that was a marvel to behold.
> So the cowboy dashed towards it, and he waved his gun
> 'Cause he didn't want no hassle there from anyone.
>
> *(Are you sure Angel's in the bathroom, darling? Oh, here's her phone, she can't have gone far. Goodness, I do wish those bikers would go away, why do they have to rev their bikes to the limit right outside OUR window? Okay, where were we? . . .)*
>
> But an angry priest was watching, in his white lace dress
> The sort of guy with whom you would NOT want to mess!
> He grabbed the heavy cross and got the cowboy on the head
> And he BASHED that cowboy with it till he was quite . . .
>
> *(Oh, sorry, I forgot it was supposed to be the other way round. Well, you know, in a fair fight these things . . . Christ, this noise really is impossible, don't cry Des I'll tell the noisy men to go away and . . .)*

She jumps up and makes for the window, opens it, leans out and shouts:

H: FOR FUCK'S SAKE, MESSIEURS!! *NOUS AVONS UN PETIT ENFANT ICI ET* . . . ANGEL!!!!! WHAT IN GOD'S NAME ARE YOU . . . COME BACK HERE THIS MINUTE, OR YOU'LL SPEND THE NIGHT IN THE CELLS, I SWEAR!!!

12 July – 'The Abduction' (Angel's Dream): Episode 2

Princess Xandar stared out of the window of the StratoCar and tried not to freak out at what lay ahead. All her attempts to contact the Empress had failed, and it was becoming obvious that her dwarfish alien abductors were intent on keeping her as a slave. Thus far she had managed, by her extraordinary powers of self-discipline and plasma qi channelling, to avoid consuming their food and drink, whose horrible effects were only too visible every time the female DAA removed another layer of her tacky high-street clothing. Thank Ximba for Diet Universal Life Potion, which flowed in even the most inhospitable of stopping-places.

As she turned events over in her mind, searching for any possibility of escape, her attention was drawn to a motley parade of two-wheeled vehicles which seemed to be shadowing theirs. At first, their riders looked heineously gross and unattractive, like all the other inhabitants of this planet. But then her eye picked up on a tiny clue, a little flag screwed to the ID plate of each vehicle – the flag of her native land!!

The Princess turned around to look out of the rear window, and scanned the riders' faces for clues. Their bland expressions, almost, like, invisible beneath savage moustaches, gave nothing away, but instantly she knew that they were there to save her – to rescue her and take her home! All she could do was watch, wait and be totally up for it when the time came.

Her suspense was not lengthy in duration. Shrewdly realising that it was in her interest to lull the DAAs into a false sense of security, she made a pretence of relaxing, even deigning to, like, chat with one of them for a few moments. Luckily, fate conspired to give her an opportunity to slip away unnoticed as they chowed down yet again. She ran to a high turret of the castle where they'd bivouacked for the night, certain that very soon her rescuers would come to her aid.

And sure enough! Scarcely a few bare minutes later, she heard the sound she'd been waiting for — the roar of their powerful engines as they rode boldly up to the very gates of the castle, laughing and exchanging manly banter. She threw open her window and called out to let them know she was there. They returned her greeting, though not, annoyingly, in any language she knew, but she let that go. Could this truly be the moment of her liberation? Dared she trust them with spiriting her to safety?

She gathered up her few possessions and ran to join them, longing to be away — anywhere but here. But they seemed to be in no hurry, and the minutes ticked by endlessly as they joked among themselves in their weird language and passed around the magic potions that gave them their powers. Anxiously, she began to look up at the castle windows, dreading the moment when her captors would notice her absence.

At last, the riders seemed ready to be on their way. Enthusiastically, they competed to have her as their passenger. But as they kicked their sleeping vehicles into life, at that very moment, once again, cruel fate intervened . . .

13 July, morning – Helen

Last night, in a prolonged and humiliating climbdown, I was finally forced to admit that there is such a thing as too authentic. I probably wouldn't have slept brilliantly after that dinner, which Colum insisted would be impossible to digest without several litres of Bordeaux' finest, even without Angel's near-abduction by the massed Club Harley de Las Vegas, whose collective hostility was almost certainly down to an earlier encounter with certain Italian bike fanatics not a million microns from here.

But then there was the Horloge. Not just every hour but every fifteen minutes, plus the rumblings and clangings before and after, plus the fact that Des insisted on coming into our room to hide from it, which meant that Angel was on her own, so Colum was up every few minutes checking on her.

And as for the breakfast! If there was one place in the world where you might have thought you'd find a decent croissant at the breakfast table, it would have been the Couronne d'Or. Would you believe at first they weren't even going to give us croissants at all? They actually tried to fob us off with that jaw-breaking toasted baguette, which of course the simpering Loxleys, our role-model English friends at the next table, were Gallically dipping into their bowls of café au lait while they discussed in perfect French their art-historical itinerary for today. I had to get quite firm before the so-called waiter finally came up with a miserable object which even I could recognise as a multi-pack part-bake number, somewhat inferior to those at the motorway service station, which in turn could learn a thing or two from the in-store bakery at Camden Town Sainsbury's.

So now that we're finally on our way, some urgent reframing of priorities seems in order for our stopover tonight. I HAVE to get some sleep SOON . . .

In-Car Questionnaire – tonight's hotel (Limoges)

(Please fill in your priorities IN WASHABLE INK below your initial)

	C	H	A	D
FUNCTIONAL lift to all floors	*	*		
Cable television			***	***
In-room bath/shower	*	*	*	*
In-room minibar with/without snacks		*		***

Chocolate machine		****	***
Health club		*	***
Breakfast in bed	*	***	
Home-made croissants/pains au chocolat		****	****
Decent yet affordable wine list	****	*	
Children's meals	***	***	****
Children's play area	**	**	****
Swimming pool		****	*****
Modern plumbing	***	***	*****
Pillows not stuffed with old potatoes	*********************************		
No large clocks in vicinity	*********************************		
No-smoking rooms	***	***	****
No pets	***	***	
No motorbikes	****		
Segregation by nationality	****		
OTHER (please specify below)			

C: 1 double and 1 twin room at opposite ends of very long corridor. No patterned textiles on walls.
H: Friendly staff (purely hypothetically, of course).
A: Near international airport.
D: Swimming pewl with inflatable dinosaurs.

Guidebook: *Autour de Tours*

Among the very many and special places you will encounter on your tour through this lovely region, do no omit on any account the delightful hilltop village of Caraquembouche! Of origin almost lost in the backwards of time, situated at the termination of a precipitous and breathtaking mountain road, this most atmospheric burg sits huddled among exceptional boulders, which legend recounts were thrown down there by long-ago giants . . .

13 July, morning – In the car

A very, very hot day. Colum is driving. The road is indeed narrow and twisty. Helen, wearing her very skimpy bubble-gum-pink bikini top and skewing out of the window to reap maximum benefit from the sun, is reading the guidebook. Angel is somehow managing to pluck her eyebrows in the mirror of her vanity case. Des has given up the goggles but is wearing his water wings, uninflated on Angel's side as a compromise.

H: Hey, Des, we're going to a village with exceptional boulders thrown down by giants!
D: Real giants? Do they have giants here? I'm frightened of giants aren't I?
H: Nonsense, everybody in France goes on holiday at the same time, the giants will all be in St Tropez by now. Anyway, giants are notoriously stupid. (*to Colum*) Why is that, anyhow?
C: (*improvising*) Anatomically impossible for any neck to be strong enough to hold up a brain proportionate to a giant body.
D: Why do they have to have a neck?
C: So they can turn their heads, in case they're being attacked from behind.
D: I know I know! Why can't they have eyes in the back of their heads?
C: Well then, how would their brains know whether the signal was coming from the front or the back?
H: You might just as well ask how my brain knows my left from my right!

C: I might well, after that last involuntary detour via the Zone Industrielle.
D: Why can't they have extra brains in their hands and their feet and their chests and their . . .
C: I tell you what, how about we do something else?
D: *(jumping up and down)* Jingley Janglies!
H: How about a bath in boiling lead, Des?

Angel puts away her tweezers and gets out a pot of pink glitter eyelid powder which she opens and begins to apply with enormous concentration. She's looking even paler than usual, but nobody notices.

C: How about a nice old-fashioned game of I-Spy?
D: My turn my turn! I spy with my little eye something beginning with . . . with R!
H: *(pretending to think very hard)* Ummmm – gosh, that's a hard one. Um, rattlesnake? Are there any rattlesnakes around here?
A: *(matter-of-fact, still glitter-dusting)* Road.
D: Okay okay my turn again. I spy with my little eye something beginning with . . . with . . . with . . . C!
A: Car.

Des looks crushed.

H: Wow, who'd have guessed Angel was so good at it. Never mind, Des, let's you and I play. Your turn again . . .
D: But Angel's not allowed to play any more is she Mum?

Angel rolls her eyes, then repeats the action, admiring the rolling glitter effect.

D: Okay are you ready? I spy with my little eye something beginning with . . . with T! You'll never never guess it Mum!

Helen looks out at the three-millionth poplar tree whizzing by the window.

H: Um – toadstool? Tortoise? Gosh, this is difficult – Tardis? Anybody see a Tardis out there?
D: Tree! It's tree Mum!
H: Wow! Des, I'm so stupid, aren't I? As stupid as . . . as a giant!

Colum turns his attention to the mountain road, which is narrowing fast, with a sharp drop on the driver's side.

D: *(wildly excited, and giggling)* A giant with no neck!
H: Stupider than a giant with no neck and no head!

Des collapses in giggles. The road makes a sudden unannounced bend, spilling Angel's glitter powder everywhere and hurling Des into the front of Helen's seat. Des's nose begins to bleed, copiously. Angel takes one look and throws up her Diet Coke all over him.

13 July – Bill for lunch at 'Aire Sud de Poitiers' service station

```
Bienvenus au MiniStop de Poitiers
13/07/02   13.56

1 x assiette Héros, jambon cru          €10.50
2 x frites @ E5.00                      €10.00
1 x plateau de fromages                  €7.50
2 x petit pain @ E1.00                   €2.00
1 x grande assiette de crudités         €12.00
3 x mousse au chocolat @ E4.50          €13.50
1 x petit assortiment de fromages        €5.00
1 x pichot de rouge                      €6.50
1 x Orangina                             €4.00
```

```
1 x eau gazeuse                          €3.00
2 x Diet Coke @ E4.00                    €8.00
2 x café @ E2.50                         €5.00
1 x pièce de fruit                       €1.00

MONTANT                                  €88.00
SERVICE 15%                              €13.20
TOTALE                                   €101.20

Merci et au revoir!
Pourquoi pas découvrir notre 'Take-Away'
Gastronomique!
```

13 July, after lunch

The view from Helen's window
So much for the simple village restaurant with the breathtaking view high on the craggy hill among the exceptional boulders and the mediaeval villagers. It appears that Angel, being half-American, is so highly evolved that she can't travel on anything less flat and wide than a freeway without disastrous consequences.

I wouldn't mind quite so much about being doomed to eat all my meals on my first holiday for four years in the French equivalent of Watford Gap services, if their so-called regional specialities didn't turn out to be identical in everything but name. Des and Colum, of course, are delighted by this, as they share the convenient male quality of being able to eat the same thing 6,594 times before even noticing it's the same, and a further five thousand times or so before tiring of it, but personally I could go off those *carottes râpées* pretty bloody easily.

Still, there was one breakthrough when Colum managed to get Angel to eat something, by deploying the advanced psychological stratagem of leaving a banana right by her mobile on the car seat and telling her she absolutely mustn't touch it, then giving her plenty of time to dispose of the evidence and act dumb when we got back.

Anyhow, I'm driving now so there shouldn't be any more unexpected accidents. And the other shoulder's getting its day in the sun. You have to wonder how those couples who insist on a Stakhanovite adherence to role allocation ever get an even tan at all.

And this way I get to decide on this afternoon's entertainment. I am absolutely not travelling right through château country without visiting a château, and the Château de Joinvilliers is right on our route. I just casually mentioned to Des that it was a real castle with battlements and that it would be bound to have a shop, almost certainly with Disney souvenirs, and he's totally into it, the lamb. As for the others, if they want to spend their entire holiday in a superheated tin box, it's their loss.

The view from Des's window
Disneyland! We're going to Disneyland, Gorilla! It's that castle with the towers and the flags and the big gateway and there'll be Mickey Mouse in his armour and with a big sword and probably Tarzan and Mulan and Hercules and they're all fighting the horrid French!!

The view from Angel's window
I cannot believe what a totally pathetic loser she is. Shopping! In a castle! And why she's so antsy about me seeing all these dumb ruins and shit anyhow — it's not like my mum is even going to notice we arrive, still less ask for a 'What I Did on My Trip' essay. Spilling my glitter sucks big time, though. I guess it's too much to hope there'll be a department store with a Mister Mascara outlet anywhere near that I could sneak into while they're inside.

The view from Colum's window
This idea that you find out about culture from old ruins —

where do people get it from? I learned more than enough about French culture from the litter bins in the car park at that last service station. If people got their idea of the Brits from visiting the Tower of London and Buckingham Palace, they'd conclude that we were a race of money-grubbing, cross-dressing halfwits with bad tempers, worse food and an obsession with queues.

Then again . . .

Still, once they've all buggered off I should get a chance to give the inside of the car a decent clean. Amazing nobody's thought of making family cars with hoseable neoprene interiors. Car design is still in the Stone Age beside bike design. Maybe it is finally time for me to pack it all in and get a job in concept engineering. Might have to take a wee pay cut at first, but after all Helen could easily get a better-paid job, and once Des is out of that exorbitant nursery and into the local primary school there'll be a brief lull before he hits the designer trainers age bracket . . .

Here's the turning . . . Aha. Yet another undiscovered gem, I see.

Sign at the Entrance to the Château de Joinvilliers

> Bienvenus! Welcome! Wilkommen! Benvenuti!
>
> Le château est – OUVERT/The castle is – OPEN/Schloss – GEOFFNET/Il Castello è – APERTO
>
> Parking à péage obligatoire/Guests must pay for the car park/Parkplatz zu hezahlen/Parcheggio a pagamento solamente
>
> Tour guidé à péage obligatoire/Entrance only for guided tour/Eintritt nur für touren/Entrata solamente con guido a pagamento
>
> Suivez la route indiquée SVP –/Please keep to the path indicated – one way only/Bitte auf dem angegeben Weg bleiben/Prego di tenere la strada marcata

Les enfants moins de cinq ans ne sont pas admis/No entrance for children with less than five years/Keine Kindern unter funf jahren/Proibito i bambini meno di cinque anni

Les appareils photographiques et les téléphones mobiles sont rigoureusement défendus/Absolutely no cameras or mobile phones/Keine fotografenapparat oder Handy's/Si informa che gli apparechi fotografichi ed i telefoni mobili non sono accettati dentro

Le café est – FERMÉ/the café is – CLOSED/Das Kafe ist – GESCHLOSSEN/Il/cafe è – CHIUSO

Le magasin est – FERMÉ/The gift shop is – CLOSED/Der Laden ist – GESCHLOSSEN/Il/negozio e – CHIUSO

13 July – Helen and Des, on obligatory guided tour of the castle

They are stifled in the middle of a tightly packed herd of fifty or so sweating tourists, among whom are the Loxley family. Helen is trying to look cheerful and interested. Des is trying to look five, and to avoid being trampled by everybody else.

They are following the tour guide, a thin, pink-nosed man with 'Les Grands Châteaux SARL' embroidered on his chest, on a narrow path cordoned off through an endless series of gilded rooms. The walls are hung with darkened rococo paintings.

H: (*thinking*) Well, at least I got Des in here – pity I had to tell that little white lie about the gift shop, but by the time we're through – whenever that is – it might be open again, or if not I'm sure we'll find something to make up for it somewhere near by. There was definitely some sort of shop in that little square where we parked – glad I spotted it before we'd driven miles to their exorbitant car park, honestly most people are just so sheep-like about that sort of thing. I did tell Colum it was quite safe, just like yesterday, the French really don't care about parking rules like we do, but once Angel had refused to leave her phone he had a perfect alibi. This phone addiction of hers does make you wonder whether there's any truth in those stories about genetic mutations across entire populations from chemicals in drinking water. Not that I've actually seen her drink water, or indeed anything other than Diet Coke. So maybe it's something in Diet Coke. That must be it! The Coca-Cola company has a secret agreement with the mobile phone companies and . . .

She finally notices that Des has been tugging at her sleeve for ten minutes.

D: Mum! Mum! Where are the knights in armour?

Helen reluctantly rejoins the moment. She bends down to whisper, holding up the crowd.

H: (*quietly*) I'm sure there'll be some armour very soon, sweetie, if you keep looking out for it, but anyway you wouldn't want real knights would you, they'd be a bit scary.
D: Where's Mickey Mouse? When can we go to the gift shop?
H: Well, they didn't actually say how long this lasts, but um . . .

Looks frantically around for a distraction.

H: Oh, look, look at this lovely painting of . . . of . . . look, it's Snow White and the Prince just before he wakes her up! Isn't that lovely!

The guide has stopped in front of a baroque painting of an unspecified god about to do his worst to a very, very voluptuous nymph. His posse duly shuffles up and clusters around him.

G: Mesdames, messieurs!

D: What's he saying Mum I can't understand him can we go I want to go and see Dad!

The guide glares. Helen leans down and whispers more quietly.

H: I'll tell you all about it as we go along, and darling if you don't make a fuss, I promise you can have a Magnum at the very first shop we pass!
D: Two Magnums!
H: Okay, two Magnums. Just this once . . .

13 July – Colum and Angel, in the car

The car is parked among a bunch of other cars in a little square under the walls of the château. Colum is diligently cleaning every inch of the back. Angel has been displaced to the front seat, where she's sitting with her mobile. She dials a number, holds it to her ear. Puts it down. Repeats this several times. Nobody's home.

Her phone bleeps. A text message coming in. Her face brightens – until she reads it. She throws the phone across the seat, sniffs once, bites her lip hard, tosses her hair, curls up in her seat and stares into space, looking miserable.

Colum puts down the fine paintbrush he's been using to get into the corners, watches her for a minute, then speaks.

C: Bad news?

She turns to look at him. Making up her mind whether to engage with the enemy.

A: My dad. He's not coming to Italy.
C: That's a shame. I'm sorry.
A: Well, you know he's like, this top ambassador and like, the President needs him all the time and stuff. He's like, totally pissed that this happened. He said so.

C: I'm sure that's true.
A: How would you know? You don't know my dad, you don't know anything about me.

Colum goes back to dusting.

C: How about your mates? Any of them around?
A: Nobody I want to talk to. And they're boring anyway.

But she doesn't turn away again.

C: How about your music?
A: It's boring, it's all last week's and my phone can't get anything here on this rubbish network.
C: And that magazine you were reading earlier?
A: I finished it. It's boring.

He puts down his brush, wipes his hands and takes a deep sniff.

C: That's better.
A: It smells like a hospital in here. Or, like, my school toilets.
C: So long as it doesn't smell of freshly spilled bodily fluids, I'm happy.

He looks around the square as he packs away the cleaning things.

C: There's a café over there with a magazine rack. I could murder a beer. And you could . . .
A: I'm not hungry, thanks.
C: . . . find yourself some French celebrity gossip. Come on, the others'll be hours yet.

Back at the château

Helen and Des are now trailing some way behind the main group as they continue their endless progress through the *salles*. The guide has stopped in front of a painting of a man in a fifty-kilo wig and a breastplate, apparently about to be thrown from his prancing horse, which is trampling a very dead lion skin. He clears his throat.

G: ... Ici, dans la Grande Salle des Conquêtes, vous voyez ...
H: (*whispering*) Ooh look, Des, look at this knight in armour, I told you we'd see knights, and look at that fierce lion underneath him! Let's listen shall we?
D: Are you sure this is Disneyland Mum? It's not a bit like it looks on TV, I think you've made one of your little silly-billies again ...

The guide glares at them and continues.

G: ... le très renommé Duc Edouard, le quinzième de son ligne, juste après sa victoire formidable dans la bataille de Trouville qui, comme vous vous souvenez sans doute, s'est passée pendant la guerre de ...
H: (*still whispering*) This is the famous knight Sir Walt, father of Mickey Mouse and famous fighter, and here he is ...

Nine-year-old Perdita Loxley is looking at Helen oddly. She nudges her mother Talitha, who also starts to listen.

H: (*oblivious, to Des*) ... fighting the Cowardly Lion from *The Wizard of Oz*, who has just cunningly made himself very flat and wide to slip under the door of the prison where Sir Walt had shut him up ...

Perdita can stand it no longer. With the ringing clarity of an English private-school classroom ...

P: That's not what he's saying! Shall I tell you what he's saying?

Helen, still bent double to whisper into Des's ear, suddenly realises she has an audience. Des looks from Helen to Perdita, doubt sown in his mind. Helen addresses Perdita with grown-up politeness.

H: No, sweetheart, it's quite all right, I do understand French.

She turns back to Des and prepares to continue.

D: I want to go back can we go back?
H: Well, the problem with that, pudding, is that – well, in a word, no we can't. BUT you know the gift shop is . . .

The guide glares at both of them.

G: . . . *après les prémiers renvers de l'hiver de mille six cent quatre-vingt-quatorze à mille six cent quatre-vingt-quinze* . . .
H: (*whispering, to Des*) . . . but just as he trampled on the Cowardly Lion it suddenly STOPPED being flat and . . .
P: (*furious*) Mummy Mummy she's making it all up! Tell her to stop!
D: Mum! I want to go to the gift shop now can we go PLEEEASE . . .

Every one of the fifty tourists is now staring at them. The guide wheels round and barks at Helen.

G: *MADAME! Il est spécifiquement et absolument défendu de faire entrer les petits enfants* . . .

Des, terrified, bursts into tears. Helen feels in her pocket, pulls out her handkerchief. It's covered in blood from Des's nose-bleed. It gives her an idea.

H: (*whispering, to Des*) Quick, darling, fall down and pretend to be killed like in our fighting game . . .

She clamps the hankie to his nose. Des duly gives an Oscar-class shriek and crumples into a ball. Helen pulls the blood-soaked hankie away from his face, pretends to see the blood for the first time, and yells out in turn.

H: *Oh, mon petit! Mon bébé! Au secours! Mon dieu!*

She scoops Des into her arms. The crowd parts and they make a run for it, both screaming at the top of their lungs.

Colum and Angel: at the bar

Colum is enjoying his second beer. Angel is leafing through a French issue of *Hello!* There are two toasted cheese sandwiches oozing between them on a plate, each cut in quarters. He's eating appreciatively. Angel is furtively casting ravenous looks at them.

C: It was probably the worst holiday I ever had, which isn't actually saying that much, because I was brought up on a wee small island, and until I was fifteen I thought a holiday was a trip to the mainland to buy wellingtons.
A: I have great vacations. I go with my mum and sometimes my dad. He gets to stay in, like, huge official houses everywhere with loads of servants and the best chefs and stuff. We've been like, everywhere. Cancun, Barbados, Florida, Mauritius . . .
C: So where do you like best?
A: Oh, I don't know, they're all like, the same really. I mean, outside of England and the States everywhere's the same isn't it? Except Europe, Europe sucks. My mum and dad hate Europe and so do I.

Colum takes another swig of his beer and eats another piece of sandwich. Angel furtively reaches out and takes a tiny nibble. Colum shows no sign of noticing.

C: I have to say I've always thought it vastly overrated myself. It's all so old, isn't it? Old buildings, old castles, old toilets – I have my doubts about this beer, if it comes to that.

Angel is beginning to warm up. This is not what she expected to hear.

C: I mean, once people are dead, who cares about their stuff? Burn their property, bulldoze their houses and start again, that's what I say.

Angel finishes her piece of sandwich and takes another, forgetting that she doesn't eat.

A: *(excited)* That is SO TRUE omigod, I mean, that's what's so great about America, I mean you know LA and Florida and places, I mean there's totally NOTHING old there AT ALL and there are all these modern things like you know, malls and beauty parlours and stuff, things that are really like, useful. I mean, you can't even live in a ruined castle or, like, who'd look at paintings when you've got MTV?
C: Exactly!

Angel is now eating ravenously. Colum catches the waiter's eye and signals him to bring another sandwich.

C: So your mum was pretty smart to get out of this trip, huh?

Angel flushes and stops eating for a minute.

A: She'd have come for me, she loves being with me more than anything, we're like, best friends even though she is so old and everything . . .
C: Of course. And she must be really good at her job to be so in demand. I bet you're proud of her.

Angel begins to eat again.

A: And she's proud of me!

13 July – E-mail exchange: Madge and Ernie

    From: Madge Handelman [madge@handy.com]
    To: Ernestine Short [ernie@ernie.com]

Sweets
Well, it looks like we have our little black kid, which presented us with a minor logical snafu script-wise, until yours truly had the brainwave of sending it to Grace Jones who you know she's hardly done anything in a decade BUT! those black complections, betwen just us two, they hold up so well, she still looks really great when she's lit carfully, so she's on for the doctor, which has given us a truly neato plot twist - see italics beloow.
  So with her and Springstein we're looking at kind of an Eighties revival kind of a feel to it, which got me thiking maybe you should be souding out a few of those English new romantic bands for the mechanic parts,
  and we still need our Kelly so what's Sinead up to these days? She does repressed grief pretty good from memory.
  Can't wait to get this one nailed so I can get to the stores. Can NOT believe I've totaly midsed an entire Marni season.
  weather here glorious as usual.
  big kiss M

----

13 July – Story synopsis of major studio picture *Deadly Medicine*

STORY
Joe Mitchum is a guy everybody envies - chief car mechanic to one of the biggest stars in Hollywood, with a stunning wife, Kelly, a *grade-school teacher*, and an adored *adoptive* daughter,

Fawn, he spends his days polishing Ferrari engine blocks and his nights singing his baby girl to sleep and making passionate love to Kelly. The only other thing that marks Joe out is his amazing good looks, and from working on cars he's developed a physique that makes women swoon. But Joe is a one-woman, straight-up kind of a guy. Then tragedy strikes, as Fawn, *who is a person of colour and was adopted as a baby in mysterious circumstances*, develops a life-threatening illness. Joe spends every penny he has scouring the world for a solution, but to no avail, and time is running out as Fawn gets weaker by the day. Finally, Joe hears of a doctor in the Bahamas who may have the answer. Joe sells his beloved vintage Mustang to pay the air fare for himself and Fawn. Fawn barely makes it, but when they meet the doctor, Dr Ingrid JayeGold, she immediately produces a drug made from a secret formula known only to herself that relieves Fawn's symptoms. *Dr JayeGold is also a person of colour*, with a stunning, panther-like beauty, and something about her strikes Joe with an uncanny shock of recognition as soon as they meet. *Dr JayeGold also experiences a shock of recognition – she immediately knows Fawn as her own baby, given up forcibly for adoption at the insistence of her white high-school head teacher, who wanted nothing to get in the way of her favourite pupil's professional future. Dr JayeGold, maddened by grief at seeing her child again in this condition, gives no hint of the truth but agrees to treat Fawn*, and Joe, unknown to Kelly, remortgages his house to pay the bill. Back home, Fawn progresses by leaps and bounds. Her parents and her beloved collie Laddy are delighted to see her back to her old self. But all too soon the drugs are about to run out and Joe goes back to Dr JayeGold, this time alone. Dr JayeGold knows he has no more money. *And she is seething with secret bitterness against all white female teachers. She wants her child back – and she wants a father for her child. But first, Kelly has to be out of the picture.* She tells Joe she'll treat Fawn without money. He's overjoyed – how can he thank her? Then she tells him her price. For every month's supply of drugs, a night of passion with him . . .

But Joe's boss, megastar Silvano Stallion, has always secretly lusted after Kelly. And one day Joe, overcome by the agony of his dilemma, reveals to Silvano that without truckloads of cash their beloved Fawn will die. The next time Silvano gets Kelly alone, he offers to pay for Fawn's treatment, if she becomes his mistress.

So now both of them, unknown to each other, are racked by the same terrible agonising dilemma. But neither dares confess . . .

From: Ernestine Short [ernie@ernie.com]
To: Madge Handelman [madge@handy.com]

Yo sista
Thanks for update.
  Just so happens there's kind of a Bananarama revival thing happening at street level here so they may be out of our price range at this point, but I'm sounding out Simon Le Bon and

his mates – they'll do literally anything to get back in the spotlight. Ditto the Kemp twins – they can't act of course, I don't know whether you ever saw *The Krays*, but they think they can which is SO much more important.

Will get to it toute de suite.

Marni sucks this season – you haven't missed anything there (though Hommebody have some great pants).

Weather here back to normal thank God – all the dead-fish beer guts covered up again, streets of W1 safe for civilisation once more.

love ya E

----

13 July, afternoon – In the square

Helen and Des appear from the direction of the castle, making for the car – or where they parked the car. Des is clutching the remnants of his second Magnum. They both look a lot happier.

H: I could have sworn it was the Disney castle, it looked just like it in the brochure. Silly Mum!
D: Silly Mum!! Can we do more screaming now Mum now we're outside please please?

Helen notices a neat gap in the line of parked cars where theirs was.

H: I wonder where they've gone to? Knowing your Dad he's probably driven miles to find a car wash.

At that moment Colum and Angel approach from the other

side of the square. Angel is carrying a giant box of Cheerios, magically unearthed in the bar, and they are actually giggling together as they come.

A: And if they won't give us a bowl . . .
C: . . . you can eat 'em right from the pack.
A: You are SO right, they're better that way. And if they throw me out of the dining room . . .
C: . . . you can sit on the floor outside and scare off all their business.

Colum also notices the car has gone. Colum and Helen speak at once:

C: Hi – where's the car?
H: Hi – where's the car?

The Parents' Handy French–English Phrase Book – 2003 edition

Chapter Four – When Things go Wrong

Asking for Help
Excuse me, sir/madam, but did you happen to observe anybody removing my car? No, I am not implying that you are a member of an international gang. Yes, I do also understand that you do not spend your day standing about watching other people steal cars. What is that, sir/madam? Have I not seen the sign quite clearly displayed here on this wall? Ah, sir/madam is referring to the sign that would be clearly displayed on this wall were there not a large flag hanging in front of it. No, sadly I was not here for the great fête last night for which these flags were especially put up.

Thank you for drawing my attention to the regulations which I can indeed now read. Yes, it is quite clear, even to a foreign tourist like myself. It is indeed likely that my vehicle has been most properly removed by your most vigilant and scrupulous authorities. But why, if I may be permitted to enquire, sir/madam, is it that all these other cars have been left here? Yes, I am indeed referring to all these other French cars. Ah, now I see the small parking permit in the extreme corner of the windshield of each car. Yes, you are right, every single car. In England we also have this system. No, I cannot explain why I did not therefore expect that it would be the same here.

Asking Directions

Excuse me, sir/madam, but can you please give me directions to the police station/lost property office/customs office/animal hospital/car pound? Yes, I am on foot. Is it a long way? Is it too far to walk? Yes, two hours is probably too long, especially for my four-year-old little boy here. What time does it close, please? I will wait here while you kindly enquire over there of the kind madam the tobacconist. It closes in ten minutes? Perhaps then sir/madam could tell me where I might find a taxi. At the station?

Where is the station, please? Yes, I am indeed new to the town. The station is very near to the car pound. Yes, that is indeed a conundrum. What is that you say? The police will also have access to the car pound when it is closed? Oh, thank you, thank you very much, most kind and gentle sir/madam. Where is the police station, please? Ah, it is right behind me here. Thank you, sir/madam, very kindly. Yes, I am truly enjoying my sojourn in your lovely town.

At the Police Station

Excuse me, sir/madam, but I believe my vehicle has been towed. What is it that you say? No, I did not avail myself of the form that is to be filled in by every person making an enquiry. I will indeed avail myself of it forthwith. Here is the form. There are indeed some blank spaces on the form. I am afraid these details are contained in documents that were left in the car. Yes, I am aware that I should in prudence have made photocopies of all of these documents and kept them about my person for just such an eventuality. Yes, I am aware that in this case it cannot be established without question that the vehicle of which we speak is lawfully and veritably mine. sir/madam/Constable/Sergeant/Inspector, I would be truly grateful for your patience in allowing me access to this vehicle in order that I can determine to our mutual satisfaction that it is indeed mine. Why must I wait for half an hour? Because the car pound is not yet closed. Certainly, I will wait for half an hour. May I perhaps take my son to buy an ice cream while we wait? No, I do not want to run the risk that you may have other things to attend to by the time I return. Certainly I will wait exactly here.

Yes, sir/madam/Constable/Sergeant/Inspector, what is it that you say? Can I perhaps tell you some of the contents of the vehicle in question? Absolutely, it would be my great pleasure so to do. The vehicle contains one pink plastic vanity case, one MP3 player (yes, that is indeed the reason the twelve-year-old girl was shouting in here a few moments ago), three guidebooks, one magazine, one toy cowboy and one toy gorilla (yes, that is indeed the reason the four-year-old boy is weeping copiously in his father's arms), and several suitcases and bags. Ah, such a vehicle has indeed been found? Hooray and cheers, this is indeed good news. May we go to claim it now? Of course, I perfectly understand that you have many other things to do here. Yes, I see that sir/madam/Constable/Sergeant/Inspector is a busy and important functionary of the state whose time must be accounted for to the highest authorities. At what hour do you estimate that your duties here will permit you to accompany us to find our vehicle? No, of course an hour or two is not too long. Yes, we will indeed wait here.

Supplementary In-Car Questionnaire – tonight's hotel (Limoges)

(Please fill in your priorities IN WASHABLE INK below your initial)

                                                   C   H   A   D

Secure, locked, legal, supervised parking   ***********************************

Guidebook Entry for 'Happy Hotel Limoges'

Large, family-friendly hotel in quiet suburb with large underground car park. 60 b/r all with bath/shower and in-room cable TV, snack bar/restaurant plus machines on all floors, lift, no-smoking rooms, in-room Continental breakfast inc.

13 July – Bill for dinner in hotel restaurant

```
Bienvenus au Burger-Luxe
Date:          13/7
Heure:         20.50
Table:         23
N. personnes   4

3 x HappyBurger double de-luxe
- fromage et bacon @ €13.50    €40.50
4 x frites @ €4.00             €16.00
1 x Diet Coke                   €3.95
1 x Orangina                    €3.95
4 x bières @ €10.00            €40.00
1 x cheesecake                  €9.50
```

```
supp. Chantilly                  €3.00
1 x gateau au chocolat           €9.50
supp. glace et Chantilly         €6.00
2 x café @ €4.00                 €8.00

MONTANT                          €140.40
SERVICE @ 12.5%                  €17.55

TOTALE                           €157.95

Merci et bonne route!
```

13 July – Helen and Colum: in their room after supper

The room is large, modern, featureless and over-lit. Colum is lying on one of the two double beds, reading a bike magazine. Helen is lying beside him, staring at the ceiling and talking, apparently to herself.

H: . . . but I suppose you have to look on the bright side, it may be miles from anywhere in a hideous sixties suburb, but that means Angel's safe from rampant bikers, and Des for one seemed to like his supper . . .
C: *(still reading)* I didn't notice anybody else turning down the frites, either.
H: I was saving you from yourself. At enormous personal cost. You should thank me.
C: Thank you.
H: And even Angel seems perkier than I've seen her so far.
C: Wolfing Cheerios straight from the box in front of MTV at full volume seems to fall comfortably within the local code of etiquette.
H: And who found MTV? What a master stroke. I nearly fainted when I saw her smile. Anyhow . . .

. . . rolling over and removing Colum's magazine . . .

H: . . . they're happy now, and I've finally got you to myself on a decent-sized, non-squeaking bed . . .

She begins to undo his buttons.

C: What are you up to, woman?
H: Guess.

She gets as far as his belt buckle.

C: Have we done this before?
H: A long, long time ago.

She's undone his zip and is getting very busy.

C: I'm sure I'd have remembered that . . .
H: Don't worry, I've got the instruction manual here . . .

She slides up his naked torso and their lips meet.

At this moment there's a scrabble in the corridor and then a knock on the door, accompanied by loud wailing. Helen sighs and goes to open it. Des is standing outside, tears pouring down his face, with Angel right behind him. She peeks into the room, sees Colum half undressed, and makes a pukey face.

D: It's not fair! I want to watch cartoons and she keeps watching her silly MTV! Make her stop Mum it's not fair it's not fair!
A: He's so dumb, I keep telling him it's in French and he won't understand it.
D: I will I will!
A: And they don't have cartoons at night they have them in the morning, and . . .
H: . . . and it's way past your bedtime Des, I kissed you goodnight hours ago.
D: I didn't have my goodnight song! I want a goodnight song!
H: I don't think Angel would really enjoy it, sweetheart.

Des's face crumples ominously again.

H: So here's what we're going to do. Des is going to bed and Angel can watch MTV for HALF an hour ONLY, WITH the sound down so Des can sleep . . .
A: That sucks . . .
H: You know all the songs by heart Angel, you know you do, and then in the morning Des can watch cartoons also with the sound down because it's true Des, you won't understand the French anyhow, until Angel wakes up! How about that for a plan!

Neither of them looks happy about this, but Helen is beyond caring. She takes Des by the hand and shoos Angel down the corridor in front of her. Colum goes back to his magazine, has a better idea and removes the rest of his clothes, stowing them neatly in the wardrobe.

A few minutes later, Helen reappears, looking pleased with herself, and advances on Colum again.

H: Star diplomat or what??? Now, where . . .

She stops suddenly, tragedy-struck. Colum has left the mirrored wardrobe door slightly open, and she's just seen her post-burger, chips and cheesecake reflection.

H: (*wails*) Christ!
C: What now?
H: I'm huge!
C: Only from certain angles.
H: No wonder Angel's scared of me. I look like one of those giants we nearly visited.
C: Shame we missed them. They'd probably have welcomed you as a long-lost cousin.

Helen turns her back on him and begins attempting to tear

off her palazzo pants and bandeau top, no easy job since that supper.

H: And why I thought for one minute I could dream of getting away with these stupid ridiculous clothes! And in front of that pre-teen Britney Spears! I'm not surprised she walks ten feet behind me . . .

C: You're beautiful and you always will be. I'd rather a fat Helen than a – come back, I'm teasing you, you daft bat – than a thousand . . .

At this moment, there's another knock on the door.

H: Oh, for God's sake!

She barks through the closed door.

H: Go back to bed! This instant! If I hear one more peep out of you . . .

This time the tears are female, and hysterical. Colum positions himself behind the door and opens it on Angel – sobbing, terrified, and trailing a blood-soaked towel.

The Parents' Handy French–English Phrase Book – 2003 edition

Chapter Five: Medical Emergencies

Seeking Help

Excuse me, sir/madam, but I have a small medical emergency and I need your help. Yes, I know that it is very late and indeed I am aware that I have been ringing this bell for not a few minutes. No, it will not be necessary to call an ambulance. What sort of medical emergency can it be, then? Ah, it is a matter of some delicacy. I wonder whether perhaps your mother may be in the vicinity? It gives me much pain to hear that your mother passed away ten years ago. I am indeed sincerely sorry. Is there perhaps somebody else of the female gender who is here in the building and might advise us? No?

Describing the Problem

Thank you for your patience, sir/madam. Perhaps you would permit me to whisper in your ear. Yes, it is true that at one thirty in the morning few people are about in this hotel lobby. In fact, sir, my young friend upstairs is in want of a diplomatic neutral zone. Let us try that again. Forgive me, I was mistakenly under the impression that 'cordon sanitaire' was the phrase for which I was seeking. In fact, what she is in need of is a . . . Ah, I see sir/madam grasps the problem exactly. Yes, we English are indeed very easily embarrassed by small matters. Indeed, I have taken up very much more of your time than was perhaps necessary. Excuse me, sir/madam.

Solving the Problem

Unfortunately I do not have such an object in my luggage. Is there perhaps such an object in the hotel? No, I do not propose that sir/madam search through the bags of every guest in the hotel. Yes, I fully understand that you are a budget hotel, and not accustomed to providing maid service. Is there perhaps a pharmacy or other shop in the neighbourhood where we might purchase such a thing? Yes, I am aware that the hour is now one forty-five a.m. What, then, does sir/madam propose? Ah, there is a shop that is open at this god-forsaken hour of the night. How far is it? It is near the motorway. No, it is on the motorway. Precisely, it is at the motorway service station. Thank you very much, sir/madam. My husband will go there immediately.

An Unforeseen Hitch

Excuse me, sir/madam, please accept my one thousand

apologies but I fear I must trouble you again. Yes, this is the last thing. Yes, upon the death of my mother's mother's mother. I fear that our car is locked up in your admirably secure parking garage, and my husband will need it to go to the shop. Yes, I am conscious that I am the daughter of the devil, along with all of my compatriots. I am truly grateful for sir/madam's exemplary patience and kindness in helping me to this exceptional degree.

13 July – The Château Disney Bacon Cheeseburger Nosebleed Calypso

> There was once a brave knight who a castle saw
> And it wasn't a castle he had visited before.
> He was sure it was the castle from the Land of Disney, and he
> Shouted, 'That's where Mickey Mouse is, now isn' he?'

> *(Eisteddfod, here we come! But that would mean going back to Wales . . .)*

> So he jumped on his horse, but when he'd leapt the wall
> He discovered it wasn't Mickey's castle at all!
> He had to think quickly to make his getaway, and he
> Remembered something that had happened earlier that day.

> His nose had bled, it was a terrible sight. He said,
> 'I'll show them the blood, and it will give them a fright!'
> And indeed they were so panicked, it did the trick.
> They let him go because they thought he'd make them all sick.

> So to celebrate he planned a slap-up dinner

And when he passed a burger bar it looked like a winner.
He treated all his friends, but one of them felt funny –
It turned out she was having a nosebleed in her tummy!

(Now go to bed, Des, it's very late and Dad and Angel will be back any minute. Night-night!)

13 July – 'The Abduction' (Angel's dream): Episode 3, 'Hope and Horror'

Princess Xandar gripped the arm of her StratoCruiser berth and tried to concentrate only on the task in hand. Now she was sure the food she'd been tricked into eating by her evil, dwarfish alien abductors had been poisoned, but her only thought was to deprive them of the satisfaction of achieving their intent. 'They shall not, like, kill me!' she recited silently, like, like, a mantra.

But alas! The poison was too strong to keep down. Finally the Princess realised that she must choose between humiliation and certain death. Defiantly, she voided the poisoned banana right back at where it came from. 'You'll have to try harder than that!' she laughed, scornfully, making sure to keep it off her Mambo pants.

It seemed hours later when they finally permitted themselves to dock for a brief rest. When the Chief Abductor and her mutant spawn disappeared on yet another trivial quest, Princess Xandar, by now faint with hunger, was amazed to realise that the other – the even older, male-type one – was covertly signalling that he was, in fact, on her side. Dared she trust him? What could be his intention in going along with this tormentuous exercise thus far?

Little by little, in hints and key words, he revealed that he was as hostile to the whole episode as she. But if she confided her true identity, would he free her? Or would he lose his nerve and turn her in? It would break her heart and destroy the Empress's like, whole plan if she were to perish at this point.

So the Princess held her peace, and even allowed him to lull her into eating a little of the familiar food which he had produced as a sign of kinship with her homeland. But her weakened constitution buckled under the shock. A bare few hours later, she lay, unconscious and bleeding heavily, in the bare cell where she was once again imprisoned for the night. Would he come to her aid? Could anybody, in fact, help her at this hour of crisis? And what was this monstrous disease which had attacked her vital organs and racked her with agonising pains? . . .

14 July, early morning – *Les Teletubbies*

Tinky-Winky a perdu son sac à main!

T–W: Oh! Tinky-Winky perdu sac à main!

LaLa apparaît. Elle voit que Tinky-Winky a perdu son sac à main.

L–L: Oh! Tinky-Winky perdu sac à main!

LaLa a trouvé son ballon! LaLa est très heureuse!

L–L: LaLa trouvé ballon! LaLa heureuse!
T–W: LaLa trouvé ballon! LaLa heureuse!

'Gros étreinte, les Teletubbies!'

T–W: Grosse étreinte!
L–L: Grosse étreinte!
D: Grosse étreinte!
P: Grosse étreinte!

Les Teletubbies s'aiment vraiment beaucoup!

14 July, morning – In the car

Another blistering day. The fan is blasting away noisily, but achieving very little. Helen is wearing a baggy, concealing

T-shirt, with the sleeves rolled up as far as they'll go. Angel is even more heavily shrouded in Colum's jumper, which is clearly far too hot but which she equally clearly has no intention of removing, ever. She's listening to the music with her eyes closed, still looking rather pale, arms clamped round her tummy. Des is back to his swimming goggles, one armband and — mysteriously — wellington boots.

Helen looks round and gently taps Angel on the shoulder.

H: Are you all right, sweetie? D'you need another bootleg aspirin?

Angel shakes her head, frowning, and turns back into her corner. Helen turns back and brings out the guidebook, apparently undaunted.

H: (*shouting over the fan*) So today we go through Aubusson, everybody! Who'd like to see the beautiful tapestries? Er — there're some in the cathedral . . .
D: No!
H: . . . and some more in the . . . the . . .
C: You weren't about to mention the C- H-Â-T-E-A-U word by any chance were you?
H: Oh, come on, just because we had one bad experience . . .
D: No more castles! No more momuments! NONONO! NO!!!!!
H: I think you've made your point, Des.
C: Anyhow, you're wasting your time with that book today.
H: And why would that be, then?
C: July fourteenth — everything's closed.
H: Oh.
C: Apart from the gastrodomes, of course. From my memory we're about to enter gourmet paradise. Sausage factories, tripe preservers, foie gras farms . . . Des'd like all that.

Angel turns her music right up and hunches into the farthest corner of the car.

D: What's Foiegras?
H: Nothing darling, Dad was just joking . . .
C: *(into rear-view mirror)* It's a dear wee farm where they have lots of beautiful fluffy white geese running around . . .
D: Cool!
C: . . . and they feed them on lots and lots of delicious corn . . .
D: *(excited)* Can I? Can I feed them? Can we go there now?
C: . . . and when they can't eat any more, the men run round and catch them all because they're too full to run away . . .
D: *(more excited)* I could catch them! I run very fast I could do that!
C: . . . and then they grab them by the head and force their mouths open and shove a load more corn down their throats until they can't eat any more, or they'd burst.

Helen shudders.

H: Do you have to?
C: Then they kill them, rip out their liver, and eat it. World's most civilised nation, the French.
D: *(very excited)* I want to do that. Do they burst? Can I make a goose burst please Mum please?
H: No, Des, it's not true, and anyway it would be very cruel wouldn't it?
D: Oh Mum!!! Please we never do ANYTHING I want to and why didn't the hotel have a swimming pewl you said it would you did!
H: Shh darling, if you're good you can have another Magnum at lunch-time.
D: And you said I could have a Disney souvenir too because to make up for yesterday!

H: I promise just as soon as we reach a Disney store, Des, you can have a Disney souvenir.

Des cheers up and returns to teaching the gorilla and Teddy POdge to shin up a wellington.

C: Although I understand that I'm just here as the driver, and have no voting rights, I have also observed quite a few wine caves, which would certainly be more than open to the suggestion of a spot of *dégustation* on a national holiday. Now there's your French culture, right there. What could be more typically French than drunk-driving down a motorway in the heat of the day?
H: Now you are joking. Or had you forgotten that we have two under-age children with us?
C: No such thing as under-age in this country, they knock it back with mother's milk. Probably why they're all so cheerful and well mannered.

Helen buries her nose in the book again.

C: And as I'm driving, technically you are in my hands at this point.
H: Look, how about this – the Caves de Champincuiq. It's a wine place where they make cheese as well so you can go and do your disgustation and I can take the others to see the cheese being made.
D: Do I have to? I want to stay with Dad this time!
H: Oh come on, you'll get free cheese sandwiches, as many as you like!
D: Like Wallace and Gromit? Will it be like Wallace and Gromit with big lumps of cheese and a big knife?
C: I feel in the interests of avoiding disappointment later on, it would be only fair to point out to the poor wee mite that this is not going to be Sainsbury's Wensleydale on Mother's Pride.

H: He's never had Mother's Pride.
C: Poor waif . . .
H: And just because certain of the adult males in this vehicle are about as adventurous as the bar towels in the Queen Vic, it doesn't necessarily follow that our child has inherited this depressing trait.
C: I thought you loved my dependability.
H: Children are naturally adventurous, it's boring adults who cramp their style.
C: So which category do you put yourself in, if I may ask?

Helen realises she's been skewered. Colum is looking in the mirror at Angel, who is now slumped on the back seat.

C: And I'm not sure that it's such a good idea to . . .

Angel sits up, wrenches off her earplugs and is once again violently sick.

Les Grottes de Champincuiq – excerpt from brochure (English-Language edition)

> *Ever since the very long-ago days of many centuries gone by, in this caves has cheese been fabricated, from the milks of the many ewes who grazes around on the nearby hills. Indeed! The so-famous caves of the Roquefort, which are indeed marvellously well-renowned, have took their idea and origin from Champincuiq, where they were already well-established before a long time.*
>
> *In the while of your visit, you shall see many different stages of the fabrication of the cheese.*
>
> *Please! Be sure to know that only at the termination of the visit is the sampling permitted.*
>
> *Please also! Be very on your guard not to be parted from your childs and other members of your grouping. Here in the caves are many twistings and turnings of the way.*

14 July – The Bold Knight in the cheese cave

As the bold knight Sir GiantKiller got more and more far into the deep, dark, twisty cave, he noticed it was getting very very smelly. 'I wonder if that's the dragon's breath?' he thought. 'Dragons must have very pongy breath from what they eat and never cleaning their teeth.' He drew his huge sharp fearsome sword and got ready. Just then, he saw a tunnel that looked just like the entrance to a dank dark dungeon. That must be the place where his brave soldier friends were shut up by the dragon. He dashed along it waving his sword, but it was longer and twistier than he expected. In fact it got longer and longer and twistier and twistier and it is awfully smelly in here, have I been here before? I wish the dragon's breath didn't smell so much, it's making me feel funny . . .

14 July – Helen in the cheese cave

This is getting a bit unpleasant, frankly. Who but the French could stretch a cheese-making tour out to an hour and a half? I can believe they've been making it in here for eight hundred years. In fact the samples they offered us could well have been hanging around since the thirteenth century. Time for Des to pull one of his notable escape stunts I think. Come on Des . . .

Des? Where are you, Des? God, where's he got to now?

14 July – Des in the cheese cave

I don't like this – it's all slippery and dark and smelly and I can't breathe properly. Mum, where are you Mum?

Helen

Des? Des, where are you? Jesus, it's a warren in here, he could be anywhere – oh God and the smell, it's like that time in Wales, I didn't think anything could smell as bad as that nappy bin and he nearly suffocated then too . . .

Des

Mum? I want my mum! Please Mum I promise I won't run away ever again if you find me please please!!

Helen

Oh God Des it was my fault that time too, why do I always have these mad ideas and never listen to anybody else, and I lied to him about the bloody cheese sandwiches, how could I be such a selfish monster!! Please God if you make him all right I'll never go anywhere again . . .

Des

WaaaH!!! MUM!! I want my MUM!!! WAAAAHHH!! . . . What's that? Who are you? I saw you before, you were in that castle, where's my mum??

Helen

DES! Oh Christ, where's the bloody tour guide when you need them! *Au secours!!!* . . . Des? Is that you? Oh, thank God!! . . . Yes thank you so much, he gets carried away and runs off I'm afraid . . . Yes, a bit careless of me . . . Yes I did read the leaflet . . . Yes, in English and French . . . No, nothing else thank you . . .

14 July – Helen: in the lavatory outside the caves

Okay, I've had it. This is it. I am leaving them at the next major town and taking the first train anywhere. Here I am, doing my best to give everybody a holiday, planning the whole bloody thing and trying, AS REQUESTED, to shove some culture down the throat of that monster child in the back seat, and everything conspires to make me look like a terrible mother and a total incompetent. And to top it all off, he has to be rescued by those ghastly Highgate Loxleys asking whether I'd read the notice about not getting separated, and did I know the leaflet was available in English too?

Then we finally get out, only to be met by a mysteriously cheerful Colum, winking and shhhing Angel like a lunatic, as though the evidence of where they'd been were not filling every inch of the car right up to the roof. 'What is the point of bringing a huge car all this way, if we're not going to avail ourselves of the local produce?' chortles Colum. Anyhow, he adds jovially, after drinking so much for free it seemed churlish not to buy a few bottles. A few!! At a rough estimate, every penny we've saved by bringing Carrie on our trip has now gone into the coffers of the child-poisoners of Champincuiq.

So first off, I am now apparently driving for the rest of the day, only without benefit of either a coherent navigator or any rear vision. Then Colum has to make it worse by asking why we have with us no cheese from the famous delicious cheese caves, which would be just the thing to settle that mystery slopping noise emanating from his middle region. Of course at the mention of the caves, Des, who up until this point had been perfectly fine and rather enjoying his adventure in retrospect, IMMEDIATELY launches into a grossly exaggerated version in which he's buried under a thousand tonnes of cheese while his mother nibbles canapés.

So to console his severely traumatised infant, Colum produces, as if by magic, the EXACT 'Hunchback of Notre Dame' Disney collectable I had secretly purchased to reward Des at the end of the trip, and when I enquire where in this foetid wilderness he had come upon such a thing, it emerges that Colum and Angel also fitted in a trip to a HYPER-MARKET!!! AND ate lunch – so now Angel will eat for Colum but not for me, apparently. And Angel also, of course, got a present (more glitter powder – this from a man more phobic about mess than Howard Hughes) to cheer her up. Now all three of them are ranged against me, and Des, clearly believing that I engineered the whole thing to keep him from discovering that there were hypermarkets in France, topped it off by telling me he loved Colum more than me and from now on he's not going anywhere without Colum.

How is it possible that somebody who still saves his bogies to show you can break your heart?

Still, I suppose that's it, from now on it's just going to be a series of tiny heartbreaks, until he finally leaves home and I'm trapped alone with Mr Perfect for EVER. I am NOT leaving here for ANYBODY, and I am NOT unlocking the door, either . . .

14 July – Colum and Helen: inside the ladies' lavatory at the Caves de Champincuiq

Helen is crouched, sobbing, inside her cubicle while Colum shouts through from the other side. Angel and Des are nowhere to be seen – presumably safe from embarrassment in the car. Various female tourists trickle in and out, clearly not impressed by this latest confirmation of the incivility and barbarism of the English.

H: . . . and I am NOT squandering what remains of my first and probably only ever holiday on a tour of French post-war retail opportunities!
C: You don't have to come in, there's a nice wee café outside where you can be having your lunch while I whiz him through.

H: I would rather die than eat lunch within a kilometre – a MILE – of a French hypermarket.

C: Well, I hate to bring this up again, but don't you mebbe feel that after this morning you owe him . . .

H: How dare you! I suppose it was me who decided to dash off down an unmarked passage and get myself totally lost . . .

An extremely genteel middle-aged woman appears at the entrance, sees and hears what's going on, looks shocked and goes out again.

C: Yeah, but if you hadn't made him go in . . .

H: Oh bloody great. Fine!! You couldn't wait for that one, could you? Never miss an opportunity of showing me what a great father you are and how I don't understand my own child, or any child for that matter . . .

Colum finally begins to lose his patience.

C: For God's sake woman! Nobody's calling you a bad mother, but you can't force children to be something they're not, and it's ridiculous to expect that a four-year-old, or a twelve-year-old for that matter, will get anything out of the kind of stuff you find in a guidebook for . . . for genteel geriatrics.

Behind Colum's back, the middle-aged woman has reappeared at the door with a uniformed male security guard. They begin a polite altercation in French about whether, in these circumstances, it is acceptable for a male guard to enter a women's lavatory, solely for the purposes of apprehending a large and clearly dangerous male intruder.

H: Oh, so I'm not only the world's worst mother but a geriatric now to boot!! Well that's it, you go off to your hypermarket, take as long as you like, what do I care, just so long as I'm kept away from the child I'm ruining with every passing day . . .

And she collapses once again into a flood of furious sobbing. Colum sighs, resists the temptation to kick in the door, and turns to find himself encircled by a dozen Frenchwomen and the guard – big, uniformed and brandishing a pair of handcuffs.

Angel: Text to Madge

```
MUM! BN TRYNG 2 CLL NNSTP BT U NVR NSWR! U HVE
HVE HVE 2 GT ME OUT F HRE, ALL CRZY + M STRVNG
2 DTH + HVE LST GLLNS OF BLD, F DN'T MK IT 2
ITLY WLL B ALL UR FLT. CALL ASAP ANGEL
```

14 July – E-mail exchange: Madge and Ernie

From: Madge Handelman [madge@handy.com]
To: Ernestine Short [ernie@ernie.com]

```
Sweets
Twenty years in this business and it only
gets worse. After we bent over to accomodate
the black kid she's gone and siged to Warners
for The Janet Jackson Story.
   So we urgemtly like YETERDAY (they HAVE to
start principal photograpy in under three
weeks or they los Stallone and worse, the tax
break) - need a new black female kid, young
enough so Grace Jones can be her Mom playing
fifteen years youger than her reel age, ie if
Grace is playing thirty kid not over twelve,
and idealy kid with a great singing boice now
that this is turing out to be a bit of a
```

musical piece. I know you don't exactly specialise in kids but we're dredging the barrel here with no luck, so coudl you be a major honey and trawl the usual theater schools, agencies etc your end?

One oter thing - I got kind of a weird texxt from Angel just now - could you be a doll and call your fiend to get a sense of how things are goimg down there?

weather here glorious as usual.

big kiss M

From: Ernestine Short [ernie@ernie.com]
To: Madge Handelman [madge@handy.com]

Yo Madge
Check, on both counts. I'll get your kid if I have to have it myself.

love ya E

----

14 July, afternoon – Helen, waiting for the others to emerge from the hypermarket

So finally it was Colum's turn to come up against the forces of French bureaucracy. I have to say, I was strongly tempted to go along with their assumption that he was an intending rapist and I'd fled into the loo for safety, but the thought of dealing with Angel and Des on my own for the next two days flipped the balance. Still, it did cheer me up.

God, I'm hungry. But I'd have to be a whole lot hungrier before I'd go anywhere near that toxic parody of a boulevard café over there. Anyhow I have to say I'm going right off French food. What I really fancy right now is some nice baked beans on toast. Or rice pudding, with lovely dark brown skin and a swirl of golden syrup trickling over it. I never eat baked beans or rice pudding at home – isn't it weird how you suddenly start fancying things you never normally eat when they're not available?

A bit like men, come to think of it. I do love it when Colum gets angry. Unfortunately it only happens about once every ten years.

What's that noise? Christ, the mobile phones here are even louder than in England. It sounds like it's right in the car.

Oh shit, it is. Where the hell is it? I know I put it somewhere sensible after I couldn't find it last time when I needed to book that hotel . . . Don't go away! Hang on! . . .

14 July, afternoon – Phone call: Ernie and Helen

E: . . . and how's Colum? And the adorable Des?
H: I know nobody by those names.
E: Pardon?
H: I prefer to maintain a dignified silence on the matter. I will say only that I intend to take the earliest possible flight home and leave the lot of them to their own devices.
E: Have you got sunstroke, kitten?
H: HAH! Fat chance of that, cooped up in this bloody car, all day every day, being everybody's favourite fat geriatric scapegoat.
E: Wow. Fun factor fifty, then?
H: In fact, as we speak, guess where I'm sitting!
E: In a ducking-stool over the Seine?
H: Ha bloody ha. I am, in fact, in the scenic car park of an out-of-town retail complex in the vicinity of Clermont-Ferrand, well known for its natural beauty and wealth of architectural gems, waiting for the rest of the party to sate

its collective urge to fill the remaining few unoccupied crevices of the car with tat.

E: So they're having a good time, anyhow?
H: I wouldn't know.
E: And . . . the lovely Angel . . .
H: Lovely? Shall I itemise? Did you actually meet her at all before sloughing her off on to us?
E: Of course I did. More than once, and in daylight.
H: Ha!
E: But she's not sick, or anything that you know of?
H: Not unless it's from a surfeit of Cheerios and Diet Coke, which appear to be the only items her highly complex metabolism recognises as food.
E: Cheerios? In France? Maybe it's time to give 'em another chance.
H: She did get her first period last night. I almost felt sorry for her at 2.30 a.m., trying to strap her into a French pensioner's towel belt without waking Des in the next bed . . .
E: She's twelve, she'll make a fashion statement out of it.
H: . . . until she told Colum she wasn't surprised I didn't have a tampon myself because I must be way past all that by now. I'm only trying to do what her bloody mother asked me to, and all I get is grief from all sides.
E: Poor chickadee. Still, it seems a pity to go through all the rough bit and then miss out on Tuscany.
H: I'd enjoy it a lot more if you were there. How's it looking?
E: It's looking like a serious case of my ass hung out to dry unless I find her a cut-price child star pronto. I have to confess the prospect of palling up to a stream of thigh-high prima donnas is not doing my qi a whole lot of good.
H: I could come and help. I've been desensitised by Paint Pots.
E: Sure, but didn't you say the in-laws were staking out your house at the moment?

H: Christ.
Pause.
E: I'd stay put if I were you. Oh God, look my favourite nail person has just come free and I've got to grab her. (Maya!!! Darling, it's me!!) I'll call you again soon, okay doll? Cheer up – I love you, even if nobody else does!

14 July – Bertie

So – what have they found for me this time? Cod, by the smell of it, and even fairly fresh. Those sardines yesterday were a shock, I must say – it's years since anybody expected me to eat something that could still look me in the eye. Luckily I'd had enough steak the day before to tide me through.

Ah, the luxury of holding not one but two humans in the pad of one's paw. This bed is a bit of all right, too. Maybe the cocoa was just a blip.

Let's see if I can still reach that itchy place on the inside of my left thigh. Yes! Not bad for a sedentary old codger. Show me a human my age that can lick its own bottom, and I'll show you a hernia two minutes away. And yet the airs they put on! Hmm – what's this? I don't remember sitting down on anything this colour. Tastes like – chicken? Time for a little digestive nap, I think . . .

14 July – George, Fiona and Bertie

Fiona is camped in front of the Home Shopping Channel, surrounded by takeaway cartons, a phone and a calculator.

George shouts through from Des's room, where Colum and Helen keep their computer.

G: Hey, woman, come away here and see this!
F: *(shouting back)* A'm in the muddle of a budding war, ye muttonhead.

G: *(to himself)* Yon broadband's a revelation!

He clicks and waits for a second, and up pops the home page of greatsportingmomentsinceltichistory.com, a bargain at £50 a month plus £50 sign-up fee plus online time.

G: *(still to himself)* Och, young Colum'll thank me fer this – he'll no have to tek ma word for anything ever again.

More clicks and whirs, and a message comes up on-screen: 'Welcome Colum McCallum – your credit card has been accepted. Where would you like to go?'

G: It's no exactly ma fault if it won't tek payment from a different address, is it? And wha's fufty pound a month to him, indeed?

From Des's bed, a muffled yowl. Bertie, who has been moved in here along with his litter tray and food bowl to confine the smell, is having indigestion nightmares on Des's hand-embroidered elephant duvet cover. He flails around wildly.

G: *(to Bertie)* Pipe down, will ye, fat furball! *(to himself)* Did I no' tell her that Dundee cake wasnae a guid follow-up to a pound o' cod?

Bertie yowls some more. George gets up, grabs him and bundles him back to Fiona and the TV. There's an ominous ripping sound, and the elephant has a big jagged hole instead of a head. George settles himself again and starts typing with one heavy finger.

G: Now, where was I? Let's go for . . . Partick Thistle versus Hibs in the semis in fifty-three . . .

14 July – Text message from Ernie to Madge

ANGL APPRNTLY SF + WLL. BT PRHPS A WRD F THNKS 2 HLN MGHT NT B AMSS AT THS PNT.

14 July, afternoon – In the car

Helen is driving, looking more cheerful, and enthusiastically eating a large bar of Frigor chocolate for her lunch. Colum has succumbed to the after-effects of the morning and is deeply, loudly asleep. Angel has shed her giant sweater and is experimenting with the stick-on face jewels she got free with her new magazine, and Des is deep in a game involving the Hunchback of Notre Dame, the cowboy and a jelly dinosaur sweet.

Helen looks into the mirror. Peace at last.

H: *(to Angel, into the mirror and through the chocolate)* This is yummy. Thanks so much, that was really sweet of you.
A: *(mumbling)* Yeah, well, you, like, helped me last night. Anyway, it was his idea.
H: Even so. Normally I don't get to eat this you see, even though it's so delicious, because it's made by Nestlé and I'm supposed to be boycotting them, but when somebody else buys it . . .

Angel clearly feels this is already too much information.

A: Whatever.

The phone rings. Colum doesn't move. Helen reaches over, around and finally under him, and unearths it from beneath his feet.

H: Hello? Madge!!!

Angel sits up, excited, then catches herself and slumps back as though she couldn't care less.

H: Hi . . . Yes, she's here. Do you want to speak to . . . Oh, really? . . . *(gratified)* She did? . . . *(more gratified)* She said that?

She turns to get a good look at Angel, now staring out of the window pretending not to listen.

H: How sweet of her. And . . .
A: Watch out!!

Helen is about to shave a few paint layers off a caravan in the next lane. She turns back and rights the car.

H: *(into phone)* Oops! . . . No, just these holiday drivers, you can imagine . . . Would you like to speak to her?

Angel sits forward and holds out her hand for the phone.

H: She's right here . . . No? Oh, I see . . . Yes, you must be.

Angel slumps back, biting her lip, and jams on her headphones.

H: Yes, of course I'll tell her . . . See you, hey it's the day after tomorrow isn't it? . . . Yes, we can't wait either. She'll have so much to tell you!!

She hangs up the phone and speaks to Angel in the mirror.

H: Your mum says hi and she's . . . um, she can't wait to see you.

No response. Des puts out a chubby hand and strokes Angel's arm.

D: *(to Angel)* Is your tummy hurting again?

Angel pulls away.

A: I'm fine.

Helen tries to change the subject.

H: Wow, suddenly it's like rush hour on the Edgware Road. We must be quite near Lyons by now, I should think, maybe we'll even get your passport sorted out today Angel.
D: Where are we staying tonight Mum? Will there be a pewl? Will there be *Teletubbies* again? Will they be . . .

H: Christ!!! Sorry Des, I sort of umm – I'll ask Dad where we're . . . Hey, Col!

She jabs him heavily in the ribs. He snores and shifts.

H: WAKE UP, COLUM!!
D: *(joining in enthusiastically)* WAKE UP DAD!!!!

Colum groans, and turns into the corner. Helen jabs him again, with the mobile.

C: Oi!!!!

He very reluctantly opens his eyes.

C: Jesus, where are we?
H: More to the point, where will we be in two hours' time?
C: *(yawning)* Sorry, I don't quite . . .
H: *(loud whisper)* Hotel!
C: What's that?
H: *(louder whisper)* Tonight! Major public holiday!
C: Indeed . . .
H: *(very loud whisper)* WE DON'T HAVE A BLOODY HOTEL BOOKED!!!

The Parents' Handy French–English Phrase Book – 2003 Edition

Chapter 6: Finding a Hotel

Getting Directions
Excuse me, sir/madam, but would you by any chance be able to direct me to the Hôtel de la Gare? The Hôtel de la Gare is defunct. Perhaps, in that case, the Hôtel de la Poste? The Hôtel de la Poste is closed for renovations. Maybe, in that case, the Hôtel du Marché? Yes, I am aware that it is currently a public holiday, the greatest public holiday of the year in fact, celebrating the notable and

unique trilogy of freedom, that only the most blessed citizens of France enjoy. But foolishly I did not infer from this that the Hôtel du Marché, situated as it is in the centre of the market square, is therefore only accessible on foot, and the parking is many tens of metres distant from the hotel. No, that might in truth be not very convenient for us. Yes, our car is indeed quite heavily laden with our many purchases from your so-excellent French hypermarkets.

Suggesting Alternatives
Perhaps, sir/madam, you could in that case direct us to another hotel that might have rooms? Yes, for tonight. For four people. Indeed, we English do after all have a sense of humour. But, sir/madam, in this instance I am quite serious. Yes, I have already enquired by telephone of the Hôtel Jolly/Hôtel Ibis/Hôtel Best Western/Hôtel Sunny Inn/Hôtel Touristique/Hôtel du Parc/Hôtel des Voyageurs/Hôtel Rendezvous. I have even enquired of the Palais Hôtel and the Hôtel Château des Eaux, even though my annual income sadly would not have afforded us even one room, were they to have had a room available. No, none of them has any rooms at all. No, I do not imagine that this is a coincidence.

The Last Resort
Please, most excellent sir/madam, you see that we have a very young girl with us who is far from well. Your esteemed and well-renowned hotel is the last one in the town and she must at all costs have a bed of some sort to sleep in tonight. No, sir/madam, I do not hold you personally responsible for the existence of the great public holiday of 14 July, nor am I in any way critical of its existence, celebrating as it does all that is most noble and unique about this great and beautiful country. Nor, gracious sir/madam, do I hold you personally responsible for my

own idiotic failure to anticipate this situation.

Yes, I do see that family of four English people even now making their way to a pleasant suite of rooms on your principal floor. In fact, we have encountered them not once but several times already on our travels. Did they indeed book their rooms more than six months ago? Yes, they are indeed prudent and responsible in the extreme, compared to our miserable selves. Is there perhaps a convent, an old people's home, or a shelter for the destitute victims of alcohol or debt, where a more sympathetic welcome might obtain? No?

Yes, I will indeed wait here while you make a phone call. I will wait as long as you like.

Sir/madam, what is it that you say? You have made several phone calls on our behalf? Truly that is most unwarrantedly generous on your part. And you have succeeded in fulfilling our dreams? Ah, how can I thank you enough, kind and noble sir/madam? The last room in town? With one double bed and two beds for infants? But that is indeed luxury beyond anything we deserve! And where exactly might they be? Near to the motorway? Ah, on the motorway? To be precise, at the motorway service station.

14 July, early evening

The view from Helen's window
I have to admit that it is quite extraordinary how one's perspective can shift as a result of quite minor developments – like, for instance, having children. Who'd have thought five years ago that a French motorway service station, equipped with air conditioning, clean loos, multinational branded food products, a cafeteria selling steak and chips for a fiver, twenty-four-hour petrol, a plethora of cleaning materials and several acres of cheap plastic toys would come to represent a haven of safety and civilisation?

But there you are. No doubt Mary and Joseph would have felt pretty bloody grateful for a room at the QuikStop Motel de Lyon Ouest, even with the sixteen-wheelers coming and going and the ice machine chundering outside all night.

I could not believe it when I saw those Loxleys ahead of us at the desk of that other place. I was ready to believe Angel's father had hired them to check up on us, even though that reptile hotelier insisted they'd booked months and months ago, but having been more or less forced into each other's company while we waited to hear our fate, they turned out to be touring France with some appalling amateur theatricals, and indeed performing tonight as part of the well-known twinning of Highgate Village and Lyons, which I had to confess in the hurly-burly of world events had entirely passed me by.

The most extraordinary thing, however, was Angel's reaction. Nobody, I swear, even her own mother – or perhaps that's not a good example, but anyway – no sane adult could look at Angel and peg her for a Shakespeare fan. But no sooner had she set eyes on them – or more particularly on their son, whom she had evidently missed on previous occasions owing to prolonged sulks in the back of the car – than she's tearing the blankets off the QuikStop bed and insisting that we drive en masse all the way back into Lyons to take in their *son et lumière* terpsichorean gambollings.

I had to do a bit of swift thinking to persuade the others, but luckily Colum's always willing to believe anything that makes me look pig headed or a food nazi. Still, anything to have a smiling face on the back seat. Her own mother – sorry, bad example again – nobody would recognise her.

The view from Colum's window
Can there be a more stubborn woman in the world? Even when we're actually staying on the premises she won't eat at the perfectly decent twenty-four-hour caff downstairs. You'd

have thought after yesterday she'd finally have learned her lesson, but no, we have to drag ourselves back into the teeming holiday traffic to have our wallets ironed and our digestions worked over by the condescending bastard who gave us the heave-ho not three hours ago.

Christ, my head. Think calm thoughts. How about those asymmetrical matte black tailpipes coming out from under the crimson leather seat of that new MVAgusta. What a bike, eh? If I'd the money to buy a Porsche, I'd stuff the Porsche and get the Agusta instead.

The view from Des's window
And the French cowboy rode thundering up to the cave and said to the dragon in a shouty voice, 'PUISJ VOUS AIDER AVEC CETTE VALISE!!!' and the dragon roared back 'TROIS TASSES DE CHOCOLAT SILVOUS PLAÎT ET DES GATEAUX!!!'

The view from Angel's window
Oooooh. Oooh. Oooh his eyes. Oooh his lips. OOOOH his bum in those baggy pants! And you can see right away how totally pissed off he is having to drag around with those toxic parents and that rancid little whiny sister. I think he liked me too – well, I made sure I didn't smile at him or anything but just wait till that Rowan hears about it. She'll just DIE!

Excerpt from Playbill for *Roméo Et Juliet,* by The Highgate Players

> *Les Highgate Players Présentent* . . .
> The Highgate Players Present . . .
>
> . . . *Roméo et Juliet!*
> . . . Romeo and Juliet!
>
> *Suite à leur succès formidable à Londres, la compagnie théâtrale 'The Highgate Players' proposent leur interprétation rayonnante en*

plein air du chef d'oeuvre de 400 ans de William Shakespeare dans la cité de Lyon pour quatre représentations uniquement.

Following the formidable success of their London production, the city of Lyons welcomes 'The Highgate Players' for only four evenings in their truly astounding evocation of Shakespeare's 400-year-old masterpiece.

11/7–14/7 Hotel de Tourisme, Lyons   21.00 h
billets/renseignments chez l'hôtel sur 76 89 58 03
prix des billets   20E
possibilité de buffet/supp. 16E

PLAUDITS POUR LA PRODUCTION
PRAISE FOR THIS PRODUCTION

'Une période d'une soirée, là sous la lumière brumeuse, les vérités profondes de la condition humaine, le pouvoir terrible et cruel du premier amour, et le calme sans appel de la mort nous ont absorbés et nous ont transportés à un monde lointain et infini.'

'For the space of an evening, there in the smoky light, the dark truths of the human condition, the terrifying and cruel power of first love and the unappealable quiet of death absorbed us, and took us to a different world.'

Daphne Dalrymple, Highgate Highlights *magazine*
www.highgateshakespeare.org.uk

14 July, evening – In the grounds of the 'Hôtel de Tourisme', Lyons

About thirty uncomfortable-looking middle-aged people, mostly English tourists, are teetering on dining chairs or squatting awkwardly on cushions, on the gravel of the rather bleak hotel garden. The remains of the buffet – ham rolls and quiche – are scattered around them. Many are clutching life-saving glasses of the hotel's local red wine. It's just about time for the mosquitoes to ramp up for the evening, and a few people are already slapping and scratching.

In the distance, mysteriously never quite lit, the actors are declaiming their lines, in English. Between them and the audience, a dumpy woman with a siren voice – a local schoolteacher – is helpfully bellowing a line-by-line translation, to the evident annoyance of the players.

At the front of the audience, Angel has spread out her blanket. She's sprawled on it, under the eye, but not the ear, of Helen. Fourteen-year-old Edgar Loxley, not required for tonight's performance, is whispering in her ear.

It's halfway through the balcony scene. Juliet is speaking. Talitha Loxley is a good twenty years too old for the part, but the dusk is forgiving.

J: . . . wherefore art thou Romeo? That which we call a rose . . .
T: . . . *pourquoi tu t'appelles Roméo? Celà qu'on appelle une rose* . . .
E: . . . where the bloody hell are you Romeo? I've been waiting hours out here and the mozzies are murdering me. You coming or what?
J: . . . by any other name would smell as sweet!
T: . . . *par n'importe quel nom aurait le même parfum!*
E: I don't hang around on balconies for just anybody, mate!
J: So Romeo would, were he not Romeo called . . .
T: *Ainsi Roméo, même s'il ne s'appelait pas Roméo* . . .
E: Okay, that's it, I'll do a lot for a shag . . .
J: Retain that dear perfection which he owes . . .
T: *Posséderait toujours sa chère perfection* . . .
E: . . . I may be cheap, but I'm not THAT cheap!
J: . . . without that title.
T: . . . *sans ce titre.*
E: Where's my address book?

Her soliloquy hangs in the twilight air. Miraculously, the slapping and scratching pause. Then, behind Angel and Edgar, a horrendous snore erupts. The trials of the day – and the previous night – have finally taken their toll on Helen.

14 July – 'The Abduction' (Angel's dream): Episode 4, 'A Miraculous Intervention'.

Princess Xandar had spent the day tossing and turning feverishly, halfway between sleep and waking. Weakened by her massive loss of blood and unable any longer to endure the idiotic yammering of her abductors, she was at the limit of her endurance, convinced she would never see her home or her loved ones again. What was the odd box of Cheerios in the black night of eternal exile?

And, by a cruel turn of fate, when she finally alerted the Empress to the danger, her abductors were there before her, reassuring her with honeyed, lying words that her daughter was safe with them and would soon be delivered unharmed back to her charge.

But then! It was the last place in the Galaxy she would have dreamed of meeting her destined happiness – the yucky, cramped lobby of a transit camp where her quarrelsome abductors had messed up yet again. The Princess, still doubled over with pain, and barely aware of her surroundings, was suddenly arrested – mesmerised – by a sight more beautiful than anything her young life had yet afforded her. There, right in front of her, and unmistakable in his bearing, his looks and his chill threads, was a Prince of the Blood – her Prince!

Swooning, Princess Xandar groped her way to a seat and turned her face away, lest he witness her vulnerable state in these shameful circumstances. He, with instinctive nobility, also turned away, pretending to have, like, not even seen her. But she knew – and she knew that he knew! That lightning bolt that had passed between them was unmistakable. This, finally, was true love.

15 July – Bill for breakfast: Sandwich Village, Lyons

```
Bienvenus au Sandwich Village de l'Aire
de Lyon Ouest

le 15/07            09.45

2 x croissants beurre        @€3.50      €7.00
2 x pains au chocolat        @€4.00      €8.00
1 x chocolat chaud Nestlé                €6.00
2 x grande crème Kenco       @€5.50     €11.00
1 x Diet Coke                             €5.50

MONTANT                                  €37.50
SERVICE @12.5%                            €4.69


TOTALE                                   €42.19

au revoir à très bientôt!
```

15 July, morning – The view from Helen's window

Well. Who'd have believed it? Angel wakes us all in our luxury broom cupboard at 6.30 a.m., taking a shower and applying a full make-up, before demanding that we drive back into Lyons for breakfast. 'We have to go anyway, for my passport' was followed by 'And I promise I'll eat!!', but, inexplicably, even this irresistible enticement somehow failed. Though I did have a momentary twinge, realising this is our last morning in France and therefore probably my last chance for several years to establish whether the Perfect Croissant does indeed exist.

Still, in the end another hour in bed won the day, though sleeping four to a room is not an experience I'd recommend for a romantic getaway. But luckily her phone rang while we were chewing our way through yet another identikit Sandwich

Village breakfast, so she was considerably more cheerful on the long and ultimately fruitless trek around the ingenious traffic-calming one-way system of Lyons in search of the main post office to collect her passport. Of course, when we had finally located it, reached it and sprinted the last hundred yards from the nearest legal parking spot to the main entrance, we discovered a sign in the window which, in teeny tiny print, informed us that in consideration of the previous day (14 July) having been a Sunday, the honourable and industrious employees of the post office had taken today off instead, and it would be closed till tomorrow morning.

At which point the only sensible thing seemed to be to make a run for the border and hope that the Italians take a more relaxed view of these things. Angel spookily offered, unprompted, to phone her dad and ask him to phone the border police so they'd be expecting us. God knows what that boy is saying to her to improve her mood this much, but here's hoping they don't fall out before we unload her on to her mum.

15 July – Phone call: Edgar to Angel

E: . . . so – d'you enjoy the play, then?
A: It was okay.
Pause.
E: Mum's so embarrassing. I hate having to trail around after them.
A: Yeah.
Pause.
A: My mum's embarrassing too. She's like – so loud!
E: I bet she's not as embarrassing as my mum. Or my dad – he quotes like, Latin at mealtimes.
A: My dad's cool. I don't see him much though.
E: Oh. Bummer.

A: Yeah.
Pause.
E: Next year I'm getting a motorbike and I'm going round Cuba on it.
A: Cool.
E: Yeah.
Pause.
E: I've gotta like, split. We're packing and stuff.
A: Yeah, I've gotta split too.
Pause.
E: Okay then.
A: Yeah.
Pause.
A: See you.
E: Likewise.
Pause.
E: So . . .
A: So?
E: . . . See you around then.
A: Yeah.

15 July – Approaching the Italian border

The car, axles sagging under the weight of its occupants, their luggage and their various souvenir purchases, is crawling in a line of other cars towards the border post of Susa. Picturesque Alpine border-control huts are hung with baskets of flowers, around which bees buzz sleepily. The pastoral idyll is tainted only by the background thump of Beppe Maniglia, Italian Curved Air one-man soundalike sensation, blasting from the speakers outside the customs HQ.

Angel, wearing a backless spaghetti-strap T-shirt, distressed stretch denim hot pants and six-inch platform sandals, is staring out of the window, a dopey smile on her face. Des, apparently still inseparable from his wellingtons, has added a snorkel tube to the goggles, but left off both armbands today. Helen has forgotten she's old and fat, and has reverted to the palazzo pants and off-the-shoulder matelot crop top. In the driver's seat, Colum, in honour of their arrival into Italy, is wearing an ancient T-shirt emblazoned with the slogan 'Motocicli Gilera! Campione Assoluto del Mondo 1957!' and a huge number of red stars. This aside, he looks fairly normal.

H: *(happily)* Italy! At last! It's weird, I always forget how much I hate the French until I get there and it all comes flooding back. But now we're done with them!

She opens her bag, pulls down the passenger-side sun visor and begins applying make-up.

C: Don't speak too soon. We could all yet end up as one of those long-running stories on the *Today* programme – you know, 'British tourists held in Bastille for seventy-seventh consecutive day – consul says his hands are tied'.
H: Nonsense. The French border post isn't even open – look at it, they've all got the day off as well, lazy . . .
C: What are you doing?
H: Putting on a face. Trust me, you've seen me do this before.
C: Not since we left England. In fact, thinking back, it could have been that night we went out with that Italian so-called producer friend of yours.
H: *(blushing)* Crap . . .
C: *(exaggerated leer)* Coincidence? You decide.
H: *(rising above it)* And they can't even make a decent croissant any more. I bet we've got more chance of . . .

Luckily at this point her soliloquy is interrupted by a movie-star-gorgeous guard, Federico, in tailored whipcord jacket, stretch deerskin breeches and knee-high black patent leather boots, who strolls casually over, tips his cap and leans in at Helen's window.

F: *Buon giorno!*

Helen buckles and drops her mascara.

H: *Buon giorno — signore!!!*

He smiles. She smirks.

F: *Documenti, per favore.*
H: *(to Colum)* Passports — he needs our . . .

Colum has already handed them across her to Federico, who riffles idly through the three English ones and hands them back, then takes a closer look at Angel's. Then leans right into the car and takes a close — very close — look at Angel. Then calls out to a colleague:

F: *Eh, Giulio — abbiam'quiqualcos'dimoltointeressant'ven'vedere!*
(Oi — here's something worth taking a gander at.)

Giulio looks up from the dreary VW Corsa he's checking through and strolls over.

G: *(to Helen) Ciao!*

Federico jerks his head to indicate that the object of interest is what's in the back seat.

F: *'A'unpassaport'diPatagoniacosacipensi?*
(She's got a Patagonian passport — we could pull 'er in for 'questioning' — what d'you reckon?)

Giorgio leans in in turn and smiles seductively at Angel, who pouts back and tosses her hair, always keen to practise.

G: *Ah, m'abbiam'giasnetitadiquestatutto'nordinedobbiam'sol'far 'Ifatturaok?*

(Oh, we know about this one, it's all okay, we just have to fill in one of those bloody forms.)

... and is about to walk off.

F: *Madai!!!*
  (Hang on!)
G: *Eh?*
  (Eh?)

They turn away. Gesturing expressively, but invisibly to the occupants of the car, Federico whispers ...

F: *LaCAMERA!!*
  (You're forgetting the old 'camera' trick!)
G: *Ah!*
  (Now you're talking.)

He turns to Helen and says, in heavily accented but perfectly grammatical English:

G: Madam! We 'ave been eenformed of your expected arrival, and arringements 'ave been mide for a speshial visa to be issued to your young friend 'ere. For thees puirpose, eet ees necessary to make a photograph of 'eer there in our bureau. Eet will tike only a few minutes, eef you could please expline to 'er?
H: Oh – a photo? Well of course, how kind, and what a relief! But I think perhaps ...

She licks her lips and looks up from under her newly mascaraed lashes.

H: ... I should come along with her?

Giorgio turns back to Federico and wiggles his eyebrows to indicate Helen.

G: *Ladonn'vuol'nchemisembracheposs'aver'tutteleduecosaci pensi?*

(How about her as well? She's gagging for it.)
F: *(big Italian shrug) Ba! Mapercheno?*
(Hey, in for a penny . . .)

Giorgio turns back to Helen, leering suggestively.

G: In that case by all means madam please come thees way end the young lidy too!

The two Italians, with Helen and Angel pouting and swivelling like crazy, set off towards the sheds.

C: Hang on!

All four turn as one.

H: *(through her teeth)* Colum for God's sake don't start making a fuss, do you WANT us to be here all night?
C: If you're all going, Des and I might as well come too, what d'you say Des, get a bit of good mountain air?

He scoops Des out of the back of the car as the border guards share looks, and Helen prepares to get totally stropped up.

F: *Mainfatti . . .*
(Sir, please don't worry . . .)
H: Colum, you're looking like a . . .

At that moment Giorgio spots Colum's Gilera T-shirt. His fixed ladykiller smirk dissolves into a smile of genuine, incredulous joy.

G: *Gilera! Madonna mia! GuardaFedlacamicianocicredilngles'con . . .*
(Gilera! Fuck, man, can you credit it, an Englishman in a fucking vintage Gilera T-shirt!)
F: *EvediinfattiGilera'chemiracoloehh!*
(Gilera! It's a miracle!)

They converge on Colum, the visa, the camera and their nefarious intentions totally forgotten. Helen and Angel might as well have dissolved away, as the three men bond in a delirious huddle.

15 July – Phone call: Madge to Angel

M: So I'm here, pumpkin, waiting for you, it's juuust gorgeous . . .
A: Mom! I'm really busy right now.
M: You are? Doing what?
A: I can't tell you, anyhow it doesn't matter, look . . .
M: But you're in the car, right? So what's so . . .
A: Look, I'm expecting this like crucial call okay?
M: Crucial? From who . . .
A: I'll see you later, whenever okay Mom? I've gotta like hang up now. *(hangs up phone)*
M: *(to herself)* Gee thanks Ernie, glad I took the time to make that call . . .

15 July – E-mail: Madge to Ernie

From: Madge Handelman [madge@handy.com]
To: Ernestine Short [ernie@ernie.com]

Sweets
not sure what the fus was about Angel – she seems aokay. Could't talk for long owing to crisiss loonig over this kiddo situation. We have have HAVE to cast her this week. My ass is on the libe here and between us two they already think I took a big risk hiring you like I did, sometiems I wonder if it was wise myself, Soi you'd better come through with this!!!! and by the way you shoul probably tone down the expenses claims for them oment.

here's the latest story outline, you'll see by the italics kid can now be any colour of the rainbow, Grace'll roll with it if we top up her entourage alowances.

Weather here in Toscana glorious. (Leater separates capital of the world half an hour away.)

big kiss M

----

15 July – Story synopsis of major studio picture *Bitter Pills*

STORY
Joe Mitchum is a guy everybody envies – chief car mechanic to one of the biggest stars in Hollywood, with a stunning wife, Kelly, a grade-school teacher, and an adored adoptive daughter, Fawn, he spends his days polishing Ferrari engine blocks and his nights singing his baby girl to sleep and making passionate love to Kelly. The only other thing that marks Joe out is his amazing good looks, and from working on cars he's developed a physique that makes women swoon. But Joe is a one-woman, straight-up kind of a guy. Then tragedy strikes, as Fawn, who was adopted as a baby in mysterious circumstances, develops a life-threatening illness. Joe spends every penny he has scouring the world for a solution, but to no avail, and time is running out as Fawn gets weaker by the day. Finally, Joe hears of a doctor in the Bahamas who may have the answer. Joe sells his beloved vintage Mustang to pay the air fare for himself and Fawn. Fawn barely makes it, but when they meet the doctor, Dr Ingrid JayeGold,

she immediately produces a drug made from a secret formula known only to herself that relieves Fawn's symptoms. Dr JayeGold is a person of colour, with a stunning, panther-like beauty, and something about her strikes Joe with an uncanny shock of recognition as soon as they meet. Dr JayeGold also experiences a shock of recognition – *despite the fact that Fawn, the product of a relationship with a white boy she dated against the wishes of her strictly conventional community, is not a person of colour*, she immediately knows the child as her own baby, given up forcibly for adoption at the insistence of her high-school head teacher, who wanted nothing to get in the way of her favourite pupil's professional future. Dr JayeGold, maddened by grief at seeing her child again in this condition, gives no hint of the truth but agrees to treat Fawn, and Joe, unknown to Kelly, remortgages his house to pay the bill. Back home, Fawn progresses by leaps and bounds. Her parents and her beloved collie Laddy are delighted to see her back to her old self. But all too soon the drugs are about to run out and Joe goes back to Dr JayeGold, this time alone. Dr JayeGold knows he has no more money. And she is seething with secret bitterness against all white female teachers. She wants her child back – and she wants a father for her child. But first, Kelly has to be out of the picture. She tells Joe she'll treat Fawn without money. He's overjoyed – how can he thank her? Then she tells him her price. For every month's supply of drugs, a night of passion with him . . .

But Joe's boss, megastar Silvano Stallion, has always secretly lusted after Kelly. And one day Joe, overcome by the agony of his dilemma, reveals to Silvano that without truckloads of cash their beloved Fawn will die. The next time Silvano gets Kelly alone, he offers to pay for Fawn's treatment, if she becomes his mistress.

So now both of them, unknown to each other, are racked by the same terrible agonizing dilemma. But neither dares confess . . .

From: Ernestine Short [ernie@ernie.com]
To: Madge Handelman [madge@handy.com]

Message received and understood. Great news re leather pants potential.

See ya VERY soon E

----

15 July – In the car: heading for Turin

A general air of *dolce vita* pervades the car, except for the corner where Angel's sitting, pretending to read a magazine and willing her phone to ring. Colum is mentally reviewing the extremely enjoyable half-hour he has just spent talking sign language about the 1957 road bike championships, and Gilera's place in history. The motorway has given way to a fairly narrow three-lane road. Helen is driving in what she imagines to be Italian style, i.e. fast, dangerously, and leaning on the horn.

H: Ah, *la bella Italia!* There's only one way to drive on these roads, you know, just have an iron nerve and go as fast as they do.

She hoots a couple more times for good measure.

H: Hey, I just remembered that joke – what's the Italian definition of a nanosecond?
C: Spare me the suspense.
H: It's the interval between the lights changing to green and the car behind hooting you!!

She hoots again, and quite unnecessarily overtakes the car in front, narrowly missing an oncoming truck, and pulling in right in front of another car, which brakes sharply.

C: I feel I should draw your attention to something here.
H: Oh yeah? What's that?
C: You're actually the only person hooting between here and Turin.
D: Mum!!!!
H: Oh nonsense, they hoot all the . . .
D: Mum!!!!!!
C: If you stopped yourself for a minute, you might . . .
D: MUM!!!!

Helen swivels round. Colum covers his eyes.

H: WHAT????
D: Do they have *Teletubbies* in Italy?

Helen swerves back into the fast lane, just as the car behind her decides to get back its former ground. Facing imminent death, the other driver emits a sharp and prolonged hoot of protest. Helen rights the steering wheel in the nick of time.

H: (*to Colum*) There, you see! You're talking nonsense as usual.
D: MUM!! DO THEY???

At this moment Des's query is joined by an anguished wail from the seat next to him. Angel throws her phone at Des and collapses in tears. Des cries out in pain and bursts into tears as well. Helen nearly crashes again.

H: For GOD'S SAKE!! I'm trying to keep us all alive here!!

Colum turns, gives Des a hug and retrieves the phone.

C: *(to Des)* You're fine. More to the point, do they have Magnum in Italy? I tell you what, this is probably the world capital of ice cream we've come to here. Any flavour you can possibly imagine, they've got it.

Des makes a big effort and stops crying.

D: Do they have lion and tiger flavour? With . . . with butter and jam?
C: Absolutely. Not on every corner, mebbe, but we'll find it. What's up, Angel?

Angel mutters something unintelligible through her sobs and her hair.

C: I can't understand you. Is it your tummy again?
D: Does your tummy nosebleed hurt still? Teddy POdge had a . . .

Angel looks up, sweeps her hair back dramatically and shouts:

A: NO!!! It's my PHONE!!! It's run out!!!
H: Is that all?
C: You can charge it up just as soon as we get to the hotel . . .
A: My charger doesn't work here! I don't have the right plug!!
C: I guess if you need to make an urgent call, you could use . . . Helen?
H: Excuse me, I have to concentrate on the road.
A: It's no good!! He only has this number and I don't have his!!!!
C: Who does???

A: We have to find a plug for my charger, right now!!!
C: We do?
H: I am NOT going to spend my only morning in the historic city of Turin looking for a mobile phone adaptor plug!! I am NOT!!!
D: Mum!! I'm hungry Mum!!
H: And that's FINAL!!!

The Parents' Handy Italian–English Phrase Book – 2003 Edition

Chapter 1: At the Shops

Asking the Way
Excuse me, gentle sir/madam, but could you direct me to the nearest dealer in telephonic equipment? No, I do not need an electrician. I need a piece of equipment to insert into a wall that will enable the machine that gives power to my mobile telephone to replenish itself. What is the brand of the machine in question? It is Nokia. No, it is not Olivetti or Siemens or Italtel. Yes, I am aware that this is not an Italian brand. I believe that it is, in fact, Japanese. Gentle sir/madam is almost certainly correct in stating that had I bought an Italian telephone in the first place, I would not now be in this predicament. But alas! Too late! Is there an agent for foreign telephonic equipment here in Turin? There is! But it is where? It is in a far distant suburb.

Calling Ahead
Perhaps it would indeed be advisable to telephone them first to ensure that they can indeed provide the item in question. Ah, but my telephone is not working. How foolish indeed I was to forget that. Yes, I do have another telephone, but it is in the possession of my wife, who is with my son in an unknown location. Would it perhaps be possible to borrow the telephone here in your valued

establishment to make that call? Yes, I understand that I am intending to call a competitor of yours. Yes, I am indeed very well aware that you have a livelihood to earn and many children to feed. Gentle sir/madam is most kind to indicate to me the public telephones only a few hundred metres down the road. Thank you.

Using a Public Phone
Excuse me, gentle sir/madam, but could you kindly advise me on what sort of change I need to operate this public telephone? Yes, I said change – money. Ah, the public telephones do not operate with money. How do they operate, if you please? With tokens. And where, gentle sir/madam, might I obtain one of these tokens? At the tobacconist. Where, please, is the tobacconist? How fortunate, just here on the corner. But today is Monday? Forgive me, I do not immediately understand the significance of that gesture in which you slapped your hand to your forehead. Ah, Monday is the weekly day of repose for the tobacconist. Is there, perhaps, another place where a single token might be obtained? There is a bar that sells cards which also operate the phone. Where, please, gentle sir/madam, is the bar? Two streets away? Thank you very much.

Buying Phone Tokens
Excuse me, gentle sir/madam, but could I please buy a credit card for the operation of a public phone? What is the network of the public phone? Is it Siemens, Olivetti or Italtel? Ah, each of the networks has a different system of cards. I very much fear that, foolishly, I did not commit that detail to memory before I left the phone to walk the several hundred metres here. Perhaps, to be safe, I should buy a card for each of the networks. Yes, I am a rich foreigner with more money than brains. I also have with me here this highly distressed young girl who – yes – no,

she is only twelve. Yes, twelve. No, she is not my daughter but . . . Gentle sir/madam, I think you have misunderstood the situation. If you could just please provide me with the cards? How much do I owe you? Sixty euros? But that is a large amount of money! Is it the minimum denomination of these cards? It is not, but the cheaper cards are more popular and have run out. That is indeed a most unforeseeable and unfortunate circumstance. Yes, gentle sir/madam, that is all. Good day.

Making the Phone Call
Excuse me, gentle sir/madam, but am I communicating with the Turin representative of Nokia? I am! But how fortunate! Yes, gentle sir/madam, I am indeed in need of a piece of equipment. But you are closing in half an hour? Can I drive to you from where I am in half an hour? Where am I? In truth, gentle sir/madam, I am not exactly sure of the name of this location. But there is a taxi rank just here. Please, gentle sir/madam, do not leave before I arrive. Yes, I will make every effort to come with the greatest possible haste. Yes, I am sure it will be worth your while.

At the Shop
Gentle sir/madam, how kind it was of you to remain here waiting. Yes, I do indeed know how sacred is the hour of lunch here in Italy. I hope not to occupy more than a few minutes of your most valuable time. Yes, it is this adaptor for the charger of my young friend's mobile phone, which will enable it to be plugged into an Italian socket and recharge her telephone, so that she can make and receive calls on it. Yes, the plug adaptor. Yes, the one I have in my hand. What is it that you say? I can obtain the plug adaptor at any electrical shop? But not here? Yes, I am sure that in the centre of town, where I have just been,

there are such shops on every corner. Yes, of course I will now leave you in peace to eat your lunch. If we must wait until the shops reopen at three o'clock, perhaps we too will partake of some lunch.

Excerpt from Ice Cream Menu: Antica Caffe e Gelateria 'La Cornucopia', Torino (pp. 74–8)

LISTINO GELATI

Gelati Assortiti – Vari Gusti di Frutta
Fragola, lampone, myrtillo, fighi, limone, arancia dolce, arancia amaro, ciliege, uva, banana, coco, mango, ananas, pesca, pera – etc.

Gelati Assortiti – Vari Gusti di Noce
nocciola, mandorle, noce, pignola, praline, torrone, nocciola bruciata, marron glace, pistaccio – etc.

Gelati Assortiti – Vari Gusti di Crema
Crema, vaniglia, crema caramella, panna, pannacotta, zabaglione, yaourt, uova, fior di latte – etc.

Gelati Assortiti – Vari Gusti di Liquori
Strega, crema di banana, cointreau, grappa, Bayleys, rumraisin, amaro, amarena – etc.

Gelati Assortiti – Vari Gusti al Cioccolata
Cioccolata nera, cioccolata amaro, cioccolata al latte, stracciatella, choc-chip, cioccolata bianco, sciroppo di cioccolata, tartufo, gianduja – etc.

Affogati Vari
– al caffe, alla cioccolata al rhum, al brandy, allo Stock, al sambuca, al whisky – etc

Granite Vari
– al caffe, alla lampone, alla cioccolata, al limone, al pompelmo – etc.

Addizionata Di

- sciroppo di cioccolata, di banana, di fragola, di lampone, di amarena
- pezzetti di cioccolata, di liquirizia, di marron glace, di nocciola, di grani di caffe
- nocciole entiere, noci entieri, noci in polvere, nocciole in polvere, coco grattugiato, cioccolata grattugiata
- fragole fresche, lampone fresche, myrtilli freschi, pesca fresca, ananas fresca, banana fresca
- panna montata, panna semplice
- liquore di Strega, di sambuca, brandy, whisky, grappa, fior di vita

2 Gusti – 4E
3 Gusti – 6E
4 Gusti – 7E
Panna Montata Supp – 8E

Coppe Classiche 15E
Banana split
Knickerbocker glory
Pesca Melba
Pera Bella Helena
Cioccolata Fudge Sundae

Coppe Della Casa
Coppa Splendida
- gelati vaniglia, torrone e lampone, sciroppo di caffe, panna, noci

Coppa Magnifica
- gelati coco, fragola, marron glace e straciatella, goccie di cioccolata, fragole fresche, panna, biscotto

Coppa Olimpica
- gelati cioccolata amara, stracciatella, crema caramel, rumraisin e banana, goccie di cioccolata, sciroppo di cioc-

colata e di lampone, noci, banana fresca, fragole fresche, panna, crema di gianduja, biscotti (2)

– Possiamo anche fare le coppe 'al su gusto' – prezzi s.c. –

15 July – Helen and Des at the Antica Caffe e Gelateria 'La Cornucopia', Torino

They are seated either side of a small table, which is almost entirely filled with the Coppa Olimpica. It is a Matterhorn of ice cream, cream, fruit, chocolate syrup, nuts and other assorted local wildlife, surmounted by several cigar biscuits and a pink paper parasol.

Each of them has a spoon, with which they are making carefully planned inroads via their favourite elements. They have already eaten almost half of the original structure, which is clearly impressive, even to the blasé waiter hovering near by. It's probably a safe guess that nobody except the most gullible and greedy tourist ever orders a Coppa Olimpica, and that few of those consume more than the highest slopes before admitting defeat.

It's also a safe guess that the waiters leaven their boredom by taking bets on how much of the Olimpica will be left, and that there's a bet on this one right now.

Helen carefully loads a combination of chocolate and crème caramel ice creams, a strawberry slice, some chocolate syrup and whipped cream on to her spoon, and swallows it blissfully.

H: What d'you think, Des – do the Italians know ice cream or what?
D: *(mouth bursting)* They didn't have a Magnum! You promised me a Magnum Mum!!

Clearly this is not the first time this complaint has been heard. Helen puts down her spoon and emits an exaggerated, I'm-a-parent-and-this-is-my-cross sigh.

H: I'm terribly sorry. I somehow thought that this giant mound of everything that's most delicious in the world, hand made from top-quality fresh ingredients by master craftsmen of several hundred years' combined experience, might do instead, for once. Clearly I was wrong. Shall I send it back?

She gestures to the waiter, who immediately hurries up, believing he's about to win his bet.

W: (*leaning in to remove it*) Posso?
D: No!

... and frantically digs his spoon in, pulling it out attached to a lump of ice cream the size of a tennis ball, which he is about to cram into his mouth. Helen waves the waiter away. He retreats, grudgingly, but continues to hover near by. Helen stops Des's hand and edits the spoonful down to something he can manage.

H: A good rule of thumb, sweetness, is not to try to swallow anything larger than your head.
D: Pythons can!
H: Pythons have a week to sit around digesting.

Des suddenly remembers something else and stops eating again.

D: They didn't have lion and tiger flavour! You said they'd have...
H: (*casually*) Oh, that's in the next place. This café is the one specialising in fruit and chocolate ice creams, so the wild animal and cleaning-fluid flavours will probably be around the corner somewhere.
D: Can we go there now?
H: No, because we said we'd wait here for the others. I think I might have a coffee, though, just to help it down. I'm getting quite full, aren't you?
D: No.

15 July – Meanwhile – Ernie's nightmare: The open casting call

An anonymous industrial estate in Acton, West London. The street is bleak and deserted, but for a long, long line of little girls, stretching away to infinity. There are curly blonde moptops, sultry brunette toddlers, vivacious freckled redheads, serene, olive-skinned Japanese, even the odd pair of twins. Each of them is accompanied by a mother, laden with coat hangers, portfolios, shoe bags and make-up cases. The little girls are staring each other out, making rude faces, casually practising triple pirouettes or arpeggios up to high G – whatever will freak out and frighten off the opposition.

The line snakes twice around the outside of one of the units and in at the door. Inside, it's huge, bleak and empty, but for an office chair and table at one end, at which Ernie sits, a pad and pen in front of her, besieged by the tidal wave of infant talent. The open casting is in progress.

It appears that, owing to the proliferation of commercials work, special audition numbers have changed a bit in the last few years.

E: Next! Er – Jodie?

A blonde in a Baby Spice miniskirt and teeny bandeau steps forward, puts her head on one side and says 'Miaoww!' Her mother steps up beside her.

JM: Jodie's speciality is pet food commercials, she's a total natural with anything on four legs.

Jodie wiggles her baby hips as she recites in a high monotone:

J: Hi! I'm Jodie *(shaking a tiny, mewing kitten from her skirt)* – and this is Twinkle! *(scoops it up and cuddles it)* I love ALL animals, I never pull their hair or tweak their tails *(rising to a squeak)* – and ALL animals love me!!

JM: She only does mornings, she has to have her own chef, and I'll be responsible for her hair and make-up.

Jodie and Jodie's mother stand confronting Ernie.

E: Um – not sure we have any animals in this piece, I'll let you . . .
JM: Nonsense, if it's a kidpic it's got to have animals. They'll be in there. You haven't read the script.
E: You may be right, she's certainly very . . .
J: *(to Ernie, winsomely)* Can YOU resist the Twinkle twirl?

Jodie holds Twinkle over her head and pirouettes very fast on one toe. Ernie stares down at her pad, pretends to write and says:

E: Thanks, Jodie, Jodie's mum! Next! Next is, er, Sadie!

Sadie's mop of tangerine curls is perfectly set off by her OshKosh dungarees, cute little check shirt, and mini-bandanna. Sadie's mum barges past Jodie and her mum, and dumps a huge portfolio on the table. Sadie poses, turns and twirls as her mother recites:

SM: Sadie – IS – Food! Though you'd never know it, would you, she's a stock Age 5, look at that flat tummy and those identical profiles, perfect from any angle isn't she?

She reaches into her bag and unwraps a large peanut butter and jam sandwich, which she solemnly hands to her daughter. Sadie begins to eat.

SM: If Sadie spills, we refund her fee. Guaranteed. And just watch her lips as it goes in. Never a smudge with Sadie on the show!

Sadie's little rosebud mouth is indeed heavily coated with pearlised rosebud lipstick, which is indeed surviving the sandwich miraculously intact. Sadie's mum riffles the portfolio under Ernie's nose.

SM: Here we go, baked beans, peas with a knife and fork, ice cream – look at that, not a drop, and here in this Coca-Cola piece, show me another five-year-old who can . . .

Sadie dramatically interjects:

S: And LOOK!

She spreads her hands, pouts her lips, shakes her lovable mop – and it's true, there's not a smear or a crumb anywhere.

E: That's certainly a remarkable talent, but . . .
SM: Of course I can't have her studies interrupted, she's learning Ukrainian and Vietnamese this year so she'll be bringing her tutor, and . . .
E: *(shouting over her)* Well, thank you, Sadie, what a lovely eater you are indeed, you can come to tea at my house any time, I'll call your mum very . . .
SM: *(steaming right ahead)* So I'll have her agent call you in the next hour, come on Sadie that's enough, I don't want to be stuffing you with laxatives all day.

She grabs the remains of the sandwich from a protesting Sadie and marches her off, already speed-dialling the agent. Ernie raises her head and sees, to her horror, that the banks have broken and the entire army is thundering towards her, screaming its wares.

'Maisie does hair with no tears or tangles, look at the sheen on these curls!' . . . 'I'm Sally and I can run downstairs and up and down again and I NEVER trip or fall over!' . . . '. . . doesn't look good in plaids or stripes, we'll need total wardrobe approval' . . . 'LOOK AT THESE LEGS!' . . . 'DOUBLE BACK FLIP ON TO HER HEAD!' . . . 'GRADE NINETEEN PIANO!' . . . MEMORISE A FOUR-HUNDRED-PAGE BOOK IN TWO MINUTES!' . . .

Ernie jams her hands over her ears and tries to turn and flee, but the entire floor in all directions is waist deep in children. They reach out pudgy hands to her, pulling at her clothes and holding out phones, palms, head shots . . . Ernie shuts her eyes, opens her mouth and screams . . .

Back to the Antica Caffe e Gelateria, Torino

Helen and Des are still wading their way through the Coppa Olimpica. Helen gestures to the waiter, who rushes up.

W: *Terminato?*

He's about to whisk away the remains. Helen and Des simultaneously grab hold of it.

D: *(perfect imitation)* Terrrminaaato?

The waiter is going off these two, fast.

H: *No, grazie, non* – not *finito* yet!
W: *(grimly) Perfetto!*

He's about to be the first waiter ever to lose a bet. His fellow *camerieri* are smirking visibly.

D: *(through another huge spoonful)* Mum, why is he talking like that waiter at the Pizza Express?
H: *(to Des)* Shh, sweetie, he's Italian. *(to waiter)* But *per favore, un cappuccino? E un . . . un glassa di aqua.*
W: *Congasosenza?*
D: *Congasosenzzzzaaaa?*
H: Pardon? I mean, um – *pardone?*

The waiter rolls his eyes and speaks with slow emphasis.

W: *Lei Vuole Aqua Con Gas, O Aqua Naturale?*
D: *Leii Vuooole Akwua Con Gass, O Akwua Naturrrale?*

The waiter gives Des a full-on murderous look. Helen shushes and frowns at Des. Her phone rings.

H: (Hi? Ernie! Sweetie, how . . . hang on a minute) Er, tap water, *per favore*. (What's wrong? Darling, you're crying! . . .)
W: (*sarcastically*) Benissimo.
D: Bennisssimo!!!!!
H: Des! Stop it! (No, sorry Ernie it's Des.) Stop tormenting him, Des. And say sorry.
D: Sorrrrrry!

The waiter stalks off. Des returns to practising Italian gestures with his ice-cream spoon, to the detriment of his previously clean T-shirt.

H: (So what's up with you? Are you coming? . . . Christ, really . . . You poor thing, I can imagine – a hundred and fifty? . . . In one morning? . . . And their mums? Why did you need to audition . . . oh, I see what you mean, yes, showbiz mums, what a nightmare. Hang on, Des wants to talk to you . . .)
D: (ERNIE!! Ernie we're eating ice cream, it's bigger than a house or a planet and it's all covered in chocolate and nuts and bananas and I'm winning but they don't have Magnum here! . . . Yes!!! . . . And the waiter talks like that waiter in the Pizza Express in London, you know he says 'TerminatochevuoleMadamaCioccolatocremapiucioccolatocappucinobenissimo!!' just like that yes!!! . . . Oh okay byeee can we see you soon? . . . Mum she wants to talk to you again . . .)
H: (. . . What, Des? . . . Oh yeah, he's been doing that all through France as well, driving us all mad, don't know where he gets it from, certainly not his boring old parents, turns out to be a total mimic . . . How old? He's just about to be five, you know that. Why do you want to . . . Yes,

you know he does, he totally lives in his imagination, always has . . . What, you might come after all? Fab! So . . . Okay, sure, hasta mañana baby or – no that's wrong isn't it, Ciao sweetheart!!!)

15 July – Text from Ernie's mobile to Madge's mobile

```
OK MY HVE CHLD BT NEED 2 KNW IF VTL GIRL? UK
GRLS MPSSBL ND WY BYND PRCE BRCKT. BT IF CLD
CHNG 2 BY, KD N QSTN HS LMTLSS CHRM, SWT NTRE
ND V.V.V. CHP. LT ME KNW SNST – E.
```

Comparative Excerpts from Guide to Historic Monuments of Turin and Guide to Historic Restaurants of Turin

The Palazzo Nuova, one of the treasures of Torinese art . . .	The Poggia Nuova, one of the treasures of Torinese culture and gastronomy . . .
. . . has been in the hands of the Forlani family for five hundred years.	. . . has been in the hands of the Ostiani family for five hundred years.
Its towering battlements, serried windows and awesome, intricately decorated doorways . . .	Its towering platters of seafood, serried vegetables and awesome, intricately decorated desserts . . .
. . . give promise of the revelations to come. Once inside . . .	. . . give promise of the revelations to come. Once inside . . .
. . . choose your route, either via the sinuous, twisting corridors and jewel-like antechambers of the first building . . .	. . . choose your meal, either from the sinuous, twisting fettucine and jewel-like antipasti of the first courses . . .

... or the dark, sombre apartments and glistening armoury of the ducal family. Do not on any account omit the ...

... imposing Galleria Grande, the family treasurehouse, crammed with art from around the world, and paintings from every school of the Renaissance ...

... a heady mix of the urbane and the earthy ...

... perfectly complemented by its setting in an elegant chamber of the Forlanis' former residence. And above all, leave time for ...

... the Tesoro Cellini, a transcendent evocation of fruit, flowers and wildlife ...

... truly the apogee of the goldsmith's art, and a fitting end to your tour.

... or the dark, unctuous meats and glistening fish of the second courses. Do not on any account omit the ...

... imposing Pastucci Grande, the family speciality, crammed with spices from around the world, and meat from every part of the pig ...

... a heady mix of the urbane and the earthy ...

... perfectly complemented by its setting in an elegant case of Pasta Frolla. And above all, leave room for ...

... the Crema Cellini, a transcendent combination of fruit, sponge cake and cream ...

... truly the apogee of the pastry-chef's art, and a fitting end to your meal.

15 July – Bill for lunch at the 'Poggia Nuova', Turin

```
Benvenuti  alla  'Poggia  Nuova'         15/7/15.04

Coperti:      4

1 x fettuccini 'Poggia Nuova'            €26.50
1 x spaghetti alla Bolognese             €28.00
```

1 x antipasto misto	€31.00
1 x insalata verde semplice	€8.00
1 x Pastucci Grande	€35.00
1 x nodo di vitello Principessa	€45.00
pure di patate	€9.50
zucchini alla Giudea	€9.50
1 x bistecca alla fiorentina	€50.00
patate al rosmarino	€9.50
spinaci saltati al tartufo bianco	€20.00
2 x crema Cellini @ €30.00	€60.00
panna supp., 2 @ €4.00	€8.00
1 x gelato 'BiancaNeve'	€16.00
panna supp.	€4.00
1 x Torre di Selva Suprema merlot	€75.00
1 x grappa antica ven. 1995	€30.00
1 x acqua con gas	€5.00
2 x spremuta di arancia @ €8.00	€16.00
2 x Diet Coke @ €8.00	€16.00
3 x caffe @ €.5.00	€15.00
IMPORTO DA PAGARE	€517.00
Serv. 12.5% a scelta	€64.63
TOTALE	**€581.63**

Grazie e arrivederci!

15 July, afternoon – The view from Helen's window

There's a reason all Italian women over thirty wear voluminous black to below the knee. It's called pasta. There's also a reason why the visible remains of their legs are festooned with varicose veins like an Aran sweater, and it's called ice cream. I really thought, when Colum and Angel arrived back all triumphant with the stupid plug, that I had a chance of getting them to a museum, but his gimlet eye was not slow to notice that Des and I, given an entirely free choice where to spend the intervening hours, had occupied them not trudging round a gallery but enjoyably testing the miraculous properties of Lycra-reinforced stretch denim by attempting to prove that ice cream, being essentially all water, disappears to nothing inside you, in the same way as it does on the plate.

And when he added that there was, as I had amply demonstrated, more than one way to appreciate a national culture, and that though there were very few Britons you could stop on Kilburn High Road who would know a Perugino from an Uccello, every one of them would unerringly recognise a plate of spaghetti Bolognese, I thought I'd stop him there before he reminded me of the Harvard Business School's flawless proof that pizza was the first truly global food, and give in gracefully.

Let's just hope that Madge meant it about paying our bills, because if not Des is skipping primary school altogether and going to work as a busker with his unforgettable rendition of 'Hop Little Bunny' instead.

It was afterwards that I had my inspiration – fuelled, as usual, by a massive chocolate shock to the adrenal receptors. What is the point of having bought all these huge and informative guidebooks if we're just going to go and look for ourselves anyway? Why keep a dog and bark? (etc.) All we have to do is imprison Angel in the car until she's memorised the major monuments and artworks of all the Italian cities we're supposed to have been to, and Madge'll never know the difference.

Needless to say, Madam, having spent lunch-time sulking over a Diet Coke on the grounds that passion had robbed her of all other appetites, and anyhow she needed to sit on her newly restored phone like the goose on its first golden egg, was fairly resistant to the idea of spending the next twelve hours in a superheated mobile crammer, but luckily at that moment her phone finally rang, and it turned out — surprise, surprise — that Les Loxleys, fresh from their cultural conquest of south-eastern France, have plans for Tuscany too. Suddenly she was all for getting there as fast as possible, which seemed a perfect moment to point out that it was entirely up to us how many hours, or indeed days, it took to get to the villa, and a spot of cooperation in our harmless little game was probably the wisest course, in this light.

Of course she was furious for an hour or so, but it's amazing how rational even the most unpromising human mind can turn out to be *in extremis*. Anyhow, I'm rather proud of my Italian Cultural Quiz, especially its carefully planned slant towards subject areas where our little hostage might have a pre-existing expertise. I think I might look into its commercial possibilities, if we ever get back to England.

Cheat Your Way Through Italian Culture

Section One – Florence
1   The Duomo is also known as:
a)   Santa Maria dei Fiori
b)   Santa Lucia
c)   Santa Gotstuckupthechimni

2   Red, green and white are:
a)   The colours of the Duomo's marble decorations
b)   The colours of the Italian World Cup team
c)   The colours of Benetton's line for the autumn

3   The important Florentines buried here include:
a)   Taddeo Gaddi
b)   Luciano Pavarotti
c)   Mario Testino

4   The name of the famous Michelangelo statue in the neighbouring museum is:
a) Panettone
b) Pantene
c) Pietà

5   The Palazzo Vecchio was, until 1565, the official residence of which family?
a) Medici
b) Gucci
c) Missoni

6   It was decorated by:
a) Trussardi
b) Vasari
c) Tiffani

7   Which of these is correct?
a) It contains the charming Appartamenti Monumentali and the huge Salone dei Cinquecento
b) It contains the huge Appartamenti Monumentali and the charming Salone dei Cinquecento
c) Who knows? It's closed for restoration until 2010.

8   The Basilica di Santa Maria Novella was built by:
a) Dominican monks between 1279 and 1357
b) Franciscan monks between 1845 and 1846
c) Have you ever seen a monk laying bricks? That's what the offerings pay for.

9   Which of these is NOT buried in the Basilica di Santa Croce?
a) Machiavelli
b) Dante
c) Fendi

10 Which of these is correct?

a) The Bargello contains sculpture by Donatello and fashions by Donatella
b) The Bargello contains sculpture by Donatella and fashions by Donatello
c) Nobody wears Versace in Italy any more

11 The most famous work of art in the Uffizi is:
a) Michelangelo's *Holy Family*
b) Botticelli's *Birth of Venus*
c) Fettucini's *Alfredo*

12 The most famous family rivalry in Florentine history was between:
a) Montague and Capulet
b) Medici and Guiccardini
c) Armani and Versace

Section Two – Supplementary Questions
Each correct answer entitles the player to set a supplementary question of their own choosing.

Helen's Supplementary Questions:

1 Cappuccino gets its name from:
a) The cap of foam sitting on top of it
b) The Capuchin monks whose robes were the same colour
c) The hood of the robe of these same Capuchin monks that, to an Italian eye, looks the same as a pile of steamed milk on top of a cup of espresso

2 Which of these is NOT a film by Fellini?
a) *La Strada*
b) *La Dolce Vita*
c) *La Cucharacha*

3 Name the odd one out:
a) Baci Perugina

b) Ferrero Rocher
c) Paolo Uccello

Des's Supplementary Questions:

1   Wall's ice cream is called in Italy:
a) Algida
b) Semifredda
c) Lasagna

2   The Italian for Magnum is:
a) Magno
b) Magna
c) Magnum

Colum's Supplementary Questions

(For some reason the concept of the simple multiple-choice answer seemed to elude him. But I generously gave him bonus points for detail anyhow.)

1
Q: What is the motorcycle link between the Minardi Formula One racing car team, based in Bergamo, and ants?
A: Minardi, which currently uses Ferrari engines, used to be called FondMetal, who make aluminium castings for, among others, Ferrari. FondMetal is run by two brothers with the surname Rumi. During the 1960s their father used the castings company fortune – and lavish government grants – to diversify into motorcycles and scooters. Their most famous scooter was made in Bergamo entirely from cast aluminium, painted cream and called the Rumi Formichino. Formichino means Little Ant.

   Bonus points can be won by guessing that the Formichino won its class in the famous Italian road race called the Bol d'Or in 1962 and was henceforth known as the Formichino Bol d'Dor and from then on

. . . okay, I think we've heard enough about that. Next!!

2
Q: The Honda Goldwing is so heavy that motorcyclists call it the Leadwing. Which Italian bike had legitimate reason to use the name?
A: The world's fastest piston-engined plane was the fearsome Messerschmitt-based fighter built by Aermacchi in Rimini during the war. After the war Aermacchi were banned from building aircraft and turned their engineering resources to motorcycles. They built beautifully light, well-balanced bikes that won lots of races. Their most famous was a 350cc machine nicknamed the Ala d'Oro, which means Gold Wing. The official name of the Ala d'Oro was . . .

Owner's Directions to 'Villa Lucida' near San Gimignano, Tuscany

'Leave autostrada by exit 32, I think it's 32, anyway the one before the Siena exit, if you get to the Siena exit you've gone too far and will have to turn around at the next exit but one, the next exit doesn't have a return, then go right and under the motorway or if you come from the other direction go left and over it, and you'll pretty soon be on a small road labelled "San Gimignano" or "Lucca". Go along this for a while up a hill and down another hill only not too far down because before you get to the bottom you have to find the turning left up to the village, which isn't actually labelled as such but does have a sign saying "Festa dei Porcini". If you get to the bottom of the hill you will know you have gone too far because you will be in the cemetery.

'Once on the road to the village you will be winding up a hill, follow the road round, it will get pretty narrow and go through some woods, then it goes through some more woods but in between there's *a rather lovely view of the towers of San Gimignano but do not stop to look at it because you will be on a blind corner and the post van sometimes comes through here pretty fast.*

'Then the woods get a bit thinner and on your left there's a small track, but don't take it and don't take the next one either, which is more of a small road really, but the one after that which has a hazel thicket on the corner and usually a milk churn waiting to be picked up, unless you arrive in the morning of course.

'So just follow that little track along for about four hundred metres, you'll pass a couple of outhouses on the way and a barn and the gate of the villa is shortly after that on your right, don't be put off by the shabby paint it's to deter burglars, and hoot your horn three times at the gate but it may take a while for Andrea to answer because he's often at the far end of the garden.

'Welcome!!'

15 July, early evening – Helen, Colum, Des and Angel, driving through Tuscany

Colum is driving the car along a narrow, picturesque, wooded road. Helen, having undone all buttons, zips and anything else that will help her to breathe, is attempting to navigate from the directions provided by Madge. Des is sleeping, and Angel, who has miraculously effected a complete change of clothes, a hand and foot nail job, a face make-up and some silver highlights since lunch-time, is texting her friends. Night is closing in and the woods are getting dark.

H: . . . We'd never have learned half as much toiling round Florence, parking the car and paying those exorbitant entrance charges, AND we'd still be there now.
C: Pity about missing the exit from the motorway and having to drive a hundred and twenty miles further the wrong way.

H: Well, we'd have missed it anyhow following these directions. Keep your eyes peeled for that Festa dei Porcini sign.
C: Here's the cemetery.
H: At least we know that's wrong.
C: Finding this house by pure elimination could take a while.

He reverses out of the gate and sets off back along the road.

H: So the Festa dei Porcini sign should be on our right now, yes? I wish she'd given a few more indications of distance. I mean, it's all very well to be vague and Italian but she isn't even Italian anyhow, she's a novelist or something.
C: That explains a lot. Would you trust Dostoevsky's street directions?
H: Maybe not. And God forbid James Joyce. But Marcel Proust, now – he had a good memory. Could this be the seed of another world-beating quiz game?
C: Here's a turning.

He brakes sharply and swings the car up a narrow lane overhung with interlaced foliage.

H: I didn't see a sign.
C: This is the only turning we passed, so unless you fancy a night with the undead . . .
H: I've had more than enough of those in the last four days, thank you.

She peers out of the window.

H: Well, it's narrow enough, and here are the woods.
C: It's all woods for four hundred miles in every direction from here. This is the largest deciduous forest in Europe.
H: How d'you know that?

Suddenly there's a loud BANG! and something whistles past the car. Angel screams. Des wakes up and begins to wail.

H: What was that?
D: I'm sleepy! I want to go to sleep!
C: Probably a tree branch cracking. Here's the gap in the woods with the view we mustn't look at.

Another, louder BANG!!! and a sharp thud, followed by a hiss, followed by the car skidding at speed towards the opening with the lovely view and the precipice.

C: Christ!

He steers into the skid and somehow swivels the car round so it's by the side of the road, a few inches from the precipice, facing across it more or less in the opposite direction.

H: Am I being characteristically melodramatic, or is somebody shooting at us?

Des suddenly stops wailing and cheers up.

D: Are there men with guns? Will they shoot us? Can I have a gun?

Colum puts on the brake and gets out to examine the flat tyre. At this moment the car is suddenly surrounded by about fifty Italian men, armed with shotguns and large, noisily barking dogs. Helen panics.

H: NO!!!! Sorry Des, close the window love and sit very still and quiet and everything'll be fine.

Angel begins to text even faster. Finally she's in a real live adventure.

15 July, early evening – Text messages: Angel, Leila, Roma and Tilly

```
ANGEL TO LEILA
LCKLY MNGD 2 SHK OFF DRNGO FLM * JST N TM 2 HK
```

UP W MGDRMY ACTR NSTD — NGLSH GY FRM HMPSTD, +
FRM DSTNGSHD THTR FMLY. U MGHT HVE HRD F HM HS
NM S LOXLEY?

LEILA TO ROMA
NOOS JST N FRM ANGL, THS TM FNTSSNG ABT SM NGLSH
BY ACTR NMD LOXLEY, DN'T KNW F 1ST R 2ND NM. PR
GRL BVSLY HVNG WRST TM, LMST SRRY 4 HR!

ROMA TO TILLY
Y'RE FRM NTH LNDN — HV U HRD OF BY CTR CLLD
LOXLEY? PRBBLY SPTTY ND ABT 14 BY SND F IT.

TILLY TO ROMA
ACTLLY THR'S A BOY EDGAR (I SWR) LOXLEY NT AS BD
AS H SNDS, A BT YNG BT I MT HM @ PRTY @ XMS ND
HE WNT DWN A TRT (HA HA). WHY?

ROMA TO LEILA
NCRDBLY IT SMS 4 NCE THRS A SHRD F TRTH IN
ANGL'S FNTSIES. LOXLEY BY CNFRMD 2 XST, NO FRTHR
DTLS AS YT.

LEILA TO ANGEL
WOW U SR GT ARND GRL WHR DD U MT HIM &C! DISH!

ANGEL TO LEILA
MT HM @ THS MGARMNTC MNLT PERF OF — OMIGOD WE'RE
IN THE MIDDLE OF MAJOR SHOOTOUT MST B AMBSH IF
IM KDNPPD TLL MUM 2 PY RNSM ASAP LV U . . . HLP
HLP . . .

LEILA TO ROMA
ANGL FNLLY LST IT. FNCY MVIE 2NGHT?

Chapter 2 – Meeting the Natives

The Unforeseen Breakdown

Good afternoon, gentlesirs/madams! Yes, we are aware that this, though undoubtedly the finest view in all of Italy, and therefore of the world, is also a famously perilous location in which to stop a car. Yes, we English are not such careful or expert parkers of cars as the Italians, champion drivers of the world. Unfortunately we are not able to follow your most excellent advice and move our car, as we have foolishly and unwittingly driven into the path of at least one of your most effective and well-aimed rifle cartridges. Yes, sadly it has punctured our tyre. Yes, it would indeed have been much more costly had it penetrated the car's bodywork, although you are right that in that situation we would have been blessed indeed to find ourselves in the native home of the world's best car mechanics.

Local Culture

Excuse us, gentle sirs/madams, but could you perhaps explain to us why, in all innocence but undoubtedly most deservingly, we have incurred this minor misfortune? Ah, it is the first day of the open hunting season! Of course we knew that! Indeed, every red-blooded man in the world must surely awake on this morning with a song in his heart and a gun under his arm. But what is it that you are hunting with such zest and in such large numbers? Are there perhaps wild boar, fierce wolves, or giant wild cats in these woods of which we should beware? Yes, of course that was only the benighted Englishman's feeble idea of a joke! Indeed, no one could seriously believe that the land of the world's foremost hunters would have left such large and predatory pests to roam free into the twenty-first century.

Yes, now that you point it out, there is indeed a notable absence of birdsong in these woods. We too in England are fond of eating roasted birds, although I must confess that, parsimonious as we are with our ammunition, we generally prefer our prey to be larger in diameter than the bore of the weapon. Yes, that can indeed only be owing to our infamously poor aim which does not permit us to shoot off the little darling's useless head at several hundred metres, leaving its deliciously crunchy and edible body intact.

Help at Hand
It is indeed most pleasant to stand around imbibing the lessons of a great nation, but sadly we should be turning our attention to the problem of how to continue on our journey. Ah, gentle sir/madam would be only too willing to help with the jacking up and replacement of the wheel? Of course, such a task is simplicity itself to the youngest child in this most elevated of cultures. What is that? Gentle sir also happens to possess a vehicle of identical dimensions not two kilometres from here, whose spare tyre we are most welcome to exchange for our damaged one, in honour of the historical love and friendship between our two most ancient and distinguished countries? Gentle sir/madam is indeed excessively kind and generous. Yes, it is indeed no more than we had expected in this cradle of all civilisations.

Safe and Sound
Whither do we travel tonight? To a villa to which indeed the most gentle sir/madam may perhaps be able to direct us, the 'Villa Lucida'. Yes, the home of the eccentric and cheese-paring English witch whom, fortunately, we know not at all. No, we are the guests of another lady, whom we believe already to be in residence there. Yes, it is indeed

likely that she is scrawny, speaks with an American accent, and has been calling frequently and with urgency on the services of the expert and patient operatives of the telephone company. Yes, she is expecting us. Ah, you can lead us there after we have finished with the car? That is indeed generosity and helpfulness beyond what even the most cultivated and travelled English person could dare to hope. No, we are not surprised. Yes, we shall make sure to warn the scrawny American lady that her habit of running along these roads in the early morning could endanger her life after today. Yes, she will undoubtedly be as grateful as we for this warning.

15 July, early evening – Madge, power-stepping in the pool, on the phone to LA

M: No, Sandy, I did NOT say I had the kid, nor did I say I definitely would have the kid by today, I SAID I'd TRY to get you a . . . Look, put me on to Marty, okay? . . . Just get me Darling . . . Hi, Darl, Sandy's kinda lost it, just needta check absolute outside parameters for this kiddo situation, believe me I have met every kid under ten on three continents, I am breaking my balls for you Darl, plus I have this shit-hot talent scout scouring all of Europe who may have a lead, but meanwhile I've been taking time to do a little thinking outside the box, and I'm like, how about if we found you a real real smart and cute kind of a pooch, or something? . . . Yeah, that's right, a dog . . . It has to be able to speak? Well how many lines are there? I mean, there are some very very expressive dogs out there, or there's always the CGI option . . . Okay well how about a macaw? Ya know, kind of like a talking parrot or . . . No I'm not pissing you around Darling, I am TRYing to SAVE your ass if you'd only . . . Just hear me out . . .

The car with its variegated load rolls to a final stop outside the house.

M: Shit – Darl, ya gotta give me twenty seconds . . . Okay, fifteen seconds, my kid's just turned up from England and I haven't seen her in, like . . . No, I am not putting personal shit before work Darl, I . . . Look, just give me ten seconds, Darling – OMIGOD!!!!! Darl – Darl, I think . . . OMIGOD, HE'S ADORABLE!! I'll call you RIGHT BACK! OMIGOOOD!!!!

. . . and she runs right past Angel, to swoop on Des.

15 July, before dinner – Helen, by the pool

I don't believe this. Any minute now somebody will tap me on the shoulder and tell me that it's all a dream and actually it's my turn to make dinner and can we please not have baked potatoes with baked beans, again.

But meanwhile . . .

After Colum had changed the tyre with the help of the massed members of the Lower Tuscany Small Game Bird Appreciation Society and got us here, he clearly felt he'd done enough manly duties for the day and disappeared to inspect the contents of the cellar. As it was obvious that the so-called help would keel over from the cumulative effects of eighty years of Chianti and *carbonara* if he lifted anything heavier than a hankie, it was down to guess who to start unloading eight suitcases, a large pink vanity case, four cases of wine, a flagon of olive oil, a pair of very smelly child's size ten wellington boots and assorted other rubbish from the car, while Des very very slowly tore himself away from his 'I Am a Wild Hunter with a Huge Gun' dream and tumbled sleepily out.

At which point our hostess, at least I had to assume it was her, shrieked at about eight hundred decibels, dropped her phone into the pool, and ran at poor Des waving her arms and shouting hysterically, so of course, way past his normal bedtime and faced with a gibbering stranger in head-to-toe black, the poor lamb totally lost it.

At that moment, as if by magic, a taxi rolled up to the house and out slid Ernie, a vision in gold leather, who peered over her Persols and explained that Madge is in the final stages of casting some mega-budget Hollywood blockbuster and had been scouring the planet with Ernie's help for a child to play the juvenile lead, until earlier today when, hearing Des's pitch-perfect imitation of an Italian waiter, Ernie got her inspiration and rushed out to seal the deal. Apparently, in total oblivion, we have been nurturing a budding star in our modest house in NW5, and here is his chance to earn more money in two weeks than either of his parents will make in a decade.

It gets better! Ernie forced Madge into admitting that four and eleven-twelfths is probably too young even by Hollywood standards to make the journey on his own, so of course he'll need to be chaperoned by – you guessed it!

ME!!!

Finally, and just at the point when I'm seriously considering chopping in my unthanked life of rain-sodden, supermarket-bound drudgery, Fate gives me a brief moment in my very own spotlight (or at least my son's spotlight, which is bound to be several sizes too big for him on his own). I don't have to leave Colum for a sulk at my sister's – I can leave him for the red carpet at the Academy Awards!

He, of course, had to be the one negative element in the whole equation. Madge had already got on the phone to her minions to book our flights, limos, luxury accommodation etc., and Ernie was teaching Des to say 'Have a nice day' and 'Gimme five!' when he suddenly reappeared with a tumbler of grappa in one hand and a chamois leather in the other, and started talking about the corrupting effects of the cesspit of celebrity, etc.

I had two words for him: 'School fees!' That shut him up remarkably quickly, I have to say, especially after Madge promised to let him read the script, which luckily seems to be mostly about people cleaning very expensive sports cars. It doesn't make a whole lot of sense to me, at this point, but I'm sure after a day or two in LaLaLand it'll be as obvious as the horoscope in *Metro*.

First Two Pages of Script for *The Love Gift*, a Major Studio Picture

(NB: In anticipation of the failure of the search, 'poodle' has been substituted for 'little girl', throughout.)

FADE IN
EXT. SUNNY GARDEN IN MALIBU – DAY
A beautiful, tranquil, picket-fenced, southern California garden. In one corner, a SAND BOX, in which an adorable, pudgy, FOUR/XXXXEIGHT year old XXXPOODLE is playing with her toy cars.

The XXXXPOODLE is totally engrossed in her game, making 'Vroom! Vroom!' noises as she races the cars across the sand box.

Suddenly, a shadow seems to pass over the cloudless Californian sky, and an expression close to panic passes over the XXXXPOODLE's face. She drops one of her cars and her XXXpaw clutches her chest, as she calls out, faintly:

     XXXXPOODLE
   Dad! Mom! I feel weird . . .

          CUT TO:

EXT. GARAGE BLOCK OF SILVANO'S ESTATE – DAY

The garage is a little way from the sprawling, ranch-style mansion of SYLVANO STALLION, reclusive Hollywood megastar. The house is vast, immaculate, and ringed with a high-security fence.

The garage is big enough to hold eight cars abreast – gleaming Ferraris, Maseratis and Porsches. One of them is being lovingly polished by JOE (31/35/40), a regular guy with a kind of a XXXXXXXXXXBRUCE SPRINGSTEEN look about him and a physique toned to the max by years of working on cars.

He's singing to himself as he works – a classic rock anthem, e.g. XXXXXXX 'Born in the USA'. He has a great singing voice.

Other mechanics in the background are harmonizing his vocals. It's a laidback, XXXXXXXall-American scene.

Suddenly . . .

     XXXXPOODLE (O.S.)
     DAD!!! MOM!!!

JOE stops dead and drops his cleaning cloth.

     JOE
    (under his breath)
    No!! Not again!!!

He races like a cheetah across the velvet lawn.

          CUT TO:

EXT. SAND BOX – DAY
The XXXXPOODLE is lying motionless, her face

blue, still clutching her toy car, which is, poignantly, identical XXXto the one her DAD was just cleaning.

JOE arrives, breathless, at the same moment as his wife KELLY, a drop-dead gorgeous blonde/redhead/person of color, yet with an air of apparently being quite unaware of her own stunning beauty. Seeing her XXXXPOODLE lying there, KELLY screams:

                    KELLY
              NO!!! NO!! XXX/REX!!!

She throws herself, sobbing, on to the XXXXPOODLE, and runs with her toward the house, while JOE is left standing there, staring in desperation at XXXXXXXnothing.

And so on.

It seems that all the tedious business of auditioning, learning the craft, etc., is totally outmoded in today's Hollywood, where the job is to stand on a designated spot while the camera rolls, and the acting is painted on afterwards with a computer. I confessed – very honourably, I thought – that standing still wasn't Des's absolutely best thing, but I was sure that by repeating our secret code word every five seconds it could easily be accomplished. (Code word is, of course, Magnum.)

So, amazingly, all that is needed at this point is that he learn to lisp his few lines in a passable imitation of some kind of American accent and agree to forgo his wellingtons for a while, the former task apparently requiring us to leave the day after tomorrow. The star himself, who had been plaintively chanting 'Swimming pewl! Swimming pewl!' every two seconds until I finally got the picture and fished out his water wings, was initially reluctant to abandon it so soon after travelling for five purgatorial days with the sole purpose of having a good splash, but Ernie was able to reassure him that where he was going he'd have his very own swimming pewl with access day and night, except during the fleeting moments when his professional duties intervened.

All this time poor Angel had been hanging about, waiting with no success at all for her mother to notice she was there. Finally Ernie turned to her and said, 'And of course, Angel darling, you'll be on hand to show them around, won't you? Won't she, Madge?' To which, before I even had time to form the word 'Help!', Madge made her usual response of flapping one hand wildly to indicate that her phone call could not possibly be interrupted by anything so trivial as the next month of her daughter's life. Needless to say, the prospect of being let loose in her spiritual and cultural (not to mention financial) home cheered Angel up on the spot. Either that or she's already plotting her revenge. Oh well, can't think about that now.

Let's have some more of this rather excellent Chianti. I hope dinner's somewhere in the broad vicinity of ready.

15 July – E-mail: Madge to studio in California

> **From:** Madge Handelman [madge@handy.com]
> **To:** Sandy Mittelman [sandy@filmart.com]

```
Sandy!! Great News!!
Did I tell you I'd find a kid or did I tel
you? He's (yeah, a boy but hey, better than a
macaw) a total natural, but parrents non-pro
and they're kind of jitery about teir little
darling in the big bod world of Holywood etc,
it's no bigie but rather than have them read
the whole script, could you mail ober the
```

```
  story outline but mak it, you know, kinda
  loose and leaving out the adultery stuff and
  the blackmail stuf and the ilegitamite kid
  stuff and the racial tenxion stuff?
     I'm telling them two hundred k a week for
  two weeks - they won't know to ask for more
  and it'll pay for an extra Spingstein track
     (did I do well or did I do well?)
     Loveya M
  ----------------------------------
```

15 July – Helen, Colum, Des, Angel, Ernie and Madge at dinner

By now it's way past not only Des's bedtime but everybody else's, too. Helen and Ernie are nicely pickled in Chianti, Colum looks bored and sleepy, Angel is willing her phone to ring, and Des is trying to get the attention of whoever will listen — by now, nobody — to the three-hundredth rendition of his Pizza Express waiter act. Meanwhile Madge is, as usual, juggling her phone and her Palm. There's a lot of wine on the table and the remains of a basket of bread, but no sign of any other food.

E: *(to Helen)* . . . and in Beverly Hills, the restaurant on top of Barneys does a great Sunday brunch, and while you're there you could pick me up some of that Bobbi Brown cheek frost they don't export yet . . .
M: (So Jake said he can do the make-up test Tuesday morning at eight, which means we can swing by the camera department after and still be back for the voice tests at one-thirty, okay?)

Colum attempts to interrupt the flow.

C: Pardon me, Madge, but there I still have a few concerns . . .

Helen shouts over him.

H: It'll be fine, honestly Colum, what a fuss about . . .
C: Well, why can't we see the whole script?
H: Look, it's got Bruce Springsteen and fast cars in it, what more do you want, and anyway they're sending the outline, Madge just told us . . .
D: Ernie, Ernie d'you know how they talk here? They talk like this, 'Vuole unaltwobottigliadivinonon abbiamo acquagazzata' just like that! It's funny isn't it?? Ernie!!
E: *(to Des)* Lovely, Des *(back to Helen)* . . . but the best-kept secret of all has to be Fred Segal in Santa Monica, because there are just no crowds, and you'll want a bit of anonymity occasionally, the paparazzi will start to get to you believe me . . .
H: Ohhhh! Ohh I can't believe it! Ohh I'm SO excited!!!
M: (Yeah, just run that by the first AD and the line producer, who is it again? . . . Oh sure I know Sol, Sol and I . . . Yeah and get back to me tonight, okay?)

Colum thinks he may have better luck with Ernie.

C: *(to Ernie)* Do you have any idea what'll actually happen to him when he gets out there? I mean, we don't know any of these people, and . . .

He drops his voice so Madge won't hear, as though he needs to bother.

C: I'm sure she's a fine woman and all but frankly . . .
H: Colum, will you SHUT UP!!! Just because you don't understand it and for once you're being left out of . . .
C: For Christ's sake woman, the last place on earth I'd want to go anywhere near is . . .
H: Yeah, right, all those Harleys, I keep forgetting . . .

Ernie helps herself to the last of the wine, probably to keep it from Helen.

E: Colum darling, it's going to be a breeze, they adore kids over there you know and they adore the Brits even more. *(big swig)* Look at it this way, he'll be home in two weeks, clutching a happy old age for you in his little fist.

From the kitchen in the bowels of the house emerges the sound of a violent argument, with a lot of clattering and bashing of pots and pans. Heavy footsteps and Italian swearing approach the dining room. The door swings open and Andrea, the 'manservant', stomps in with another basket of bread and more wine. The assembled company attempts to ask him where the dinner might possibly be, but he mutters:

AND: *Prestomoltoprestopochiminuti!*

. . . and vanishes as noisily as he arrived. Des decides he's fed up with sitting, wriggles out of his chair under the table and comes up between Ernie and Angel, who shrieks and slaps him.

D: Ow!! Mum she hit me!! Dad!! It's not fair!!
C: If this is the kind of behaviour we can expect from him before he even gets there . . .
H: *(fiercely, to Des)* WILL YOU GET BACK TO YOUR CHAIR or there'll be NO TRIP and NO ICE CREAM!!
M: (. . . okay, now put me on to Mia . . . Mia, I have a . . . *(looking at Des)* call him four, a little stocky, legs a tad bandy, shortish arms but not bad head, blond, big feet . . . Yeah, the kid . . . Yeah, I'm looking at Wednesday morning for the first fitting, d'ya have an opening?)

Helen dumps Des back in his chair. Des bursts into tears. Angel's phone rings. She jumps, answers it, turns puce and runs out of the room.

At this moment, Andrea crashes back into the room holding a big china platter high over his head. Everybody looks relieved. Five white napkins are spread expectantly on five laps.

H: Food! At last!
M: (... okay we set then? ... Loveya!)

Madge finally puts down her phone.

Andrea sets down the platter in the middle of the table. On it are eight skewers neatly threaded with small dead birds, plucked and roasted but still complete with heads, feet and beaks. That's it.

The silence of total shock engulfs the table. Then Madge takes some bread, turns her best fixed smile to Helen, and asks:

M: So! How was the trip down?

15 July, bedtime – Helen and Des

It's very late, and Des can barely keep his eyes open. Helen, who is feeling the effects of all that wine and all that excitement on an empty stomach, is putting him, the cowboy, the gorilla and Teddy POdge into a large white bed in a large white bedroom. Downstairs, Madge is still shouting into her phone, but otherwise the house is, finally, blissfully quiet.

H: So have you had enough to eat, sweetness?
D: Yes I REALLY REALLY like those crunchy birds can we have them again?
H: I don't think so, and since you had everybody else's as well as your own ...
D: Will they have birds on a stick in Hollywood? Can I have a gun and shoot my own? Do they have soldiers with guns there?
H: I hope very much that neither of us will be needing a gun, I think we'll have a lawyer instead. You're going to

have a wonderful time, it's just like a giant make-believe game only you won't have to play on your own, AND you'll get ice cream every time you say your words right!
D: I want a gun! Dad said everybody has guns there he did he did!
H: I think he was just teasing us, lambkin, you know he's funny that way sometimes. Now go to sleep, and tomorrow you can spend all day in the pool.

She tucks him in and begins to drag herself wearily towards the door.

D: You haven't sung me my song! I want a song!

Helen pauses. Somehow keeps her cool, turns around and says:

H: How about an extra-long one tomorrow?
D: No! No tonight, or (*wailing*) I'm going to be frightened, I don't like it here, I'm all on my own and . . .

Helen comes back, slumps on to the bed and takes a deep breath.

H: Fine. Have it your way. What do you want a song about?

The Hollywood Blockbuster Small Dead Bird and Shotgun Calypso

> I'm going to sing you a song, but it's only short, about
> Some little tweety birds that the huntsmen caught.
> They'd stayed up to play, though Mum said it was late,
> And their reward was ending up on Des's dinner plate.
>
> Now Des is off to Hollywood to be a star,
> It'll feel just like home even though it's far.
> There'll be hamburgers and ice cream and lots of TV
> And that's enough bad poetry for now from me.

15 July – 'The Abduction' (Angel's dream): Episode 4, 'Encounter with Destiny'

Princess Xandar lay wide eyed, too excited to sleep. Finally, despite all the thwartings of her evil, dwarfish alien abductors, she had made it back, not yet to the Empire, but to one of its colonial outposts, where the Empress herself, still wary of showing too much favouritism to her beloved only child, nevertheless had secretly, like, made a sign to let the Princess know how much her courage and bravitude had pleased her.

Now, her reward was only hours away. Surely it could not be mere coincidence that the Prince's travels were bringing him so close to where her enforced sojourn was enforcing her to stay? Unable to eat or sleep or think of anything else, the Princess lay tossing in her bed. She could no more think of sleeping than . . .

16 July, next morning

The day is well advanced by the time Colum, in shorts and another antique Italian T-shirt, staggers into the dining room, where he's greeted by the stink of the empty wine bottles and the sight of sixteen little avian skeletons on Des's dirty plate. Nobody has touched the table, or anything else in the room. He groans and moves out on to the terrace by the pool, which is also still scattered with last night's glasses and bottles.

There's a drop of mineral water in the bottom of one of the bottles, which he glugs back before moving slowly round the terrace, tidying up. On a sun-lounger in the shade, wearing a huge hat and sunglasses and covered with sunblock, Angel is flipping through a magazine. She gives no sign of having noticed him.

C: Hi.

No reply.

C: Anybody else around, d'ye know?
A: I saw the maid and the old guy leaving with their bags a while back.
C: Ah. Well, that explains a certain amount. In which case, I'd better go and do some shopping. D'ye fancy coming?
A: What for?
C: Och, you know, in case I have a heart attack at the wheel, or we drive into another small-arms ambush . . .
A: I MEANT, like what are you shopping for?
C: Well, I had a quick look in the kitchen cupboard and I thought I'd start with Jif, bleach, a couple of bottles of washing-up liquid, some scouring pads . . .
A: No thanks.

She turns back to her magazine, the same French one she's been 'reading' for three days.

C: D'ye think I'll get all of that in San Gimignano?

She looks up suddenly.

A: Where?
C: San Gimignano or however ye say the damn thing, I believe it's the nearest town.
A: Oh. Well . . .

Colum fishes out his car keys and sets out towards the car. Casually . . .

C: You're the expert shopper . . .

Angel wriggles around in her chair, unable to bear either to go or to stay. Finally, she sighs heavily, as though making a major sacrifice.

A: Okay, I guess you're bound get into some like totally embarrassing situation otherwise.
C: I'd be very grateful.

Angel climbs with some difficulty out of the sun-lounger and slouches towards the house.

A: But you'll have to wait for me, okay?
C: No problem. I'll be making a list.

16 July – Colum's shopping list

> Fernet Branca
> Mineral water
> Alka Seltzer
> Aspirin
> Jif cleaner
> Mr Muscle bathroom
> Mr Muscle kitchen
> Toilet Duck, or equivalent
> Bleach (thick)
> Washing powder/liquid
> Fairy Liquid or equiv for washing-up
> Scouring pads
> Washing-up sponges
> Dishcloths
> Paper towel
> Bin bags
> Loo paper

A little later – Colum and Angel: in the car

Colum, who refuses on principle to wear sunglasses, is shielding his headache against the white-hot sunshine as he drives slowly through the busy streets of the quaint Tuscan tourist showpiece of San Gimignano, looking for a parking place. His concentration is not helped by Angel, who is once again in full make-up and jailbait clothes, and has suddenly become a relentless chatterbox.

A: . . . and the bike path in Santa Monica is like, SOO cool, there's like people blading with their dogs and their pet lizards and stuff, and all these beach cafés where they play the best music, and . . .

C: Baby sunblock.

A: Say what?

C: Remind me to add it to the list. How about playgrounds, are there good playgrounds?

A: Oh yeah well like, you know, all the celebs take their babies to the beach playpark on the weekend, so he'll get to do some like major networking there . . .

C: Terrific. Hey . . .

He's seen something or somebody in the distance.

C: . . . aren't those our theatrical friends over yonder?

Angel squeaks, turns bright pink and squirms down into her seat. Colum appears not to notice.

C: They're leaving, that's lucky. We can take their parking space.

He cruises alongside the Loxleys' formidable vintage Saab estate car. Piero Loxley is already in the driver's seat but Talitha, Perdita and Edgar are waiting on the pavement. Colum rolls down his window.

C: Are you following us, or are we following you?

Talitha giggles and looks up over her shades. She fancies him – she probably fancies most men. Colum turns to Angel.

C: (*innocently*) Did you have any idea they were heading here?

Angel shakes her head furiously, and turns away from Edgar.

T: Well, WE have a genuine excuse, don't we darlings?

She nods towards the window of the nearest café, which displays a flyer for 'La Compagnia Teatrale di Highgate' and its series of local performances.

C: I guess that makes us the stalkers. Tell you what, give us your parking space and we'll promise to leave you alone for the rest of the day.

Angel is staring at a fly on the windshield as though entomology is her favourite subject. Edgar is staring coolly at Angel. Talitha laughs, winningly.

T: Well actually the two of us have to rehearse, can you believe on this glorious day, and Perdie's got a little friend staying, but poor Edgar's at a bit of a loose end in fact, aren't you Ed?
A: (*looking right at him*) Edgar? Ed is short for EDGAR?

She giggles. Ed's turn to blush, which totally destroys his Mr Cool act.

C: Well why don't you come back with us for lunch then, eh Angel?
E: (*fully recovered*) Well thanks, ANGEL.
A: Hey . . .
C: . . . and I'll run you back later on, okay? We've just got a few bits to pick up here, but there's a nice shady garden with a pool where we're staying. How about it?

Angel and Edgar are speechless with embarrassment and mutual lust. Talitha and Colum are both well aware of this.

T: Oh, well . . . well, how kind of you! I don't see why not . . .

16 July, morning – Back at the villa: Helen's dream

Helen and Des, both surreally beautiful and gorgeously dressed, are standing in a giant sandpit in a giant garden, which is lit by a giant sun which is, itself, part of a giant set (think *Truman Show*, only bigger). In the sandpit are three immaculately detailed toy cars, big enough for Des to climb in and out of, which he is doing with huge glee. Helen looks up and sees Bruce Springsteen, in his prime, running, running, running towards her over the endless acres of perfectly sprinkled green lawn. She smiles, giddy with joy, and holds out her arms, heart pounding.

He keeps running – but somehow never gets any nearer – or any larger.

Suddenly a shadow falls over her and Des. They look up and see Colum, a giant standing over them, holding a squeegee in one hand and a chamois leather in the other. 'WHY ARE THERE NO ITALIAN BIKES IN HOLLYWOOD?' he bellows, and looks over to where Bruce, now also carrying a squeegee and a chamois leather, is still running, running towards them.

Helen looks up at Colum and down at Des, and suddenly realises that she and Des have both shrunk to the size of toys – it's Colum who's normal size. Colum reaches into his pocket, pulls out a wallet, opens it and takes out a giant ice-cream cone. He lifts it up and starts to lower it towards Des. Helen realises Colum is planning to suffocate Des with the ice cream. She tries to move, but cannot. She shouts out: '*NO!!!!!!!!*'

. . . and sits bolt upright in bed, with a terrible hangover.

16 July, late morning – Angel and Ed: in the garden

They're lying some way from the house on the other side of the pool, on a blanket under the shade of a big old Italian pine. They seem to have got over their shyness. Ed is teaching Angel how to make grass squeak, a technique her education has somehow omitted. They are lying very, very close, but not quite touching.

Angel tries to produce a squeak, instead produces something

like a fart, giggles, and rolls over artlessly on to her back, where she lies sprawled like Marilyn in those beach shots. Ed takes his grass and very carefully begins to find out where she's ticklish. She seems to be enjoying herself, though from time to time she giggles, unconvincingly, 'Stop it!'

Then Ed puts down the grass stem, raises himself on one elbow, and looks down straight into her eyes. A real Mr Wolf gaze. A flicker of something like panic runs across Angel's face, but she tosses her hair and tries to laugh it off. Then Ed lowers his face towards her and parts his lips. She looks back at him, licking her own lips, a bit scared . . .

16 July, midday – Helen

Boy, am I glad I'm never going to see twelve again. Or a hundred and twelve, from the way I'm feeling today, but that's a different story. Ernie and I were just catching up on the gossip while supervising Des in the swimming pewl when Angel suddenly appears, shaking and hysterical, and wanting to know why boys are so vile and horrible.

I was just trying to think where to begin, when it became obvious that this was a purely rhetorical question, as Ernie leaped gracefully out of the pool, fetched Angel a glass of iced water and sat her on her knee, stroking her hair while she drank it. It wasn't totally clear what had happened, but it obviously had something to do with the Loxley boy, who at about the same time found Colum doing a spot of cleaning and demanded to be taken back to San Gimignano immediately.

Luckily they'd only got about half a mile when the local bus rumbled up behind them, and I suspect the content of Colum's send-off to young Ed at that point was something along the lines of 'If you're old enough to do whatever you've just done, you're probably old enough to find your way home from the bus station'.

Anyhow, the whole situation had obviously been compounded by poor Angel's continuing delicate condition, but luckily at this point Ernie was able to distract her with the offer of a fabulous new hairdo, and they went off together quite happily. Who knew Ernie had such depths of fellow feeling for the travails of adolescence?

Madge then appeared to take delivery of our air tickets, and interrupted her telephonic torrent just long enough to explain that, as she was sloughing me, Des and Angel off on the next jumbo, and as Ernie was only here to make sure Des got the job, there wasn't much point in keeping the villa on for two weeks *à deux* with Colum. So she's cancelled the villa, which basically means poor old Colum gets two whole days of holiday and then drives right back the way we've just come. Ernie offered to chop in her return plane ticket and go with him, apparently requiring time to 'unwind' after the stress of the last few days, and after the embarrassing spectacle I made of myself last time I thought they were spending too much time together, I could hardly object.

So they're even now huddled over Fernet Brancas and the map, working out a route that can mutually accommodate maximum vineyards (him) and maximum shopping (her), and avoid anything that could ever be suspected of being a monument. Which seems to leave me to sort out the lunch – surprise, surprise. Still, only one more day of domestic drudgery, and then Cinderella WILL go to the ball . . .

16 July, afternoon – Phone call: Colum to George and Fiona in London

C: Mum?
F: No thank you, not today.
She hangs up the phone.

Second phone call

F: (George? George ye'd better speak this time.)
G: *(in distance)* Just finding me other slipper . . .
C: MUM – it's me, you daft . . .
G: Please stop this immediately, or I shall be obliged to call the police.

He hangs up the phone.

Third phone call

F: (What will I do this time? . . .)
C: MUM!!! MUM IT'S ME COLUM DON'T PUT DOWN THE . . .
F: Colum? Could ye lower your voice, for the love of God we've the cat sleeping just here. (I've made the tea George, I'll leave ye to put the milk in yours will I?)
C: Mum, are you there?
F: And where else would I be, haven't we been looking after this house for you these five days and only just getting the hang of the plumbing? (D'ye fancy a biscuit wi' yer tea, George?)
C: Mum, it's costing me a fortune to call from here . . .
F: Never mind what it's costing me to listen to ye blathering on . . .
C: . . . I just wanted to tell you that I'll be coming back a bit sooner than we expected. Nothing wrong, only Des and Helen are going to America for a bit and . . .
F: And wasn't it me told you right from the start she'd be off with the first man who took her fancy? A fillum star is it? (George! George, come here I can't be disturbing the puir wee cat again, and Helen's left Colum for a fillum star . . .)

16 July – Bertie

I knew it. I could have told them, if they'd bothered to consult me, that nothing good ever came from eating out of another person's food bowl. Of course, nobody did bother to consult me, but then nobody ever does. I'm just part of the furniture around here. They think I lie about all day in a flatulent torpor, with nothing going on between the ears. Did it never occur to them to wonder how Einstein arrived at his Special Theory of Relativity? He certainly didn't get there by running after mice instead of eating what was put in front of him, or perching on a wall every night yodelling about his virility.

Absolutely predictable that they should spring this change of plan on me just when I was getting the new tenants properly trained, but probably just as well, in view of the lessons of history. They may seem harmless and suggestible enough this time around, but if they're capable of that hot cocoa incident once, it could happen again – or worse.

I trust they'll take all these bin bags and toilet rolls with them. This place is cramped enough at the best of times.

Meanwhile, I could swear there's still a bit of that cod around in this bed somewhere . . .

16 July, bedtime – Colum and Des

Colum is tucking Des into the billowy white bed, along with his animals. Des looks very small, very blond, and very innocent. And very excited.

D: . . . and Mum says that's where the cowboys come from too, like in all the cowboy films, and I might meet them! Only I don't want to ride on a horse.
C: I've a feeling they all drive eight-cylinder jeeps these days.

He sits on the bed, strokes Des's head.

C: Now go to sleep.
D: Can I have a song? Mum always sings me a song.
C: I'll send her up later. Are you okay about this trip?

Des looks puzzled, then worried.

D: What about? Okay about what?
C: Silly old Dad, of course you are. How about those rowdy animals – are they asleep yet? They've got a big journey tomorrow.
D: Ummm – I think so, only that teddy does snore so, he kept me awake ALL NIGHT before.

He puts up his face to be kissed. Colum kisses him and touches his cheek again.

C: How do cowboys tell their teddies off, d'ye suppose?
D: *(weird twang, but great verve)* Yee Haw you bear! Shut it!!
C: You're going to be a star, son. Don't forget to come home.
D: Will you be there when I come home?
C: I will.
D: Will Grandma and Granddad? Will I get presents?
C: We'll have to see about that. Night-night.

Des burrows under the covers with a happy little sigh.

D: Night-night.

16 July – 'The Abduction' (Angel's Dream): Episode 5, 'The Journey Home'

It was late at night by the time Princess Xandar finished her final preparations for the return home. Every muscle in her beauteous body ached, every nerve was alert, as though all the stresses and torments of the past week had lain in wait until now, kept at bay by sheer will-power and mind-blowing discipline.

She was near the end of her precious reserves, but she knew she had to stay vigilant for just one more day – that until she was actually safe in the Empire, behind the ramparts of the MetaGlass Castle, with the nano-cameras primed and the virtual memory locks reset, an attack could still come at any time, and from any quarter.

She could still hardly believe the perfidy of the Warrior Prince. Remembering the encounter, her body shook all over. To suffer the pain and shame of her illness was bad enough, but to have it brought to light so unexpectedly, and received with such – you have to say – loathing had taxed her royal demeanour to its utmost. Let him just once be wounded and vulnerable at her feet, and she would show him! And how! But no, that would, like, demean her too. All she could hope was that, in the vast starry reaches of the Galactic Empire, their paths would never cross again.

But now it was late, and she had her beauty sleep to consider. If she had learned one thing from the recent forced association with her evil dwarfish abductors, it was that it's never too soon to start taking really good care of your complexion.

17 July – American Airlines first-class in-flight menu, Rome/Los Angeles

Good morning!! And welcome to American, the premier airline of the free world. Here in our new upgraded UltraFirst™ Class, we aim to give you an in-flight experience of unparalleled luxury and service. So sit back in your fully-reclinable 'Sleepaseat'™, relax, enjoy our services, and remember – if there's anything at all you need, at any time, the touch of a button will bring it right to your side.

>ON DEPARTURE
>Assorted canapés of smoked fish and Beluga, or help yourself from our mini-buffet in the central aisle.
>SERVED WITH:
>Dom Perignon '97, Buck's Fizz, Stag's Leap Chardonnay special

Reserve '98, freshly squeezed juice, soft drinks or mixers.

LUNCH

Rosette of foie gras and 10-year-aged pancetta affumicata, served with warm olive crostini, prosciutto and walnut rolls, and a finocchio truffle garnish.

OR

Mixed salad of baby leaves, wild rucola and garden herbs, with a warm walnut-truffle-smoked ginger vinaigrette.

FOLLOWED BY:

Neapolitan of florentine beef, baby artichoke and wild garlic, with a salsa verde, potato risotto cake and mixed wild mushroom ragout.

OR

Fresh lobster al'Armoricano, flash-grilled over five-spiced wafers of eggplant and treviso rosso.

OR

Fettucini all'Alfredo with unpasteurised farm-aged grano di Padana, crema di mascarpone and grated alba truffle.

SERVED WITH:

Dom Perignon '97, Buck's Fizz, Gringrich Reserve Chardonnay '99, Coppola Estates Cabernet Supreme '97, freshly squeezed juice, soft drinks or mixers.

FOLLOWED BY:

Twice-cooked Valrhona pudding cake with fresh yellow raspberries and semifreddo di vaniglia.

OR

Assorted farm-aged Italian cheeses with celery wafers and mountain butter.

OR

Tropical fruit basket.

SERVED WITH:

Dom Perignon '97, Buck's Fizz, Weeping Cedar Rose Muscat '99, freshly squeezed juice, soft drinks or mixers.

FOLLOWED BY:
Godiva chocolates and assorted mints.
SERVED WITH:
Cognac 5*, Stock Riserva Grande, Glenfiddich, Jack Daniel's 25-year prime, Baileys or other liqueurs upon request.
Coffee, tea, tisanes, infusions.

UPON AWAKING:
Freshly baked viennoiseries with mountain butter and assorted jams.
Assorted mini-muffins.
Granola with honey, almonds and Greek yogurt.
Tropical fruit basket.
SERVED WITH:
Buck's Fizz, coffee, tea, tisanes, infusions, freshly squeezed juices, soft drinks or mixers.

THROUGHOUT THE FLIGHT
your American Superflight™ staff will be glad to furnish you with drinks, snacks, fruit, candy, potato chips and other light refreshments.

17 July – Helen: on the plane

It's a good thing these SleepaSeats™ are made for middle-aged chief executives. I'm spilling out all over this one after that lot. Lucky I'm not the type to get her head turned. A person could all too easily become accustomed to wallowing in this grotesque stew of gluttony and obsequious personal service.

Funny thing though, however they describe it, the food still tastes of nothing at all. Maybe it's something to do with the air recirculating in the cabin, but I could swear I had that same beef dish on a Poundstretcher flight to Malaga in . . . whenever it was.

I still can't believe we're actually in the air, en route to the adventure of a lifetime. Nor could I believe Madge had managed to forget the little detail of Angel's passport, either, but it's amazing what a fistful of first-class reservations can do to a minor bureaucratic tangle.

(Christ, my head. I'm sure I only had the one glass just to relax with the canapés – at least, that was definitely my intention.)

I do hope I'm not making a terrible mistake. It's been so hectic up to this point, and it seemed like such an amazing opportunity for little Des, but I could easily be walking him right into a lifetime of grandiose fantasy and therapy bills. Colum obviously believes after a day in Hollywood I'll be taking bids for Des on eBay, but you can't just turn your back on this sort of opportunity when it plummets right into your lap. Unless you're Colum, and you never want to go anywhere or do anything, as the last five days have amply demonstrated.

(And then, of course, I had to just try a drop of the red with the main course, because Colum's always going on about how he had the Coppola wine once and it's actually quite good and he's not just saying it because it's made by the director of his favourite movie. Pity I'm not drunk enough to ask them for a bottle to take back to him. Or am I? Did I?)

But Des is so little and innocent and unspoiled, look at him now playing Happy Families with that nice Superflight™ lady, with absolutely no idea what he's in for. And look, by contrast, at Angel, barely enough orifices for all the mindless gratification she's sucking up from the in-flight entertainment console. If this is what LA does to children, our own happy little family is certainly doomed.

I'll just have to make up for all the attention by sticking to Des like a limpet and being absolutely firm that at the first movie-star tantrum he's sent to bed early with no supper and no calypso. After all, it's not going to change me, and consistency is the most important thing with small children –

everybody says so. I mean, in Angel's defence, you only have to look at Madge. If Angel had had one per cent of the quality time Madge devotes to her phone, she'd be a model child.

(And then of course there was the rose muscat. I don't normally touch dessert wines because I never used to like them, so it seemed – not having anything important to concentrate on afterwards – like an ideal time to find out whether I do yet, or not. Can't quite remember, but there's always the flight back to make the final decision.)

I suppose I'd better heave my astonishing bulk into full recline to prepare for the paparazzi on the tarmac – only kidding, at least I hope I am. Des seems fully bonded to his Superflight™ surrogate – she's tucking him in right now. Must stay awake long enough to toddle over and kiss him goodnight . . .

17 July – Helen, Angel and Des: unpacking at the Ocean Shores Hotel

Helen, straining the credibility of her H&M palazzo pants, and Des, in Buzz Lightyear shorts and a grubby T-shirt, are standing, dazed, in the middle of the huge living room of a huge hotel suite, which is furnished in ultra-cool beachside style with a lot of pale, dry-clean-only textiles. The aesthetic effect is only slightly marred by a giant arrangement of purple-and-orange bird of paradise flowers, and two huge gift baskets full of Doritos, Cheetos and Taquitos, with a pink helium balloon shouting 'Welcome!'

Late afternoon California light floods in from giant windows overlooking the ocean. As it is now 2.45 a.m. by the time they got up, they'd be feeling fairly woozy even without the massive ingestions of inappropriate in-flight food and drink, and the blinding light everywhere.

A huge black guy, with the body of a very expensive personal trainer rippling through a cream-coloured Giorgio Armani suit, and a peaked cap worn backwards, adds Des's wellingtons and goggles to the pathetic pile of luggage in the middle of the room. This is Omar, their dedicated limo driver.

O: That's it. Anything else I can do for you guys?

Helen fumbles in her handbag for her purse . . .

H: Um, er . . . Oh, no thanks, er here before you go . . .

. . . desperately rifling through a wad of apparently identical bills . . .

H: . . . here, I'm afraid I've only got a fifty-dollar bill, but if you could . . .
O: That's cool.

He pockets the bill, clearly not about to give her change.

O: See you at eight, right?
H: Really?
O: The welcome party? The card's right there? There's a babysitter fixed up for Mr McCallum? So . . .
H: Please. He's called Des.
O: Cool.
H: Oh Christ, that's less than . . .
O: By the way, you'll be speaking to Mr Elfstein at the party, right?
H: Mr? . . .
O: Like, the director? Of the movie? Only . . .

With incredible dexterity he pulls a thick A4 document from the inside pocket of his suit and holds it out to Helen.

O: . . . I wrote him with the logline of my movie and he was, uh, pretty jazzed, so if you could, like, just slip it to him . . .

Helen, confused and on autopilot, takes it, just as Angel appears from one of the two bedrooms, grabs it from her and hands it back to Omar.

A: Elfstein's agent is Lydia Martin at CAA. You know where that is. Come at seven fifty and you can drop me off on the way.

Her accent has flipped over to perfect mall-drawl. Omar, knowing when he's beaten, touches his cap and leaves. Angel is perusing a large, stiff invitation she's found.

A: By the way, you don't tip your driver. He gets tips from every restaurant and bar he ever takes you to, plus he's on studio salary with pension and benefits. Plus he does *Baywatch* in between. I'll bet he makes more than Mom.
H: Oh. Thanks.

She picks a couple of sorry old suitcases from the pile, making for the other bedroom, just as Des hurtles out of it, carrying a black object.

D: Mum!
H: Des, I *told* you the wellingtons had to stay behind.
D: Mum! Look! It's for me!

He puts on the black object, which turns out to be a mini-baseball jacket with 'The Love Gift' embroidered on it in florid gilt, and a matching mini-baseball cap embroidered with his name.

D: And there's one for you and there's lots of chocolate and that wine you like and . . .

He takes Helen's hand and drags her into the next room, where sure enough, next to more flowers and champagne, another, adult-sized jacket is draped over a mini-director's chair with 'Desi MaCallum' written on the back. Helen tries it on and goes to the mirror.

H: Hey, I'm a movie star . . .

She peers more closely.

H: . . . John Travolta in *Get Shorty*.

The doorbell rings. Angel lopes towards the door and opens it. Another huge basket is suspended outside. A voice from behind it:

M: Ms McClackum's suite?

Helen appears behind Angel. The messenger thrusts the basket at her. She begins to stagger off with it and the bags.

M: I'm to wait.
H: Wait? For what?
M: The signature?

Helen puts down the bags and realises that buried under the fruit, flowers, YoYos and Oreos are an opened document and a pen.

H: Oh, sorry, okay.

She opens the pen and is about to write when Angel leaps at her and grabs the pen, knocking the basket flying.

A: STOP!!

Helen, the basket and Angel land in a heap on top of the bags, with an ominous tearing sound.

A: NEVER sign ANYTHING without your lawyer! Don't you know ANYTHING?
H: But it's a delivery note!
A: It so is NOT, it's his contract!

She extracts the document and hands the basket back to the messenger.

A: You can tell your legal people's people that our legal people

will be forwarding our response to your legal people.
M: But . . .
A: Here's your pen.

She slams the door.

17 July, early evening – Helen

I'm beginning to realise that Angel has her redeeming qualities. After all, context is everything. A Siberian tiger would hardly be a welcome neighbour in the queue at Tesco, but in the snowy steppes of Siberia it's a wonder of nature. Angel has clearly been custom designed for southern California, which is turning out already to be a bit of a minefield.

We were just in the swimming pewl, trying to sober, er, wake up enough to put in an appearance at this do tonight, which is apparently entirely in our honour and will feature more stars than there are in the Milky Way, and I was trying to get Des to memorise the four lines which have been thoughtfully highlighted for him on the script, when I suddenly saw a long black object sticking out of a nearby bush. Long black object turns out to be – no! – the 400mm lens of a camera taking pictures of me and Des, which wouldn't have been so bad if I hadn't had on the Bhs candy-striped bikini I borrowed from Georgie when I couldn't get into mine after Des was born. I have kept meaning to replace it, but . . .

Anyhow, Angel immediately took control of the situation and had hotel security eject the poor guy. I did try to put in a word for him, after all everybody has to earn their crust and he was amazingly good looking, but apparently this sort of thing doesn't go down at all well with the studios, who like to be able to charge through the nose for photos of their Properties, which is apparently what we have now become.

Not sure about the sound of that, but apparently the next step up is to become a Brand, which sounds even worse.

Anyhow, it became obvious that purchasing a new swimsuit is a matter of urgency, as is losing about a tonne of blubber. What a happy accident to find ourselves in the world capital of liposuction, on massive expenses. Angel is clearly the gal to sort all this out. She's already telling me what to wear for the party. The invite clearly says 'casual' which I would have interpreted as my lovely palazzo pants, had they not met with a tragic accident when she kickboxed me to the ground earlier, but she swears it means black, with little heels. As the only black I have is the Elmore Leonard XX-large bomber jacket, which might flatter the production team but is not exactly the first impression I'd choose to make, they're going to have to be taken at their (literal) word. Everybody knows body surfing and frayed jeans were invented here. Angel has clearly been in Sussex too long.

Visitors' Handy Cut-out-and-keep Guide to Hollywood Vocabulary

Section 1 – The party

What a great outfit!	=	Didn't you read the invitation? Did you even get an invitation?
I get so bored wearing black all the time	=	... but at least I don't look like a dork
I wish I had the courage to dress like that!	=	Yeah, and go home at night to a locked ward
You're British, aren't you?	=	You don't know anybody – why am I wasting my time with you?
Haven't I seen you in those beautiful Merchant-Ivory movies?	=	You need to shop at Barneys more often

I'll bet you cook like Nigella	=	I'll bet you're a great lay
You do?	=	You cook? For yourself? Wow, I didn't know things were that bad over there.
Is it true she's, like, a big star in the Old Country?	=	So if she's on regular TV, what's on the porn channels?
Can I get that for you?	=	I can't believe you actually tried to pour yourself a drink. We're paying ten thousand for help tonight.
Just help yourself, we're real casual here	=	Did I just hallucinate, or did you go into the kitchen and grab that food from the side? Maybe you'd like a doggy bag to take home?
You English are so brilliant!	=	Pity about your tits
You English are so witty!	=	You're drinking like a fish
That's hilarious!	=	I can't understand a word you're saying
You can't go – the party's just beginning!	=	You ARE the party – or at least the floor show
You're in town for a while, aren't you?	=	You'll end up hanging on for years, thinking it's all about to happen for you
May I call you?	=	At least that way you won't be bugging me
We'll do lunch next week – it'll be great!	=	By next week I won't even remember meeting you

17 July – Timetable for the evening: Des and Helen

	HELEN AT PARTY	DES WITH STUDIO BABY-SITTER
8.00	Arrive, meet, all smiles	Arrive, meet, all smiles
8.15	First-ever margarita. Yum!	First ever Dr Pepper. Yum!
8.30	Need to eat, urgently. Waiters nowhere to be found. Help self from kitchen, fearing reprisals later.	Need to eat, urgently. Room service nowhere to be found. Help self from hamper, fearing reprisals later.
8.45	Second drink. Even better.	Second drink. Even better.
9.00	Begin to feel woozy.	Begin to feel woozy.
9.15	Notice other guests don't seem to understand a word I say	Notice baby-sitter doesn't seem to understand a word I say.
9.30	Begin to feel miserable and homesick. Have another drink.	Begin to feel miserable and homesick. Have another candy bar.
9.45	Definitely time to get out. Vent bad temper on driver.	Definitely time to be sick. Vent bad temper on baby-sitter.
10	Get home in nick of time.	Get to loo in nick of time.
10.15	Realise need big hug before can sleep.	Realise need big hug before can sleep.
10.20	BIG HUG!!!!!	

17 July, very late – Helen, in bed

Mmm – what a relief to be horizontal at last. I have to say they're all very charming here, and such wonderful manners, if a bit more formal than I'd expected. I think I actually made quite a hit with the hot pants, several people complimented me on them, and not just men, either. I made myself quite useful too – here they all are, running media empires on gigantic salaries, but nobody had the first clue how to open a wine bottle, let alone uncap a beer in the door frame. The best action was in the kitchen, as usual, but they were all speaking Spanish so I couldn't really join in. Still, they were friendly enough – just as well I went exploring in there, I could have starved to death before those dozy waiters came by.

Didn't notice any major stars, which was a bit of a disappointment, but even the parking people look like movie stars, so I probably missed half of them. I did meet one v sweet guy whose name was actually Cary! He swore he was no relation, but with those eyes and that dimple he could well be some kind of secret illegitimate offspring or something. Anyhow, he said I looked just like Lauren Bacall (I must admit people have said that before, if not very much in the last five years) and that with my wit and vocabulary I ought to be writing screenplays. Which, having had a quick look at the garbage they want Des to say, I could probably do in my sleep. Maybe I should have a go – give me something to do while Des is having his fittings or whatever.

Anyhow, Cary said he'd call me. He seemed very keen, especially when I told him where we're staying. For some reason this made me feel guilty – no reason, I wasn't even really flirting after all, and flirting is not only acceptable but vital to the survival of a modern marriage.

And it is EXTREMELY nice to be treated like a woman for a change, and an attractive and witty one at that, instead of a not very bright general trainee from the Jobcentre.

God knows what time it is back there . . .

18 July, morning – Colum and Ernie, in Bordeaux

They are sitting at breakfast under the dripping awning of an unhygienic café in Bordeaux. On the table between them are four large coffee cups, two dead and two on the go, and a basket of – finally – perfect, flaky, home-made croissants, which they are obliviously tearing and dunking as they eat.

E: Don't worry, they'll be fine, it's not like they've gone into uncharted territory or anything. It's just Eastbourne with better weather. And Des has his head screwed on, it'll just be one long game to him.
C: Des! I'm not worried about Des! At least he knows the difference between make-believe and reality.
E: What, and Helen doesn't?

He raises an eyebrow and dunks another croissant.

E: Well, even if it does go to her head a bit at first, what harm can it do? The poor thing deserves the odd treat, she's had a pretty dreary life these last three years.
C: And I haven't, I suppose?
E: Men are used to dreariness. You invented the office.

She drains her coffee.

C: I just hope she doesn't do anything silly.
E: If she didn't do anything silly she wouldn't be the Helen we know and love. But I'm sure she'll keep it within the bounds of redeemability. Come on, the rain's stopped, I need to get these shoes into a dry car.

18 July – Guest list for Informal 'Getting-To-Know-You' Playdate, at home of Aaron Mumby, boss of American Studios

> Desmond McCallum star
> Wade Mumby   son of Aaron Mumby, chairman, motion
>   picture division, American Studios

Tennison Speed	son of Max Speed, head of worldwide distribution, American Studios
Lydia Darcy	daughters of Darling Darcy, producer
Louella Darcy	
Macarthur Elfstein	son of Lorenz Elfstein, director
Carsey Solkov	daughter and son of Paul Solkov, cinematographer
Milton Solkov	

chaperone to Mr McCallum
chaperone to Mr Mumby
chaperone to Mr Speed
chaperone to the Ms Darcy
chaperone to Mr Elfstein
chaperone to Mr and Ms Solkov

Please arrive between 3.30 and 3.40 p.m.
Please ask your driver to collect between 5.00 and 5.10 p.m.
PLEASE NOTE: security gates will ONLY be open between these times.
If required, drivers and assistants may wait in the staff block to the right of the pool house.

18 July – Des and Helen, at Playdate

A long table has been set out on the beautifully landscaped twenty-acre lawn a few feet from the pool of Aaron Mumby's Bel Air home. It's a very, very hot afternoon, and the sprinklers are sprinkling energetically. Between the table and the pool is a metal fence, tastefully disguised with bamboo, and a large notice reading:

> WARNING! GUESTS USE THIS POOL AT THEIR OWN RISK.
> NO UNACCOMPANIED CHILDREN AT ANY TIME!
> FOR LEGAL DISCLAIMER, SEE BELOW

followed by a screed of tiny writing.

The table is set with expensive china featuring characters from American Studios' latest hit, and scattered with merchandising figures from others.

In each chair sits a child, immaculately dressed in miniature designer casuals, varying in age from four to nine. Behind each chair stands a Guatemalan or Filipina nanny. Behind Des's chair stands Helen, looking cross and uncomfortable. Des has insisted on wearing his black wool mini-blouson, which is not totally appropriate for the 95° heat, provoking nudges and contemptuous whispers from the other children.

Most of them are squabbling over who gets which movie character. Tennison grabs the two he wants, shoves them at his nanny, and turns to Des.

T: So who's your agent?

Puzzled look.

H: *(to Tennison)* Our ... oh, well, d'you know, we've only been here a day or so ...

Tennison turns to Wade and whispers loudly:

T: Get this – I bet it's not even ICM!
H: ... and to be perfectly honest ...
W: *(whispering back)* I bet it's some junior at William Morris! I bet ...
H: *(persevering anyhow)* ... I don't think he quite has an agent, yet.

The squabbling stops dead. Eyes bug out all round the table.

W: He's OPENING a TENTPOLE MOVIE and he doesn't HAVE an AGENT?

They sit and stare at Des, who hasn't yet understood one word of anything, but has noticed a uniformed waiter approaching, carrying two large plates of pizza slices, which he deposits on the table.

H: *(to the neighbouring nanny)* Food! That looks good, doesn't it?

The nanny, who doesn't speak English, nods and smiles. Nobody moves except Des, who makes a grab towards the nearer plate. Lydia Darcy gasps, and says to Louella:

LY: Did you SEE what he DID?
LO: He helped himself!!

Helen blushes.

H: Des, perhaps you ought to offer it to the others first, sweetheart.

Des picks up the plate in both hands, and holds it out towards Lydia, who ignores it. Lydia and Louella share amazed looks with the others. Wade addresses his nanny.

W: Tell her *(indicating Helen)* to tell him I get it first, because my dad's the head of the studio.

Helen takes the plate of pizza from Des.

T: Hey! Not so fast! My dad's head of distribution, WORLDWIDE, and without him nobody would see the picture! I get it first!

Tennison's nanny is about to take the pizza from Helen when Macarthur sighs, patiently:

M: Lookit, guys, without MY dad there wouldn't BE any picture! He's the creative force, right?

Mac's nanny tries to snatch the plate from Tennison's nanny . . .

M: Plus his next picture's with George Clooney AND he's on pay or play with two per cent!

. . . and succeeds, but before she can give Mac any, Lou and Lydia chorus:

LY: Oh, so who put the deal together and got the green light?
LO: My mom can get your dad fired!
LY: . . . so how big does that make him, Mr Creative Vision, huh?

The girls' nanny is now in possession of the plate of pizza, over which everybody is squabbling, oblivious of the other plate at the far end. Carsey and Milt, clearly used to being at the bottom of the pecking order, sit in front of it mutely, while their nanny tries to muster the nerve to give them some.

Des, who wisely took three pieces, has been eating steadily. He finishes, burps and wipes his hands on the snowy tablecloth.

H: Des! Where are your manners?

Helen is desperate to get away. She looks around for escape.

H: (*whispering in Des's ear*) Hey, do you see what I see over there?

She's boiling hot in her sensible car-ferry slacks, the only clean clothes she had left. Des follows her pointing finger, and spots the pewl.

D: Swimming pewl! MUM . . .

She clamps her hand over his mouth. She needn't have bothered. The other children have progressed from shouting to hitting and hair-pulling. The nannies stand like so many impassive deities, making no move to inhibit them. Unnoticed, Helen and Des sneak over the fence, strip down to their undies, and jump in.

18 July, late afternoon – Helen

It seems that everybody here has a pool, but nobody dares swim in them. Or at least, nobody dares invite anybody else to swim in their pool, except resident family, that is, and not even necessarily then, if they happen to be a litigious family.

How was I supposed to know that a quick dip in Aaron Mumby's lap pool could threaten the entire insurance status of the movie? At first I thought they were upset by my two-year-old M&S balcony bra, which did get a bit waterlogged, but apparently the problem is that if we swim in the hotel pool and, God forbid, anything happens to young Des, the unfathomably profitable Ocean Shores group can be sued for many millions and everybody comes out happy – except, presumably, Des and me – whereas somehow Aaron Mumby doesn't fancy coughing up personally to compensate one of his studio's own properties.

Anyhow, it was getting very boring, so it was a good excuse to leave. Luckily Omar had chosen to stay and network with the other 'drivers', so all we had to do was hack into the security code and we were away, just in time for Des to have a quick nap while Omar watched *RugRats* and Angel and I did a bit of vital wardrobe upgrade in the mall.

What's that song about a kiss without a beard and an egg without salt? It is now searingly obvious that Angel and shopping are two halves of a perfect whole. She laughed! I swear it, and not just when I tried to find Ernie's cowboy-fringed bikini in my size. She was literally unrecognisable as the snarling brat we dragged down France, as she skipped in and out of designer outlets, evaluating the cut of rival brands of jeans, and making sure I didn't doom our social life at birth by buying Ray-Bans.

In fact, apart from her disappointing insistence on avoiding any exposure to the sun, she's shaping up to be a charming and useful companion. I now have a complete 'casual' wardrobe of interchangeable black garments in forgiving stretch mixes, and this bikini, fringeless it's true, but which makes me look about six inches thinner all round. Either that, or my brain has already succumbed to the crude psychological trickery of labelling everything several sizes down. Most of the shreds of clothing Angel tried on seemed to be size 0, which makes one wonder where they go from here. I'd be very surprised if the intellectual capacity of the average local sales assistant is up to minus numbers.

I suppose I ought to go and rehearse Des again. He doesn't appear to have a very firm grasp on what he's here for yet, but it is early days.

Mr McCallum's Lines for Major Motion Picture: *The Love Gift*

```
'Dad! Mom!'
'Dad! Come quickly! I feel weird!'
'Dad! Will I be okay?'
'Dad! Give Laddy a big kiss for me, okay?'
'Dad! Why is Mom crying?'
'Mom! Why is Dad crying?'
'Dad! Please make me better - please!'
'Mom! Dad's going to make me better - it's okay!'
'You're not my mommy, you're a bad doctor - I
hate you!'
'Doctor! Doctor! Please don't hurt my mom!'
'Dad! Dad! Please don't hurt the doctor!'
'Mom! Is Dad in heaven now?'
'Mom! I love you!!'
```

19 July – Des and Helen, at Des's first rehearsal

They're in a small office at the studio with Mark, the first assistant director, and Jolene, one of the stand-ins. Mark is a flamboyantly casual dude with a ponytail and baggy shorts. He's about twenty-four and earns indescribable sums. Jolene is a motherly woman who is used to being ignored and humiliated in the name of art. Mark is drilling Des on his lines, while Jolene sits staring into space, and Helen scribbles notes for her screenplay.

M: So, like let's just try you repeating each line after me, okay?
D: Why?
M: Because you have to learn your lines, okay?
H: *(hastily)* And then you'll get an ice cream.
D: When? Is it a Magnum?
H: When you've learned all your lines. There aren't many. Now do what the nice man asks.
M: Okay?
D: In my voice or in that funny voice?
M: 'Funny'?
D: *(to Mark)* Like your voice is funny.
H: *(mortified)* I think he means your accent. He's never travelled before. Say sorry, Des.
D: Why?
M: Let's try the funny voice, okay? So, here's the first line. You just repeat, like, *exactly* what I say, okay?
D: *(perfect southern California drawl)* You just repeat, like, *exactly* what I say, okay?
M: *(slight fraying on the cool)* No, that wasn't the line . . .
D: No, that wasn't the line . . .
H: Des! Concentrate!
D: *(Helen's voice)* Des! *(his own voice)* Oh sorry, did I lose a tum? It's like Simon Says isn't it? When he says it I do, and when you say it I don't!

Mark shoots Helen a look, but she's busy trying to think of titles.

M: Okay, let's try this a little differently. When I hold my arm up, like this *(holds arm up)*, I'm saying lines, and you say them after. When I have my arm down, like this *(puts arm down again)*, I'm just, like, speaking, and you don't repeat it, okay?

Des is silent.

M: *(distinct slippage on the cool)* Okay? Did you get it?

Des nods furiously, still silent. Helen looks up and realises things are not going too well.

H: Des, he didn't mean you can't talk at all. Come on, it's not complicated!

Des's lip begins to tremble.

D: So it's not Simon Says?

Mark pushes his chair back rather suddenly. Jolene, who has been dozing, jumps.

M: Um, maybe we should, like, take a break?
D: *(near to tears)* I want my ice cream! Please please I promise I can do it!!

Helen drops her notebook, comes over and crouches down to hug Des.

H: You're doing brilliantly, petal, and it's a very very good voice. It's not quite like Simon Says, but if you imagine it's a make-believe game, and when his arm is up you're playing the game, and when his arm is down, you're not – okay?
D: *(nodding vigorously, eager to please)* Okay!!

Helen returns to her chair and her muse.

M: Okay, let's try the scene with the doctor. Jolene, if you could feed him . . .

J: Sure, hon.

M: So Desmond, she'll say this . . .

J: (*totally expressionless*) 'Come sit on my lap pumpkin just like you do with Mommy.'

M: . . . and then you say, 'You're not my mommy! You're a bad doctor! I hate you!' And then you like, hit her with your fists.

Des looks a bit worried, says nothing, but looks at the floor.

M: Okay, Jolene, in your own time.

J: 'Come sit on my lap pumpkin just like you do with Mommy.'

Des continues to stare at the floor.

M: (*small sigh*) Okay now Des, you remember, it's 'You're not my Mommy' . . .

D: (*almost inaudible whisper*) 'You're not my Mommy' . . .

M: 'You're a bad doctor! I hate you!'

Des says nothing but continues to stare at the floor, shuffling his feet and shaking his head.

M: (*big sigh*) 'You're a BAD DOCTOR! I HATE YOU!'

D: (*little frightened sob*) I'm not allowed to say that! That's naughty!

Mark looks for help over to Helen, who is lost in the fantasy of her script.

M: Excuse me, Mrs McCallum – Mrs . . .

Helen jumps.

H: Oh! Sorry! Oh Des, whatever is the matter darling?

Silent tears are rolling down Des's cheeks as the ice cream seems to retreat further and further. Helen jumps up and hugs him tightly.

D: *(wailing)* He said I had to say naughty things! I'm not allowed to do that and to hit people! I want my ice cream!
H: Oh, sweetheart! It's okay! It's acting, that's what acting is, darling, doing things you don't do in your real life. That's what you're here for! Now stop crying, you're doing really well, I'm very proud of you.

Des takes a big sniff, and stops crying.

D: So I can say those naughty things?
H: Of course!
D: And I can hit that lady?

Helen looks over, unsure. Jolene nods and smiles, encouragingly.

H: I guess so.

A world of possibility dawns over Des's face.

D: I like acting! Can we do it again? Can we do it lots????

19 July – Memo: Studio to Des

From the desk of   Arthur Lipschitz
                            Lipschitz, Dipschitz and Moloney, Inc.

To: Legal representatives of Desmond McCallum

19 July

Dear Sirs,

RE: 'The Love Gift'

Acting on behalf of Aaron Mumby and of American Studios, Inc., and in light of the fact that we, acting on behalf of said persons, have not yet received your confirmation of the terms and conditions of the contract of employment on the above major motion picture, being a property of the above studio our client, this is to inform you that your client's services are terminated forthwith, and all monies owing for accommodation, travel, amenities, per diem et cetera are to be repaid with immediate effect, under penalty of California and federal law and incurring interest at the rate of ten per cent (10%) per day with immediate effect.

Yours
Joyce Wellbeloved
pp Arthur Lipschitz

19 July – Mobile phone conversation: Helen and Angel

H: Angel! Thank God! Did you get my message???
A: (*background noise of surf breaking*) Yeah? 'Ssup, dude?
H: Angel, this is a major emergency, they just hand-delivered this note from the studio lawyers and they say Des has been fired and we owe them thousands of dollars in expenses!
A: Oh. Sure. No biggie. (Dude! Wait up!)
   (*sound of rollerblades scrunching into hi-speed mode*)
A: Say, I'm at the beach right now, I'll catch you later okay?
H: ANGEL! You have to help us! Where's your mother?
A: Hawaii. (WAIT UP!!!!) Look, it's nothing, okay? It just means we have to get moving on the legal shit. I'll call Todd right now okay and we'll go by his office later?

Visitors' Handy Cut-out-and-keep Guide to Hollywood Vocabulary

Section 2 – Legal and Contractual Terms

Termination	= minor quarrel
Legal action	= average quarrel
Federal action	= lawyer needs to pay off mortgage

You're fired	= you were late in this morning
You're barred from the studio	= you were late this morning, again
Star	= somebody the studio has contracted to use and needs to find a role for
Major star	= somebody who can afford to demand a salary that will bankrupt the production (see also 'profit participant')
Deferral	= way of being paid on a movie nobody has any faith in
Back end	= you, if you agree to deferral
Budget	= amount the studio can afford to lose on the movie to avoid tax this year
Gross	= amount the person above you in the cast list makes
Net	= amount left after the profit participants have had their shares (see also 'residuals')
Profit participant	= Mafia connection
Residuals	= ice cream money

19 July – Helen, Angel and Des: first meeting with lawyer

The offices of hiArts, a nouveau boutique law firm, are in a converted gym near the beach, and there are still pieces of gym equipment scattered among the driftwood work tables and top-of-the-range Macintosh computers, presumably so Todd and his magna cum laude Harvard Law colleagues can work out during the precious hundred-dollar minutes in between clients.

Des is playing on the floor, where his gorilla is savagely attacking two of Aaron Mumby's merchandising characters. Angel is watching MTV on Todd's computer. Helen is watching Todd's lips, not because she's interested in what he's saying, but because she's never seen anything so gorgeous in her life before, and certainly not swinging its legs casually over a desk a foot away from her.

T: . . . so that just about wraps it up, apart from a couple points I've highlighted . . .

He leans towards her, indicating the contract. In her head, a scene from her movie is playing out.

T: . . . here . . .
H: *'He leans towards her, every nerve trembling with the strain of holding back'* . . .
T: . . . and here, which we should maybe chew over.
H: *'. . . She looks back at him, and for a few electric moments, their eyes meet . . .'*
T: I have a few ideas, foremost with respect to this first item . . .
H: *'. . . until her gaze breaks and she looks tremulously down, unable to resist or deny the force of his passion.'*
T: . . . the weight penalty clause? Have you read it?

Helen just stares dumbly back at him. He tries to get her attention to the contract, again.

T: Here, look, where it says about the progressive financial penalties for any weight gain, culminating in termination?

Helen's lips are moving silently as she plunges into fantasy.

T: Mrs McCallum?

Helen suddenly realises what he's talking about.

H: What, he has to be weighed?
T: Every day. They'll do it at the lot. It's totally standard.
H: And if he puts on weight . . .
T: First they fine him, starting with a thousand a day for each extra half-pound, and then after a week or three

pounds, it kicks in to ten thou, with an optional contract break. At that point production is suspended until he drops back to where he was when he signed, and you pay the total costs of keeping everybody on stand-by, until that happens.

H: *(stunned)* How much are they?

Todd flicks through his notes casually.

T: Hard to say exactly but – don't hold me to this – around the three hundred a day mark.
H: Three hundred dollars?

Todd smiles, indulgently, as at a wayward child.

T: Three hundred thousand dollars.

Helen looks down at Des.

D: Rarrr!!! This is MY jungle, and . . .
H: Des, sweetie, stand up for a moment.

He does so. She bends down and lifts his T-shirt, to reveal a normal, bulging four-year-old's tummy.

D: I'm hungry, Mum. When can we go and have a hamburger? Will it be like in France that time? Can I have cheese and bacon?

Todd turns his arc-lamp smile on Des in turn.

T: Hey, sport. How about a yummy Chinese chicken salad instead?
D: No, my mum said I could have a hamburger and then another ice cream for learning my words.

Helen is now fully back in possession of her faculties.

H: *(to Todd)* The thing is, you know, it may be perfectly standard, but it's also perfectly standard for four-year-old boys to grow. I mean, he's not exactly pudgy, is he? What if he puts on weight because he's getting taller?

T: I'm afraid that wouldn't go down so great, either. There's a penalty clause relating to costume fittings that . . .

H: Please!!

Todd puts down the papers, and gives her his best 'I'm your friend so long as you keep paying me' smile. She breaks into a sweat.

T: I'll fix it. Don't give it a thought.

Angel, bored, switches off the computer and wanders over. Todd ruffles her hair.

T: Hey, witch.

She resents it. She's known him all her life.

A: Are you guys done yet?

Helen recovers herself enough to look at the notes she made in preparation.

H: Oh! I just had one question – it's a bit embarrassing but . . .
T: Go right ahead, don't be shy!
H: Who pays for all this – I mean, for you doing this contract and sorting out the eating stuff and . . . er, stuff?
T: *(unabashed)* You do. Or Junior here does, out of his fee.
H: *(gulps)* Ah. And . . . um, well, roughly how much d'you think it'll cost?
T: Let's see . . .

He whips out a Palm and begins calculating.

T: . . . an hour this morning plus say two for phoning and another couple for the redraft – say five hours at eight hundred an hour – four k at this point, maybe?

Helen sways and props herself up on the desk.

H: Four thousand dollars? Already?
T: You okay?

He puts out a hand to steady her. It burns into her arm.

H: Sorry – still a bit jet-laggy, you know. Look, don't worry about doing any more work to change it, how many hamburgers can he eat in the next two weeks?

Des triumphantly holds up all the fingers of both hands.

19 July – E-mail: Madge to Helen

> **From:** Madge Handelman [madge@handy.com]
> **To:** Helen McCallum, care of [mail@oceanshores.com]

Hiya Helen darling
Just a quickie to keep you up to sped – Spriggstein has had to pull out, his mannager figures asociating him with the image of a maried man will pay haboc with his sales, so we're on a slight hiyaitus with the scedule but don't wory – the studio is fine covering your expenses and it'll only be a wek max before they replac him.
 Haring great things about your adoreable son. So glad it's workig out with Angel too. Isn't she just the bestest?
 Gotta scrable! Madge

----

19 July – Phone call: Helen to Colum's mobile

C: ... D'you have any idea at all what time it is?
H: Oh – sorry – what time is it?

C: I don't know and I don't want to know, but I was asleep.
H: I said sorry.
C: Yeah, well.
Pause.
H: Where are you?
C: Le Mans. Great croissants, by the way.
H: Thanks.
Pause.
C: So – how's the impossibly glamorous world of the silver screen?
H: If you must know, it pretty much is impossibly glamorous.
C: Let me guess – personal limos, little director's chair for young Des to sit in, perfect weather every day, and all the men look like Brad Pitt.
H: I tend to prefer the ones who look like George Clooney, but otherwise you're bang on.
C: I see. Well, rather you than me.
H: Yes, you probably wouldn't fit in very well here.
C: And what exactly do you mean by that?
H: Nothing. Why are you so grumpy?
C: I'm not grumpy. I'm having the time of my life with the lovely Ernestine. She's a brilliant navigator. Knows her way around, if you get my drift.
H: I refuse to rise to your puerile provocations . . .
C: Fair enough.
H: . . . I only called to say that we're going to be staying a bit longer than we thought.
C: Oh yes? How's that then?
H: Oh, just some problem with the star. But don't worry, Des is loving it.
C: Can I talk to him?
H: He's not here right now, he's in the pool with Omar.
C: Who the fuck is Omar?
H: The limo driver. He's really nice, he's got two undergraduate

degrees and he's really a writer but he's just doing this to give back. You know, to the world.
C: Oh really.
H: What do you mean, 'Oh Really'? God, you're so NEGATIVE!
C: I am not negative, I'm just not quite so pathetically gullible as . . .
H: Are you calling me pathetically . . .
C: Look, it's late, okay? Let's just speak in the morning.
H: Don't worry. I'll call you when the tinsel wears off. Goodnight!
C: And sweet dreams to you too!

19 July, late – Helen, in bed

I fear I may have spoken too soon about Angel. Des was totally impossible at bedtime, refusing to go to bed, refusing to eat anything but junk food from room service for supper (even in LA I'd never have guessed that a burger could end up costing $1,000) and hitting me when I tried to help him clean his teeth. When I asked him, quite politely, what had got into him, he said that it was his Method. Method of what, apart from provoking an early demise, I wanted to know, and it turns out that Angel has been telling him about Method acting and he's decided that this requires him to behave like a spoiled American brat twenty-four hours a day for the duration of the shoot.

I'll give him Method acting. Actually, I think the poor lamb was mostly just jet-lagged – lunch-time feels like midnight, which is probably why I was a bit grumpy with Colum earlier. But you really start to notice that awful British cynicism in a place like this, where everybody's so open and enthusiastic.

He's probably dreading having to deal with George and Fiona. God, it feels like a million miles away.

20 July – George and Fiona, having breakfast

They're chomping their way through yet another spread of exotic cereals not yet available in the Outer Hebrides, with GMTV blaring from the giant screen. Bertie, by now spherical, is polishing off a piece of wild salmon with potato rosti on the side.

The doorbell rings. George gets up to open it, which is easier said than done, as the Bertie trap is still in place, and the rest of the hall is entirely filled with mountains of loo rolls and giant extra-strong bin bags. On the step stands a burly delivery man holding a clipboard.

DM: McClashan?
G: McCallum.
DM: That'll be it, sign here please.

He waves back at another burly man standing by the tailgate of a lorry, who begins to manoeuvre a large and bulky object out of it.

G: Sign? And for what?

The two men together get the bulky object up the front path to the door. George shouts back over his shoulder to Fiona:

G: Wife! There's another one arrived! Come quick!
F: (*in distance*) Another what? I've the celebrity horoscopes only half over here.
DM: So where d'you want it guv?
G: What is it? (*to Fiona*) Come away here will ye, woman, before I heave a brick at yon TV!

The delivery man consults his notes.

DM: Says 'ere it's a rolling stair-climber. There's the paperwork.

He hands a fat envelope to the bemused George, just as Fiona appears in the background.

F: Och, that was awfu' quick wasn't it?

The delivery men hold out the pad for Fiona to sign.

F: Would ye be good enough to bring it in for us laddie afore ye go? Only it'll take me a wee while to figure out the book of words here.

G: And what have ye done now, woman, with yer special-offer mania?

F: It's no' a mania George, it's absolutely free for a month, it says right here, and then when we're away home they can send it back.

She moves herself and George out of the way of the men, who shove the stair-climber over the doorstep.

G: But we're leaving in two days, ye mad bat.

F: Aye, well I didna know that when I ordered it, did I? An' mebbe they'll keep it, yon Helen's always been an idle slut.

The stair-climber slides into the front hall, where it crushes Bertie's cage and completely blocks the space left beside the bin bags and loo rolls. The delivery men take their pad and leave.

F: Och, move yerself George, ye're as useless as a peg leg to a blind man, and give me room to think.

20 July, morning – Phone message from Cary for Helen

C: Good morning good morning good morning! Remember me? I sure hope so – it's Cary. We met at the party? Can it be two whole days ago? Well, I truly enjoyed that evening, and I was just wondering, on this superlatively glorious day, whether you might like to drive up the coast to Malibu with me for lunch? There's a great little place nobody knows about and the food is to die for, if you do seafood and dairy of course. But I'm sure to be at least tenth in line, so I'll wait to hear from you. Later!

20 July, morning – Phone message from Helen for Cary

H: Hello Cary, how lovely to hear from you, and it sounds terrific, only I did promise Des I'd take him to the aquarium after his costume fitting, he's bonkers about animals and fish and stuff, and also I sort of promised my . . . I promised I'd stay with him the whole time because he's only little, so if you wanted to come with us, and then maybe we could all have lunch afterwards somewhere?

20 July, morning – Helen and Des at costume fitting

Helen and Des, the latter stripped to his Thunderbirds underpants, are standing in an endless corridor on the studio lot, hung on either side with racks and racks of costumes. A wardrobe assistant is taking Des's measurements, and consulting with the movie's costume designer, Mia Tolare, as they scrutinise Des from every angle.

Next to Des stands Spencer, his body double, who is more or less the same size and shape, and a veteran of forty movies.

MT: The legs are the big issue.

The wardrobe assistant bends to touch Des's perfectly normal knees.

WA: Yeah, see this bump here? And it's the same both sides.
MT: They'll have to keep the camera frontal in long shot.

Helen looks hurt. Des is much more interested in Spencer's career history.

S: So it was on *Free Willy 2* right . . .

D: With the whale! You saw the whale! Was it really really huge?

S: Saw it? Boy, I was like practically in its mouth I was so right there with it, and it was just me and him with these humungous teeth and they couldn't even like put any safety harness stuff on or anything . . .

The wardrobe assistant looks at her notepad and consults Mia again.

WA: Then there's the . . .

Mia has obviously already clocked whatever it is.

MT: Yeah.
WA: It's big, huh?
MT: Real big. Not a lot we can do with it, unless . . .

Helen positions herself behind them and stands on tiptoe to get exactly their view of Des's stomach. It looks just the same as before, i.e. totally normal.

MT: *(to Des)* Turn around, honey.

Des obediently turns around. Now he's facing away from them.

S: . . . and I had to like swim all around it . . .
D: Can you swim? Without arm bands?
S: Man, I been surfing at Zuma since I was three.
D: My mum won't let me go in the big pool without arm bands, but I bet I could if I tried.

Mia shakes her head, despairingly.

MT: That's worse. And it's not like we can hide it.
WA: Yeah.

Helen is totally baffled.

H: *(nervously, to Mia)* He did have quite a big breakfast, but I don't think he'll eat much lunch, he's not a greedy sort of child.

Their turn to look baffled.

MT: If you need to feed him right away, the commissary'll be open in a few minutes, I could have somebody run over . . .
H: No, no, only I thought . . . I thought you thought . . .
MT: *(to her assistant)* You know what? I bet a haircut'd fix it!
WA: Really?

Mia reaches over, grabs a clump of Des's hair, which has indeed got quite long lately, and lifts it away from his head.

MT: See? With an inch off all over, it's almost normal size.

Helen's face clears.

H: Great! Des! It's all fine! It's just your head! And you can have that burger!

All four of the others stare at her. They have no idea what she's on about.

20 July, afternoon – Helen

The longer I spend here, the more I realise that all that tosh about people in LA being stupid and uneducated and primitive is the result of sheer envy or ignorance. Cary is evidently one of nature's gentlemen, and an avid reader too – all the way round the aquarium he kept quoting me from somebody called Kalil and Deepak Chopra, and talking about Buddhist Sutras, and how they help him achieve deep spiritual harmony between the conflicting pressures and temptations of his life here. It must be hard being so multi-talented, with everybody wanting a piece of you, and not knowing which of your many gifts to develop first.

He was very sweet with Des too, offered to take him to a

baseball game which I'm sure Des would love if he'd only give it a try, and he'd have paid for us all to go into the aquarium, which was quite a lot of money, only it turns out they have reductions for tourists, so it made sense for me to do it. Then when we came out we were right by the hotel, so we just had lunch here and put it on the room.

Des, however, was not at his most charming, demanding that Cary tell him the name of every single fish, crustacean, jellyfish and mollusc in the aquarium, plus what they were saying at any point, and whether they were real fish or only acting fish. Somehow Des seems to have got the idea that everybody here is an actor, which is probably not a million miles from the truth – waiters are actors acting as waiters while they wait to act as other people, etc. Cary's response – I thought quite witty – that they were all called Brad and Jennifer evoked only contempt from Des, and an opportunity to trot out his PhD-level knowledge of marine taxonomy.

Anyhow, after spending all my time since I arrived tending to Des's needs, I deserve a friend of my own, and it will be very nice to have somebody to go to premières and openings and parties with. After all, I might as well make the most of it, and Cary seems to know absolutely everybody. Pretty flattering that he chooses to spend time with frumpy old me and my lovable encumbrance.

Whether it was that wild raspberry margarita he made me try at lunch, or just the unusual experience of an entire conversation with a man who's not micro-dusting at the same time, I felt quite dizzy afterwards. Probably just as well we're not here for long – found myself quite unconsciously fiddling with my wedding ring. Somebody once told me that, however much weight a person puts on, their wrists stay the same, but I now have the sorry evidence that this doesn't apply to hands. If – God forbid – I ever lose my marriage, I'll have to lose a finger as well.

Anyway, who cares if I helped finish Des's burger as well as my own. I was saving us thousands of dollars in fines, and it's all going to be hoovered off next Thursday at 12.45.

Might have to have a little lie-down now. Des has demanded that Omar teach him to dive like a killer whale, but I'm sure they're safe for a few minutes. Des is technically Omar's pay cheque at the moment, so he has some incentive to keep him alive. Better just check the messages first I suppose . . .

20 July – Phone message from Colum

C: Hiya – you there? Helen? I guess not – big surprise. 'Catching rays,' I presume.

    Any road, just calling to say we got back fine, deposited the lovely Ernestine and her pantechnicon of luggage, before arriving home to discover Bertie missing and the entire house full of toilet paper and bin bags. It seems, despite our planning, that my parents were no match for the mental dexterity of the Kentish Town con artist, and answered the door to a man claiming to be taking bulk orders from Sainsbury's. The bad news is that they also seem to have been confused into buying a brand-new video recorder and DVD player, which they thoughtfully offered to take with them, until I discovered they'd found your John Lewis account card while storing the excess bin bags.

    Anyhow they're off now, thank God, and Bertie was unearthed when I went to find their bags in the landing cupboard, which I apparently made parent-proof but not cat-proof. He seems fine, a wee bit traumatised mebbe, but that could have to do with an incident with the Miracle Rolling Stairclimber my mum took it into her head to welcome into our home on a month's free trial the day before they left, which evidently rolls over anything, including things that don't get out of the way in time. Still, you don't want to be bothered with all of this, it'll be history by the time you're back.

Are you there yet? No. Of course not.

What else? Your sister and mother send their love, something about Des's birthday presents and measuring him up for a jumper you asked her to knit. I'm just opening the post here – mostly bills of course, letter from the health centre for Des and your film club calendar – nothing else to report except it's bloody hot and sticky everywhere, so Camden Council has decided this is the perfect weather to impose an indefinite preservation order on the rubbish we left out two weeks ago.

Well. Better stop throwing money into this thing. Give young Des a kiss from me and get him to give us a shout some time will you?

20 July, early evening – Helen, sunbathing by the pool

Here I am, sitting under an oleander by an Olympic-sized swimming pool, sipping a papaya-and-passion-fruit smoothie, and staring out at the deepest, bluest ocean you have ever seen, while my baby cavorts with Omar the Black Whale and butterflies dance around the lavender planters.

I have to say, the vagaries of the Camden Council sanitation experts seem rather a long way away.

I mean, I love Colum and we've spent half our lives together and everything but – sometimes it's just time for the caterpillar to shed its old skin and move on, and moving on isn't something Colum is exactly cut out for, even if he wanted to, which he obviously doesn't. I actually don't think at this stage he's physically capable of adapting to a new environment.

But for me – somehow the minute I arrived here I just felt totally at home, as though it had been waiting for me all along.

All my life I've believed that it was my duty to live in a hideous stinking city and do a dreary brain-numbing job with a bunch of asinine nerds for company, holding my tongue and keeping my longings and dreams in check because they seemed impossible – and here suddenly I discover that I don't have to, that there are thousands if not millions of people who've just come here to live in paradise and follow their dreams – and they came true!

Des, in the pool with Omar

Whoosh!! Whoosh! Wah wah! I'm a killer whale and I'm going to SNAP this baby seal's head right off and eat its blood and now I'm diving whoosh whooosh oh urggh splutter . . . now I'm gliding gliding along and . . .
    I don't want to do this any more.
    I want to talk to my dad.

Helen, by the pool

. . . even if Des doesn't get another film for a bit and I don't sell my script right away, we wouldn't need a lot of money, property here is incredibly cheap and because the weather's so great you'd hardly need anything for clothes or heating, and the food is all fresh and costs nothing, too.
    And I mean, I'd never take Des away from Colum or anything of course, but he could always visit whenever he wanted . . . Oh, hi Des, wow you made me jump, have you had enough? I think it's probably time for supper and bed, don't you?

20 July – Helen and Des: bedtime

Des and Helen are in the second bathroom of their suite, which has two whirlpool omnijet tubs, two basins, two lavatories, two bidets, two telephones, a pull-out multigym, a make-up corner with magnifying mirror ringed with daylight bulbs, a wall-mounted pivoting TV, and an electronic weighing scale, calibrated to a tenth of a gram, set flush with the floor.

Helen is avoiding the scales while she dries Des after his swim. He's squirming around, trying to get a better view of *Nickelodeon* on the TV, and arguing. Helen is trying, without success, to distract him from his purpose.

H: ... Ooh look, poppet, you've got a little tan mark already! How grown up! God, I hope there's not a penalty clause about that in the contract too ...
D: I want to call him NOW! He left that message and he said I was to call him ...
H: How do you know?
D: I heard it. Angel showed me how.
H: Oh she did, did she?
D: Yes and I miss him and I miss Teddy too, my real teddy I want to call him NOW!!!
H: Sweetheart, you can't call him now, it's the middle of the night.
D: *(squirming away)* No it's not it's not even bedtime, and he goes to bed much later than me!

Helen grabs him again. It's like trying to dry a squid.

H: Come here.

He wriggles away again.

H: Come here or I'll turn that damn thing off!

He stops squirming.

H: It's bedtime here, but in England it's the middle of the night.

Des looks out of the window.

D: No, look it's sunny still.
H: You don't understand darling, when the sun comes up here, it goes to bed in England.
D: It can't, there's only one sun, you told me. How can it be in bed and not in bed all at once?

He breaks away and makes for the phone. Helen grabs him, wedges him under her arm, snaps off the TV and marches into the living room. He starts to wail.

D: Let me go! Let me go!
H: Not until you promise to stop behaving like a brat. You're just going to have to take my word about the sun, until I can get access to an orrery and an astrolabe.
D: You're lying! And it's my money anyway and it's my phone and I'm more important than you and ...
H: STOP THIS RIGHT NOW OR THERE'LL BE NO MORE TRIPS TO THE ZOO, EVER!!

Des bawls even louder.

D: I want a hug! I want to go home!!

She sighs and cuddles him to her.

H: Sh, poppet. Sh.
D: *(through his sobs)* I can't! It's my Method!!
H: Well what if my Method is to be a sabre-toothed tiger? Grrrrrr!!

A faint giggle breaks through the tears.

H: That's better. You don't want to go home yet, we've only just got here.
D: I want to call Dad.
H: We can call him tomorrow, I promise. When the sun's just getting up here, it'll still be day over there.
D: Which day?

H: Tomorrow. Tomorrow starts earlier there than here. It's ... never mind.

She jumps up and reaches for the room service menu.

H: So, what's it to be? A Chinese Chicken Salad with crispy noodles and mandarins? A Zesty Fresh Seared Tuna Niçoise? Or ... (*seeing his face*) well, maybe just one more, but that's absolutely the last burger until after the shoot ...

21 July – Phone message from Madge

M: Hiya kiddo, don't want to wake you so this is just a quickie to say that the studio just adores young Des, and the dialog coach is real jazzed at his ability with accents, but the producer feels it would be a good direction to make the character English anyways (I'm faxing you the new outline to keep you on the same page, as usual changes are in italics), and the director unfortunately wasn't able to go along with that so they've let him go, which means just another teeny hiatus until the new director comes on-stream.

    Which is great because it means you guys get to spend time exploring!

    I'll be here in Maui through tomorrow and after that I may have to go to Peru for a few days but you can always reach me on my service. Loveya!

21 July – Story synopsis of major studio picture *The Love that Kills*

```
STORY
Joe Mitchum is a guy everybody envies - chief car
mechanic to one of the biggest stars in Hollywood,
with a stunning wife, Kelly, a grade-school
```

teacher, and an adored adoptive *English son, Hugh*, he spends his days polishing Ferrari engine blocks and his nights singing his baby *boy* to sleep and making passionate love to Kelly. The only other thing that marks Joe out is his amazing good looks, and from working on cars he's developed a physique that makes women swoon. But Joe is a one-woman, straight-up kind of a guy. Then tragedy strikes, as *Hugh*, who was adopted *recently on one of Joe's trips to the UK to race Silvano's vintage Ferraris*, develops a life-threatening illness. Joe spends every penny he has scouring the world for a solution, but to no avail, and time is running out as *Hugh* gets weaker by the day. Finally, Joe hears of a doctor in the Bahamas who may have the answer. Joe sells his beloved vintage Mustang to pay the air fare for himself and *Hugh*. *Hugh* barely makes it, but when they meet the doctor, Dr Ingrid JayeGold, she immediately produces a drug made from a secret formula known only to herself that relieves *Hugh's* symptoms. Dr JayeGold is a person of colour, with a stunning, panther-like beauty, and something about her strikes Joe with an uncanny shock of recognition as soon as they meet. Dr JayeGold also experiences a shock of recognition – despite the fact that *Hugh*, the product of a relationship with a *British aristocrat she met on a business trip*, is not a person of colour, she immediately knows the child as her own baby, given up *under pressure from his father who at first wanted a son to secure his inheritance in the Scottish Highlands, but then married and spurned the child in favour of his baby son* by *his new wife*. Dr JayeGold, maddened by grief at seeing her child again in this condition, gives no hint of the truth but agrees to treat *Hugh*, and Joe, unknown to Kelly, remortgages his house to pay the bill. Back home, *Hugh* progresses by leaps and bounds. *His* parents and *his* beloved collie Laddy are delighted to see *him* back to *his* old self. But all too soon the drugs are about to run out and Joe goes back to Dr JayeGold, this time alone. Dr JayeGold knows he has no more money. And she is seething with secret bitterness against all *wives*. She wants her child back – and she wants a father for her child. But first, Kelly has to be out of the picture. She tells Joe she'll treat *Hugh* without money. He's over-joyed – how can he thank her? Then she tells him her price. For every month's supply of drugs, a night of passion with him . . .

But Joe's boss, megastar Silvano Stallion, has always secretly lusted after Kelly. And one day Joe, overcome by the agony of his dilemma, reveals to Silvano that without truckloads of cash their beloved *Hugh* will die. The next time Silvano gets Kelly alone, he offers to pay for *Hugh's* treatment, if she becomes his mistress.

So now both of them, unknown to each other, are racked by the same terrible agonising dilemma. But neither dares confess . . .

21 July, morning – Helen, Angel and Des at 'Happy Nails'

Helen and Angel are seated at adjacent stations in the Happy Nails parlour, having manicures and pedicures from two busy Vietnamese women.

Des is crawling on hands and knees among the other stations, examining the various toe designs on display, and occasionally making gorilla noises. All the other women seem to think this is very sweet.

Helen holds out one completed hand for Angel to scrutinise.

A: You need another coat – something like, pearlised. *(to manicurist)* Ginger Satin, number 23, one coat.
H: Pearl? Isn't that a bit *Cosmo*?

The manicurist waits for a decision.

A: *(patiently)* Pearl like, catches the light. It's for where it's sunny. In London, it'd be like – why bother? *Pink* pearl is *Cosmo*. *Ginger* pearl is like – Hollywood Hills classic.

Her own nails, which are not pearlised at all, are coming up the colour of a very old Christmas pudding. She seems pleased.

H: I still lust after those adorable stars and stripes with the little diamond stars.
A: So what, you never had your teen years? *(to manicurist)* Ginger.

The manicurist duly gets to work again.

H: I certainly didn't spend them getting my nails done for an hour and a half.
A: So like, what are you supposed to do while you hang around? By the way, did you call Todd yet?
H: Todd? Why?
A: *(patient sigh)* He can get you a ton of money in nuisance fees for the delay.
H: And charge me another ton for doing it.
A: It's worth your while, believe me.
H: Well, I'm not repelled by the thought of another meeting with him.
A: You did get that he's gay?

Helen blushes like a fool.

H: I knew it was too good to be true. Still . . .

She coyly studies the nail in progress.

H: . . . there's always . . .
A: Always what?
H: Um — more of a who than a what. I mean, I barely know him, but . . .
A: Uh-oh. Want an expert critique?

Across the room, Des growls, then yelps:

D: Mum!!
H: I don't know . . .
A: Believe me, I have razor instincts. My mom uses me *all* the time.
D: MUMMM!!

Des comes bounding over, still on hands and knees.

D: Mum MUM!! There's an alligator in the corner!
H: How lovely, sweets. We're nearly finished here and then we can go for one of those lovely non-fat sugar-free . . .
D: No no no really Mum come and see come and SEE!

He grabs Helen's hand, ruining forty minutes of careful work at a stroke.

H: DES!!!! *(to manicurist)* God, I'm SO, SO sorry!

The manicurist smiles, pats Des on the head and says:

M: Hah!! Vey cute boy huh!!

Des drags Helen off to the other corner of the room, where there is indeed a two-foot-long pet alligator, curled up in a Magic Toes vibrating foot bath.

D: Look look and he's got real teeth!
H: I can see that.

His owner looks up over last month's *Allure* and squirts a plastic water bottle over the alligator, Des and Helen.

O: He's fine so long as he's damp. It's like, a real deep tissue massage for him. Keeps him calm.
H: I'm glad to hear it.
D: Can I have an alligator Mum? Can we take one home please please!!
H: Probably not, sweetie. But how would you like a lovely lunch out, with non-fat sugar-free ice cream?

She squeezes his hand, then looks at her own.

H: Somehow I don't think our lifestyle is compatible with seven-layer manicures, do you?

21 July – Helen and Cary, on the phone

H: So, I know it's a bit soon after yesterday, but we've got another delay on the production and it's so gorgeous again, I thought this time we could try that place up the coast you suggested . . .
C: (*cheerily, like Tom Hanks*) It so happens my plans got cancelled this minute!
H: Oh, great. I mean, are you sure . . .
C: (*smoothly, like Cary Grant*) I'm all yours.
H: Oh!

On the phone, he really could be Cary Grant, with a humour bypass.

C: (*suggestively, like Richard Gere*) So, just the two of us, huh?
H: Er – well not exactly. There's Des of course and my friend Angel, but you'll like her she's very . . .

C: (*zestfully, like Jim Carrey*) She sounds wild! I'm gonna love her!
H: Oh!
C: (*concernedly, like Jeff Bridges*) And how are you? And how's the screenplay?
H: Oh, fine – I mean, slow, of course, but I think it's got real . . .
C: (*Jim*) It sounds terrific! (*Jeff*) You and I must get together for that *one-on-one* tutorial *(Richard)* – real soon.

First Page of Helen's Script, *City of Dreams*, eighth draft

```
FADE IN
An opulent hotel suite by the ocean in Los
Angeles. HARRIETXXXxHONORXXHILARY, a quite
pretty/stunningly beautiful in an English sort of
way thirtyish WOMAN, dressed all in black and with
an air of recetn tragedy about her, is . . .
    THINK WHAT SHE'S DOING . . .?? unpacking?? Too
drab. Looking through photos? Good setup for
backstopry!!
    Suddenly, an adorable four-year-old BOY also
dressed in black comes into the room, carrying
his teddy bear. This is her son XXXDARENXXX-
TEDXXXDAN

                    DAN
         (holding out his teddy bear to her)
       Look, look, Mum! Look what I've done!

Hiulary looks at the teddy bear, IT is wqearing a
black armband.

                    DAN
       Look Teddy is in mourning for Dad too!
```

For some reason this makes HILARY burst into tears. She gives him a big hug throug her sobs.

                    DAN
        don't cry Mum! We're starting a new
        lifehere like you said! I't what Dad
                woudl have wanted!

                   HILARY
              (through her tears)
    Oh yes, love, you're such a comfort to me,
          and thank goodness Dad left us tons
       and tons of money. That reminds me, I must
    call the lawyer. I wonder what he's like . . .

FROM HERE - meeting with lawyer toi settle will, they fall in love but he's not nice to Dan, so what will she do, torn between love for him and for her son, then just at moment when shes' abou to take plunge, she meets CORY, who is man of her dreams. But CORY has a secret . . .

Visitors' Handy Cut-out-and-keep Guide to Hollywood Vocabulary

Section 3 – The Attractive, Available Man

As it happens, my lunch plans just got cancelled this minute!	= I was just beginning to wonder who was going to buy me lunch today
Why don't we meet at the bar on the corner?	= My place is a dump
My car's at the shop. Jaguars are just so unreliable!	= I don't have a car
I have to be a little careful with what I eat	= So long as it's more than fifty bucks, I'm fine

There's this gorgeous little place, and nobody knows about it!	= I won't be spotted by any of my exes
It's not exactly cheap, but it's worth every penny	= You're paying
I'm kind of a multiple hyphenate – you know, actor/writer/producer	= I'm unemployed
We're just waiting to iron out the contracts	= I don't even have a temp job
You are so fascinating! I could listen to you all day!	= I'm certainly not telling you a thing about myself
I feel a deep spiritual bond between us	= I'm going to stick to you like a limpet . . .
Money is such a trap, isn't it?	= . . . so long as you're paying, that is
We really should go for a massage/reiki workout/hot stone treatment together	= That way you can pick up the tab, again
Your little boy is just adorable!	= But *I* wanna be your little boy!
He seems totally at home already	= He's just as much a brat as all the other kids in town
The studio is never gonna let a little star like that go	= Imagine the money he's gonna make for us . . .
I so adore LA, don't you?	= Just checking that you really have bought the hype
This place is too good to be true, isn't it?	= Just like me
You must have a dessert,	= Who cares if you're fat, so

the desserts are to die for! How about if I have one too?	long as you're paying? = That way I can skip dinner
So tell me your impression of the people you've met so far	= I wanna talk about ME!!
Would you say English men are emotionally colder?	= Let's both talk about ME!!
I'm so glad you're here for a little while	= I might get to clear my credit cards before you leave
I guess I really should go make a few calls to my lawyer	= If I don't keep swapping the debt between cards, I'll be in gaol by tomorrow
I can't believe it!	= Here it comes . . .
I must have left my wallet in the Armani jacket!	= . . . Hey, you knew it was coming!
Let me speak to them, I can work something out	= I can always embarrass you into paying
I feel truly terrible about this	= I can't believe I got away with it, again!
Let me buy you lunch tomorrow to make up	= So why stop now?

21 July, afternoon – Helen, in her room, with a headache

Can it be that only yesterday I was singing Angel's praises and welcoming her into my confidence on matters dear to my heart? Talk about vipers and bosoms! No sooner had we arrived than she was subjecting poor Cary to a merciless interrogation, of a kind not seen since WWII movies on Saturday afternoon TV. What did he do, how much did he earn, what

341

EXACTLY was he working on right now and with whom, whom had he worked with before, etc etc. I was so mortified I didn't know where to look.

And hinting – no, downright suggesting – that he didn't, in fact, know all these movie stars nearly as well as he claimed, if at all. None of which was helped by Des co-interrogating him throughout about the availability of alligators in the local pet stores, and would Cary go and buy him one right away, please?

Then when the poor man tried to change the subject to the interesting cultural differences between modes of emotional expression in British and Angeleno men, Angel decided it would be really helpful to tell Des that Cary was slagging off his father for an uptight repressed old stiff, which thank God Des only got a faint whiff of, but enough that he then switched to insisting that we leave RIGHT NOW to go and phone Colum, Angel being unaccountably unwilling to let him make long transatlantic calls on her ubiquitous mobile. Luckily her maths was not up to refuting my little white lie that it was midnight in England at that point, and not the perfect time to catch him at his affectionate best.

So I nearly died for Cary when the poor man discovered he'd left his wallet at home. I mean, I know how terrible I felt the only time that happened to me, luckily I was with Georgie and it was only a bag of fish and chips, but I could just project that multiplied a hundredfold, to which Angel, far from sympathising, had the nerve to imply that even this was some sort of deliberate ploy to get us to pay. As though he had no reason for wanting to see me, other than my temporary flushness with studio dollars! So what does that make me? I asked her on the way back, after we'd dropped poor Cary off at the yoga studio. I'm glad to say that shut her up for the rest of the journey, and she's now gone off pogoing with her idiot mall-rat friends, or something.

Anyhow, they needn't think that any of this is going to put me off him. He's gorgeous and kind and funny and warm and gorgeous and modest and he's INTERESTED in ME!! And he eats pudding. So what if he's not a millionaire? Name me one millionaire who's all of those things, or indeed any of them, apart from George Clooney of course.

Anyhow, what a stupid fuss about a friend. He's only a friend. I'm allowed to have friends still, aren't I?

Bugger that phone. Oh well, I suppose I'd better answer it, it might be about Des's alleged job.

21 July, afternoon – Helen and Colum, on the phone

H: ... brilliant timing, in fact, we were just about to call you.
C: Indeed.
H: What do you mean?
C: I mean indeed, it's a word in current English usage, I believe.
H: I didn't want to call too soon, on the assumption you'd be enjoying a protracted welcome back with the boys at the Bog and Badger.
C: As it happens, I've been home all evening.
H: Cleaning the house, I suppose.
C: Maybe you've forgotten that here in the cradle of democracy we don't have a bottomless pool of illegal labour for these menial tasks.
H: Do you love me?
C: What's that got to do with anything?
H: Maybe it just means that for once I'd rather talk about meaningful things like emotions and relationships than cleaning the house, AGAIN.
C: How long have you been in LaLaLand?
H: God, it's so childish, calling it that.
C: In fact, I did try to call you a couple of hours ago, but you were out.

H: Well, even I have to be allowed to eat lunch, don't I?
C: Was it good?
H: Lovely, thank you very much.
(sound of Des erupting into the room in the background)
D: Mum! Mum! I'm awake can we call Dad now is he up yet?
H: (D'you know what, I'm talking to him right now sweetie, here he is.)
D: Dad! Dad!! I miss you Dad!!!
C: I miss you too.
D: Dad can I have a pet alligator Dad please please they have alligators here Mum won't let me buy one it's my money please!
C: I'm not so sure an alligator would be that happy back here. But when you're home, mebbe we can talk about getting a friend for Bertie.
D: Dad, I don't like Cary he's boring and he doesn't know about animals!
(sound of Helen in the background)
H: (Des! Dad doesn't want to know about Cary!)
C: Who's Cary?
D: We had to go and have lunch with him and he forgot his wallet and Angel says he said you're re . . . repress . . .
(sound of Helen snatching the phone from Des)
H: (Go and learn your lines, Des, you can talk to Dad again later.)
(sound of Des wailing in background, 'I want my Dad!!!')
C: So who's Cary?
H: God, honestly, he's just this really nice guy who I met who . . .
C: . . . who thinks British men are repressed. I bet he does a lot of yoga and eats brown rice and tofu.
H: As it happens, he eats everything.
C: I'm not surprised, if he only gets to eat when somebody else is paying.

H: Oh for God's . . .
C: Does he tell you he loves you?
H: I refuse to continue with this conversation!
C: Does he?
H: FOR CHRIST'S SAKE!!!
(sound of Des's wails rising to a crescendo in background)
H: He's just a FRIEND!!!!!
C: Just don't drag Des into it, that's all. Get off the phone now and see to the poor wee scrap!
H: How DARE you!!
(sound of phone being slammed down, at both ends)

21 July – Helen, after the phone call

Clearly I have come to a crossroads in my life. It's going to be painful for everybody, but all change is. I've spent the last year longing for something to happen, and now it has, I have to face the reality and embrace it. Colum and I had something wonderful once – or at least I thought we did – or at least the me I was then thought we did – but that was then, and though it may sound harsh, I have moved on, and he has not.

But before I do anything hastily, and remembering always that the most important person in all of this is still young Des (how DARE he imply I wasn't looking after DES! The BASTARD RAT FINK SODDING BASTARD SON OF A SEWER RAT'S ARMPIT!!!!!!!!

Now now, you know he only said it because he knows it's the thing that will hurt most. He fights dirty, and he always did, and he always will. Remember that . . .)

Anyhow – I have made comparative lists of their respective qualities, in order to be able to arrive at a reasoned decision that I can stick to through what are bound to be intensely agonising and difficult times to come, in the next few months or years. I think I have managed to make it fair and evenly balanced, bearing in mind that I have known Colum for many long years and Cary for . . . my God, not very long at all.

But you know, don't you? Everybody says so. When it's The One, you know.

But then I thought I knew with Colum . . . very poignant, thinking back. I was so young then and, more important, so young in experience.

Here it is.

COLUM	CARY
Never talks about emotions or relationships	Will talk about anything and everything
Never asks how I am (says instead, 'I assume you'll let me know if there's something wrong, you usually do')	Asks how I am all the time and REALLY MEANS it and LISTENS
Never comments on my appearance (except to tell me there's lipstick on my teeth)	Tells me I'm beautiful (and knows a LOT of beautiful women)
Never praises my talents	Notices everything I do, and is thrilled by it all
Never wants to do anything new	Is always up for a new adventure or experience
Does work which involves sitting at a grey desk in a smelly office drawing up legal documents	Does work which involves drawing on the full range of emotion and creativity with unflinching honesty and courage
Spends spare time hanging about in Bog and Badger, or with head inside a bike engine	Spends spare time exploring the boundaries of human perception and experience on the way to spiritual peace

Best friend is Billy Giddens, certified mental defective and bike nut	Best friend is Brad Pitt's next-door neighbour
Lives in Kentish Town	Lives in Malibu
Looks like everybody's favourite brother	Looks like Cary Grant
Slurps his tea, and has been known to stick his buttery knife right in the marmalade jar (and has the body to show for it)	Has perfect table manners and great taste in food (and has the body to show for it)

I could go on, but it's more painful than I expected. How can I do it to Colum, and to Des? But how can I not? Surely in time they'll see it's for the best, and thank me for . . . oh hang on, there's the phone.

21 July, late afternoon – Helen and Georgie, on the phone

H: Hello?
G: Helen?
H: Georgie!
G: Hi sweetie, aren't you impressed that I found you, I certainly am.
H: Well . . . yes, and . . . but isn't it some unearthly hour of . . .
G: Is it? Christ, so it is. No, well, you know how it goes, the only time I get to do stuff like sort out the baking cupboard is around now, and I suddenly remembered when I got to the . . . oh hang on, I'm making my list – currants, brown sugar . . . I remembered it was Des's birthday soon and I wondered what sort of cake you wanted baked for his party? What's this? Dates – rather prehistoric dates by the looks of them, ha ha. Helen? Are you there?

H: Yes – yes, I'm here but . . . well, you've caught me at a rather painful time I'm afraid.

G: I knew it. When Colum told me where you'd gone, I said to him, 'She'll be red as a lobster by day two, she always overdoes it in the . . .'

H: That's not what I meant. I meant painful in the . . . look, things are a bit up in the air round here and . . .

G: I do pity you with all those pinheads, Colum said they sounded just awful . . .

H: THEY'RE NOT AWFUL! And he doesn't know anything about it.

G: Well you don't have to bite my head off, I'm just . . . cocoa we have, now how much treacle is left in this . . . hang on, Helen . . .

H: What I was trying to say was . . .

G: Enough treacle but . . . damn, now I've got it all over the phone. I was offering to bake a birthday cake, you don't have to jump down my throat.

H: It's very kind of you Georgie but . . . well, I don't think it would be fair to anybody to go into detail at this point.

G: You know, you do sound a bit weird. Colum said . . .

H: I DON'T GIVE A FUCK WHAT COLUM SAID!!

G: Helen, he's your husband.

H: Look, I know that, dammit, at least he is *for now* but . . .

G: (Tamsin! What on earth are you doing at this hour dressed like that??? Get to bed this minute and TAKE IT OFF!) Sorry Helen, what . . .

H: Look, Georgie, all I can tell you is I don't know when we'll be back . . .

G: Oh, okay then . . .

H: . . . if at all.

G: Well, I'm sure he'll have a great birthday out there, they love parties Americans don't they?

21 July – Letter from Todd to American Studios

From: Todd Mulwroney
            Perlheim, Mannheim and Harvey, Inc.

To: Arthur Lipschitz
            Lipschitz, Dipschitz and Moloney, Inc.
            Legal representatives of American Studios, Inc. in the person of Aaron Mumby, President and CEO

21 July

Dear Sirs,

RE: 'The Love That Kills'

Acting on behalf of Desmond McCallum, and in light of the fact that, as a result of delays, prevarications, disputes, foreclosures, changes of personnel and of schedule, the aforementioned Desmond McCallum has suffered loss of income, loss of incidental income and defrayment of expenses, loss of personal and professional well-being, mental and emotional trauma and distress, as well as actual and potential damage to earnings and to the value of the property known as 'Desmond McCallum':

WE HEREBY DEMAND the immediate renegotiation of terms of employment under contract of the aforesaid Desmond McCallum with particular respect and application to the above-cited major motion picture, 'The Love That Kills', under penalty of the immediate and permanent withdrawal of Desmond McCallum and of the brand and property of that name from participation in this or any other motion picture initiated or instigated at or by American Studios, Inc., and/or Aaron Mumby, President and Worldwide CEO.

Be it known that in the absence of any such renegotiation, Mr McCallum and his representatives will consider themselves free and clear of any legal obligation with regard to the above.

Be it further known that, in the event of an unsatisfactory response or none to the above demands, major legal action will be instigated forthwith by us on

Desmond McCallum's behalf against American Studios and against the person and property of Aaron Mumby.

Yours
Lyle Grossmith
pp Todd Mulwroney

22 July – Internal Memo, American Studios, Inc.

From the desk of:	Shawn Sliver
	Assistant to the Senior Vice-President of Creative Affairs
To:	Janice Golightly
	Senior Assistant to Shawn Sliver
Date:	7/22

Janice

Have a big bunch of flowers messengered over to the McCallum kid with a bottle of Cristal for his mom, will you? Better yet, make that a magnum.

SS

22 July, morning – Helen and Des in the bathroom

Helen and Des, both looking rather bleary, are standing either side of the electronic scale, surveying it warily.

H: Look darling, it's not as though it's going to hurt you, you just have to jump on and then jump off again.
D: But I like hamburgers and you're going to stop me eating them.
H: Not necessarily, pudding, you don't look to me as though you've put on an ounce since we've been here.
D: Then why do I have to . . .

Helen takes a deep breath.

H: Look, how about if I go first, just to show you . . .

Meanwhile, outside in the corridor, Cary, fresh as a daisy and twice as fragrant, is approaching the suite from one direction, just as the studio messenger reaches it from the other, staggering under the weight of yet another enormous bunch of flowers and a huge gift-wrapped bottle of champagne. The messenger is about to knock on the door when Cary taps him on the shoulder.

C: (*with total conviction*) I'll take those for you, I'm on my way in.
M: But . . .

Cary removes the flowers with one hand . . .

C: I'm his dad. They're not up yet.
M: Oh. But . . .

. . . and grabs the champagne with the other.

C: Kid gets pretty aggravated if he's disturbed too early, know what I'm saying?
M: Uh – sure.

Cary waits outside the door for him to leave . . .

C: Later, dude.
M: Oh – uh, sure, later.

. . . and watches as he disappears around the corner.

Meanwhile, back in the bathroom, Helen and Des are still standing either side of the scales.

H: Look, sweetheart, if I don't know I'm going to have to stop the hamburgers, just to be on the safe side.
D: You said they were going to cut my hair.
H: So what?
D: So then I'll weigh less anyway!

At that moment, the doorbell rings.

22 July, morning – Helen

Now I really don't know what to do. I was just up, not even dressed in fact and feeling terrible, because of course I couldn't sleep a wink last night, when the bell rings and suddenly there's Cary, with his gorgeous smile, and the most enormous bunch of flowers you ever saw in your life AND champagne, inviting me to go up to Santa Barbara with him to work on my script.

He was so sweet when I explained that I was upset about how horrible Angel and Des were to him yesterday, and he said of course he understood, and Des was bound to be suspicious of him, and wasn't that just like a plucky and loyal little tyke to protect his mom and stick up for his dad. God, I could have thrown my arms round his neck and wept then and there, but luckily Des grabbed at this opportunity to get on the phone to room service – he's still after the giant walnut-and-honey breakfast waffle with strawberries and whipped cream – so that defused the atmosphere somewhat.

And then Cary had what I have to admit was the quite brilliant inspiration of asking how would Des like a trip to Disneyland while we're gone? Of course Cary can't take him personally, because he's going to be with me in Santa Barbara, but he pointed out that Madge is back in town tomorrow, at least that's what she told us, and she sort of owes us one on account of dragging us here and then leaving us hanging around endlessly waiting, and she's lucky we're not suing her as well as the studio, so she can take him, and Angel can go along as well.

So after that Des was almost nice to him for the rest of breakfast.

Anyhow, can't think about it now, I have to get Des to a

meeting with this new director who wants to meet him to 'refresh his creative vision' apparently.

Do you suppose the residue of a banana muffin with giant hot chocolate will outweigh an inch of hair? It had to be less fattening than the waffle.

22 July – First meeting with new director of *The Love that Kills*

A large, rather bare rehearsal studio with a mirrored wall. Helen and Des are being addressed by Brett Rittner, wunderkind director, on his vision for the film, while his (unpaid, trust-funded) assistant Johnston, wearing an unfortunate pair of baggy homeboy shorts on his very spindly legs, takes notes. Des, fascinated by the sight of such a huge mirror, is making alligator and fish faces at himself in it, while Helen wonders why her first encounter with an A-list Hollywood director is somehow so . . . underwhelming.

B: So, conceptually, it's like a tragedy wrapped in a love story wrapped in a family saga wrapped in a courtroom drama with, like, a kernel of fish-out-of-water.

Over his shoulder, to Johnston . . .

B: Got that, JayJay?

Johnston nods, busily. Helen nods, earnestly. Brett appears not to know she's there, or care. Johnston types into his mini-laptop while fielding calls and e-mails on his mobile.

Des roars at himself in the mirror. Helen kicks him and he roars again, but silently, seeing how many of his teeth he can show at once.

B: At the core is the father–son relationship, which naturally represents the thwarted dreams and desires of Joe the father, in conflict with his love for his wife and sense of duty to

      his family. Kind of a Capraesque thing with a touch of *Big*. You with me, JayJay?
J: *(typing)* All the way, Brett.

Brett suddenly snaps out of his film-auteur mode and squats on his haunches, appearing right in front of Des's face just as Des cracks his fiercest snarl yet. Brett does a comic mock-scared double-take.

B: Hey! Don't bite, Tarzan!
D: I'm not Tarzan, I'm a ALLIGATOR.
B: Why, so you are. Hard to see in this big dark swamp.
D: It's not a swamp it's a room.
B: Hey! A womb! Fascinating! And why d'you say that, Desi? Don't mind me calling you Desi, do you?
H: *(under her breath)* If you don't mind him biting your ankle.
B: Say again?

It's the first time he's taken any notice of her. He knows what he thinks of Hollywood moms.

H: Nothing. Sorry. Tell Brett what you're doing, Des.

Brett leaps to his feet again and holds up one hand dramatically, as though stemming a fast-running tide.

B: No! Wait! I have it! *(to Des)* Jump up, big boy, we're gonna play a game.
H: Stand up, Des, and do stop looking at yourself.

Des reluctantly stands, and turns away from the mirror to face Brett.

D: *(suspiciously)* What kind of game?
B: Well, you know, Desi my man, this is kind of a sad story, this movie we're making, and d'you know why?

Des shakes his head.

B: Because the little boy — that's you — is going to die, and there's nothing his dad can do to help him without hurting his mom. So — why don't you just kind of . . . just play one of your games and show me how that makes you feel?

D: What makes me feel?

Brett squats again and takes both of Des's hands. Des squirms away and looks up at Helen for help, but she's totally absorbed in her own agonising, but highly enjoyable, moral maze.

B: Like, you're gonna die, and leave your dad and your mom and your pet dog behind. Show me that — go on, just like, wherever you feel like going with it.

Des thinks for a moment and then falls to the floor, writhing around viciously and snapping his jaws in the direction of Johnston's bare legs.

D: ROARRRR! Roarr roarr!!

Johnston is not sure an unpaid internship is worth this. Des makes another little dash at him. Far from intervening, Brett watches, amazed. Finally Johnston slides off his stool and makes a run for it across the room, clutching his laptop and mobile, and pursued by Des at amazing speed on all fours.

B: Okay, Des. OKAY!! YOU CAN STOP NOW!!

Des finally hears, and rather reluctantly turns around and comes back. Johnston, pink and huffy, waits in vain for an apology from anybody.

B: Wow! So that was a real . . . interesting improvisation, Des. Can you tell me just a little bit of how you came to that place?

D: Well. I was the little boy you see and that man was Cary and he was going to take my mum away . . .

Helen swims back from her daydream in time to hear Cary's name.

D: . . . only I didn't want to die and leave my mum with him so I just turned myself into a ALLIGATOR and just SNAPPED his head off and then his feet and his hands and his bones and his blood and ate him all up and he was deaded!!

Brett stands listening to this in total silence, quite oblivious of Helen, who would clearly like the job of killing Des herself, next time it's available. Johnston is typing again, fearful of missing out something that might turn out to be the kernel of the next *Citizen Kane*.

Then, suddenly, Brett throws back his head, roars with laughter, and slaps Des on the back, which clearly offends him.

B: You know what, kid? You're a comic genius. And you've given me a brand-new take on the goddam movie.

22 July – Studio memo

American Studios US Inc.
STRICTLY CONFIDENTIAL – DO NOT CIRCULATE

7/22

From: Darling Darcy, Producer, 'The Love That Kills'
To: Aaron Mumby, CEO
            Head of Worldwide Distribution
            Head of Marketing
            Head of Press
            Head of Production
            Head of Post Production
            Head of Development

> Head of Story
> Head of Merchandising
> Line Producer

RE: *The Love That Kills*

After a long story meeting with Brett Rittner today, Brett feels that he can take the show in a powerful new direction that will dramatically optimise its appeal to the core blockbuster demographic while limiting damage at the over-40 margins.

New direction will transform the show into a teen comedy, with family elements and a CGI twist.

I'm thrilled to report that Joe Barrelly ('Squishy Fingers', 'Pork Barrel Peckerwood', etc.) has agreed to step in as writer, and they will be brainstorming it intensively over the next couple of weeks.

In the meantime, please apprise all relevant personnel in your departments that the picture is on hold and no action should be taken without prior reference to the Line Producer.

As usual, Amy Sorkin will be finessing press. We hope to achieve an early build on this one that will segue right into Spring Break opening season.

22 July – Studio note, Darling Darcy to Madge

> *Hiya 'M'*
> *See attached memo – we're in shit creek with this one. Rittner hasn't a fucking clue but Mumby owes him a picture and it had to happen before the fall or his pay-or-play kicks in.*
> *But hey, who knows? Could be he's a genius after all.*
> *Anyways it means the kid's still pending but we can't let it show on the bottom line. So do what you need to, okay? They've hired that little asswipe Todd Mulwroney, but he'll roll over for you. Just send me the small receipts and bill the rest to that turkey you worked on for Universal (ha ha)*
> *Loveya D X*

23 July, morning – Phone call, Madge to Helen

M: ... so it's great great news because with Brett on board the show will do mega business. You liked him, huh? Is he a genius or what?

H: He was ...

M: And he said the same about you. Wants to read your script in fact.

H: He does?

M: Plus ya can take Des all those places you weren't going to have time for, ya know, Disneyland ...

H: Well, it's amazing that you mention that.

M: ... Universal Studios ...

H: ... because I know how fond you are of him and you've barely seen him ...

M: God, I tell ya it breaks my heart but ...

H: ... so I was wondering whether you and Angel would like to take him to Disneyland, say perhaps on ...

M: Honey, I'd love to but ...

H: ... Thursday? In fact I was going to call you because Todd was actually making some rather nasty noises about you getting us into this deal, and it not being a great one for Des, and how maybe he was going to have to reconsider representing you at all ...

M: Todd said THAT?

H: ... or even cite you in the lawsuit – you know we already have a lawsuit, or in fact several I think – with the studios.

M: ME??

H: I thought it was awfully harsh myself, but he said ... What was his phrase? He said in any case they'd probably 'let you take the rap' and there wouldn't be a thing he could do ...

M: Ya want me to take the kid to Disneyland? For a whole day?

H: Gosh, that would be so great, and he and Angel really get on these days. I'll be back early on Friday and I can pick him up on the way . . .

M: You're gonna be gone OVERNIGHT?

H: Just the one night, but we can't very well leave him on his own in the hotel can we? I mean if anything happened and you were liable . . .

M: I . . .

H: . . . it's his life's dream, he'll adore every minute of it, thanks SO MUCH for suggesting it! So can we say eight thirty on Thursday morning at your place?

23 July, morning – Phone message: Madge to Angel

M: Angel, honey, I was thinking you and I need quality time together, I've barely seen you. Let's spend the day Thursday, okay? And I'll bring the check for those new blades you wanted.

23 July, late morning – The view from Helen's window, en route to tell Cary

I hope this cab-driver knows where he's going. Hard to tell, given the total lack of any common language. Somehow I don't think they have the Knowledge here. Now, if I needed a cut-price Kalashnikov . . .

Silly of me to take a cab anyway. Why should I be ashamed of Omar knowing where I'm going? Especially as I'm going to put an end to it all.

I have to tell him in person. It wouldn't be fair otherwise. Not after letting him think I was going to . . . I just can't, that's all. I can't. It was a silly fantasy but after all, one has duties and responsibilities and just because I only have one life and I'm chucking it away and I'll miss this place and Cary every day of it . . .

It was Des's little face that did it. He just looked back at me and he knew, right away. Damn him. I mean I'm offering him the equivalent of a free pass through the pearly gates and he looks at me and says 'You're going away with Cary aren't you? Without me?'

And what if I am? Don't I have any rights too? Just because I have a child, do I have to forget about any dismal remnant of my own life that might be left over from caring for him twenty-four hours a day?

Oh help. I think . . . in fact, mm, yuck, I definitely forgot to have a bath this morning. And my hair has reacted very oddly to the sun. Cary is always so immaculate, maybe I should turn back and . . .

Stop making excuses. Do what you have to do. What does it matter what you look like anyhow? You're beginning to sound just like Colum's worst nightmare of the people here.

Colum. Good old reliable, ordinary Colum. World's Best Father. Think about all the good things he is. Just like Celia Johnson's hubby in *Brief Encounter*, famously the most romantic film of all time. She did it, she renounced the love of her life for her family and her children. And did she die of it? Well, of course we don't know. She could have thrown herself under the next shoppers' express, for all the film tells us. We do know that *Brief Encounter – Return to Cosy Domestic Life in the Home Counties* was not considered sequel material.

She was fine. And we don't live in the Home Counties. We live in Kentish Town, where the streets look like Tracey Emin's in charge of rubbish collection. There's something to look forward to.

My God, are those dolphins in the sea . . . sorry, ocean? They are! Dolphins! I must tell Des, he'll go bonkers. How can I say no, when every fibre of me is saying yes? And how can it be wrong to keep Des in a place where he'll be seeing dolphins and pelicans every day and . . .

Anyhow, we're not talking about for ever, or indeed anything at all except one day and one night, at the moment. I mean practically everybody I know has had one lapse, even if it's only with some slimeball at work. At least I truly love Cary and he truly is worthy of it. And he couldn't be more different from Colum. If somebody wants to give you something you long for and need, and the other person can't . . . or won't . . .

Colum isn't exactly a saint either, remember.

And I'll let him keep the house so it won't disrupt his life, and once I'm selling my scripts and Des is earning too we'll have loads of money, even if we only let him do one movie a year. Which means he'll be able to go on lots of long visits to Colum. After all, there are children whose parents are diplomats or whatever who go to boarding school and hardly see them at all. Look at Angel. Her parents aren't even separated, technically. It's all to do with how you manage it, everybody says so.

I swear those shadows on the beach are blue! And that sunset last night! How can people say it must get boring seeing the sun all the time? You might as well say it gets boring eating chocolate every day.

God, how can I be thinking about chocolate when my whole life is in the balance?

But it's ridiculous expecting one person to be your best friend and domestic partner and co-parent and lover and life companion. Colum will always be my best mate, and Des's father, and the person in the world who knows most about MotoGuzzis, but he may not always be all the rest . . .

Oh God. I can't believe I'm even thinking about it. Until a week ago – less! – I thought Colum and I'd be waking up to the Last Trump in a king-size double bed. Not being grandparents together will be a bit sad. But who knows what will have happened by then? One of us could well have died, even if we'd stayed together. Or Des might turn out to be gay, or not into it, or . . .

What am I going to say? Look at me, I'm sweating and shaking like a teenager – and not a very toothsome one at that.

Can this be right? Sepulveda Boulevard, and this is . . . yes it's the right block, too. Maybe I should have called first, but I thought if I didn't come right now . . .

23 July, midday – Angel and Des, at the hotel

Angel is standing on the atomic-precision scale in Des's bathroom. Doesn't like what she sees. Gets off and steps on again, balancing on one leg. Slight improvement. Steps off and steps on with the other leg, right on the edge of the scale this time.

From the living room come the faint sounds of what appears to be a wildlife programme – elk in mortal combat, perhaps.

A: You okay out there?

No reply. She tries hopping off, then hopping on again, right to the middle of the scale. Apparently this is worse. She sighs and slouches through into the living room, where Des is sitting in front of the TV in his swimsuit and goggles, eating a bacon double cheeseburger, and watching a porn movie.

A: Des! Are you allowed that?
D: It's my lunch. I'm hungry. I'm a alligator. Alligators have to eat lots.
A: You do know you have eighty-five grams of fat just in the patty, plus thirty for the cheese and ten for the bacon, which is like, eight times your whole daily allowance.

Des hunches over it and takes a huge bite, apparently fearful she's about to take it from him, and chokes.

A: Hey, big boy, don't do a Mama Cass on me.

She pats him on the back, then slumps down in front of the TV and finally registers what's on screen.

A: Eeeugh!! Gross!
D: It's supposed to be cartoons. Can you find the cartoons?

Angel picks up the remote, then gets fascinated despite herself.

A: Can you believe the size of that?
D: Elephants have bigger ones. And rhinos. But hippos' are weeny. Anyhow I saw my dad's willy lots of times.
A: Like that?
D: Like what?

Angel flips the channel, to Disney's Playhouse.

A: So where'd you think your mom went? She was like, weird.

Des wolfs down the last of his burger and dutifully trots to put the plate on the tray, which is next to the phone.

D: I want to call my dad, I miss my dad. Please!
A: Sure thing. Gimme the phone over here. What's the number?
D: Ummm – it has five in it. And eight, I think. And there's four twice.

Angel picks up the handset and dials.

A: Yeah – Information? Britain. London. Kentish Town. McCallum. Sure, put me through . . . (*to Des*) No reply – could be he's at . . . (Oh, hi, Colum . . . Yeah, it's me . . . Yeah, it's cool . . .)

Des is jumping around next to her, shouting.

D: Dad! DAD!!
A: (Here he is.)

She hands over, retreats to the sofa and switches to E! Entertainment.

D: (Dad? Dad!! I'm going to Disneyland Dad I miss you and Mum is going away without me for a whole day and a night and I'm going to Disneyland! With Angel!!)

Angel looks round.

A: You are?
D: (She's . . . think she's going away with Cary and . . . Yes. Yes Dad I don't like Cary he's creepy and . . . okay here she is . . .)

Angel takes the phone again.

A: (Hey . . . No, I don't either . . . Yeah, he's an A-grade slime-ball but he's WAY gone on her, or rather her expense account . . . No, I have no idea, but it was bordering on heavy yesterday . . . He's good, porky but good, here he is again . . .)

About to hand the phone to Des, she has another idea.

A: (Hey Colum, don't sweat it, I have a plan, but you know like, in 'The Rules'? . . . It's this like, dating guide . . . Yeah, but it works, and it says when you want to get somebody back, even if you're mad with them, it says 'Don't get mad, get flowers'. You dig? . . . Sure, okay and I'm on to it this end, trust me.)

Puts down the phone and mutters passionately:

A: I DESPISE Disneyland.

23 July – Story synopsis of major studio picture *Goofy Racers*

STORY
Joe Mitchum is a guy *who just can't get it right*

– *handyman and janitor* to one of the biggest stars in Hollywood, with a *ballbreaking, loud-mouthed, pet beautician* wife, Kelly, and a *runty, nerdy son, Ellis*, he spends his days *digging holes in the lawn and poisoning the carp in the pond* and his nights *filling in supermarket coupons*. Joe is the kind of guy everybody's glad not to be – just thinking about him is like acid indigestion. But *at least Joe* is a one-woman, straight-up kind of a guy – *after all, who else'd have him?* Then *triumph* strikes, as *Ellis, who has been staying out of school since he had the shit kicked out of him in the school yard by the local bullies*, develops a *fantasy that he is, in fact, a man-eating alligator and returns to terrorise his classmates*.

Joe *is thrilled that his son is back at school and no longer terrified*, but *the school board is none too thrilled by Ellis's attacks on the other kids* and time is running out as *Silvano also gets more pissed off* by the day. Finally, Joe hears of a doctor in the Bahamas who *may be able* to cure his son. Joe *enters and wins a cracker box contest* to pay the air fare for himself and *Ellis. Ellis barfs all over the plane, attacks the other passengers, bites through the blouse of the bosomy female stewardess and* barely makes it *through the flight, and Joe also gets into trouble to hilarious effect as he somehow gets tangled with the belt of the baggage conveyor which pulls his trousers down around his ankles in front of the entire plane and all the bag handlers* but when they meet the doctor, Dr Ingrid JayeGold, she *falls into Joe's arms as though he's the man of her dreams.*

Dr JayeGold is a *hypnotherapist and bodybuilder*, with a *stunning, reptilian stare and arms like tree trunks*, and something about her strikes Joe *on the back of the neck* as soon as they meet. Dr JayeGold also experiences a shock of recognition – despite the fact that *Joe is out cold* she immediately recognises *that both he and his child are uniquely suggestible, and perfect subjects for her latest technique*. Dr JayeGold, maddened by *excitement* at *the opportunity of testing this out*, gives no hint of the truth but agrees to treat *Ellis and Joe. While Joe is still unconscious she persuades him that he is, in fact, a six-foot-plus god with movie-star looks, and entirely without fear. Meanwhile, she persuades Ellis that he is not an alligator, but a peaceful, home-loving tabby cat who does no harm to anybody so long as he gets a tuna sandwich every day*. Back home, *Ellis* progresses by leaps and bounds *and stretches and purrs*. His parents, *though not* his beloved collie Laddy, are delighted to see him *home from school unscathed every day*, even though he begins to smell badly of fish. But all too soon Joe *is in trouble, convinced that Silvano ought, in fact, to be working for him*, and . . .

(at this point, exhausted by his creative efforts, Joe Barrelly went out to lunch and took in an action movie, which so confused his muse that they were both obliged to take the remainder of the day off)

Visitors' Handy Cut-out-and-keep Guide to Hollywood Vocabulary

Section 4 – The 'Working Lunch'

Oh, that's not my home – that's just my office	=	That's my home
It's so much easier to concentrate without a phone ringing all the time	=	They cut off my phone months ago
Often I don't even notice the time passing . . .	=	. . . I'm asleep
But for you, I have all the time in the world!	=	You *are* my work, right now
Normally I work right through lunch	=	Sure reading the paper is work – where else do you find story ideas?
But just this once, I guess I can take a break	=	So long as you pick up the tab, again
Finally, I have you all to myself!	=	Now we can get down to business
Of course your kid is adorable . . .	=	Hey, I was a kid once . . .
. . . but let's forget about him just for an hour	=	. . . but enough with this guilty mom stuff already
After all, you're not just a mom, you're a beautiful woman	=	Keep on like that and you'll never get a man
Let's celebrate!	=	I haven't had a drink since last night
Did you bring your script?	=	You can always borrow one from the waiter, the car valet, the maître d' . . .

You forgot? Damn!	=	Good – off the hook for another day
Just run the story by me again	=	I need to read the menu
It sounds totally awesome!	=	It sounds just as dumb as every other first script
It's bound to make you a ton of money	=	It's bound to make us a ton of money
I'll just have the special	=	It's always the most expensive thing on the menu
Are these margaritas great or what?	=	Drink up, I need another
C'mon, just one more – you'll make me feel like a lush	=	I am a lush
Wouldn't it be great if we could do this every day?	=	Just open your checkbook, honey . . .
Sure, I understand . . .	=	I knew it was too easy
Things are happening real fast	=	Can't be fast enough for me – the bailiffs are due any day
It's bound to be confusing	=	Especially on the third margarita
I'd hate you to feel you were being rushed into anything	=	I guess I need to keep you happy
But you know you can trust me	=	Believe me, there are far, far worse around here
Just remember – life's too short for looking backwards	=	I can't remember last night, let alone my last fuck

23 July, early afternoon – Angel and Des, going to the studio

They're sitting in the back of the limo, bowling along the palm-lined boulevards of west LA, en route to the American Studios lot. Omar has the glass door open and is head-banging to Eminem. Angel is irritated.

A: *(shouting through the open partition)* Hey, homeboy! We're working here!

Omar looks around, shrugs and closes the glass. Angel turns back to Des, who is wearing the dirtiest clothes she could find, plus his wellies, which have ripened considerably in the heat.

A: Now, whatever he says to you, what do you say back?
D: *(miniature Omar-like shrug)* 'Huh?'
A: That's good, but it still needs something – hey, I have it.

She bangs furiously on the glass. Omar reluctantly opens it.

A: Stop the car!

He does so, nonchalantly crossing three lanes of traffic and parking in a three-hundred-dollar fine zone.

O: Man, that power is sweet.

Angel scrabbles in her pocket and hands him a bill.

A: Go in that liquor store and buy a couple packs of Juicy Fruit.

Omar, bemused, does so.

D: My head is itchy.

Des is not just dirty. He's had his hair cut – half an inch all over, with a sticky-up bit on top. He looks like an evacuee with a bad case of nits. About as far from adorable as Angel could manage.

A: Your mom said they needed to cut your hair. This way, we've done it for them, they'll thank us.

Des presses his nose against the tinted window. Suddenly gets excited and bangs on it.

D: Mum!! MUM!!!! It's Mum, look!

Angel looks out, but sees nothing at first. Des is wrestling with the door handle, which is child-locked. Fails, hits the electric window instead, and is about to shout out of it when . . .

D: Oh – she's with that horrid Cary.
A: So she is . . . Hey, let's leave them be, we're still . . .
D: What are they doing?

On the sidewalk terrace of a fancy restaurant, Helen and Cary are entwined in a passionate kiss. Angel hits the window and it closes again.

A: They're acting. Everybody round here acts all the time, remember? They're just like, rehearsing for a movie, or something.

Des's lip trembles.

D: I don't like him. I don't like acting. I want to go home!
A: And if you do EXACTLY what I say, that's where you'll be, quicker than a rat's shit.

Omar returns, tosses the gum in at Angel, and sets off again, Eminem louder than ever. Angel unwraps a stick and hands it to Des.

A: Okay, get chewing. Now let's try that again . . .

23 July, afternoon – Helen, in the cab home

God, what have I done? I was totally sure when I arrived there – after the confusion about that horrible little cabin he works in – I had it all worked out, I was just going to get Des through the film and whizz him back in time for his birthday . . .

What happened? I mean the restaurant was beautiful, and I suppose I shouldn't have had that drink – the third one, anyhow – I always forget how disastrous lunch-time drinking is for me until it's too late. And then . . . and then . . . God it makes me blush just remembering it. I'm a married woman with a child. I don't do things like that! I don't!

But I did. And in public. Thank Christ I don't know anybody here. Yet.

It was wonderful. It was, I can't deny that. You forget, when you're grinding along in your dreary woolly-socks monogamy, you kind of make yourself forget what passion is because it would be too painful otherwise, knowing you'd given it up so carelessly and for ever, along with vodka luges and topless bathing. And he's right, I mean I'm not just a mother, I'm a woman. That was what my body was responding to. I AM WOMAN, and I HAVE NEEDS!!!

I guess it was the intensity of being alone for the first time. It was so sweet of him to take such an interest in Des, wanting to make sure we had a good lawyer and Des was getting the top rate for the job. Come to think of it, we should have had the first cheque through by now. I must remember to ask Todd.

I'll be home in five minutes, and what am I going to tell Des? I can't change the plan again, I can't – not after Cary booked the room. I can't imagine how much a place like that costs, but it must be a fortune if he had to use his platinum Amex just to reserve it – hope he does find his wallet when he gets home, it's probably wherever he left it when he was making the booking.

Well, I'll just tell him . . . I'll just have a little lie-down first, and talk to Des later. Or maybe – maybe I'll just get the cab to go round the block one more time. Why is it that taxis suddenly find a short cut the one time in a million you're not in a hurry?

23 July, afternoon – Angel and Des, at the studio

The limo purrs up to a white guardhouse in the centre of a big, elaborate gate with 'American Studios' written over it. Omar hits his window button and mutters something to the guard. The guard scans his clipboard, ticks something off, tips his cap and bows them in.

The car drives through a parking lot packed with late-model Lexus jeeps and vintage sports cars, and down a road between two gleaming white, beautifully landscaped office buildings.

Makes a turn down a somewhat smaller road, between plainer office buildings.

Makes another turn down an even narrower, rutted road, by the sound stages, with dumpsters and empty prop crates outside the doors. Can't make the next turn, so Omar just idles the engine, blocking the way, and lets Angel and Des out.

They walk down a narrow alleyway between scruffy beige Portakabins. This is where the writers work. Angel peers at a sign on the furthest Portakabin and bounds up the steps, towing Des.

Inside, an unshaven, very overweight man in a polo shirt and bermudas is chain-smoking in front of an ancient PC, under a No Smoking sign which is the cabin's only ornament, apart from his Harvard graduation certificate. Beside the computer are the *Wall Street Journal*, *People* magazine, and a copy of Kant's *Critique of Pure Reason*. This is Joe Barrelly, blockbuster machine.

He looks up, trying to pretend he's just this minute been typing. Sees Angel and Des, and decides not to bother.

A: Mr Barrelly? I'm Angel Handelman, I manage Mr McCallum?

He looks dubious, but can't exactly contradict her. She shoves Des forward. He stands in front of Joe, slouching, frowning and chewing like a pro. Joe jumps up, takes Des's hand and bows low over it, simultaneously wheeling forward the ancient swivel chair he's been sitting on.

J: Well, a surprise. And an honour. Our little English gentleman.

Des looks about as far from an English gent as the human race can accommodate. In a brilliant moment of inspiration, he spits his gum on to the floor and pops another stick.

A: Yeah well, we just stopped by to see how you were getting on, and to give you a sense of what Mr McCallum is capable of.
J: Very thoughtful.

Angel seats herself in his chair and, unasked, begins scrolling up the screen. Joe wishes she wouldn't, but not knowing who she really is, doesn't dare stop her.

A: So. How's it going?
J: Great. Great. This animal thing is . . .
A: So, why don't you ask Des – Mr McCallum – a few questions? He's got like, a great story sense, right Des?

Des scowls even more deeply, scratches his itchy scalp, takes a deep breath, rearranges his gum, and says . . .

D: Huh?

Joe looks depressed.

J: Well, little fella, so you had a great meeting with Mr Rittner!
D: Huh?
J: I hear you're big into alligators?
D: Huh?
A: Give him a little time, he's just like, getting a feel for the vibe in here. He's real sensitive to atmosphere.

Joe tries again.

J: So, we're doing a little kind of semi-Dr Dolittle thing with the story here – so you kind of turn into all these different animals. It's kind of goofy but a lot of fun, whaddya think?
D: Huh??

Angel, who has been reading the various versions of the story synopsis on the screen, appears to have had a sudden idea.

A: So – whose is the overarching point of view – I mean, narrative-wise? Are we talking eye of God or subjective here?
J: Well, I thought – a little of both . . .
A: Because – I mean, you're deep into it and I'm not of course, but wouldn't it be kinda cool if it was all, like, the son's POV? So we see the whole thing THROUGH the eyes of a child . . .
J: Or an alligator . . .
A: . . . kinda like a Spielberg like, innocent world-view thing. And you get the morphs via the adults' response, so they get to do loads of like, outrage and horror shtick. Which the audience will, like, go wild for.
D: Huh?
A: Which then of course, I mean he could be anything, he could be a fire-breathing dragon, you could go totally wild and crazy with all these changes and these delusions, if you . . .

Joe is suddenly excited.

J: If you see it all THROUGH his eyes, never see him at all . . .
A: *(hastily)* Well, that might be going too far . . .
J: *(reassuring)* He'd be there, of course, sure he would, kinda – off screen . . .
A: *(apparently anxious)* . . . but there on set, all the time, right? I didn't mean like, to totally write him out, God forbid.
J: *(absently)* Right. Absolutely. God forbid.
D: Huh?
J: *(suddenly wildly excited)* You . . .

Kisses Angel, which she wasn't expecting.

J: . . . You are a genius! This solves everything!

Angel jumps out of the chair just in time to avoid being crushed by his bulk as he jumps back into it, rabid to start work again.

A: *(sotto voce)* I am, and it does.
D: Huh?

23 July – Memo: Aaron Mumby to Legal Department

American Studios US Inc.
STRICTLY CONFIDENTIAL – DO NOT CIRCULATE

From: Aaron Mumby, CEO

To: Marvin Brownski Head of Legal Affairs

7/23

RE: 'Goofy Racers'

Marv

Can you find out what our exposure is with the British kid? The writer has managed to dump him which could be great news considering he has zero recognition and we would've been into building a whole new brand just for this one movie. Try to get us out of it clear will you and get back to me?

23 July, late afternoon – Helen, back at the hotel

Helen staggers up the corridor, dead on her feet from tequila, heat and heartbreak. Outside the door of the suite is a modest, scruffy Interflora gift arrangement, perfectly adequate for NW5 but woefully pathetic in this setting.

She reaches down, picks it up, reads the card – and bursts into tears.

She opens the door and carries the flowers in. The message light on the phone is blinking energetically.

23 July, late afternoon – Phone message from Madge

M: Hiya Helen, I was hoping you'd be there but, look, there's been a mini change of plan with the movie, they've kind of reworked it into a kind of Steve Spielberg meets *Jumanji* fantasy role-play kind of thing with a Dr Dolittle comedy edge, and the kid's been written out. But it's great, this way you get to go home and see your . . . he'll be missing you won't he? Anyways, I'm off to Lodz in . . . is it Poland? One of those cheapo locations anyways on this period piece so can't say bye-bye in person but they'll look after ya, thanks for the help with Angel too, gotta go . . .

23 July, late afternoon – Greeting on Cary's voicemail

C: Hi! Great that you called! Leave a message and I'll get RIGHT back to you!

23 July, late afternoon – Phone message from American Studios

AS: Mrs McMillam? This is American Studios artist relations speaking, we have authority to pick up a director's chair, two baseball jackets and two caps from you and will be coming by momentarily, if you could please have them waiting at the front desk for our messenger, thank you.

23 July, late afternoon – Note pushed under door of suite

```
Ocean Suites™ Resorts Worldwide
Santa Monica, CA 90401

7.23

Dear Guest

We hope that you have enjoyed your stay with us
and that you will continue to accept the hospi-
tality of Ocean Suites™.

   However, we have to inform you of a change in
the terms of your stay as per attached invoice,
and would request that you settle it immediately
to avoid further action.

BILL FOR GUEST SERVICES

Room/Suite:            314
Day Rate:              $949.00 plus tax

Itemization:

7/17 Room              $949.00
Tax                    $87.00
Pool bar               $15.00
Room service           $45.00
Minibar                $35.00
```

7/18 Room	$949.00
Tax	$87.00
Room service	$153.55
Minibar	$45.50
7/19 Room	$949.00
Tax	$87.00
Room service	$245.00
Telephone — international	$85.00
Minibar	$24.50
7/20 Room	$949.00
Tax	$87.00
Room service	$185.65
Phone — local	$10.00
Pool bar	$51.25
Minibar	$35.00
7/21 Room	$949.00
Tax	$87.00
Room service	$53.00
Minibar	$12.35
7/22 Room	$949.00
Tax	$87.00
Room service	$243.35
Minibar	$33.75
7/23 Room	$949.00
Tax	$87.00
Room service	$32.65
Minibar	$12.00
Premium rate cable	$45.00
TOTAL TO DATE:	$8,614.55

```
TERMS:
Payable immediately on receipt
Please note we cannot accept cash, personal checks,
out-of-state cashier's checks or Diners Card
We appreciate your business and hope you have a
pleasant day
```

23 July, late afternoon – Helen, on phone to reception at hiArts

H:	Hello? Hello, can you put me through to Todd—
R:	Todd Mulwroney?
H:	Mulwroney that's it – please?
R:	Who can I say is calling?
H:	Helen McCallum – and it's urgent, please, terribly urgent.
	Long pause.
H:	(*to herself*) Come ON!!! God, where are they when you need them . . .
R:	I'm sorry, Mr Mulwroney is unavailable . . .
H:	He can't be! I'm his . . . we're major clients of his!
R:	. . . but I'm putting you through now to . . .
H:	Oh, thank God . . .
	Several clicks on the line, then a new voice says:
A:	Accounts Receivable – Ms McCallum?
H:	Er, yes, that's me but I need to speak to . . .
A:	We have an invoice for you here, Ms McCallum which we'll be messengering around, if you'll please be at the hotel with your certified cashier's check in about . . .
H:	Hang on, we haven't been paid yet, how can I . . . ?
A:	I'm sure I don't need to remind you of the procedure in the event of defaulting on accounts, Ms McCallum, and your account to date is in excess of twenty thousand dollars . . .

H: Twenty thousand dollars!
A: ... which is well in excess of our normal limit for unbonded clients with no credit history.
H: This is a nightmare ...
A: Our terms of business are clearly stated on your contract. So, say, about fifty minutes? Thank you. *... and the phone goes dead.*
H: No!!! DON'T HANG UP ON ME!!!

23 July, early evening – Greeting on Cary's voicemail

C: Hi! Thanks for calling! I'll be out of town for a few days, but leave a message and I'll get back to you right away!

23 July, early evening – Helen, in the hotel

Helen, more bedraggled than ever, drops the phone with a clunk and murmurs pathetically:

H: *(to herself)* What am I going to do?
A: About what?

Behind her, Angel and Des are coming through the door. Des bounds ahead, carrying a huge stuffed alligator. Helen rushes to him and hugs him.

H: Where have you been?
D: We went to the aquarium Mum, Mum she bought me this look Mum it has teeth!!!
H: I've been worried sick!

Suddenly she notices his hair.

H: Des! Your beautiful hair!!
A: Yeah, well when you'd been gone for, like, hours ...

Helen blushes.

A: . . . we didn't know where you were either . . .
H: Anyhow I'm glad you're back now because there's been some sort of huge mix-up and I can't get any sense out of anybody.
A: I know.
H: Your mother left a message saying . . .
A: I know.
H: You do?
A: Omar got a call on his cell phone and put us on the street way over at Seventeenth, so we had to walk, which is the other reason we're late.
H: Omar's gone too?
A: You're lucky he didn't come by for his tip yet.
H: Anyhow, it's like the ravening wolves of Siberia, suddenly everybody wants money and I don't have any money and I tried to call that jumped-up little lawyer of yours but . . .

Des stops cavorting round with the alligator for a moment.

D: Mum Mum Angel says I don't have to do any acting any more does that mean I can eat as much ice cream as I like Mum I STILL haven't had a Magnum Mum!!
H: Oh for God's sake Des! Ice cream! We're about to be bankrupted on a scale that'll make Black Monday look like a . . . a blip, and . . .

Angel brings Helen a glass of water and heads for the phone.

A: I'm calling Todd on his cell. He needs my mom's business. This is just, like, more acting.

Helen, about to take a sip of water, stops with the glass in midair.

H: This is tap water, right? I'm not going to get charged for it?

A: *(already dialling)* Relax, will you?

Helen glugs thirstily, then pulls Des on to her knee and gives him a big hug.

H: Remember, darling, whatever happens, we'll always have each other, and Mum will always love you, okay?

Des looks slightly worried.

D: Mum I'm hungry Mum can I have a hamburger?
A: (Todd? Pick up, I know you're there, the . . . Yeah, I know but this is a major bonus opportunity for you . . . Yeah, the McCallum kid . . . Yeah, no reasons, no notice, no fault on his side at all . . . Sure, but they know they can't do it either . . . Sure you'll get it back, c'mon Todd don't be a wimp . . . Okay, if this is hardball, how about thirty? . . . Eighty! Dream on, Toto . . . Okay, forty-sixty plus you guarantee the outlay so far . . . Well I guess the hotel and a ton of burgers – oh, and a porn movie earlier . . . Fifty-fifty?? You're a chiselling weasel-eyed sonofabitch . . . Yeah, it's a deal.)

She slams down the phone triumphantly and turns to Helen and Des.

H: What was that about a porn movie? I'm not putting Des into porn, if I have to wash dishes for . . .

Angel flaps her hand, suddenly a mini-Madge.

A: So, he's gonna write off your fees to date plus cover your hotel until tomorrow morning against fifty per cent of whatever he gets out of the studio for breach of contract.
H: Tomorrow morning? Then what?

At that moment there's a ring on the doorbell. Angel goes towards it. Helen rushes in front of her.

H: (*theatrically*) Don't let them in!
A: You're getting this all ass-backwards, they're the ones who're in shit here.

She opens the door on the studio messenger.

SM: Pickup from Ms Camillam?

Helen wearily waves him in. He knows exactly where he's going – he left them there, after all – and emerges with the chair, the two blousons and the two caps.

D: Mum! He's taking my . . .
H: You don't want it, sweetie, believe me.

The messenger collides in the doorway with two hotel porters, who march straight up to the huge TV and DVD player, unplug them and, with some effort, carry them towards the door.

H: Hey!

The first porter manages to turn his head far enough to say:

P: We got orders. The extras gotta go.

Des dumps his alligator, drops on to all fours and makes for the nearest one's ankles.

D: I want to watch cartoons! I'm going to . . .
H: Stop it, Des!

She scoops him, kicking and screaming, under one arm, follows the porters to the door, grabs it with the other hand and slams it behind them – right in Colum's face.

25 July – Bertie

They're back, finally. Thank heavens, and not a moment too soon. When that Juggernaut rolled through the door at me I realised, in a split second, that all the lavish diet and personal services had been mere trifles from the arsenal of perfidy. A moment later, and I'd have spent eternity as a hearth rug.

And as for the alpha male — when he finally got around to rescuing me — if he thinks he's so busy and important he can 'forget' to open the odd tin from time to time, he should see how he likes it when I 'forget' to wake him up in the morning. I'll give him busy and important. Luckily the oestral female is neither of those, and she did make a gratifying fuss of me at first, but what did it amount to, in the end? We're back on Felix and those gravelly biscuits, and I have to say it's getting harder to tell the difference between the dinner plate and the toilet every day. It'd be enough to drive a person back to hunting, if the cat door hadn't mysteriously shrunk in the heat.

She came back looking as though she'll need to watch it in doorways herself, if she doesn't start chasing the odd squirrel up a tree. Whatever they fed her over there, it certainly wasn't what the Felix tin calls 'a perfect balance of nutritional elements for bright eyes and healthy fur'.

29 July – Helen

Hello trees! (Well, tree. It's still a tree, even torn up by the roots and splattered with biryani.) Hello sky! (It's grey, but it's a sky. God loves the clouds as much as the sunshine. Clouds are what give us our rolling meadowlands and our dewy English-rose complexions. No wonder those LA crones need all that cosmetic intervention, living under an arc lamp all year round.) Hello, overflowing rubbish bins and ancient dumped sofas! Hello Kentish Town Road, with your enticing motley of game arcades, cut-price convenience stores and boarded-up banks!

I never thought I'd be glad to be back in NW5. But there

it is, the trip achieved something nothing and nobody has ever done before. Actually, it did more than that. It confirmed that the food in first-class is, indeed, identical, give or take the odd slice of star fruit and glass of rose muscat. And with any luck, at least according to Angel, by the time Todd has factored into his legal arguments breach of contract, emotional trauma, psychiatric counselling, loss of education, loss of future earnings, false enticement, emergency repatriation and treatment for sunburn, we'll have enough to put Des through a dozen educational establishments stinking of gross privilege, and still get that stars-and-stripes nail job. (There's a place round the corner that was doing them all the time! Who knew?)

I have to admit Colum has been no less than saintly throughout. He could have said any number of things, coming across us as he did, but all he permitted himself was 'Hi Des, glad you finally got a haircut' and a request that I remove my foot from the flowers he had dispatched with some difficulty and expense via Bunty's Bouquets on Camden Road. He did make a point of telling me that the croissants at Le Vieux Truckstop in Bordeaux were exceptional, but I'm afraid they're going to have to wait several decades for my attentions. Greedy I may be, but I have some vestigial self-protective instinct left.

Even the aggravation of shopping for Des's birthday party hardly dented my sunny mood. Who needs to see the real sun when you have the sun of family love in your heart?

Le 'Handy-Guide' du Parent Occupé – Edition 2003

Chapitre 5: 'On Prépare la Fête de L'anniversaire'

Example: Le liste des invités
Jack
Sara
Zoe

Shakira
Max
Billy

Phrases utiles:
Hello, did you get the party invitation? No, it was posted more than a week/two weeks/two days ago. Yes, of course you can bring the baby. Yes, of course you can bring the baby's best friend. Is Grandma staying for the weekend? Yes, of course Grandma can come too. No, the birthday cake will not contain nuts. No, the birthday cake will not contain dairy. It is possible the birthday cake may contain eggs. Would Billy like his own birthday cake? What would Billy like in his birthday cake? Sadly, it is not possible to make a cake without eggs, milk, flour, fat or dairy. No, we are not having an entertainer. No, not any kind of entertainer. The last entertainer was frightening. And, indeed, exorbitantly expensive. Instead, we will be playing several enjoyable and traditional games. Yes, the games will be non-competitive. No, Zoe does not have to join in the games. We look forward to seeing you, then.

Example: Le Liste des Cadeaux Désirés
Pop-Up Animal Safari Book
Doctor Dress-Up Set
Cowboys and Indians
Toy horse – plastic, not furry, not black

Phrases utiles:
Hello, do you still have that Animal Safari Book? No, I was not here yesterday. No, I do not remember the ISBN number. Yes, you did have it last week. What a pity you sold the last copy five minutes ago. Please could you order a copy for me? No, next week will be too late. No, it would not be convenient for me to travel to your Brent Cross

branch. Yes, I can give you my credit card details. Yes, I will give you £50 under the counter if it arrives before Friday.

Excuse me, I have to buy a white blouse to sew a red cross on. Where can I buy a white blouse for a girl of eight? No, my son will be five, but it is to make a doctor's white coat for him. Do you have one with a soft neckband of the sort worn by girls, please? Do you have one with long sleeves? Yes, it is indeed a big girl's blouse. Yes, I also enjoy a joke on a Monday morning.

Do you have any red felt? How much would I need for a cross/for two crosses on a five-year-old's white coat? What is the minimum quantity you sell? How much is it per yard? What can I do with ninety centimetres of leftover red felt? Yes, I am sure it will be very useful. Is this felt self-adhesive? Do you sell glue?

Good morning. Could you direct me to the model figures department, please? Do you have any Cowboys and Indians? No, I did not know that Cowboys and Indians are no longer politically acceptable. Yes, I am grateful to you for this information. Could you perhaps direct me to a place where political correctness has not yet arrived? What a pity, I was in France only days ago. Do you have the phone number of the French company you mentioned? No, I do not mind waiting forty minutes while you serve eight other customers. Yes, I am still here. May I read you back that phone number? Yes, perhaps it would be best for me to check it with Directory Enquiries anyway. Yes, that is all. Thank you and good day.

Hello? Do you sell toy horses, please? Yes, that is indeed a relief. No, I do not want a soft, furry horse. No, I do not want a fuzzy plastic horse. No, I do not want a set of farmyard horses. No, that horse will not do as it is black. No, that one will not do as it is too small. No, I am not trying to be difficult. Yes, you are probably right. Thank you, I will try elsewhere.

Example: Organiser le goûter
Pizza
Sausages
Honey-and-banana sandwiches
Crisps
Jelly
Cake

Phrases utiles:
Excuse me, are you using that trolley? No, the trolleys over there in the stack are too small. Yes, I know that there are people shopping with two or more small children whose need is far greater than mine. Yes, I will go back outside and find one. Where is my list? Where is my supplementary list?

Do you have any organic chipolata sausages? Do you have any ordinary chipolata sausages? Do you have any in the back, perhaps? Yes, I will wait here. Forgive me, am I blocking your way? No, I cannot move, I am waiting to hear about some sausages. Oh, what a pity. Yes, I will make a special trip tomorrow. Will you definitely have more tomorrow? Yes, I will telephone in advance.

How many pizzas will twelve children eat, if they have already eaten sausages? How many will they eat if there turn out not to be any sausages? Do most children prefer deep-crust or crispy pizzas? Yes, I am talking to you. No, I know we have not met, but I saw from your trolley that you had bought ChocoLoco Cheerios, so I guessed that perhaps those pizzas were for children. Please forgive the intrusion into your privacy. No, I am not winding you up.

Excuse me, do you sell vegetarian jelly here? What is carnivorous jelly? I'm sorry, I don't understand. Are you saying that you don't know the answer to my question? Yes, I am sure there is such a thing as vegetarian jelly.

Please, where has the cocoa moved to? No, I have looked with the baking ingredients/the cake mixes/the hot drink mixes/the chocolate products/everywhere else, and it is not there. Yes, I am sure.

Excuse me, have you ever used this green food colouring? No, not this particular bottle, but this brand. Yes, it is for a birthday cake. No, the icing on a birthday cake. To be precise, an alligator birthday cake. You may of course be right that the brown mixed in with the green just at the tips of each scale would achieve a more authentic effect. No, I was planning to apply it with an ordinary knife. No, I do not possess a reptile-skin nozzle for my piping bag. Unfortunately, I may not have time to go to Bedfordshire to obtain one from your most excellent-sounding supplier. Yes, I had guessed that you might be a professional cake decorator. Of course, had I known, I would have been delighted to use your services, save myself time and trouble, and achieve a cake that my son was likely to recognise as an alligator. No, I think that having bought all the ingredients I will struggle on in my inept amateurish way. Oh look, there is my best friend ten aisles over! I must not detain you another minute. You have been most kind, madam. Oh, thank you, yes, I will indeed take this card and call you next year. Yes, well in advance. Bye-bye!

Is this all the honey you sell? Do you sell any thick honey? Is this where it would be if you had any? Yes, I did hear you the first time. Thank you very much.

No, I do not have a loyalty card. If I had loyalty to a shop, it would not be to this one, after today. No, that was not me talking. No, I am not trying to start something. May I have my change, please? Yes, I am sure it was a twenty-pound note. Ah, this other customer also saw that it was a twenty-pound note. Thank you, madam. You have restored my faith in humanity. Yes, I am leaving now.

5–6 August – E-mail exchange: Colum and Billy

From: ColumMcCallum [colum@laverda.demon.co.uk]
To: Billy Giddens[billy@goat.freeserve.co.uk]

Hi Bill
If this is the result of letting the dog out for a walk, I should consider doing it more often. Ever since she got back, considerably improved on the grooming front apart from anything else, she's been all over me like a bad suit, night and (on occasion) day. Not even the revelation that every child at Des's nursery was expecting to turn up for a bunfight shortly has clouded the sunshine, which is becoming, to be honest, a bit unnerving.
    Still, she's due back at work next week which should restore things to normal pretty sharpish. I haven't been so sleep-deprived since Des was teething.
    As it looks like we may after all succeed in extracting a few bob from the moguls, I think you and I deserve a little outing too. Fancy the superbikes at Donington on the 18th?
    Col

From: Billy Giddens [billy@goat.freeserve.co.uk]
To: ColumMcCallum [colum@laverda.demon.co.uk]

```
col old miucker
egiytnteet souns good, i may hgave to masage
teh truth aroud the edges a bit to get a
passout from teh Stalag but i've had pektny
of practise as you know. steve might come
along. I\ll give him a bell
   glad thingd restored on dometic front -
doesn't do to let dogs get too fancy, it only
hitsd them harder when they reach forty and
canbt afford the reonstructive surgey.
   yrs bill
```

----

7 August – Helen and Ernie, decorating Des's cake

They are standing in the kitchen, drinking Australian Shiraz, or rather Helen is standing as Ernie goes through a variety of yoga squats and stretches, while buffing her nails. Helen is bent, frowning fiercely, over a long sausage-shaped cake with four mini-rolls sticking out of it sideways, to which she is attempting to apply gloopy grass-green icing. Crumbs of the cake are breaking off and making lumps in the icing. This is not a professional-quality job, but her heart is in it.

H: I had this brainwave in the middle of last night that if I squished raspberries into the cake mix it would make it pink, sort of like flesh.

E: *(over her shoulder)* Des will appreciate that.

H: Yeah. It would be even better if I'd had some raspberry jam to ripple through it, so it'd bleed when you cut into it, but . . .

E: *(through her legs)* I think, if you'll allow me to say so, that you may have been spending a bit too much time with young Des over the last few weeks.
H: Tell me about it.

Ernie is finally satisfied with her nails. She bends in half from the waist, and with straight legs splays her perfect fingers on the floor.

E: *(under her armpit)* That's better. I was going through ten deniers like a rat through a sewer.
H: Please! We try not to mention those around here.

On the way back up, Ernie notices Helen's hands.

E: Christ! What have you done to yours?

Helen's nails, where they're not clumped with icing, are adorned with wildly asymmetrical, very garish stars and stripes.

H: What?
E: 'What?'!
H: I think it's rather cute. It'll give me something to stare at when things get slow at the library.
E: You want to watch those little diamante thingies around that cake. One of Des's precious friends bites down on one of those and you'll be paying dental bills for months.
H: In LA I certainly would be. Legal bills too. God, I can't believe how paranoid and litigious they are! Did I tell you about the swimming pool . . .
E: Yes.
H: And the inanity of the conversations! The men were the worst, they just would not shut up about their problems, their emotions, their relationships, their careers, or more often lack of them — God, the lies they tell! . . .
E: You told me.
H: . . . and talk about skinflints! I handed out more free meals than the Red Cross!

E: So you're not sorry to be back after all.
H: Put it this way, I . . . oh hello Angel! You got your key then?

Angel has slid unnoticed into the kitchen. She is dressed quite normally in jeans and a T-shirt with front, and back, and sleeves.

A: *(perfect English public school accent)* Yup, thanks.
H: You didn't have anything to do with that large lump of money that arrived in our bank the other day, did you?
E: Can I have one?
A: Yeah, well — you said she owed you for the trip down . . .
H: Oh, but it wasn't that much, next to the . . .
A: She won't even miss it. I do it all the time.
E: You do?
A: Yeah, I have all her codes and stuff. Reverse engineering is my best thing in computer studies.
E: You and I should definitely talk.
H: Ernie is the Harry Houdini of the virtual world. There is no computer she can't get into, or out of, undetected.

Ernie is now giving Helen a neck rub as she works.

E: Just a sideline.
A: Cool.

She sits at the table and notices the green sausage.

A: Ugh, what's THAT?
H: That, blossom, is a birthday cake. You ought to love it, it's certified free of all natural ingredients.
A: Yeah, but what IS it?

Helen has finished glooping the icing over the cake. It now looks like a child's drawing of some kind of lizard. She fishes in a cupboard and brings out an ancient packet of blanched almonds.

H: Ernie, you've got a PhD, how many teeth does an alligator have?

A: That's an alligator?
H: It's as much of an alligator as that thing you bought him that he insisted on dragging all the way home on the plane. Thanks for that, by the way.
A: Don't mention it.

She grabs a couple of almonds from Helen and stuffs them in her mouth.

H: Hey!

She carefully applies the remainder around the front end of the sausage. They look surprisingly convincing. Angel turns her attention to the leftover icing in the bowl, which Ernie has already worked over.

A: *(to Ernie)* Omigod! My mum's SO furious about that job you stole from her.
E: Stole! I like that! Just because Alan Parker happened to recognise that I had a natural empathy with teenage Melanesian throat singers . . .
A: . . . and it just *happened* to involve a trip to the South Seas . . .
E: Well, she's gone somewhere exciting on her new job, where is it again?
A: Eastern Poland.
E: There you go. Very stimulating.
A: She actually asked me to, like, go along with her . . .
H: That's fantastic!
A: . . . only I said I was coming to this A-list party instead.
H: Really? You're coming?
A: Yeah, the only thing worse than Mum on her mobile is Mum in a place where she can't get a signal.
H: Well, I hope it lives up to your expectations, sweetie. We're not expecting the paparazzi, you know.

Ernie takes a big slug from her glass.

E: It can always be arranged, darling. Just tell me when and where . . .

From outside, the sound of little feet running towards the kitchen.

H: *(calling out)* Not just now Des, Mum'll be out in a minute.
D: Mum! Mum, I feel . . .

Helen whisks off her apron and heads for the door.

H: I'll be right there!

Too late. A scrabble at the handle, followed by the unmistakable sound of a child's projectile vomit hitting the door.

8 August – The We're Very Glad to Be Back But We Wish We Weren't Sick Calypso

>Now here's a sorry tale, though it started okay
>With Des very pleased to be no longer away.
>The life of a movie star is all very well, but when
>The bills arrive it turns into a living . . . *not very nice experience, at all.*
>
>It was grand to be greeted by Bertie and Dad
>Though the former was in shock from the adventures *he'd* had
>And the latter did admit it hadn't been all bad – he'd been
>Cleaning, drinking wine and riding bikes like mad.
>
>Now Des was looking forward to his birthday party
>Though he doesn't much enjoy having to dress up smart, he knew the
>Cake was an alligator, teeth and all, his mum was
>Making it from scratch and she was having a ball.

But what is this? Poor Des suddenly felt queasy
He tried to hold it in, but it wasn't too easy.
He was making for the loo, but thought he'd tell Mum first . . .
Unfortunately of all choices, that was the worst.

For Mum had locked the kitchen door, and in the time it took to
Open it, Des poured forth an ocean of— (*hey, let's not go there, shall we? Yeah, I know it's my fault, but sometimes the muse'll just take a rhyme and run with it, ye know?*)
Now the poor mite's tucked in bed, though he says he'll be okay – he just
Doesn't want to miss out on his big day.

(That'll do for now, chum, I'm not the natural bard your mother seems to be. You get some sleep, and we'll see how you are tomorrow before we do anything rash, okay? Yes, I promise . . . I love you too. And remember, next time somebody promises to make you a star – run!)

8 August, very late – Helen, in bed

Anybody who claims that the life of a middle-class wife and mother is sheltered from the great ethical dilemmas of the human condition has clearly never had to deal with the discovery that the birthday boy may or may not have chickenpox, on the night before twelve of his friends plus all their carers are due round for a major social event.

I did think about cancelling. I did, for a few moments. But first, it may be a false alarm, and secondly, chickenpox is a very good thing for children to get over in their youth. They'll be grateful. Eventually. If it is.

And thirdly, how could the temporary and minor discomfort of a few women I barely know, and their rather boring little sproglets, outweigh adding yet another crushing blow to what poor Des has heroically endured lately?

Anyway he's fine, barely a temperature and only about two spots on his tummy. It could be anything, or nothing.

Anyhow, I can't. Not after finishing the cake, with those almond teeth and those hand-cut liquorice claws and those amazing gumball eyes. A whole year's worth of frustrated artistic creativity went into that alligator. What self-respecting child wouldn't take the risk of a passing bout of chickenpox for the sake of tucking into that?

What time is it?

Oh God. I must stop worrying about this and get some sleep. If he hadn't happened to be sick, and if I hadn't decided he needed a particularly thorough bath as a result, I'd never have known, and there'd be nothing to lie here worrying about.

If I am going to go through with it, I'm not doing it on no sleep. I'm sure I had one or two sleeping pills left in the bathroom somewhere – let's not wake Colum, now he's finally stopped snoring. That was one undeniable benefit of being six thousand miles apart, but the price was probably rather high.

Bathroom – light – cupboard – what am I looking for again? Arnica, chilblain plasters, Calpol, dental floss – tampons. Poor Angel, it must have been . . .

Hang on.

How come there's still a full box there? How come I . . . Jesus, how long is it since—

Oh no. I can't be.

It's the worry. And the change of time zones. It has to be. Doesn't it?

My God, could it be . . . No, I didn't in the end, did I? Think, Helen, think back through the murk of that third margarita . . .

No, I definitely didn't. Well, that's something.

Anyhow, I can't be. I mean, what chance did we have on that . . . Ah. The night before we left for LA. Oh. Ah.

Well, so much for getting to sleep. If I'm going to be awake anyhow, I might as well make a list for Colum to take to the supermarket tomorrow. I think we've got most of what we need for the party itself, but I've still got loads of catching up on all the things I've been missing in the land of idiotic salad combinations and food-free food. Not that I would ever normally go near a chocolate teacake or a pork pie, of course. I wonder whether Americans of taste and refinement return from abroad to an orgy of ReddiWhip and CheezWhiz?

9 August – Helen's shopping list for Colum

PARTY STUFF
Jungle Book napkins, 2 packs
Jungle Book paper cups, 2 packs
Jungle Book paper plates, 2 packs
red wine, cheapest you can find (for parents), 2 bottles
 white wine, ditto
potato crisps, any flavour children won't steal, 2 large
 packs (better give parents something, we had smoked
 oyster canapés at the last one I took Des to)

HELEN'S STUFF
Instant custard, full fat and high sugar
Jammy Dodgers/chocolate digestives/custard creams
 (any or all) chocolate teacakes (those chocolate-
 covered marshmallow breasts)
crumpets, 2 packs
KitKat, family pack
(I know what you're thinking, and I DON'T CARE . . .)

ready-to-eat spotted dick, family size (if I'm not family size yet, I will be soon)
or alternatively bread and butter pudding, ditto or both, what the hell
kippers (see, they're healthy)
Wall's Farmers Recipe Pork Sausages (I KNOW the farmer's a money-grubbing sadist and the pigs suffer all their short lives – I'll go back to happy pork next week, okay?)
pork pie with egg, crispy bake
back bacon, smoked and unsmoked (American bacon is rubbish)
thick sliced white bread
DairyLea triangles
Fray Bentos steak pie in a tin (are they still legal?)
Heinz baked beans (NOT WeightWatcher)
Lindemans Bin 69 Shiraz (not wasting that on the parents)

(oh, and just in case you pass it, and purely to have it in the house, because you never know, not for any other reason . . .)

Predictor

Le 'Handy-Guide' du Parent Occupé – Edition 2003

Chapitre 6: 'La Fête de L'anniversaire'

Example: L'horaire de la fête
3.30 Arrive, random play
4.00 Games
4.30 Tea
5.00 Cake
5.30 Party bags and depart

Phrases utiles:

Hello, Zoe/Zoe's sister/Jack's grandma/Billy/Shakira. Yes, you are a little early. No, it's no problem, please come in. Yes, it is difficult to judge the traffic in London these days. Of course, there is not a single café within a radius of several miles where you could have waited until the time the party is actually scheduled to begin. Please put your coats in the bedroom. Please excuse me while I go and put some clothes on. Yes, of course you can make a cup of tea/a Martini/a long-distance phone call/put Billy's special food in the oven. Please excuse the mess in the kitchen. Oh, is there no room in the oven? I'll be right up to sort it out.

Here is the birthday boy! Des, show your friends the playroom. No, you must not hide all the presents you were given earlier. Please share your toys. Yes, even the ride-on digger. Oh, look at the lovely book/construction set/modelling clay/gun/farmyard animals he/she has brought you. Sh, that's not polite. No, I am not whispering. Yes, I know you have one just like that already. Aren't you lucky to have two!

Ah, there is the phone. Hello, Max's mother. Oh, what a shame Max will not be able to join us. Chickenpox! No, I'm sure Des has not had chickenpox. Yes, it would probably be impractical to poll all the parents here now as to whether they want this to become a chickenpox party instead. Ha ha. No, you have not inconvenienced me in any way. Yes, I quite understand how disappointed he must be. Of course it will not be too much trouble to put his party bag in the post to him. What was that? And some birthday cake? I will certainly see what I can do. Well, I cannot swear that it is not made with artificial colourings. Perhaps it would be best not to try to send it to you by post. Thank you so much for letting us know, even at this late stage. Perhaps you could put Des's present in the post in exchange? Ha ha, yes, of course I was joking. Bye-bye!

Example: Les jeux
Pin the Tail on the Elephant
Dead Lions
Stepping Stone Cushions (aka musical bumps)
Pass the Jungle Parcel

Phrases utiles:
Now, children, we are going to play games. Who would like to pin the tail on the elephant? No, there is not a lion/a zebra/a giraffe, there is only an elephant. Yes, Shakira, you must close your eyes. Are you sure that's where you want to put it, Jack? Shall I take off your blindfold now? No, I am very sorry, you can't have another turn right now. Please don't tear the elephant, some children have not yet had a turn. Here, would you like a sweet? Yes, I know it's just a stage they go through. Perhaps you would like to take him into the garden/the park/another continent for a few minutes? Who knows how to play Pass the Parcel? No, I am not going to tell you what's inside the parcel. Yes, I did wrap it myself. Please sit down, Zoe. No, Sara is sitting there. Please move along a little, Sara. Please do not hit each other, children, or we cannot start the game.

Are you hungry, children? I too am hungry. Sadly, Dad has not yet returned from the supermarket with the napkins, paper cups and balloons I somehow omitted from the last shopping list. Yes, they were to be *Jungle Book* themed napkins with alligators and monkeys on them. Yes, Sara, I'm sure you had them for your party. But Billy had *Toy Story 3* cups and napkins. Was Billy not a lucky boy? And Zoe had specially custom-printed napkins with her name and photograph on them. So Zoe was even luckier.

No, Zoe, I am sure we cannot do better than that. In fact, I think we will just use ordinary cups and torn-up paper towel. Who would like to help tear off the squares of paper towel?

Example: Le goûter
pizza
sausages
banana-and-honey sandwiches
crisps
jelly
birthday cake

Phrases utiles:
Who would like some tea? No, we do not have passion fruit juice, we only have orange/apple/pineapple/cranberry/grapefruit juice. No, there is no meat on the pizza. No, we have no pizzas with meat. Yes, you may leave the rest, but please not on the floor. No, the sausages are not hot. Oh, the sausages are hot. I'm so sorry, I forgot the sausages had been microwaved. They will cool down very quickly. Would she like a cold drink? She would like some ice cream. I think there is some ice cream in the freezer. Eat your sandwich before you have any more crisps, Des. These are the sandwiches without butter. These are the sandwiches without banana. Can she eat honey? No, the honey in the sandwiches is clear honey. No, unfortunately I could not buy any thick honey.

What is that funny smell? It's Billy's food. I am so sorry, I did not realise you had left it in the oven. Can Billy eat bread/cheese/jam/honey/bananas/jelly/ice cream/cream/pasta/any kind of cereal? No, I'm afraid I don't have any corn pasta left. Has everybody finished? Don't worry, I can wash the carpet/the upholstery/the curtains/the floor later.

Happy Birthday to Des! Who would like some cake? No, Des, you can have yours after your guests have been served. Yes, I will save the alligator's face for you. Yes, there is plenty for everybody. The cake is organic. Yes, the icing is also organic. No, the green colouring is not organic. Would she like a piece without any green? Would she like a piece without any icing? Is that piece too large/too small? Who else would like some cake? Yes, I did make it. Thank you, I did enjoy piping the alligator's nostrils at 1.30 a.m. No, I did not know that Sainsbury's make very good alligator birthday cakes. How surprising, I was in Sainsbury's only yesterday.

Yes, I am still working at the public library. Yes, I really do enjoy it. No, I was not for one minute tempted to swap it for a life of overpaid luxury as a Hollywood screenwriter, ha ha. If this is not anybody else's cake, I will just finish it up. Would you like a glass of wine? I am going to have a glass of wine. Where is the corkscrew? The corkscrew is lost. But lo, we do not need a corkscrew, I have found a bottle of champagne. Who would like a glass of champagne? Yes, I am sure there is enough for everybody. No, Des, I did not mean for you.

Oh look, here is Dad back from the supermarket with all the things we needed for tea, just in time to miss the cake and Happy Birthday, and to finish off the champagne. What do you mean, are we celebrating something? What could possibly have given you the idea that we have anything at all to celebrate? Something on the shopping list? Let us talk about it later.

But of course, we are celebrating Des's birthday! Dad, may I introduce Zoe. Zoe, may I introduce Dad. Zoe's mum, may I introduce Dad. Sara and Sara's mum and dad, may I introduce Dad. Billy, Billy's grandma . . . oh, sorry, Jack's grandma, Billy's little sister, may I introduce Dad.

Please forgive me, my mind is like a culinary receptacle full of many holes today. I did not sleep at all last night. No, I am not ill. No, we are all quite well. Yes, really, even Des. Jack, may I introduce Dad. Where is Des? Come here, Des, the knife was for cutting the cake. Yes, the alligator is already quite dead. No, it does not need to be stabbed a thousand more times with the knife. DES, PUT DOWN THE KNIFE!!!

Do not cry, Zoe. No, Billy, I am not cross with you. Who would like some more cake?

Now it is time for the party bags. Yes, there is one for everybody. Can you find the bag with your name on it? I'm so sorry you don't like your present, Zoe. No, I am afraid I don't have another. Oh look, Sara doesn't like her present either. Would you like to swap with Zoe, Sara? Thank you very much for coming, everybody. Say thank you to everybody for coming, Des. Yes, it was lovely, wasn't it? No, no trouble, honestly. Yes, I'm sure we'll see you very soon. Tea next week would be lovely. Or possibly next century. No, I did not say anything. Is that everybody now? Bye, everybody! See you very soon! Bye!!!

Now, if you'll just excuse me, I have to run to the bathroom for a few minutes . . .